I Shall Be
Near to You

I SHALL BE
NEAR TO YOU

ERIN LINDSAY MCCABE

THORNDIKE PRESS
A part of Gale, Cengage Learning

GALE
CENGAGE Learning·

Farmington Hills, Mich • San Francisco • New York • Waterville, Maine
Meriden, Conn • Mason, Ohio • Chicago

LIBRARY OF CONGRESS CATALOGING-IN-PUBLICATION DATA

McCabe, Erin Lindsay.
 I shall be near to you / by Erin Lindsay McCabe. — Large print edition.
    pages ; cm. — (Thorndike Press large print basic)
    ISBN-13: 978-1-4104-6865-9 (hardcover)
    ISBN-10: 1-4104-6865-8 (hardcover)
    1. Soldiers—Fiction. 2. Husband and wife—Fiction. 3. Impersonation—Fiction. 4. United States—History—Civil War, 1861–1865—Fiction. 5. Large type books. I. Title.
PS3613.C3233I17 2014b
813'.6—dc23   2013050970

Published in 2014 by arrangement with Crown Publishers, a division of Random House LLC

Printed in the United States of America
1 2 3 4 5 6 7 18 17 16 15 14

MAY   2014

For Douglas and Dallas
And, of course, the women who fought

All of us are clean for once, hair slicked back, our new kepis on, our trousers still creased, standing in the dim shop, a blue curtain draped across the wall behind us. The photo man, he makes us six press together like horses in a rainstorm. Jimmy and Henry stand on one side, then Jeremiah and me, then Will, and Sully on the end, looking even more tall and gangly next to Will. The photo man keeps telling Sully to stand still. Jeremiah's hand rests on my shoulder and my arm is round his waist. My spine shivers like we've been caught kissing in church.

The photo man finally sees what the rest of us already know about Sully and his chances of staying put. There is a burst of light. None of us jump at that, but Sully ain't still of course.

When I've given over four bits and am holding my tintype in my hand, I almost holler at Sully for ruining the picture, him nothing but a fuzzy blur leaning forward. Anyone looking will think we're good friends, all of us joined up together. Anyone will see one boy shorter than the rest, younger too maybe with that smooth face, but just as hard when it comes to the eyes. Papa will see the only son he'll ever have. Mama will see different when she gets that tintype in the mail. She will see us holding each other. She will see I still ain't ever the daughter she wanted. But all I see is me and Jeremiah, his head leaning toward mine, his fingers tight on my shoulder.

■ ■ ■ ■

HOME

NEAR FLAT CREEK, NEW YORK:
JANUARY–FEBRUARY 1862

■ ■ ■ ■

'Sit still, my daughter, until thou know how
the matter will fall.'

— *Ruth 3:18*

CHAPTER 1

JANUARY 1862

I know it when I see them. Jeremiah. The boys, Henry and Jimmy O'Malley, Sullivan Cameron. The four of them in a tight bunch across the churchyard, a bushelful of excitement between them, looking sideways with smiles only half hidden, that handbill paper all soft from too much of their hands on it. I know right then they are planning on joining up. It makes me so mad I could kick shins, but I stay put next to Betsy, listening to Mama talking about Mrs. Waite's baby, how sweet, how pretty, and her so young and her husband gone already, killed at Bull Run and his enlistment almost done.

And then I just can't stand still. I march through the snow to the boys' corner, watching their mouths clamp shut as soon as they see me coming. Jimmy hides himself farther behind Henry, always trying to stay out of a fight, and Sully snatches that paper

11

out of Jeremiah's hands and hides it behind his back, but it's Jeremiah I want. I grab his elbow and yank.

Sully whoops, 'I told you she'd be mad!'

'It ain't like it's tough getting Rosetta riled,' Henry laughs, showing all his crazy teeth.

I don't pay them any mind. I just drag Jeremiah back around the church's corner so none of them gossiping churchladies can see.

'What you think you're playing at?' I ask.

He leans his long body against the church, reaching out to pull my hand off my hip, smiling the whole time like it's nothing, his hand cool and smooth with calluses.

'What do you mean?' he says, like I don't know. Like everyone don't. Like the men ain't been talking about the war for most of the year, my Papa standing with Mr. Cameron and Jeremiah's Pa, their voices loud, their hands moving, complaining on Lincoln or McClellan or talking about how if we had more Generals like Grant the war would be over already. Now more than ever I am wishing it was.

'What makes you think you need to be the one teaching those Rebels a lesson?' I ask him.

'Rosetta, that ain't the only thing —'

12

'You marry me then,' I say, and I ain't even scared.

'What?' he says, his back straight as the steeple.

'Marry me. If you aim to go off and fight, well I don't aim to be a spinster. You make me your widow before you go off and die, that's what.'

'I don't aim to die,' he says, eyes gone all to pupil, arrowhead shiny.

'You do this, you might as well. Mr. Waite, he's gone for sure. You want to be like him?'

'Rosetta,' he says, 'you know a man's got to —'

'A man!' I say, pulling my hand away. 'You kiss me by the creek and make me think things and plan on leaving the whole time?'

He looks down, his jaw clenched. 'Rosetta, it's good money,' he says, meeting my glare, taking up my hand again. 'You know when I get back, we'll have money enough for Nebraska, get ourselves that farm —'

'No,' I say to him. 'No more dream talk. Don't you leave me here like nothing. You marry me. Next Sunday. Or the week after. I don't care when. But you do it before you go and join. Because if you don't —' I can't even say it.

'Don't cry,' he says, reaching for the handkerchief in his pocket.

'You just marry me,' I tell him, wiping my eyes with the back of my hand before walking past the boys, ignoring Sully and Henry pulling faces as I go back to Mama and Betsy.

Betsy's breathing is so loud and my mind won't quit.

All day I waited, but Jeremiah ain't come by to help Papa fix tools or make rope like he always does. And me, staring out the window and slamming doors and clattering dishes the whole time 'til Mama threw me out of the kitchen for giving Betsy fits.

I kick at the quilts, sliding away from Betsy and the warmth coming off her. The floorboards are cold but I go to the window. Nothing. Not a thing but snow outside and my breath turning to mist against the inside of that glass.

Out there in the dark, the creek winds through the trees to our back fence line, to where it crosses over onto the Snyders' land. The creek is where I first learned something of Jeremiah besides his name and that he didn't read good for being two years older, the first time Eli got to bothering me on account of our papas' quarreling. I was feeling easy that day, outside our grieving house, proud that Papa was trusting me with a job

14

so grown up.

The water rippled past my shins, the trout darted past my ankles. But fishing always ends in pounding heads with rocks. My pail sat on the squishy mud by the bank of the creek, four trout in there, brushing the sides with their silver-brown tails. My toes old-man wrinkled from being in the creek since first light. Eli came crashing through the bushes behind me, his face red like a dried apple, and his friends, boys whose papas sometimes did day labor for Mr. Snyder, hanging back in the bushes, ready to run.

'You can't fish here,' Eli told me.

'I can fish anywhere I want. You don't own this creek,' I said, wondering if I should run or swim or scream, and standing frozen like a deer instead.

'My Papa owns the pool where those fish hatched, and these fish are mine,' he said.

When he picked up my pail I screamed, 'No! Those fish are for my Mama! She's sick!' but he dumped my four brown trout in the calm water by the bank. They looked sad and stiff bobbing there in the water and I wanted to be everywhere at once, saving my fish before they floated away, pounding Eli's head. Instead I ran at him, clumsy in the water, and stabbed into his belly with my pole. I didn't know that was a mistake until too late.

'How dare you!' I said. 'My Mama's so sick and you throw away our supper?' And then I said things that didn't make no sense. 'That's for the baby! You take away everything and I don't even have no brother!'

He grabbed my pole, making my arm jump like I'd got the biggest fish in the world on the line. I wouldn't let go and he jerked and jerked.

I slipped and fell hard on the green slime creek rocks and when I came up sputtering, he shoved me back in the water before breaking my pole over his knee.

Only the splashing and yelling stopped me from the murder I was thinking.

'You can't push a girl!' one of them boys was saying. It was tall and skinny Jeremiah Wakefield, sticking his chest out, stomping through the water, pushing Eli's shoulders with both hands, pushing him away from where I was standing. 'It ain't right.'

I cried then, everything hurting so bad I sat back down in the water, watching a snot string dangling from my nose like spiderweb and then dropping in the water; I cried for the fresh mound on the hill and the new baby born dead and my Mama sick with fever, but I said, 'The fish . . .'

I pull that curtain shut. What kind of fool

16

have I been, thinking Jeremiah would want me for a wife with that as his first real memory of me?

Betsy sprawls across the whole bed. Maybe I ain't leaving this house after all. Maybe I'll be sharing this bed with Betsy until she's the one getting married, until her husband is the one taking over Papa's farm because a spinster daughter don't get nothing if there's a man around to claim it. Maybe Jeremiah didn't mean a thing by making Eli leave me be, by helping Papa with the rope and the horses. Maybe he was only ever being neighborly and all those kisses I let him steal really were only for practice.

But then I think of his hand on my arm, how he stood me up, saying, 'You go home, Rosetta,' his blue eyes a surprise with that dark hair, and him holding out my pail with four fish back in it but cleaned and gutted too, and how I listened when he said, 'You go home now.'

'There's more sewing and mending than Betsy and I can get to,' Mama says, settling down Papa's plate of eggs.

Papa looks up at Mama 'cause he knows I want no part in a sewing circle, but she has already turned back to the popping eggs. Then he looks at me. I shake my head, begging him to take me with him. There has always been Mama's world inside, and Papa's world out there, and me toeing the path between.

He shrugs, telling me he ain't up for a fight. 'Course,' he says. 'I've got to fix the North gate, since that fool horse kicked through it. But I suppose I can get it hung without my farmhand.'

'Well,' Mama says, sliding my plate in front of me, 'I would be grateful for the help.'

After breakfast, Mama sets me to peeling and chopping potatoes for the supper soup, and when that is done we all sit down around the woodstove with the sewing. Mama is still trying to teach me about being a good farm wife and Winter is the best time for women's work, but that don't mean I want to be kept inside with her and Betsy, pricking my fingers and drawing beads of blood.

All Summer Jeremiah helped us bring our hay in, telling Papa he knew farmhands were scarce, and I thought it was a good thing, him seeing me be Papa's right hand, him knowing I could do what needs doing. But now I am stuck inside mending and he hasn't come and I ain't so sure.

The skirt I am holding slips down to the

floor and I can't sit another second. I stab my needle into the pincushion and stand up. Betsy giggles when Mama asks me, 'What is in your bonnet?' but I just let her question fall like the curtain I keep pulling back and make for the door, banging on the way out.

I am off the stoop and across the yard, moving fast as I can through the snow, glad to escape Mama and Betsy. Chickens flap and squawk out of my way because they know better. At the barn, my hand stops on the rough cold metal handle of its sliding door. I can't believe the voices coming from inside.

'It's good wages, Sir,' Jeremiah says, and my hand won't move on the handle, not for all the world, no matter how fast my heart pounds, not before I know why he's come. 'A hundred and fifty dollars for joining plus regular pay after.'

'Seems to me there's a damn sight more important things than money,' Papa says, high and mighty like he knows best.

'Well, Sir' — Jeremiah uses his polite voice — 'a man can't live without money. I aim to buy us a farm, supposing you agree. The Army's paying.'

I want to laugh to hear him say *us* after waiting two days. After I've been convincing myself I was wrongheaded for all my wishes about Jeremiah.

'I'm sure Rosetta'll have something to say about that,' Papa says. 'She knows every farm in this valley.'

'We've got ideas, Sir. Rosetta's the only girl I ever met who cares about farming the same as me.'

It's like Papa don't hear Jeremiah talking proud about me. He asks, 'You ain't got the money to support a wife, why you aiming to get yourself one?'

There's a funny strangling sound before Jeremiah says, 'It was mostly Rosetta's idea, Sir, getting married now. Before —'

Whatever tool Papa's working on fixing clatters to the ground. He's laughing. 'Well, don't she just beat all. Been near to the death of her Mama, but that girl's the best farmhand I ever had. Can't imagine hiring a better one, but I suppose if it's her idea I can't say no.'

'Thank you, Sir.'

Hearing how Jeremiah has spoken for me, I lose track of my feet and slip right there on the icy snow, clutching at the barn door handle to keep from falling.

There's footsteps in the hay and I scramble, running to look like I've come straight from the house, throwing off my dirty apron and shoving it beneath the lilacs that are no more than sticks jutting straight up out of the snow.

I skid on the stoop's frosted planks as the barn door opens. Out walks Papa, clapping his hand on Jeremiah's shoulder. Jeremiah is taller than Papa and his legs don't look so spindly no more. He is wearing his Sunday best to come calling, nicer than anything my Papa has ever worn, but it don't hide how his arms are thicker than Papa's.

'Rosetta,' Papa calls when he sees me shivering. 'Looks like you got yourself a nice young man here, says you're after marrying him and now he's trying to make it right by asking my permission.'

When he climbs the steps, I tell him what I told Jeremiah, the thing he will understand most, not all the things I'm feeling.

'I don't want to be no spinster, Papa. And if he goes off —'

Papa squints. Then his hand is on my head, messing my hair, and he says, 'Then I guess we might as well tell your Mama, ease her mind on one account anyway.' He points at Jeremiah, opening the kitchen workroom door. 'You stay for dinner.'

It is warm inside and we three squeeze in among the butter churn and the washtub and Mama's spinning wheel. Jeremiah's heat is behind me and I turn to smile at him, his ears looking wind-chapped when he says he'll stay.

'I imagine you two got things to be discussing, now you're fixed on each other,' Papa says. He sits down on the bench and pulls off his work boots, the soles almost worn through. 'How about I'll head in, get Mama working on another plate for supper, and you two can sit right here until it's ready?'

I nod. Right before he goes in the door, he turns back and adds, with a shrug and a glint in his eye, 'But then, you can't be upset if it turns out I can't keep the news to myself.'

After Papa goes, we stand as close as we can get, looking everywhere but each other, like we are strangers, like there must be some new way of talking now everything is settled between us but we don't have the knack of it yet. When Papa's voice comes through the wall, rumbling too low to make out the words, Mama trills back like a bird and I don't need to hear what she's saying.

'She's pleased,' I say, and look at Jeremiah full on.

'And what about you?' he asks, a smile starting. 'You pleased too?'

I throw my arms right around him then,

squeezing tight.

'What took you so long?' I ask, my ear to his chest, his heart pounding as loud as mine.

'That's all you got to say?' he says, and cocks his head to look down at me, the smile gone.

'I thought you weren't coming! I been waiting for near on three days now and —'

'You counting Sunday?'

I draw back. 'Course I'm counting Sunday. You didn't ask my Papa on Sunday, did you? Made me wait most the day Sunday, all day Monday, and now it's supper on Tuesday. That seems like something close to three days from my way of thinking.' Without my telling it, my hand has pulled free and got itself on my hip.

'It ain't so simple as just asking, Rosetta.' He reaches out, tickling at my hip, working to gather my hand back into his.

'No?' I say, and let him pry my fingers loose, closing them in his warm ones.

'No. There's arrangements that have got to be made. Like where we're going to live. How soon we can be living there. Getting Pastor Bowers' permission. I've been making arrangements these past two days.'

I ain't really thought about a thing except

what I want, but it ain't for him to know that.

'So when are we getting married?'

'Unh-uh.' He shakes his head. 'You ain't answered my question, I ain't answering yours.'

'What question?'

'I asked if you was pleased.'

'Course I'm pleased! You think I'd be mad if I wasn't pleased?'

'You don't make a lick of sense,' he says, but he is smiling now and he takes a step closer to me.

I move into the circle his arms make. 'You ain't told me how soon we're getting married.'

'Pastor Bowers said he could marry us the Sunday after next,' he says into my hair.

'And where are we going to live?'

'On my family's farm,' he says. 'We've got my Ma and Pa's Little House, the one Pa built first.'

'We get our own place?'

'Course. I ain't bringing no new wife into my parents' house.'

'But — even when you're —' I can't finish saying it.

'Even when I'm away. You can live there. It's ours. 'Til we get our own farm,' he whispers, and kisses my forehead. It is a dif-

24

ferent kiss altogether from the one at the creek, 'til he cups my cheek in his hand and I raise my mouth to his. Only then Betsy bangs through the door and yells for supper like we ain't standing right in front of her.

Later, at supper, after Mama apologizes for not having something more special than beef soup and bread, she tells how Papa, only he was the farmhand then, showed up, knocking on Granpappy's door. How she pretended not to take notice of him, but she remembers him turning his hat round and round like a wagon wheel in his hand.

'Oh, but he was funny looking!' Mama laughs, running her hand down the back of Papa's head, smoothing his hair. 'Those raggedy clothes and his hair sticking every which way! Looked more like a scarecrow than a man. And him telling Granpappy what a good worker he was!'

Mama don't spy it, but Papa looks up from his bowl to shake his head.

'Woman! I don't know what you see in this story. There ain't nothing to it. The trick to winning a woman's love,' he says, looking at Jeremiah, 'is to work for it.' And then he laughs and reaches his arm to hook round Mama's waist from where he sits next to her.

She swats at him but he don't care because she is smiling.

He puts his hands out and says, 'Girls, don't ever settle for a man who won't labor for love.'

'Betsy, you fetch the double wedding ring quilt.'

'But Mama!' Betsy whines, like she's been counting things as hers and thinking on what might be going in her own hope chest someday.

'You hush now. Soon as we get Rosetta's chest filled, we can start working on another quilt for yours. Lord knows there's scraps of fabric waiting, and now you can have some of Rosetta's wedding fabric pieced in.'

Betsy pouts, but she brings the quilt from our room and then sits herself down. I ain't had much use for Betsy since she started promenading with Carrie Jewett and all the other town girls. The giggling when Carrie told Betsy she'd better not let any more of me rub off on her was worse than anything Eli Snyder ever done. Betsy used to hold my hand walking to school, used to call me her best friend besides Tillie Nilsson. She ain't bad, my sister, she just aims to please folks in a way I've never seen the sense in doing.

I reach for a pillow slip, but Betsy gets it first.

'Rosetta ain't filling my hope chest,' she says, staring down at the hem, but Mama pretends she don't hear.

Mama has my wedding dress on her lap, hiding the new knot of thread in the lining, careful with even the smallest thing.

She says, 'This can be your something blue. And besides, you always look prettiest when you wear this shade,' and I almost jump at how warm her words are.

Papa shoulders his way through the door, his arms full of wood. After he builds up the fire, he sets the lantern on the table between his and Mama's chairs.

'And what shall I read tonight, my ladies?' Papa winks at Mama before taking the Bible from the mantel to read Scriptures for her like he always does.

Mama pauses and then says, 'The Book of Ruth, I think.'

'The Book of Ruth? You aiming to teach our girls about getting widowed?'

'Of course not!' Mama's sharp voice comes back, and then she looks at me and her face softens. 'But Ruth tells us how a marriage makes new bonds, don't you think?'

'Making new bonds doesn't mean you

have to break the old ones,' Papa says, his eyes on me. He looks back at Mama. 'Seems if you're looking for marriage advice from the Lord, other books got more instruction than Ruth.'

'Just read Ruth,' Mama says, poking her needle into the fabric.

Papa sighs and thumbs to the right place. 'Now it came to pass in the days when the judges ruled, that there was a famine in the land. And a certain man of Bethlehem went to sojourn in the country . . .'

Hearing Papa's molasses voice fill the room, I almost start missing home already, until Betsy reaches across me for more thread and ain't careful about her elbow in my side.

CHAPTER 2

Bundled up in the wagon, Betsy chatters on
about how she wouldn't want a Winter wedding, how she would want wildflowers for
her bouquet and a picnic on the church
grass. I never cared to think on such things,
not before now. I am about to tell her how
Winter is best for a farm wedding when she
says, 'After seeing how pretty you look, ain't
nobody can ever get married in blue in Flat
Creek again!' and Mama turns to smile at
the both of us, the same smile as when she
saw my reflection in her looking glass, tears
brimming to see me looking how she's
always said I ought, almost handsome with
my hair still fresh-washed, the freckles from
Summer almost faded.

It is too cold in the churchyard to be mill-
ing with folks waiting for the start of Sunday
services, and anyway we ain't got time for
socializing. Papa keeps hold of my arm and

Mama and Betsy lead the way, walking up the steps to the church door. I don't like feeling as if people are seeing good in me for the first time now I've got my fancy dress the color of bluebells and my hair done up in twists at the back and curls hanging down at the sides.

Inside it is quiet and white, the Winter sun beaming in long shafts through the windows, lighting the walnut pews. We walk right to the front and Mama slides into the first one. I don't dare look for Jeremiah, not with the whole congregation watching. Preacher Bowers takes the pulpit and I ain't ever been keen on his sermons before, but with all those eyes on me for once I am glad for anything to keep my mind busy.

'At this time of great discord in our nation,' he says, his voice grave and slow, 'when so many of our men are battling so far away from their earthly homes, we can draw wisdom and comfort from remembering Eden and Heaven, our first and last homes, the purest examples of harmony and perfection . . .'

Seems to me a wedding ain't the time to trot out war talk, like there ain't a new casualty list posted outside the church door and enlistment posters up at the Mercantile calling for fresh volunteers, but I keep my

FEBRUARY 3, 1862

mouth shut and focus on the stained-glass window behind Preacher's head.

'What then, are the principles of unity, of marriage, set out by our God? God tells us in Genesis that it is not good for man to be alone. He also tells us in First Corinthians that a wife must not separate from her husband . . .'

'Why ain't God said a thing about husbands going off to war?' I say under my breath, making Betsy giggle and Mama give me a look.

'. . . for although Eve led Adam astray, he did not forsake her, but was cast out in sorrow and in pain with her, to create a new home out of adversity. This same sorrow and pain and adversity strikes within our nation now, taking so many away from their communities, their homes, their wives, breaking apart our unity. I say to you that as a wife must submit to her husband and remain loyal to her husband, so must a state with its nation.'

Once Preacher says that, there is a stirring in the pews. I twist and crane my neck to look across the aisle and behind me and there is Jeremiah, jiggling his knee, sitting so straight and looking so handsome, like a man I don't hardly know in a fresh brown suit and his hair all neat. I am willing him

31

to look at me when Mama clamps my thigh.

'Without Love,' Preacher says, 'there is nothing, and that is why I charge you to take the love you bear for each other and build a new Union . . .'

I don't hear a word else that Preacher Bowers says. Instead I tug at the tips of my fancy lace gloves over and over, until Mama clasps my hand tight in hers. She only lets go when Papa reaches out to help me stand.

Preacher asks my Papa, 'Who gives this woman to be wedded to this man?' and there is Jeremiah standing right across the aisle.

And then Papa leads me forward and with the whole church at my back he puts my hand on Jeremiah's elbow. Jeremiah looks at me and before he walks us to the altar he whispers in my ear, 'You look so pretty,' and it is different than when Mama says, 'You look prettiest *when* . . .'

Preacher is still talking but not one bit of it stays in my mind. There is just Jeremiah taking a deep breath. His hands shaking. His eyes meeting mine: my something blue.

When it is my turn to say the vows sealing me to him for the rest of my days, I barely hear my own words until Jeremiah gets that soft, hungry look of his as I promise to be his faithful and loving wife. Then Preacher says we can kiss and Jeremiah's mouth is hard on mine. I hold him fast even with the whole church of people watching because at least for now he is mine.

An icy snow covers the churchyard, but Jeremiah steadies me through the gate and across the schoolyard, every step crunching until we climb the schoolhouse steps and there is the hollow sound of wood beneath our feet. That schoolhouse don't hold good memories, nothing but Miss Riggs' ruler or Eli Snyder telling everyone I had hair full of nits, or Carrie Jewett singing songs about my cow-stink. I haven't stepped foot in here since Papa got Mama to let me quit schooling and Jeremiah keeps his hand at the small of my back, pushing me forward, like he knows it's no place I'd choose to be.

The woodstove inside is already burning, but I am shivering with cold, my leather boots soaked through. Jeremiah closes the door behind us and then he comes to me.

'You're so cold,' he says. 'Maybe we ought to stand by the stove . . .'

'Maybe you ought to come and keep me warm,' I say, and smile up at him, at this thing we can do now that what we are to each other ain't a secret.

We stand right inside the door, Jeremiah

at my back, his arms around me, waiting for everyone to come give us their congratulations and best wishes.

The desks are pushed back along the walls and the churchladies have all laid their best tablecloths and set out cookies and sweetbreads made special. At the front, on Miss Riggs' desk, is Mama's linen embroidered tablecloth, and sitting there is our wedding cake, a ginger cake from my new sister-in-law Sarah.

'You all right?' Jeremiah asks.

'I just want to go home,' I say, turning into him. 'It's too much, all these people looking at us, talking about us.'

'It's only nice things they'll be saying.'

But I know how those churchladies talk, and their daughters judge, and I don't tell him how I already heard Mrs. Jewett saying if people wanted to make a fuss over something they ought to be baking for soldiers' boxes instead of some farm girl's wedding.

Jeremiah takes my hands, holding them out wide as he takes a step back. 'I ain't missing this for the world,' he grins. 'When else do I get to show off my pretty new wife?'

My cheeks flush but I look from under my eyelashes at him, trying not to think what he means by *when else*.

The schoolhouse door opens and Jeremiah

moves to stand beside me. My stomach drops like we're standing back in front of the whole church.

Our families come ahead of the rest of the congregation, Jeremiah's Ma, Mama and Betsy, our papas behind and then Jeremiah's brothers and their wives and children. Jeremiah and his brothers are cut of the same cloth, their straight mouths and blue eyes and coffee-colored hair from their Ma, their long bones like their Pa. But Jeremiah is like cloth that has been washed to a softness, where James and Jesse are stiff and dark like fabric fresh off the bolt. Their wives, Alice and Sarah, ain't a thing like me. Alice is big eyed and Sarah is quiet and both of them ain't a thing but gentle.

They come at us fast, all at once. Mama beams like she has got every one of God's blessings and takes her place next to me, kissing me on the cheek. Jeremiah's Ma stands straight in her lace collar next to him, looking at me like she is counting my flaws. But Papa takes my shoulders in both his hands and kisses my forehead. 'You make me proud.'

It warms me from the inside out when Papa turns to Jeremiah and says, 'You take care of my girl.'

Somehow Sully, standing a head taller

than the rest, and Henry and Jimmy get themselves to the front of the line, and with their huffing they must've run across the schoolyard to get here quick. Those three boys are all proper with my Mama, but when Jimmy lingers over Betsy, too nervous to even shake her hand, Sully bumps past and takes mine like he aims to kiss it, like I am some fancy lady.

Henry pumps my arm up and down and then leans in to whisper, 'You ain't taking Jeremiah away from us, are you?' and before I can say how I ain't the one going anywhere, he turns to shake Jeremiah's hand.

When Jimmy can't hold up the line any more, he comes, saying, 'You look real nice, Rosetta. I told Henry you'd clean up good.'

Henry and Jimmy's Pa put his stamp on every one of his babies, giving them each his same sturdy build and ruddy coloring and crazy teeth, except Jimmy got all the freckles and smiles.

The people keep coming: the Prices with their daughter Harmony who only ever looks down at the floor, old Miss Weiss who tells me I look real fine when everyone knows she's as blind as can be. Mrs. Waite, who used to be Elsie Callison, only two years ahead in school, steps up to me, her face pale against her black mourning dress, little Charlotte on her hip, that baby wearing black ribbon armbands too. Mrs. Waite glowed like a lantern the first months after she married Clarence Waite, was round with child not even six months later. Then Mr. Waite left for his ninety days, thinking to get a nest egg before the baby was born, and now he ain't ever coming back. She rests her hand on my shoulder, swallowing back tears, and says, 'I hope you'll be happy,' before hurrying past Jeremiah without saying a thing.

And then my attention snaps to the Snyders, who oughtn't to have bothered showing, not when Mr. Snyder and my Papa don't do a thing but argue over water rights and Eli Snyder ain't ever caused nothing but trouble for me. But of course they are here, with Mrs. Snyder being a particular friend of Jeremiah's Ma. Jeremiah takes my hand tight and I hold everything inside a deep breath, reminding myself to be a good daughter-in-law. Mama is gracious to the Snyders and I make myself be like her for once, shaking their hands pleasant as can be.

When Eli steps forward I pretend he is nothing more than one of Sully's carved figures come to life, with thick bones and coarse features. Eli grabs for my out-

37

stretched hand but before anyone can see how bad it's shaking, Jeremiah moves to meet him, standing right in front of me.

'Eli,' Jeremiah says, 'I didn't think you'd be coming.'

Jeremiah's Ma purses her lips together and then Eli's eyes meet mine over Jeremiah's shoulder. 'Congratulations on getting yourself a wife,' he says. 'She managed to look real pretty today.'

Jeremiah says, 'I think she does every day,' and drops Eli's hand to take up mine again. ' 'Scuse us, we've got a cake to cut.'

And then he drags me forward, putting his arm around my waist, and I let myself lean into him. He nods, all polite to everyone as we thread our way to the front, but out the side of his mouth he says, 'We'll go soon. Just wait 'til you see the big bed we've got at home.'

Jeremiah drives the cart right on past the Wakefields' barn. 'I ain't having Mrs. Wakefield walk from the barn to the house in her wedding dress,' he says when he sees me looking confused.

And then he turns the horse off the main lane, 'til we come to a small clearing and the Little House, a box of a cabin with a window on either side of the door where me and Jeremiah used to sneak to play marbles. Jeremiah only barely has the horse pulled to a stop next to the porch before I am peeling off the quilts, to see what he has made of this place.

'Don't move,' Jeremiah says, and he jumps out and runs in front of the horse, wrapping the check rein around the porch railing before coming to my side of the cart. When he holds out his hand like I am something special, I laugh. But he don't hand me from that cart like a fine lady. As soon as I gather my skirt to step down, he gets one arm behind my back and the other at my knees and swoops me off my feet.

'Hold on!' I shriek, and it ain't what I mean, but Jeremiah grabs tighter and carries me up the two steps onto the porch before kicking open the door.

'Our house,' he says when he sets my feet down on the freshly white-washed floor. 'What do you think?'

He leads me into the kitchen. There is a faded blue braided rug, and below the front window at the table is the bench my Papa made as a gift, a folded-up quilt on the seat. Jeremiah has tried to make it nice.

He takes my hand, his mouth starting to go straight. 'You ain't saying anything.'

'It's just right.' It is so easy to make him smile.

'The horse,' he says. 'Don't go anywhere.'

And he walks out of the house, leaving me there to dig through the hope chest for the sheets Betsy and I hemmed and the double wedding ring quilt, to take out the few dishes Mama could spare. Seeing those things don't make the place feel like home, don't make me feel like a wife. Without Jeremiah beside me, all I feel is like a guest in someone else's house. But that is just because we ain't had a chance to make this Little House ours yet.

'We've got two days,' Jeremiah says when he comes back, banging the door shut, his boots clomping on the floor.

I am keeping my hands busy, working to get a fire going using wood from the full box next to the hearth. I spin to see him, dropping the flint, my heart sinking to think he is leaving so soon.

'Two days for what?' I ask, the words out of my mouth before I see Jeremiah is smiling.

'For our honeymoon. For learning to be together, like man and wife, without worrying over chores. For practicing,' he says.

I blush to hear him say it.

The first time we practiced together was almost four years ago, for a different thing altogether, back when I asked Jeremiah to teach me about fighting.

It took me days to finally get Jeremiah alone because the O'Malleys never did take a hint and there's no good excuse to walk all the way to the Wakefield farm.

I finally caught him as he turned the corner past the Mercantile, calling his name so loud it scared even me.

'Jeremiah! I've got something to ask you,' I said when I got up next to him.

'Okay.' He stepped back like I was a wild animal, might bite him any minute.

'Can you teach me to fight?'

His breath came out so loud I wondered how he could keep so much air inside him. Then he grinned.

'What do you want to learn that for?' he asked. 'Is Eli still bothering you? I swear that boy ain't fit for the slaughterhouse.'

'It ain't Eli,' I lied, because I didn't want no more trouble. 'Do I need a reason?'

Jeremiah squinted at me. Then he shrugged. 'There ain't a thing to it. You've just got to punch and not get punched.'

'There's got to be more than that!'

He shook his head. 'No, it's about that plain. And you go for weak spots.'

'You talking about male parts?'

His mouth dropped. 'It ain't only that. There's other weak places.'

'Like what?' I tugged on his arm. 'You've got to show me.'

Jeremiah looked up and down the dirt road, like he was checking for spies. He took my elbow, dragging me to the side of the road, under the shade of an oak. Then he put his hands on my lower back. I almost jumped away, but for his stare.

'Here, where the kidneys are,' he said. 'You punch there. And then here —' His hands brushed across my stomach and I sucked in, quivering but standing firm.

'And here.' He touched the very tip of my nose. It was the first time he touched me since Carrie made me so mad I broke Miss Riggs' inkwell and Jeremiah walked me all the way to Doc Cuck's. I can still feel his arm around my shoulder like he thought I might faint from the blood my hand was dripping.

I tried to think about anything but Jeremiah touching me. About where I'd like to punch Eli the next time he said something mean. About the trees behind Jeremiah's shoulder, their leaves going orange and red.

'Now let me see your fist,' he said.

I balled up my hands, making him shake

his head.

'Not like that. You'll break a thumb that way. See, it's sticking out?'

He curled his fingers into a fist and showed me his thumb, going across the front of his first three fingers.

'That's better,' he said. Then his hands burned into my shoulders, shoving me.

'What're you doing?'

'C'mon! Punch me! Anywhere you want. Punch hard.'

He meant it. My arm drew back and flew for his shoulder, but he dodged left and brought a light fist into my waist, aiming for one of those weak spots.

'When you punch,' he said between quick breaths, 'you've got to be ready to get punched. You've got to move.'

I saw my advantage while he was talking and tried for his stomach but he was fast and blocked me, his forearm pounding down on mine before he threw his fists up again. He aimed to spar so I tried again, my wrist throbbing. My fist glanced off his shoulder and then we were dancing and throwing punches and circling like dogs meeting until his breath and mine were heavy.

My hands were up for blocking when he threw me down to the scrawny grass, still wet from the last rain. The damp went through my dress, Jeremiah pressing me into the ground, his body stretching more than the length of me, trapping my hands against his chest.

'Can we practice again tomorrow?' I asked between breaths that made me feel how my bodice didn't fit right no more.

'Sure,' he said smiling with everything, his eyes so focused I thought he saw through me, 'I'll practice with you.'

He's looking at me like that now as he takes my elbow. 'Here,' he says, his hands moving to my lower back. 'Here.' He brushes my lip with the tip of his finger, moving down to my chin, tracing my throat on his way to my chest.

'What have we got to practice? I already know how to fight,' I tease, turning back to breathe onto the tinder nest and kindling. It has barely caught fire, the flames licking at the dry wood.

'Oh there's plenty for us to do, just you and me,' Jeremiah says, his arms coming round my waist.

'You mean like getting this stove burning hotter?' I wriggle away from him, moving to get another log out of the box. 'Ain't you hungry?' I ask.

Jeremiah looks at me, his eyebrows raised,

his cheeks still pink from the cold, his hair sleek, and rubs his hands together. 'I ain't talking about cooking,' he says. 'We already had cake.'

He is a fine-looking man with his bright blue eyes and clean-lined face and maybe it is too much, having him even for the two weeks before he is gone to enlist. I swallow past the lump in my throat.

'What is it?' Jeremiah asks, coming to put his hands on my shoulders.

'Nothing,' I say. 'Nothing except I like being here with you.'

'I like being here with you,' he says, and I have to bite my tongue not to ruin the thing.

'I ought to get supper started,' I say, but his arms tighten.

'You know, I've never seen your hair loose,' Jeremiah says, and then his fingers are teasing gently at Mama's tortoiseshell combs, my hair falling in waves. 'I have always wanted to do that,' he murmurs, sweeping it back away from my face and turning me to look at him. He runs his hands down my arms and leads me across the hall to that big bed. When he crushes himself against me I feel everything and when his hands go under my skirt I let him touch there, I want to feel more. When he asks if I am cold, if that is why I am shiver-

45

ing, I shake my head no and that is the truth.

CHAPTER 3

WAKEFIELD FARM: FEBRUARY 1862

When Jeremiah is but a few days from leaving, we go for family supper at the Big House. I wear my wedding dress because that is the best I've got, and my thoughts are of butterflies new out of their cocoons. But sitting at their big table laid out in its own room, I don't care how fine the Wakefields' spread is with all their matching dishes the color of cream right before it turns to butter. I see how Jeremiah's Ma and Pa don't sit next to each other, how they put their children between them, their sons on one side and their daughters-in-law on the other, the grandchildren in the kitchen.

When everyone has sat, Jeremiah across from me and his brothers' wives on either side, Jeremiah's Pa says grace. For years I have seen him silent in the church pew, never even singing the hymns, but his voice is loud now.

Then the table is so quiet, quieter even than at home when Mama and Papa are fighting. There is the sound of bowls passing from hand to hand, of knives scraping across plates, of Jeremiah's Pa chewing loud. It feels like holding my breath, serving myself at this table. I put a lamb chop and potatoes and a biscuit on my plate. It is a feast, even without the canned peaches that Jeremiah's Ma says Alice brought special. I look down so no one will catch me wanting more, so no one will think how I have brought nothing for this meal.

Every time I look up from my plate, Jeremiah is quick to smile, his eyes shining. Alice and James don't look at each other once, and her hands shake when she passes a plate to me. Sarah clears her throat but says nothing, and I try to keep myself small. When James finally speaks, there is a hardness in his voice.

'I don't know how Jeremiah came to break the brush harrow's tines,' James sighs, and looks at Jeremiah. 'It can't be mended.'

'We've got to have one,' Jesse says, like he has eaten something sour.

'Of course we do,' James answers quick. 'I ain't saying we'll do without, but who knows with the war where we'll be able to find a

48

new one.'

'This is not the time or place to speak of this,' Jeremiah's Ma says, her voice sharp and her back straight, and the table goes quiet again. Jeremiah keeps eating, his eyes on his plate. When the bowls of food are passed again, his Ma watches and only the men take more food.

The ladies all stand and so I do too. We take our plates to the kitchen, and even the children get quieter when we come in. I wonder where it is that Jeremiah has learned to talk, has learned to smile. Jeremiah's Ma sets Sarah and Alice to washing and me to drying while she clears more plates. When she comes back, she stands next to me and it don't matter that she is short and thin, I fold myself inward.

'I know what your father would say, but what is it you do best, Rosetta?' Jeremiah's Ma asks, her voice quiet but firm.

I have not said a word since we came through the door of this house, I have only nodded my head and smiled. I look at this woman, at Jeremiah's Ma, and clear my throat.

'I can do most anything needs doing,' I say, my voice too loud. 'I can tend animals, milk cows, help with slaughtering. I can work a kitchen garden if you have one. I

49

like to help my Papa with harvesting, mending fences.'

'Our menfolk do most those things. What of household tasks?' she asks. 'I don't recall you at any of the church quilting bees, not since you were a child.'

I think on Jeremiah, how he promised our own farm, and then steel myself and say, 'My Mama taught me to sew a fair seam. I can make soap and do the wash.'

'I see,' she says, because she has heard and seen things about me. Because I am a disappointment already.

I lay with my head resting on Jeremiah's shoulder, breathing his smell, nicer than anything I ever dreamed back in the bed I shared with Betsy. But even with his hand petting down my hair, I can't stop from wishing Jeremiah ain't ever brought news of this war to us. My heart nearly stopped that Saturday in April when Jeremiah came banging on our door, shouting, 'They've gone and done it! They've fired on Fort Sumter!'

Papa dropped the ear of seed corn he was husking, all the blood drained from his face, but before he could even go to Mama, she was already crying, 'No, it can't be true! It just can't! Oh my poor sister, down there in the thick of it!'

I reach a hand to Jeremiah's cheek, turning him toward me in bed. 'Why you want to fight for the Union so bad, anyway?'

'I don't know . . . Don't you think loyalty ought to mean something?'

'But what about Nebraska? Don't you want a farm no more? You said —'

'It's all to get that farm, Rosetta! It's the best way —'

'You could do that right here — you could hire yourself out. There's no good farmhands left —'

'That ain't it — my brothers — my Ma would never let me — Besides, I've got a hankering to see something different than the haunches of a plow horse. It's only for this little bit —'

'Can't I go with you?'

'No,' he says, but he pulls me tighter against him.

'Sure I can,' I tell him, my voice small.

'What would you do?'

'What would I do here?' I ask. 'Can't I do the same anywhere?'

'You can't,' he says, running his fingers down my back.

'Why not?' I ask. 'What if I want to see something more of this world too?'

'A wife's got to stay home,' he says, his

51

voice getting louder.

'I don't want to stay here without you,' I say. 'I don't want to be all alone.'

'You won't be all alone.'

I wrap my arms around him. 'What if I just up and follow you?'

He laughs and kisses the top of my head. 'Stone Lady,' he says, teasing me. 'So stubborn.' He turns on his side, his head propped on his hand, his fingers sliding down my cheek to jaw to bosom. 'You ain't really serious about coming.'

'Why can't I be?'

'A wife stays, Rosetta,' he says, his mouth set. 'It ain't a nice life. You've got a life here.'

'And you don't?' I ask. 'Your folks don't want me here.'

'That ain't true,' he says.

'It is. Your Ma don't like me. You can't go off so soon and us only fresh married.'

'You knew about this,' he says. 'This was the plan.'

'But it ain't a good plan! I don't like you being gone.'

'It's the fastest way to get enough money for our farm,' he says.

'I could earn money maybe,' I say, 'get us our farm sooner. Work as a laundress. Or a nurse.'

'I ain't having my wife washing other

52

men's underthings. Or worse.'

'When the fighting starts you can send me home.'

Jeremiah looks at me and that is when I think maybe I win, if doing laundry can be called winning.

'It'd be nice, having you there. But not once the fighting starts,' Jeremiah says.

'I promise I'd leave,' I say.

'Rosetta,' he sighs, 'don't make it worse than it already is.'

I say, 'A man should cleave to his wife. I am cleaving to you. You can't leave me.'

'You always try to drive such a bargain, Mrs. Stone?' he whispers, and I nod, my head rubbing against his cheek, my hair catching in the stubble there.

'That ain't my name,' I say.

'Ought to be. Everything about you is ornery and rock hard. 'Cept for a few places —' he says, his mouth brushing mine as his fingers circle across my chest. 'You don't ever take things easy.' He smiles, his cheeks apple blossom pink.

'Easy ain't always good,' I say.

The next morning, I visit Mama and Betsy. Mama smiles to see me, saying, 'I've been saving something for you,' and goes into the kitchen workroom, gathering canning jars

53

from the shelves, still dreaming of me in my own kitchen like she taught me.

'We don't need all these, and I know how you like canning,' she says. 'This way when it's the season, you'll be ready.'

I don't remind her how it ain't the canning I like but the being outside picking fruit. Still, I take those jars and say, 'I'll make you some preserves in the Fall, when it's time.'

Mama shoos Betsy off into the kitchen, sending her to check on the stew. Then she says, 'Rosetta, I never told you some things,' and turns to straighten the shelves. There is a long pause and then, while her back is still turned, she starts talking.

'Now you're a married woman, there's things you ought to know.'

I don't say a word. All I want is to be banging out the door and running down the steps. Mama keeps her back turned and sets herself to dusting each jar on that shelf.

'There's a time for everything,' she says. 'There's a time for a wife to lie with her husband if she wants a baby, and a time to lie with him if she doesn't. You understand what I'm saying?'

I've been living on a farm my whole life. Of course I know what she is saying, but I just say, 'Yes,' and let her keep talking. I get

54

to wondering why she ain't told me this before I got myself married.

'The time before and after your courses, that's when it's safe if you don't want to be having a baby quite yet, if you don't want to be raising your child alone while Jeremiah's gone.' Mama turns to me, holding out another empty jar. 'I'm not saying what you should do,' she says.

I take the jar and open my mouth to ask her if she ever took her own advice, or if she is still trying for Papa's son, but then she says she'd better check on supper, even though she sent Betsy to do it already.

When I say I'm going to go visit Papa out in the barn, Betsy follows me back into the workroom. Once the door is closed and I reach for my coat, she looks at me, all serious. 'You and Jeremiah going to have a baby before he goes?'

I think of Mama lying in bed, the curtains and the door shut tight so I could only get my eyes inside that room a sliver at a time. Or seeing Mama sick and Mrs. Lewis in this kitchen workroom washing the blood out of Mama's bedclothes and cooking us up one supper and then leaving me and Papa waiting in the parlor while that baby cried. The whole night.

Papa didn't smile for four days after Mrs.

Lewis left and we didn't name the baby for near to a week. Not 'til we knew it might live and Mama too. Papa didn't say so, but I knew if Mama didn't live what the baby's name would be. When Mama was feeling better, Papa was back to smiling even though she was all mean asking, 'What's wrong with you and you don't give the child a proper name?'

Papa said, 'Since we done the easy part of having a baby I don't think we should be the ones to name it, but if you don't have no ideas I was thinking of Hepzebah.'

She laughed until she cried and when she could breathe again she asked me, 'What were you thinking, Rosetta?'

I said, 'Violetta so we could be a bunch of flowers,' and she laughed and laughed so hard there wasn't no sound.

Finally she said, 'Thank the Lord I didn't up and die, or this poor child! I was thinking Elisabeth Violet.'

Anyone could see she wasn't thinking about it. It was done and she used both our names and made something better.

'Rosetta,' Mama said. 'You bring Elisabeth Violet here.'

I opened my mouth to say I ain't never held no baby before and I don't much want to, but Mama's face was turned away and

Papa was sitting on the bed holding her hand so I didn't have a choice in the matter.

The oaken crib was pushed along the wall on Mama's side of the bed. It was the one Papa made for me and I must've looked like that in it, so small and flower-petal white, the veins showing through. The baby — Elisabeth — she was all swaddled up. I put my hands around the bundle and I didn't know how tight I could hold, thinking of pumpkins and overripe tomatoes and what they do when someone drops them. I moved my hands and petted the peach fuzz of her head with its soft spot like a fruit bruise.

I didn't know Papa was coming until he rested his hand on the back of my neck.

'Here, Rosetta. You put your hand here and your other one here,' and he slid one red chapped callused hand under her head and one under the middle of her bundle. I thought then that I was getting out of picking her up, but he took his hands away and said, 'Now you try.'

I held her, thinking of the time I broke Mama's special china teacup and feeling scared what would happen if I dropped this, the only sister I've ever had, if it would be like that baby bird all skin and dark lids and what happened when it fell out of its nest. I couldn't get to Mama's bed fast or slow enough and when Mama reached her hands out over her special wedding ring quilt for the baby, I had to sit because I made it without dropping my baby sister.

'No,' I say to Betsy now. But I can't find my tongue to tell her the rest. I don't tell her how babies are too delicate, how I am scared of having one after watching Mama labor over our dead brothers or how I can't see myself raising a child with Jeremiah's Ma hovering over me and Jeremiah gone and never seeing it, not even once. I don't want a baby to remind me of Jeremiah, I just want him. I don't tell her how I've come to ask Papa something, so maybe after Jeremiah leaves I won't have to stay at Wakefield farm, lonely in that house by myself.

Betsy says, 'Oh. I thought maybe . . .'

'No,' I say. 'That can wait for Jeremiah to come back.'

I take up those jars Mama pulled down for me.

'When are you going to come visit again?' she asks.

'Soon, maybe. But I'll see you at church,' I say, and am out the door before she can ask me any more questions.

I button my coat against the cold wind. Inside the barn the smell of cow is thick on the air because they ain't been out to pasture since the last storm. Papa is dumping a bucket of water from the barn well into the tie-up trough, water sloshing down his pant leg and bits of hay sticking to his hair and clothes.

After he gives me a hug, he says, 'You look happy. Jeremiah being a good husband?'

I nod and wonder if Papa will think I am happy or that Jeremiah is a good husband once he hears what I am asking.

Papa says, 'The farm misses you.'

'I miss it too,' I say, and start to tell Papa that I aim to keep on helping him.

But before I can say a word, Papa says, 'I talked Isaac Lewis into being my farmhand now you've gone and grown up.'

Papa has to think about the farm and can't see any other way, but it smarts to hear he has filled my shoes already. I hug those canning jars to my chest and say, 'We aim to have our own farm someday, me and Jeremiah.'

Papa gives me his sad smile and says, 'I know you do. You've always been a farmer at heart. But I bet about now you've got a husband getting hungry at home.'

I hear how I am dismissed, so I just say, 'Good-bye, Papa,' and show myself out. I walk down the lane and along the road where the snow ain't so deep and look over my shoulder to the hill where all my baby brothers are buried.

I can still see Papa there, the last time he took his shovel, me watching from the kitchen window, him stabbing the earth over and over, his back turned to the house. Betsy, she was in with Mama, both of them quiet like snow falling. There was that world out there and another world in Mama's room and then there was me staring out the window.

I didn't know my mind was made up to help him until my hand was on the door handle and the bitter wind was pulling at my hair. The chickens cackled as if there weren't nothing different about today than any other day. Except for Papa on the hill again.

In the barn the cows were waiting, lowing because they had full udders. When I went through the tie-up and opened the lean-to door, the horses nickered their sweet talk to me, hoping on getting some breakfast.

'You just have to wait some more,' I said to them. 'Like we all have to wait sometimes for nothing. Or for nothing good.'

Papa took the best shovel so I clattered around the lean-to looking for the other one. I found it, my hand on the splintery handle, and took it up that hill, tripping over the frozen mud.

At first there was only the metal punch of the shovel and Papa grunting. But the closer I got, the more it sounded like talking and then I had to stop because of the words he was saying and I heard how he didn't want no audience, not for anything in the world. Not with the things he was saying.

'God. Damn. You.' After every word, the shovel pounded the ground. 'Why can't you keep to yourself! And what kind of God would? What kind of God, damn it! Taking all my sons! All my sons! Leaving me nothing but daughters!'

I should've stayed looking out that window. My heart was near to breaking, but that made me freeze right through. I listened too long and then I left Papa on that hill and took my shovel back to the lean-to. In the barn the horses and the cows were all waiting the same as before.

I threw down enough hay to keep them still and got to work milking. My head against warm cow flank, short hair drying my wet face. The metal pail rang with hot milk and the long scruffy barn cat came running, winding himself around my legs, hoping for the first squirts but we all hope for things we don't get.

When I finished the first cow I dragged my stool to the next. The cat came too; he just wouldn't give up but I wouldn't give in neither, not even when he bit my leg through Papa's old work pants. I kicked that cat but he kept coming back for more, and I wondered how he could be so stupid to keep trying the same thing.

I milked every last cow, trying to forget everything but the hair smoothing my cheek, the rubbery teats in my hand, the cat twining my legs.

But I ain't ever forgotten. All I can think is the hard work I've done and how it's never enough. Not ever.

I spend the last few days with Jeremiah organizing and packing things for him while he works the farm with his brothers. The last night we practice one more time in the big bed. Feeling Jeremiah's seed spilling from me, I think maybe Betsy was right, maybe I should have thought more about getting a baby on me, on having something of Jeremiah's to keep while he's gone, but it's too late for that now, the moon only a sliver in the sky.

In the morning, I wake to Jeremiah getting out of bed to stoke the fire. Watching his back as he leaves our room, I swallow back the tears.

When he comes back, he holds out a thin parcel, folded in his Mama's parchment paper and tied with a blue grosgrain ribbon.

'What's this?' I ask, sitting up, gathering the quilt to my chest.

'Open it,' he says.

I undo the ribbon and as Jeremiah looks on, I tie my hair back with it, all the time watching him, memorizing the lines of his face.

'You are the slowest,' he says, shaking his head at me.

I carefully unfold the parchment. The packet inside reads *The United States and Territories.* I wonder how Jeremiah can smile like that.

'It's a map. So you can follow where I am.' He taps the word *Territories* with his finger. 'And remember where we're going.'

It is nice, but I can't get any words out and that is what does it then. I reach to put that map on the bedside table, so Jeremiah won't see the tears get to welling, but I don't hide it good enough.

'Let's forget all about everything. Make our last morning nice.' And then he leans across the bed to kiss me.

'You can't leave yet,' I say, and pull him to

me, kissing him until his breath comes fast.

'I've got to chop some more wood,' he says, breaking away.

'You ain't got to do that.'

'I want you to be provisioned,' he says.

'There's other things I can't do by myself . . .'

'I won't be easy if that woodbox ain't full,' he says, sliding away from me.

'Then I'll come help —'

'No, you stay here,' he says. 'Get a nice supper on . . . and then maybe . . .' He opens his mouth like there is more he wants to say, but he turns around quick and heads for the door.

When I stop hearing the ax, I start supper like a good wife does, setting the table with our two plates and the gingham napkins from my hope chest, laying out the big spoons, buttering thick slices of bread. I've just got the pea soup boiling when the door bangs.

I say, 'Oh, but it's not ready yet!'

Only when I turn around, it ain't Jeremiah standing there, it's Timmy O'Malley, the littlest one, holding another folded paper out at me.

'From Jeremiah,' he says, and then he runs out the door before I can even ask a thing.

My hands shake, unfolding that paper. It is crisp and white as laundry from the line. Inside is Jeremiah's bad penmanship that schooling ain't never made nice. That writing makes me want to take my pea soup and scald him with it, throw the whole pot at his head.

February 19, 1862

Dear Mrs. Wakefield,
I am writing this letter as your Husband, and that is something Good. It don't mean a thing is different about my Feelings that I am setting off without you knowing, or seeing you one more time and telling you all my Thoughts. You will cry to Hear them said so that is why I am Going this way, so I can Make myself Leave without causing you any more Pain.

I always knew you were someone Brave, the way you didn't take Nothing from no one. And every time we talked about Farming, and Nebraska, I saw you weren't scared about going. There ain't another Girl who would Do for me. That is how I know that you will hold up while I am gone, because you are Strong, Mrs. Stone.

It's no easy thing, Parting, but it helps thinking of you in our house with all our People close, taken care of and Safe. We will have Our Farm when I am back. It is only because of what I want for us Together that I do this. It will be but a short while I am Gone and I'll send you letters all that time.

Already I am missing you.

Your Faithful Servant and
Loving Husband,
Jeremiah Wakefield

He thought real hard, wrote nice things in that letter, but I can only think about how he has gone and I ain't said good-bye, not really. I run to the lean-to and see what I ain't seen before, how he must've moved his pack when he went out to the privy this morning. Seeing that empty space, I sink down to the floor. Days ago, I snuck up behind Jeremiah and wrapped my arms around him the moment the ax came down on the stump. But now, when I heft logs from the stack Jeremiah left me, I'll think of how the wood split in two.

Near twilight I get up and go to the wash-basin in our room. Next to the pitcher, tucked under my brush, there is a folded-up piece of paper. Inside it says *I love you, Stone Lady.* I throw that paper down on the ground, but there's a sweetness in what he's done. I will be like that name he gave me. I won't stay mad, but I will be strong, I can make this place my home, even without him. I can wait here for him.

Back in the kitchen, I eat my supper at the table, across from his empty place. I wash dishes and make everything clean so no one can say I ain't doing my wifely duties. When there is nothing else, no other chores, I straighten our bed one more time. I go to the chest of drawers and take out a work shirt Jeremiah left, burying my nose into it. I lie down, holding that shirt, feeling how we will be together again because he has been bound to me almost since the first I knew of him.

And then I see the map, still on the bedside stand. I sit on the edge of the bed and unfold it carefully. Jeremiah has made a heart at Flat Creek and a star at Herkimer. But in the Nebraska Territory he has written, *I shall always be near to you.*

CHAPTER 4

WAKEFIELD FARM: FEBRUARY 1862

All night I play over one memory from the Summer. I was standing at the barn well, my back to the field, working to fill the jug with water because Mama's lemonade don't last longer than a lightning bug's flash. The buckets for the horses were already as full as I dared make them, if I wanted to make one trip. But then there were legs swishing through the rye grass behind me.

'I came to see if you needed help,' Jeremiah said.

'That bucket is ready for taking,' I said, nodding at it sitting at the base of the pump.

He came round to take the bucket while I kept pumping.

'I'm almost done, but the horses'll be thirsty in this heat,' I said.

'This one'll hold a little more,' he said, looking me full in the face before he bent to move the jug and put the bucket under the spigot. I slowed my pumping so as to waste less water, my breath coming hard from the work or the heat or both. The warm wind coming off our hill blew loose hair from my braid into my face where it stuck to my sweat-damp skin, working its way into my mouth. When he'd got the bucket set, he went back to watching me. I didn't know what he was staring at until he reached for my face and trailed a work-rough dry finger down my cheek, pulling the hair loose. I was still sweating and my face got hotter, but my arms turned goosefleshy and there weren't a thing I could do to hide it.

Jeremiah smiled and ducked to take the buckets. He pushed the jug back under the pump and then I stared after him walking, the weight of the buckets on his arms tilting him like a wind-crooked tree. He didn't look back even once, and when he disappeared over the hill I was still standing at the well forgetting to even pump.

It hardly seems worth building a fire and setting breakfast oats to boil when there is only me to eat them. The rest of the day stretches out before me and there ain't a thing in it that seems pressing with Jeremiah gone. But I know this feeling, I have seen it before with Mama, and the only thing for it is to keep moving.

The sun is full up when those first chores are done and breakfast eaten. I am drying the last dish when footsteps come loud across the front porch and then there is knocking. Maybe it is Jeremiah coming back to say good-bye like he should have, but when I fling open the door of course it is Jeremiah's Ma calling, a basket in her arms, the cold rosy across her cheeks.

'I came to see how you were faring,' she says.

'Come in,' I say, even though she ain't the company I want. 'I've just been laying out plans for my day.'

'Oh? And what are those?' She moves past me to the middle of the kitchen, taking measure of the house I keep.

I say the first thing that comes to my mind. 'Thought I might start making soap.'

'Good. At least you keep a tidy house.'

'Thank you,' I say. 'I try.'

'I brought along some mending, needs doing,' she says, and sets down her basket. Inside are chambray shirts and trousers and woolen socks.

'I can do that,' I say, even though there is nothing I hate more.

She gives me a pointed look and then acts like I ain't said one word. 'The men discussed it and Mr. Wakefield thought you might be of help with the sugaring.'

'I'd like that better than mending,' I say, thinking of being outside, tapping the maple trees and collecting the syrup. 'I can drill taps — you only need tell me where the tools are kept —'

Jeremiah's Ma frowns. 'That's work for James and Jesse. The mending needs doing. And it's the sugarhouse tending you'd be best suited for, since you don't have anyone else to mind.'

She wants me indoors, is what, sewing or else working over the sugarhouse stove, boiling sap down, keeping all hours. She is reminding me of Alice and Sarah with their homes full of children to watch and husbands to feed. All I have is an empty house and it ain't enough.

'I can tap the trees easy. I'd like doing it.'

Her mouth goes tight. 'You'd do better to remember you've come up in the world and do what you're asked.'

The mending ain't much. Split seams. A hem come undone. Socks rubbed threadbare at the heel. From the kitchen window the trees' empty branches sway in the wind, and I try to prove myself with my smallest stitches. But I get tired of hearing my own

71

breathing and the pull of thread through fabric.

Out on the porch, the weak sun feels nice, but that ain't where I want to stay. I 'am down the steps and into the fallow cornfield, heading for the woodlot. I pass the tin-roofed sugarhouse, moving along the creek, walking where Jeremiah must've gone when he left, seeing things the way he saw them. Trees send out new tips to their branches, and ice crusts the banks of the creek. I tuck the hem of my skirt up in the waistband of my apron to keep it from dragging in the mud.

I am watching my boots mash their prints into the slushy mud, not paying any mind to where I am going, when a voice says, 'Rosetta Edwards. You're a ways from home yet, ain't you?'

'That ain't my name no more,' I say, my heart pounding to see Eli Snyder in the middle of the path.

I kick myself for walking this far when I've got other things to be .doing. By avoiding one hurt, I have just brought myself a different kind of trouble.

'That's right. You're a married woman now. What are you doing here then, Mrs. Wakefield?'

'Going visiting,' I say, and square my

shoulders, meeting his look dead-on.

'Your think your new family is going to get your Papa those water rights? That's why you got married now, after hanging on Jeremiah all this time, ain't it? And everybody knows Jeremiah only married you to get the bigger enlisting bounty.'

Eli steps closer, his hand stretching out, reaching for my skirt. I think how the boss mare in a herd don't wait to kick, and I aim for his man parts. He catches my leg, twisting and shoving until I fall back into the slush. Then he bends over me as I scrabble backward, my feet slipping in the mud. He is panting now but he keeps coming. I can't get my feet under me to stand and he lurches forward, pinning me and snatching my hem. My shriek is so loud I can't hear my gathered skirt seam pulling free of the bodice, but I can feel the ripping fabric.

Jeremiah's voice says, *You've got to punch hard and not get punched.* I ball up my right hand, thinking of weak spots. Eli's hand clamps my leg. The other grabs my left wrist, pushing it into the ground, digging each one of his fingers and every rock into my wrist. His fingers scratch and claw at my thigh, but I aim for his nose like Jeremiah taught me, hearing him say, *When you punch, you've got to move,* and then I smash

73

my fist into Eli's face.

Before I even see the blood, I am shoving up off the ground, quick, ready to punch again. Eli rolls away from me in the slush.

'Don't you touch me!' I scream.

Eli keeps his eyes trained on me as he sits up off the ground, blood coming between the fingers of the hand he has clamped over his nose.

'There's something wrong with you,' he says.

'I ain't the one who's wrong,' I yell. 'You get away! Unless you want another crack to put downstairs with you.'

'You know Jeremiah's Ma won't take up your part against mine, don't you? This ain't over,' Eli says, and then he stalks off, his shoulders hunched forward, one arm hiding his bleeding nose.

By the time I can fill my lungs proper, Eli is down the path and through the trees. I stand there dumb, using what's left of my skirt to wipe my nose. My knees shake and my hands and wrists and thigh burn. Right before Eli disappears, he turns back to look at me, making my teeth go to chattering.

Walking up the steps to my dark Little House, I start feeling shaky again, like somehow Eli could be here waiting for me, or maybe he has already made up some story about me and how his nose came to be bloody, but it is just as quiet inside as when I left. Safe in the bedroom, I get myself fixed up right and get hold of myself because my insides go to warbling again and no one can know a thing. I pluck my other dress out of the chest and a scrap of paper flutters to the ground. *I miss you already,* it says. And then I start crying.

Even after I wash myself and put on a fresh dress, my thoughts won't quiet. I sit to mend my dress. I am fine. I am strong. Eli won't bother me again. But everything would be better if Jeremiah was with me and none of this would have happened if he'd stayed. Only maybe that ain't true.

But Eli ain't the whole of it. Even Jeremiah himself, writing that letter, has been dreaming on how I might make something different of myself, how I might be a good wife.

I drag the woodpile ax back into our bedroom, leaning it against the wall. Laying there on our bed is Jeremiah's work shirt where I left it, the map unfolded beside it. And then like a hornets' nest in the hot dust that you almost don't see until it's too late, but once you have, you can't not see it for the buzzing in and out of the crack in the dirt crust, the idea of it just comes to me.

CHAPTER 5

WAKEFIELD FARM: FEBRUARY 1862

I take the sturdy shears out from the bottom of my hope chest. I carry them through the hall to the kitchen hearth and I don't stop to think; I sit in front of that woodstove, still throwing out heat from the morning's cooking, and plait my hair into one thick braid hanging down my back. Then I push those shears to the base of my braid and force down, using both hands to make those scissors saw my hair bit by bit, cutting it all off. It falls to the floor with a heavy thump, a light brown snake coiled behind me.

I stare at it there and Betsy's voice is in my head saying, *'Why you got such pretty hair? All wasted on someone who don't care none about it?'*

Then I feel Jeremiah running his fingers through my hair, but I've got to stop that. I snatch that braid up, the top thick and splayed, the bottom curled to a tip, and fling it into the cinders. It almost chokes out the fire, but I breathe on it and use fresh kindling from the box to poke it down until the flames lick at the braid, filling the room with its awful smell.

In our bedroom, there's a pair of Jeremiah's old trousers, ones he's got the hems frayed and worn down on. I step into them, trying not to look at Eli's fingerprints pressed into my thigh, turning up the legs to fit. I fold my apron and my mended dress and the petticoat and lay them in my chest, where they will be waiting when we come back. Those sheets Betsy worked at hemming so carefully tear easily into long strips. When I have rolled up all the strips but one, I hold it against my bosom with one hand, getting it under my arm and then wrapping it tight around myself. It's hard at first but I keep pulling it tight and then it's working. I cover myself with Jeremiah's old shirt and roll the sleeves before getting Jeremiah's straw hat from the hook by the door. In the looking glass that used to be Mama's I make my face look like stone, with tight lips and my jaw pushed out. I tip the mirror down to see the shirt and trousers, how they fit loose enough to hide everything. I could do it so easy, earn a soldier's pay instead of just a nurse's or a laundress's and stay with Jeremiah for as long as this war drags on.

He will be happy to see me, his face lighting up like our wedding day, all the more handsome in his uniform. He will tell me he is sorry for going like he did, that he never should have done it, how it was the boys that made him leave, that he was wrong to tell me I couldn't come along.

Only maybe it won't be like that. Once Jeremiah blacked Henry's eye after school, all because Henry whispered 'son of a whore' after Jeremiah's name at roll call and the whole class snickered. Jeremiah simmered for hours, the heat of his anger enough that Henry broke for the outhouse as soon as Miss Riggs' bell tinkled.

I ain't ever made Jeremiah mad like that. We ain't ever argued for real. Not even once.

But I have to do it now, I have to go, because I can't show my face to Jeremiah's Ma with my hair like this. Jeremiah won't care that it don't look good, it won't matter with a cap on, covering it. Plenty of people don't have nice hair.

Back in my own clothes, I sit myself down to work, staying up past the moon's rising, making neat hems on Jeremiah's old trousers and cutting down the sleeves on two of his shirts.

I wake at dawn, my neck cricked, still sitting in the chair by the fire, the last of the hemming just a few stitches from finished.

In the kitchen I dig for a burlap sack. There is hardly a thing for me to pack. The map. Jeremiah's letter. Flannel rags for my woman's time, extra socks, a wool blanket rolled up tight, two boiled eggs, two thick slices of bread, and some side meat, all wrapped in cheesecloth. I wind a scarf around my neck and tug Jeremiah's hat down over what's left of my hair. I am just about to go through the door, when I remember the mending for Jeremiah's Ma. I scratch out a note saying *Gone Visiting* and leave that with the basket on the porch. Then I lift my sack and sling the canteen across my chest and walk out under the gray sky, bracing myself for what is a day's hard ride on horseback. I look back once at the Little House, a thin trail of smoke still drifting up from the stovepipe. I think on Papa and Mama and Betsy reading every night around the fire. Words from Preacher Bowers' sermon come back to me, about Adam and Eve being cast out in sorrow. Only I don't feel sad to be leaving when that place ain't my home no more, and without Jeremiah, this place ain't my home neither.

CHAPTER 6

I don't even make it to the church before I start thinking on the first casualty list Preacher posted on the door, back when the little boys, Tommy O'Malley, Phin Cameron, and John Lewis, were still lining up to march back and forth with Lars Nilsson yelling orders. Back before those little boys' mamas made them quit playing soldier on Sundays.

The only good thing about that list was how it made Jeremiah get around to making things official, him coming to Papa, his hat in his hands, saying, 'Good morning, Sir,' and then his eyes flicking toward mine before adding, 'I was coming to ask permission to walk Rosetta home, Sir.'

All those weeks he walked me home from school, he ain't never asked permission.

I wish I were walking down Carlisle Road

81

like that now, with Jeremiah crooking his elbow like he is a fine gentleman and I am a lady, feeling the heat coming off him through his cotton shirt, my steps matching his. Leaving Jeremiah's Ma standing straight in her lace collar, her two daughters-in-law and Mrs. Snyder beside her, prying after us.

Back then the first thing he said was, 'You look real nice in that dress,' and when I told him, 'It's the same dress I always wear to church,' he pushed me with his elbow, laughing as I staggered sideways.

'Maybe you always look nice,' he said.

I wonder if he'll think that now.

At the old oak, where the path veers off from the road, I can almost see Jeremiah shuffling down the slope to the creek before me, down into the ferns, and holding out his hand, smiling at me with his head cocked to one side like it is a question or a test. I took his hand that day and ain't ever felt anything so nice, even when our hands got to sweating.

Down by the creek, Jeremiah's look made me get to feeling nervous, like there was something different between us, the way the air changes before a storm.

I said, 'I want to cool off a bit,' and undid the laces of my boots, rolled down my stockings, slipped them off.

Holding my skirt out so it wouldn't get wet, I squished the silt between my toes, the water cool enough to almost make me forget the sweat-damp dress sticking to my back. Dipping my free hand into the creek, I skimmed it along the back of my neck. Jeremiah stood rooted.

Just to make him stop staring, I said, 'You remember the last time we were here, just us? You remember how you said you wanted your own farm?'

'Course,' he said.

'You still want that?' I asked, standing so quiet a fingerling fish brushed up against my ankle.

'I do,' he said, 'I've been keeping those ideas in my head. But the war —'

'You still thinking on Nebraska?'

'Yeah,' he said. 'I've been thinking on that. Could get a whole farm, a hundred sixty acres, for maybe two hundred dollars.'

I don't know what made me do it but when I stepped out of the creek, I brushed against him as I headed for my shoes. He turned to watch me, that look coming back.

'How you going to get that kind of money?' I asked, stooping to get my things. 'My Papa can't pay you none.'

'I ain't working for your Papa for money. I've got other ideas.'

My cheeks went hot and I couldn't say a thing so I washed off the dirt and leaves sticking to my feet, dunking my toes into the water before standing on one leg, trying to get that clean foot back into my shoe.

'Here,' Jeremiah said, walking to the edge of the water and holding out his arm. I grabbed hold to steady myself, planning on saying thank you or else asking what other ideas he has got, but those words stopped in my throat. I didn't move as he bent closer, his arm reaching across my back, his mouth pressing to mine, and it was hot and wet and my arms went right around him.

When he drew away from me, I didn't want him to quit. My eyes opened onto his blue ones and I couldn't remember closing them. I looked at his jaw and the stubble growing there. He bent to me again, but before his lips touched mine he said, 'You still want that farm too?' and I didn't have to say yes, I just let him kiss me.

I wake under a bare-limbed tree at first light, my head resting on my pack, my blanket tucked up to my chin, my back aching from the cold or all the walking. Off in the distance there's the rumble and creak of a wagon, and that gets me up. When it comes close, the old man sitting on the

84

bench nods all friendly while his skinny bay horse draws him past.

I jog after that wagon until the farmer says 'Whoa,' milking the reins until the gelding stops.

' 'Scuse me,' I say, my voice catching in my throat.

The old man leans a bit closer. Maybe I should have let him keep driving.

'You heading to Herkimer?'

'No,' he says.

'You know how much farther it is?'

'Most of a day's ride, I expect,' the man says.

It makes me want to kick rocks or throw sticks after walking so hard yesterday and I ain't barely halfway there.

'You mind giving me a ride?'

'I'm only going up the road a little piece,' he says, 'but it'll save you a bit of walking.'

I croak out, 'Thank you,' and haul myself up onto the wagon. I have only just sat when he clucks and slaps the reins on the bay's back, making the horse lurch into the trot.

'What's your business in Herkimer?' the man asks over the sound of the horse's hooves. 'You looking for work?'

'I aim to enlist.'

'Well, now!' He turns to give me a quick look. 'Ain't you awful young for a soldier?'

Before I can think what to say to that, he pulls up his pant leg, showing me the long, jagged scar running from his knee down into his boot. 'Got this in Mexico. I was luckier than most. Got to keep the leg and never got yellow fever or the pox or none of it. Fared better than most everyone I knew, that's for damn sure.'

When my silence gets too long he says, 'You're mighty brave, going it all alone.'

'I've got a cousin I'm meeting.'

'The friend I joined up with never even made it as far as Texas. The bloody flux is what got him.' He looks me over again. 'But you look healthy enough.'

And then he is stopping at a lane and saying, 'I guess I can't convince you to help unload this timber then, can I?'

'No, Sir,' I say, and clamber down fast.

'My wife will have a hot supper on . . .'

'I thank you kindly, but I'm already late getting there.'

'Best of luck to you then. The march ahead of you ain't nothing a good soldier can't manage in a day. You'll know you're getting close when you start smelling the tannery. Damned if it don't make me think of Texas every time . . .'

I look back the way I've come. Papa's always saying there's work enough on the farm for a dozen farmhands and how I ain't got to be married if I don't want. If I'd asked, he would have sent Isaac Lewis on his way and let me be his farmhand again.

But then there is that farmer, putting his hand up to wave as he turns down the lane. I can almost see Jeremiah in him, driving home to his farm, to his wife, and the life I want.

I look up the road. All those miles between me and Jeremiah.

■ ■ ■ ■

CAMP

MOHAWK VALLEY, NEW YORK: FEBRUARY–MARCH 1862

■ ■ ■ ■

'I'll tie back my hair, men's clothing I'll put on, I'll pass as your comrade, as we march along. I'll pass as your comrade, no one will ever know. Won't you let me go with you? No, my love, no.'
— *'The Cruel War'*

CHAPTER 7

HERKIMER, NEW YORK: FEBRUARY 22, 1862

It is my shivering that wakes me early the second morning and I walk fast along the wide river. Already the houses are closer together and then there is the rotting stink of the tannery and then a real town, with a jail and a courthouse and a newspaper and four hotels, one saying *Herkimer* on it.

Being in that town not even five minutes makes me feel like a simpleton. There's ladies in silk and satin dresses with ruffles and flounces and not one made from calico, dresses Betsy'd be happy just to touch. There's so many wagons and carriages all together, more than are ever parked outside Flat Creek Church, even on Independence Day. The only thing that reminds me of home is the mud and smell of the horses, only the smell here is worse than a closed-up barn in Winter. There is too much to look at, windows with signs saying *Arrow's Iron Tonic,* and *Carter's Little Liver Pills,* and *Lilly's Washing Machine Sold on its Merits,* and a door saying *Tintypes and Daguerreotypes.*

Someone knocks into me. It is only a little boy, skipping past, holding on to his mama's hand, but as I turn, I catch sight of a poster on the wall. RECRUITS WANTED! PRESERVE THE UNION! it says so big even blind old Miss Weiss couldn't help but see. 97TH NY VOLUNTEERS! GET YOUR BOUNTY! $152! WEDNESDAY FEBRUARY 19 AT THE COURT-HOUSE IN THE TOWN OF HERKIMER.

I am three days late. Jeremiah is gone already, probably on a train bound to New York City or maybe even Washington, D.C. I will have to go home alone, walking back all the way I've come. I will have to listen to people whisper about my hair and where I've gone to for the rest of my days. I will have to face Eli again. I almost die of shame right there.

I can't make myself turn for home, not yet, so I start down the street, only my way is blocked.

'I want to show Dada at supper!' the little boy yells, hopping up and down.

'Dada's in Utica, remember I told you?' his mama says as he drags on her arm. 'He's a soldier for the Army now, and soldiers can't come home for supper.'

I don't hear anything else the little boy says because I am turning back to that enlistment poster to see what I missed before, the words NOW ENCAMPED AT UTICA stamped in smaller letters at the bottom.

There is still hope for it; maybe Jeremiah is there with those men in Utica. I pull out Jeremiah's map, trace the route. Utica is fifteen miles more on the Mohawk River, the Erie Canal going right through it, same as in Herkimer. The canal is mostly drained for Winter and all iced over, but if I follow the tow path I can't help but get there. If I just keep walking, I will find what I am looking for.

'Are you thinking about joining up?'

I jump out of my skin and almost fall off the boulder I'm sitting on. There, standing on the road behind me, is a girl maybe my age, a shawl wrapped around her shoulders, a book in her hands.

'Me?' I say before I remember myself and what it is I am supposed to do. After four hours' walking, my food gone and the water in my canteen so cold that drinking it sets my teeth on edge, I've been resting, watching the field beyond where a small herd of men marches in columns and rows, waiting 'til something tells me the time is right. 'Afternoon, Miss,' I say, and tip my hat.

'Good afternoon,' she says, her voice light and quiet. She is a willowy thing, her skin pale, her eyes hazel and her auburn hair swept up in twists too fancy for living in the white tents set back from the road a piece. Even in her shawl and plain brown wool, she can't hide being other than a town girl.

'You guessed right,' I say, working to keep my voice low. 'I'm after enlisting.'

'Oh, then you should speak to my husband, Captain Chalmers. I can take you to him,' she says.

'No need to trouble yourself. You can just point the way.'

'It'd be nice to walk,' she says. 'It'll keep me warm. Come with me.'

Mrs. Chalmers sweeps in front of me, down the packed-mud path leading away from the road, her skirt skimming the ground. I don't like having one more person witnessing me getting myself enlisted, especially not a woman who will see the detail of a thing more than any man.

Outside the biggest tent, where the Stars and Stripes flag is flying with a small blue banner underneath it, Mrs. Chalmers says,

'Why don't you wait here,' and ducks to go in.

I don't know what I'm going to say to her husband, but it's easier than figuring what I'm going to tell mine. I pull my cap down low and run my hands down my front, checking all my buttons. And then I try and see inside that tent, listening hard to hear Mrs. Chalmers say, 'There's a young man outside who wants to enlist,' but it don't ease the feeling that I've got bees buzzing inside me. Isaac Lewis got sent home for having bad eyes, and if a doctor's exam don't smash my plan all to bits I don't know what would.

When Mrs. Chalmers comes back, there is a man following behind her, older than I thought her husband would be and her so young. He looks at me long enough I count the seven buttons on his blue coat.

'My wife says you'd like to enlist?'

'That's right.' I stand taller. 'I'm hoping you've still got some numbers to fill.'

'What's your name?' Captain Chalmers says, passing the black-bound ledger in his hand to his wife.

'Ross,' I say, 'Ross Stone.' It ain't what I planned, but there it is. I aimed to be Ross Wakefield, Jeremiah Wakefield's cousin, but my head has gone soft. 'I've got a cousin, I think joined up a few days ago in Herkimer. Jeremiah Wakefield?'

Captain Chalmers looks at his wife. She nods and says, 'That's right,' and then his smile cracks his beard open like a nut. 'Family affair?' he says.

'Uh-huh.'

'What county you born in?' he asks.

'Montgomery,' I tell him, and watch Mrs. Chalmers write it in the ledger.

'Age?' the man says.

'Eighteen,' I say.

'Occupation?'

'Farmer.'

'Height?'

'Five foot two,' I say, standing straighter so maybe it will be true. He looks up for a second like he's got rulers for eyes.

'Health?' he says, still measuring.

'Good. Strong.'

'Run for me, along there.' He points to the path Mrs. Chalmers and I walked to get here.

'Run?' I ask, my throat closing.

'Yes' — he waves his hand — 'to that tent and back.'

'All right.'

I turn around and when my boots land on that path, I pretend it is just my toes hitting the spitting line, Sully saying, 'Let's see if

Rosetta can spit like she talks,' and me working up a ball of it, my back arched and ready to strike when Mama's voice comes from around the church corner, yelling, 'Rosetta Florence Edwards! It's bad enough you're always with the boys but now you're acting like one, too!'

I take long fast steps, turn right back around and run as fast as I can to where Captain Chalmers and his wife are standing. He looks at me with his head cocked, listening to me breathe for a good long minute, long enough I start sweating under my binding.

When he sticks his hand out, I grab it firm and shake like I've seen Papa do. The man nods and says, 'Pass,' while his wife writes. I can't read as good upside down, but I see she puts *Good health.* Then she turns the book to me and pushes the pen and says, 'Make your mark.'

I let out the breath I've been holding and sign my new name.

'Welcome to Company H of the Ninety-seventh Volunteers, Private Stone,' the Captain says.

CHAPTER 8

UTICA, NEW YORK: FEBRUARY 22, 1862
Captain don't waste any time. He leaves his wife and takes me straight away to where the Regiment is drilling across the muddy parade ground, the men shoulder to shoulder in rows of ten, moving across that field like plow horses at harvest time. With no uniforms or rifles they look more like a town militia than the Federal Army, and now I am bound to join them. My stomach knots itself to think of hiding in all these men, but then I remind myself of why I have come all this way.

Jeremiah. I can't get a good look at any of the men because from somewhere in the ranks, a man orders, 'Company, Right Flank!' and they all turn away. The same voice yells, 'Company, Extend to the Left!' and the men fan out into long lines stretched wide across the field. He calls, 'Company, Close March!' and they move back together into a bunch, their backs still to us.

'Companies G and H,' Captain says, pointing. 'The rest of the Regiment will join us before we leave for the Capital.'

'How soon is that?' I ask.

'I expect within a month,' Captain says.

The Companies drill until they march themselves back around, standing at attention right in front of Captain Chalmers, whose hand has slid inside his frock coat.

'Sergeant Ames!' Captain Chalmers calls.

A kind-looking man, not much younger than my Papa, steps from somewhere in the middle of the ranks and comes forward. He is a mite taller than me, and his brown eyes crinkle at the corners, a smile hiding behind his beard.

'Yes, Sir?' Sergeant Ames says.

'I have a new recruit for Company H,' Captain Chalmers says. 'This is Private Ross Stone. You'll see him settled?'

It is something odd to hear myself called *him,* but I keep staring past Sergeant's shoulder, to the men lined up behind him.

'Yes, Sir!' Sergeant Ames says to Captain Chalmers. 'Follow me.'

Some of the men I pass are young, just boys, and others are older than my Papa. When we have passed more than half the rows, a swarthy, thickset man with a black eye starting to go from purple to green gives a low whistle and calls, 'Hey, Fresh Fish!'

Sergeant says something but I don't hear a word of it because there not five yards away is Jeremiah.

His hat is pushed back, the sun bright on his straight nose and across his high cheekbones. He don't even notice me. He is too busy watching Black Eye clap the wiry man beside him on the shoulder, the two of them laughing. To see Jeremiah all mixed in with these coarse men puts me in mind of Doc Cuck's Thoroughbred saddle horse next to Papa's plow horse.

I find my place in my row, doing the best I can, pulling my feet up out of the mud, following the orders of 'Company, Forward March!' and 'Left, Right, Left!' and 'Company, Halt!'

I look straight ahead, but sometimes I can't help myself and stray to watch Jeremiah marching just two rows ahead. I ain't ready for him to see me. It is good just knowing he is near and safe. I don't want to be thinking about a thing else, about what he will say as soon as he knows I am here.

'Private Stone!' a voice barks, and my mind flies away from Jeremiah. 'Do you aim to stick out like a sore thumb?' Sergeant Ames asks, and I look around to find myself marched clear out of my column.

'No, Sir,' I say, and move over two steps. The boys in the rows ahead are all craning their necks to see what I have done, and Jeremiah is one of them. I drop my chin, holding my breath.

When I glance up again, Jeremiah has turned away. If he even saw me, he must not have looked close enough to know it, and I let out a long sigh. Maybe he wouldn't know me even if he did look hard.

'Company, Forward March!' Sergeant yells, and this time I keep my mind where it should be.

It don't take much before I march better than most these boys. Course, that ain't saying much when the ranks are filled with the likes of Jimmy O'Malley who can barely tell his two feet apart.

I let myself get lost in the music of it — Sergeant calling, our feet tramping, the men breathing around me. That is the only way I can keep from wondering what it is that makes Jeremiah elbow Sully or shake his head at Jimmy. Finally we are done and Sergeant dismisses Company G to their tents. But then instead of excusing us, he shouts, 'Private Stone, come forward!'

101

I don't know what could make Sergeant call me out except he has seen me for what I am. I walk to Sergeant slowly, looking away past where Jeremiah stands, feeling the men watching, hoping Sergeant will send the rest of the Company off before he drums me out of the Regiment.

I stop next to the first row of men, but Sergeant waves me to him, has me face the Company. My throat closes right up and if Sergeant asks me to say a thing for myself, I won't have the breath to do it. I look to Jeremiah. He is staring right back at me and the moment our eyes meet, he knows me.

But then Sergeant's voice booms, 'Which of you has space in your tent for our new recruit, Private Stone?'

Jeremiah's face is blank as ice, colder than the wind blowing off the river, but his hand shoots up fast. A few other hands come up besides, but I keep looking on Jeremiah, willing him to help me. And then Jeremiah calls, 'Sir, permission to speak?'

I have never seen Jeremiah so serious or heard him sound so proper, not even asking Papa for my hand.

'Granted,' Sergeant says.

'The new recruit is my kin,' Jeremiah says, 'and there's room in my tent.'

102

Sully's head jerks toward Jeremiah's, and I let out the breath I didn't know I was holding. I don't know if I should be glad Jeremiah has seen me right away and if it means he will let me stay or if I should still be scared of what he'll do.

'In that case,' Sergeant says, 'Private Stone will join with you. Company, dismissed!'

I stand there while the lines scatter and boys and men walk away, heading across the field toward their tents. After a moment there is only the boys from Flat Creek left, and me along with them. I stay where I am, planted in that field, and finally Jeremiah comes toward me, his face stern, his mouth straight like his Ma's. I'm afraid to look at the others.

When they get close Jeremiah says, 'You all go on ahead.' His voice is so flat that the others stay quiet. Not even Sully has a joke before they walk off.

For the first time I feel the aching in my knees and the emptiness of my stomach and the sleep I ain't had and then it is like the grit just washes out of me. All I want now is to put my arms around him. My mouth opens, but no sound comes out. We stand there staring at each other in the empty field, far-off laughter coming from the tents, the wind ruffling Jeremiah's hair.

'Rosetta —' Jeremiah starts.

'Ross,' I say. 'You've got to call me Ross.'

'What are you doing here? I told you, you weren't to come!'

'I'm a soldier. Like you.'

'A soldier? But, you didn't really — You're not serious.'

I stand up straight and say loud, 'I ain't funning. I did it. I enlisted.'

'I can't believe Captain Chalmers —'

'It's already done. I signed the ledger and everything. I'm getting paid, same as you.'

'Rosetta —'

'Ross!'

'You can't — What are you thinking?'

'When you left, I couldn't . . . I tried . . . You left me!'

'That was the plan! I was going to get the money for our farm!' he yells, his fists clenched at his sides, his face red. I have never seen him look so mad. 'That was always the plan!'

'I can't live that way! And I can't go back now, not after —' I stop before I say too much.

'Why can't you?' he asks.

'You think I can go home looking like this? After I already enlisted? You think your folks will have me when I just up and left and didn't say a thing about where I was going?'

Jeremiah shakes his head. 'This is too much. You've got to go home. You can't run about doing whatever you please.'

'Is that it, then? You tell me what to do now? You ain't listened to me one word when I said I didn't want you doing this thing, so I don't see why I've got to do what you say neither.'

'But you can't stay here! You're a — you're not —' He lowers his voice to a hiss. 'You're a married woman, for Christ's sake!'

'I don't see what being married has got to do with it, save for me wanting to be with my husband.'

He kicks a frozen clod of mud, making it go to pieces in the air. 'I want you safe!'

I think on Eli shoving me down, his hand wrenching, stitches ripping, fingers digging into my skin. I don't know how to say those things to Jeremiah. I don't want to see how it changes the way he looks at me. I don't want to see him take on the weight of knowing the whole of it.

So I say something else.

'It's too hard with you gone. What friends have I got with you all leaving me?'

'Did you ever even think about the boys? You think they'll want you here? You think they'll be happy you've come?' He has got

105

himself worked up so he can't hear a thing I say.

'Are you saying they ain't real friends to me? Is that it?'

'This don't have a thing to do with friendship! Your Papa — I don't know what he was thinking, letting you get ideas —'

'You keep my Papa out of this. I'm not even his farmhand any more. He's got himself Isaac Lewis for that now. And I ain't keeping house for just myself on your Pa's farm, your Ma coming and making me feel like something less.'

'That ain't what she's — She's never called you something less! It's the way you —'

'Don't! Don't you defend her! You don't know what it is, being there all lonesome and getting told I've got to do mending and stay inside and — You've never seen the way she looks at me! You never hear!'

'Rosetta, it ain't like that.'

'It is! I can't do it! I can't be your wife if you ain't there!' My voice is too loud but I can't stop it. I look around us quick, but no one's close enough to hear me call myself *wife.*

'You're not safe here!' Jeremiah says.

'This don't seem so dangerous,' I say, throwing my arm out to the empty field.

'You see any Rebels here?'

'You don't belong here! Can't you see that? And I can't be worrying about you all the time,' Jeremiah says.

'Is that what I am to you? A worry? You think you're the only one that worries?'

Jeremiah looks down. There is hurt and something harsh about his air that I ain't ever seen in him before.

'This ain't good.' He is done arguing.

'How? How ain't it good? Me being with you?'

His voice is level. 'You don't make a lick of sense.'

'You already knew that, and you married me anyway,' I say.

'You come with me,' he says, and grabs my elbow. 'We've got to fix things.'

Jeremiah takes off across the field, but instead of going toward the tents, or for Captain Chalmers, we skirt the trees at the edge of camp until we are far enough that the sounds of men talking and laughing and the smell of campfires fade. Then Jeremiah veers into the woods. I have hardly stepped from the parade ground to the gritty snow in the shade when he turns, grabs my shoulders, and kisses me, his lips rough and chapped. It ain't a nice kiss. It is something else, but I forget everything, just for a moment. Then I remember and shove him off.

'That don't fix anything,' I tell him, looking all around. 'It's a good thing there ain't a soul to see us.'

'There ain't a good fix for what you've done,' Jeremiah says, and takes my hand, marching farther into the trees until he finds a log sheltered by a thicket of sticks and branches. He hauls me down next to him, but he don't talk. Just sits there, staring off into space, his jaw tight, his thigh warm against mine.

Finally he takes my hat from my head and looks me over.

'What did you do to your hair?' he says, like that is the most important thing, and reaches to touch where it stops above my ears. I should pull back but I can't. I'm too glad for this little touch.

'You look —'

'Don't you be mean,' I say, and cross my arms over my chest. 'It can't be helped now.'

'I ain't being mean,' he says. 'You look . . . it looks different, is all.'

'I ain't any different,' I say. 'And it'll grow back.'

And then his fingers are in what's left of my hair and he kisses me again, gently. 'You ain't got it right,' he says. 'Only ladies wear a part down the middle.'

His hands, all shaking, go from my hair to the strap holding my canteen across my chest. 'And you can't sling your canteen like that,' he says.

'You are plumb full of advice,' I say, tugging at the leather while he stares at where it cuts across my chest. 'Does this mean you're letting me stay?'

'Rosetta,' he says, looking and swallowing hard.

'Ross,' I say.

'Always Rosetta to me. I can't not touch you.'

'We'll be secret,' I tell him. 'You call me Ross, and when we're secret you can say Rosetta. But now we've got to practice.'

And then his eyes go hungry and he says, 'Practice what?' And then his hands, they shake still, but he takes the canteen over my head and then he kisses me while his fingers work at the buttons of my coat and then my shirt and I do the same to his. When he has got to the binding around my chest, he stops.

'What —'

'It's to hide —' I start, but then he unwinds it, unwrapping like he's turning a wheel and I am the hub.

He sits back to look at me, catching my

left hand, pressing it to his mouth and I know what at least one part of him is thinking.

I shiver in the cold and try to draw my hand away before Jeremiah can see the bruises and scratches marking my wrist. He holds tight and a fluttering feeling rises in my chest and all I want is for him to drop my hand.

'Let go,' I say. 'That hurts.'

'What's wrong?' he asks, his blue eyes darkening as they go to my wrist. 'What's this?'

'It's nothing.'

'It ain't nothing,' he says, looking me full in the face.

'I got lonesome. And I thought I'd go see my Mama and Papa and Betsy.'

Jeremiah's eyebrows knit together, making two creases above his nose. 'And?' he says.

'And I didn't get there.'

'You didn't get there?' he repeats, and stares at me.

'Eli stopped me.' The words come fast. 'But I punched him and he was done with me.'

'Eli did this?' Jeremiah's voice climbs.

I look down, the shame of it coming over me as I nod.

'That white-livered son of a bitch! He

110

touched you?' Jeremiah jumps up, standing over me.

'He just grabbed me and shoved me. It wasn't nothing I couldn't handle,' I say.

'I promised to protect you,' he says, sinking back down on the log.

'You weren't there!' I turn away, dragging my shirt up from the ground where Jeremiah dropped it.

'Is that why you came all this way?' Jeremiah asks, his voice pulled like harness traces.

'I ain't going back there, not without you,' I say.

Jeremiah is quiet a long time, looking down, his hands opening and closing in his lap. The cold breeze moves through the trees, moves between us, and I don't know what he is thinking.

'I wanted something to make it back for,' he says.

That does it then. The feelings coming over me are all mixed up. It is maybe the best thing anyone has ever said to me, but I ain't thought about us not making it back, not really, not if we're together.

'There's other things to make it back for! We've still got our farm. We've still got a family to raise. With me making the same pay, we can get all that sooner.'

'It's a three years' enlistment, Rosetta. It wouldn't matter if we got the money now, there ain't nowhere to go but with the Army.'

'Then we'll go where the Army does. Everybody says this war'll be over soon.'

Jeremiah shakes his head, pushing furrows in the mud with his toe.

'I never want to see you hurt,' he says, and stands. 'We've got to get back.'

CHAPTER 9

UTICA, NEW YORK: FEBRUARY 1862

I don't know at first what Jeremiah means to do. We walk through the melting snow and mud, through a small village of men. Most of them look to come off farms like we've done, but as we pass one of the tents, that wiry-looking man says, 'That fucking mill don't pay damn near enough for the three of us. 'Specially not if that shit work is going to kill me.'

The Black Eye man answers him, 'Don't I damn well know it! That mill took my brother's arm and I can't hardly keep us fed on what it pays.'

'Canal work ain't no good either. I about break my back doing it and couldn't even pay for a pine box to bury my wife in,' says the serious-faced man who was marching near me.

Those men are in their old clothes, dirty now from days of wearing and traveling and drilling, but that ain't what gets me thinking of Mama's thick squares of soap, the foul mouth on that man worse than anything I ever tried saying, worse than anything Papa said when our cows busted through the fence and trampled Mr. Snyder's corn. I stay close to Jeremiah as we walk between the rows of tents, wishing I could grab his hand, how maybe then I'd know something of his mind.

There's a laugh I know and Jeremiah stops in front of the tent it's coming from. He catches my eye before calling out, 'Hello!'

I step from behind Jeremiah and there, gathered around a campfire, are Henry and Jimmy and tent-pole Sully between them.

'What took you so long?' Sully asks from where he sits on a wooden crate, his long skinny legs folded up like a grasshopper's.

Those three look between each other. Henry snickers and digs his elbow into Sully's ribs.

'We thought you might need some time to work things out, but damn! That was a while!' Henry says. Jimmy turns away, his face red enough to almost hide his freckles.

'This is important,' Jeremiah starts to say, but Sully ain't paying him any mind. He has got his knife out, whittling away at a stick, keeping his hands busy. Henry looks at me, every part of me, and then Jimmy asks, 'What did you say you're calling yourself now?'

'Ross Stone,' I say, and Sully's head snaps up then too.

'Ross is staying here,' Jeremiah says. 'With us.'

'For tonight?' Jimmy asks, and the air goes still like when a herd of cows is about to do something stupid.

'No. She's — Ross is coming with us. With the Regiment,' Jeremiah says.

Henry looks between us and takes off his cap, rubs his ginger hair, so greasy now from days of going unwashed that it almost looks brown. He slaps the cap back on. I can't think of a time when these boys ain't let me join in with them.

'Have you lost your mind?' Henry says. 'This ain't no place for a woman. You got to get your wife in hand —'

Jeremiah takes a step closer to Henry. 'You keep your voice down.'

I stay where I am.

'You mean just 'til we get orders,' Henry says.

'I'm enlisted,' I say, and stare at Henry. 'I ain't going home.'

'Rosetta — you hush for once!' Jeremiah's hiss almost knocks the wind out of me.

Sully says, 'You ain't kidding?' and Jimmy keeps his head down, like his feet are something special to see.

'Is that the most fool-headed plan you ever heard?' Henry asks, looking at Sully and Jimmy.

'Pretty much,' Sully says.

'Well, it ain't my plan!' Jeremiah yells. 'But it's what happened.'

'You think you're going to be a soldier?' Henry turns on me.

'Being a soldier don't seem so tough,' I say, straightening up. 'I already marched with you and nobody thought a thing about it.'

'Jeremiah — you agreed to this? It ain't right!' Henry says.

'It look like I got another choice?' Jeremiah says, throwing his hands up.

'The other choice is you send her home!' Henry says, like I ain't even standing there.

'I ain't going. Captain Chalmers has got his wife with him,' I say.

'Maybe you ain't noticed, but she's wearing a dress!' Henry practically shouts.

Jeremiah clears his throat, his face looking pained. 'Ross is staying. If that don't suit you, maybe you'd best find another tent.'

There is a long silence. The boys look at each other and then Jimmy shrugs, shaking

116

a crick out of his back, and smiles at me and shoves his hands into his pockets. When Sully sees Jimmy's smile, he throws the stick he's been holding into the fire, making a spray of sparks.

'I'll find myself another tent,' Sully says, and my stomach drops, thinking I am breaking the boys apart and that ain't what I meant to do at all.

'If that's how you feel, I ain't stopping you,' Jeremiah says.

'I sure as hell ain't sharing a four-person tent with no newlyweds,' Sully says low, and then he shoves himself off the crate and toward the aisle.

'Damn it!' Jeremiah shoves the crate that was Sully's and then sinks down onto it without even offering me a place to sit. 'Lord knows it's madness,' he mutters.

'Madness don't even begin to cover it.' Henry shakes his head, looking straight ahead, past me.

I forgot to take any of them to mind, to think how Sully can't hardly keep his mouth shut, and how Henry gets meaner every year since his Pa up and left, and how the three of them could get me sent home just as easy as Jeremiah can.

Next morning, I am up before the sun even

117

starts creeping over the hills because I've got to be, because I barely slept the whole night for fretting. That and sleeping on the hard ground, Jeremiah's back to me and the cold seeping through my blanket. Jeremiah is still breathing deep and slow next to me, but now his arm's across my belly, his mouth curved into what almost looks like a smile, now that he is too sunk in sleep to remember to be mad. I can't help myself, I turn to him and kiss his cheek.

'Mmmmm,' he says, not moving a bit.

Jimmy and Henry are two lumps under their blankets. I wriggle out from under Jeremiah's arm and our covers, bending to keep from touching the roof of our tent. I want to stay under the scratchy wool, in the heat coming off Jeremiah, but there ain't any other way to get my business done.

My breath comes in puffs and my teeth are chattering before I even find the tent flap in the mostly dark, trying to stay quiet so I don't wake the boys. The ties on that flap ain't easy to undo, but before long I am out in the morning frost, sucking in the clean air. It don't matter it's cold; after a night under mildewy canvas anything fresh is a blessing. Down the wide aisle between our row of tents and the next, it looks like these boys have been living here for weeks

118

with the lanterns and crates and knapsacks left lying about. In the dim light there ain't another soul stirring, but the snoring and coughing of men sleeping comes through the tent walls and I hope Jeremiah has the sense to pull our blankets apart when he gets up.

The camp has got one big long latrine trough dug off a ways, but that don't stop the bitter smell of piss from reaching all the way to the tents. There is burlap strung up to make a wall shading the trough from sight, but I can't be using that, and anyhow it is more foul than even the old school privy. Heading away from the main camp, I weave through the trees and down into the woods. The ground crunches beneath my feet until I find cover enough for my private business.

When I get back near our row of tents, there is a man still keeping farm time, dragging a wet comb through his thinning hair before getting to the day's work. He is wearing the homespun clothes and leather skin of a farmer. He don't say a thing, just looks and nods at me. I don't trust my voice to ask his name, so I nod back. There's other boys stirring now too. The wiry foul-mouthed millworker pushes out of his tent right in front of me, rubbing his hands across the stubble on his face. He says, 'Cold as a witch's tit, ain't it?'

All the times the boys used words like that around me, they sucked their lips in and made like my ears might bleed, and for a second, I don't think he's talking to me. Then I see there ain't no one else close.

I make my voice go low. 'Sure is.'

'Anybody around here got a fire going?' he asks.

I shake my head, 'Not that I've seen.'

'Goddamn it!' Foul Mouth says to my back as I hurry off. 'Fucking useless!'

Farther down the aisle, in front of the tent Sully moved himself to, a narrow-faced, towhead boy looking younger even than Jimmy sits cross-legged on the ground, his lips moving as he reads the Bible cracked open on his knees. I think about asking after Sully, but the boy don't look up so I keep on past and slip back into our tent. Jeremiah stirs under the blankets but I don't try waking him. Both O'Malleys look dead to the world. I sit myself down, tired already from worrying on getting caught and pretending for even an hour alone. But there ain't no other way.

The blast of a bugle comes blaring. Jeremiah jumps out of the blankets, his hair every which way, and looks around like he's lost something. He sees me and a hint of a smile lights and then fades. He rakes his hair with his fingers and it is good he has got all his clothes on so he can pop right up and go. Grumbling voices gather outside and Sergeant yells, 'It's reveille! Get moving to the parade ground!'

'Let's go,' Jeremiah says.

'I ain't keeping you,' I say, and haul our blankets apart. Jeremiah takes one look at the O'Malleys still sleeping and starts in on them, pulling at their feet. 'Hey! Henry! Jimmy! Wake up!'

Henry kicks out and says, 'Leave me be!' and I get to wondering how he ever got to any farm chores, but everybody knows the O'Malley farm don't prosper and maybe their Pa being gone ain't the only reason.

Jeremiah practically drags those boys out of their blankets and into the sun, Henry grumbling and complaining the whole time while Jimmy trails after us, keeping out of the fray like always.

We line up on the parade ground, me taking Sully's old spot beside Jeremiah, Sully off in the back row somewhere, Jimmy still sucking himself back. Leatherskin and wiry Foul Mouth and stocky Black Eye are in the row ahead of us. And then there is Captain Chalmers at the front with his wife looking small beside him, that black ledger back in her hands. She marks things in that book while Captain calls roll.

'Levi Blalock!'

'Yes, Sir!' a short and squat boy not much older than Jeremiah answers.

'Ambrose Clark!' Captain says loud.

'Here, Sir!' says that serious-faced canal-man to my right who has got the same liquor smell as Mr. Lewis back home.

Captain walks up and down the line yelling out names, and that is how I learn that Towhead Boy is Will Eberhart and Leather-skin is called John Morgan and the younger man beside him is his son Frank. Foul Mouth is Hiram Binhimer and his friend Black Eye is Edward Stiles, the two of them making a naughty pair. When Captain calls out 'Ross Stone,' there is a long pause and Jeremiah elbows my side before I remember myself. I forget to make my voice deep when I call out, 'Present, Sir!' My throat almost closes up to see dainty Mrs. Chalmers staring at me, but Captain keeps on down the line.

When all our names have been called, Mrs. Chalmers takes a small book from her apron and gives it to Captain before she swishes away in her long skirt. He opens it, flipping through the pages.

'I ain't ever seen book learning be any help when push comes to shove, but Captain can't get enough of that manual,' Ambrose Clark says, his voice thick and slurry.

'It's his wife I can't get enough of,' Hiram laughs from ahead of us. 'Don't know how he found a sweet-assed angel like that, but I'd sure like push to come to shove with her!'

My neck prickles. I want to get farther away from Hiram, but instead I stand tall, pretending not to see Henry's smug face and the eyebrow he raises at Jeremiah.

'We move together to keep safe,' Captain tells us.

As soon as the words are out of his mouth, Ambrose says, 'There ain't no place safe on a battlefield.'

But Captain don't hear him, one hand stroking his beard as if he's ironing it, his eyes pasted to that book in the other hand. Finally he yells, 'Company H as Skirmishers, by the Left Flank, Take Intervals, March!'

It ain't a drill we did yesterday, but the other boys turn left so I follow.

We march forward twenty steps more and then Jeremiah whispers at me, 'Stop right here and face front and then move ten steps to the right!'

I do like he says even though there ain't no more orders coming from Captain yet and I don't see how I'm going to get this drill straight, learning after everyone else already did. When I turn, the whole line of our Company is stretched out, some men kneeling and some lying down. I keep standing. I don't see either how kneeling or making a left flank is going to help when the bullets start flying, but I feel better when everyone is doing the same thing.

Jimmy says, 'Ross, take cover,' and he kneels down on the ground so I do too.

And then Captain yells again, 'Company H, Assemble on the Right Flank!' and as we stand, Jimmy whispers at me, 'Go back into fours!'

We keep drilling, going from marching in column to fanning out in line of battle and back again, 'til the ground that started out icy has turned to mud again. We get to where we move in a herd, only we don't do it smooth on the flick of an ear or the turn of a haunch. After every new order, Captain looks up from his book to see if we're doing like he said, his ironing hand sliding inside his frock coat.

'Private Blalock!' he bellows after he has sent us out ahead of where Company G waits in reserve. Only one man in front of us is standing.

'Have you forgotten yourself?' Captain yells. 'Are you offering yourself as a sacrificial lamb for Company H? Why have you not taken cover? Why are you STILL standing?'

The words ain't even out of Captain's mouth and Blalock is down on the ground, but Captain keeps yelling. Jeremiah bumps my elbow.

'You've got to stop that.'

'Stop what?'

He points to my hand on my hip. I screw my nose up and stick my tongue out at him, but he just shakes his head real small at me. I see I've got to mind what I do without thinking and be like Jimmy standing with his legs spread out, or Henry scratching under his hat and then at places no lady would, or Sully spitting off to one side every time I look over at him.

'And you can't run like that,' Jeremiah scowls while Captain stands over Blalock, yelling something about incompetence, and I guess Captain ain't the only one I've got to worry about watching to see I get things right.

'Like what?'

'Bigger steps,' he says.

When Captain is finally done making an

example out of Blalock, he orders us back into line of battle. A man who is older than my Papa and all string and sinew, who I remember being called Thomas Stakely, claps my shoulder as I'm falling back. I jump in my skin.

'You're a quick study,' he says, and I smile to hear it.

That smile don't last long, though, because then he says, 'Bet your family is real proud.'

I never had so much of nothing to do before in my whole life. No cows needing milking. No chickens needing scraps. No troughs to fill. No garden hungry for manure or fences for mending or laundry for scrubbing. There is just mustering for drill, or roll, or inspections, all of which mean getting up before the sun even though it seems to me there ain't a thing to be done in our Company that needs such early rising.

The next morning, I've already taken care of my necessaries and found five things to do before most of the boys are even stirring. Being first up, I start a fire, getting water from the jug at the end of our row, and putting it on for the coffee Sergeant rations out to us. Jeremiah must smell the idea of coffee 'cause no sooner do I get that

126

water on, he crawls out of the tent, carrying a sack of cornmeal and sowbelly from his pack. He tosses the provisions at me like I am nothing but a farm dog waiting for a bone and disappears into the trees without even a kind word.

He just ain't used to the idea of me being a soldier yet. Or else he is sore he can't boss me around like maybe he thought. I buck up and with the few things I've got I figure on making biscuits. I ain't got milk or butter, but water and sowbelly grease might do and anybody who sees fit to complain don't have to eat none.

When Jeremiah gets back, I pretend he ain't been rude. I give him sowbelly in a tin cup, a biscuit, and tell him, 'I don't aim to cook for everyone. It ain't smart.'

'How ain't it smart?' he says, wiping grease from his tin cup with his biscuit.

'I can think of one reason bigger than a hog before slaughter. Ain't you been telling me things I can't do all the time?'

'When it comes to cooking there ain't a soul better equipped,' he says. 'You're the only one with any kind of experience. Except maybe for Mrs. Chalmers.'

'That's what I'm saying,' I say, my spoon clattering. 'Won't someone think something?'

'Lots of soldiers cooking over fires from what I see,' Jeremiah shrugs. 'Might as well use the one skill you got while you can.'

The only thing that keeps me from snatching that tin cup away from Jeremiah is Towhead Boy from Sully's new tent coming to stand by me, his narrow shoulders even with mine. That boy is careful around the rest of us. I ain't sure I like him pairing up with Sully who can't keep his mouth shut, especially if he's mad, but there's no choice in it.

While I'm turning the sowbelly over in its pan, I raise my brows at Jeremiah but he don't pay me any mind.

'Smells good,' the boy says.

'Mmm-hmmm,' is all I've got for him.

'I have some sowbelly needs fixing,' he says, holding out a dark-stained haversack.

'Sowbelly ain't tricky,' I tell him because it's more than I want, all this cooking. 'You can use the fire and pan if you want.'

'I'd be pleased to share it,' he says, still holding that greasy bag out to me.

I can't help thinking of my Mama then, all the times she forced me into the kitchen, setting me to work scooping flesh out of roasted pumpkins or rolling out pie crust or chopping tomatoes for canning or shelling dried beans for Winter. Maybe she would

128

smile to see me working over a fire, at how her teaching finally took some.

'You ain't here with any people of your own?' I ask.

'No,' he says quiet. 'I came alone.'

'Put it in there with the rest.'

He does as he is told. Jeremiah watches, but I pretend not to see him.

'Good. Now just push it around a bit so it don't stick to the pan. That's all there is to it.'

'Thank you. You're kind to show me,' he says so nice I feel bad for not being more friendly. 'My name's Will.'

'Ross. You want a biscuit? They ain't very good, but it's something to fill your belly.'

'Things taste better when you share them,' he smiles.

'Well, in that case,' Jeremiah calls real loud from where he is sitting in a small patch of sun, 'maybe if you can get Sully to stop sulking and come on over, between the two of you, our food will get to tasting like home-cooked!'

It gets my dander up, to hear him judge my cooking and all the other boys laugh. All the boys except Will.

'You want to come try? You think you can do better?' I ask, fighting to keep my hand from going to my hip as I stare over at

129

Jeremiah.

'No, Ma'am!' Jeremiah says with a smirk I want to slap off his face. 'But I think maybe we could improve our chances of getting a decent meal, if what he says is true.'

Sully swaggers into our camp from where he's been sitting across the way at Will's tent, saying, 'I ain't been sulking. I was only making room — I can see when I ain't wanted.'

As he passes me, he shoves my shoulder. 'Looks like you're doing the sulking now,' he says.

And that is how Will and Sully along with him come to be at our fire most mornings.

CHAPTER 10

UTICA, NEW YORK: MARCH 1862

'Soldiers!' Captain calls from the front of the parade ground where a wagon has been parked since first thing this morning. He stands prouder than ever. 'Today is the day many of you have been waiting for!'

Every head snaps forward, but eyes keep wandering to the wagon on Captain's right, filled with wooden crates. Sergeant Ames and Sergeant Fitzpatrick from Company G clamber up into the bed and work with crowbars at prying off those lids.

'You thinking what I'm thinking?' Sully asks Jeremiah, only he don't give anybody a chance to answer. 'I bet he's got our orders!'

'It is my privilege to issue each of you a Springfield Model 1861 Rifled Musket,' Captain says, and Sully whoops, 'Hot damn!'

A smile flickers across Captain's face, but he goes back to being stony and serious

131

when he says, 'These weapons are entrusted to you by the United States Army. This weapon is your life. It is your safety. It is the life and safety of our great nation. You must take proper care with it.'

Jeremiah watches me, but I don't do a thing but stare straight ahead. I ain't forgiven him for calling me *Ma'am* in front of all the boys, even though he hasn't said a word about me going home. He ain't been the least bit tender or easy with me. I'm not easy either, especially not thinking about that gun, thinking about what I might have to do with it, but I can't let that show. Most of these boys can't hardly wait to get their hands on that rifle and so I've got to be pleased too. I step in line behind Jeremiah and the rest of them making their way toward that wagon.

'Now here is something might help us win some fights,' Thomas Stakely says from the front of the line. 'Get me home to my girls sooner.'

'I'd like to meet your girls,' Hiram says, and it is a wonder how he makes everything that comes out of his mouth sound foul.

Thomas turns on him, the sinews in his neck standing out even more than usual, and Leatherskin John Morgan steps closer behind him.

'You ain't to talk about my girls,' Thomas says.

Hiram puts his hands up and backs away, 'Oh, I see. You think they won't do for a rowdy like me, eh?'

Thomas says, 'Something like that.'

'Well, most times I can make any girl serve the purpose just fine,' Hiram says, thrusting his hips.

Thomas don't look away from Hiram, but John puts his hand on his arm, nodding at the officers. 'He's only blowing off some steam.'

'I'm looking to blow more than steam!' Hiram shouts. 'But I ain't got to fight you old men for permission to do it!'

'Come time to use those guns up there, I think you'll find these old men got more than enough fight,' Thomas says, shrugging off John's hand and taking a step closer to Hiram.

'I can take anyone here and any Rebels that come at me. You name your day, old man, and we'll see who walks away with one of your girls over his shoulder.'

'Hiram, ain't you wanting your Rebel-killing rifle? We're all waiting on you!' Jeremiah hollers, and he must be daft to do it.

'Hell, yes, I want me a rifle! These old

133

fellas got me distracted, talking about pretty girls!' And then Hiram turns away from Thomas like he ain't done a thing.

Sully finally gets to the head of the line, and there's never been a blind baby bird looking so hungry as Sully is for that rifle. When Sergeant Ames sets his rifle in Sully's hands, he don't notice the weight, how it makes them sink. He turns and lifts that gun over his head, saying, 'Gonna get me some Rebs!' forgetting to move until Jeremiah pushes him forward.

Sergeant Fitzpatrick holds out a cartridge box to me, and I take it, slinging it over my shoulder so the brass oval saying us is right across the middle of my chest and the leather pouch rests at my hip. Then I raise my arms to Sergeant Ames and he puts my rifle right into my hands. It is even more of a burden than I thought, heavier than Papa's gun for sure, and I don't know how I'll ever keep the barrel up to aim while I'm running at our enemy. All of it is so much to carry.

'Ain't none of you worried how killing is a sin?' Jimmy asks as we're heading back to our row.

'I told you to stop thinking so much about it,' Henry says.

'Ain't you listened to a word Pastor Bowers said these past six months?' Sully asks, and I can't believe he ever sat still long enough to hear. 'All that about protecting the Republic and establishing God's kingdom on Earth?'

'God has sent armies into battle many times to stop the wicked. This is a righteous war, not murder. There's no sin in it.' Will's words make me think of Mama's hand laying a cool cloth across my fevered forehead, wiping away some of the worry I didn't even know I was carrying.

Henry slaps Jimmy on the back and says, 'See? I told you it was nothing.'

As soon as we are lined back up, Jeremiah has his belt halfway off and is sliding his cap box onto it. The other boys all do the same, and so I unbuckle mine rough like a man and fumble at getting the leather through those loops.

'I'll race you,' Sully says, holding up his belt.

Jimmy joins in, like he's already done fretting over what it is we're meant to do, but Jeremiah don't. He is opening and closing his cartridge box, training himself.

I flip open the main flap of my cartridge box and two smaller ones to get to the wooden holder sitting neat with two rows of paper cartridges. I'll never be able to do it fast enough to be any use on the field.

'I win!' Jimmy hollers. 'I beat Sully!'

Sully looks like he can't even believe it. 'There's a first time for everything. Bet you can't do it again.'

Henry says, 'Why do they put so many flaps a man's got to open between him and his Secesh pills?'

'Secesh pills?' Jeremiah asks.

'Yeah,' Henry laughs. 'You ain't heard how we're going to give those Secessionists their medicine?'

Henry keeps laughing, but Jeremiah don't.

'You getting cold feet now, Jeremiah?' Henry asks. 'Didn't you hear Will?'

'It ain't that —'

'Good, cause you'd have some explaining to do after marrying a girl like Rosetta! She's meaner than any Secesh!' Henry slaps his thigh and Jeremiah laughs. I grit my teeth and finger the edge of the cartridge box flap until I can't even feel its coarse stitches.

When all of us have a rifle in our hands and our two Companies are back in rows, Captain looks us over. Then he waves his hand and Sergeant Ames and Sergeant Fitzpatrick step to the front and side, bringing their muskets with them. Ames stands holding the barrel of his rifle and resting its butt on the ground between his legs.

'Company, Loading, Nine Times!' Captain yells.

The ripple going through the rest of the soldiers tells me those words don't mean a thing to any of them either. There is a long pause, until we see the only thing to do is move our rifles to look like how Sergeant Ames is holding his. I hold the cold barrel in my hands, that rifle so long it comes up past my shoulder.

Somebody kicks my heel. When I sneak a look over my shoulder, it is Henry.

'Sure you can handle a big rifle like that?' he says.

Before I can say something smart, Captain yells, 'Load!' and I snap frontward to see Sergeant Ames moving his musket to his left hand and opening his cartridge box with his right. I can't find the latch to my cartridge box and already Captain is yelling, 'Handle Cartridge!' and 'Tear Cartridge!' and Sergeant is putting the cartridges in his mouth and tearing the top off with his teeth. The *ptuh!* of boys spitting is all around me before the dry paper and bitter taste is in my mouth. I spit the paper out to the left side and Henry kicks the back of my heel again.

'Charge Cartridge!'

137

'Captain!' Hiram yells, and a scowl settles on Captain's face.

'Private Binhimer,' Captain says, 'your OUTBURST is UNWELCOME!'

'Captain, Sir. Are we shooting blanks?'

Captain marches along our left flank until he comes to Hiram's row. When he stops in front of Hiram, I am surprised to see Captain is taller.

'You think we have Minie balls to WASTE so the LIKES of YOU can LEARN TO SHOOT?' Captain yells into Hiram's face, and I wonder if Captain has been paying mind to Hiram and his big talk.

Hiram don't even move. 'Sir, no, Sir.'

When Captain snaps himself around and struts off, I try pouring powder into the barrel of my rifle the way Sergeant Ames looks to have done. Only I can't even see the top or the hole I'm pouring into and as soon as Captain is back to the front, the orders keep coming. 'Draw Rammer!' 'Ram Cartridge!' 'Return Rammer!' All around is the metal scraping sound of knife sharpening and sword drawing as we pull our ramrods from their holders, shove them down the barrels, and sheathe them again.

'Prime Cartridge!' he yells.

I am still fumbling with my cap box while there's men all around me hoisting their

138

rifles and the murdering ratchet of hammers being half cocked, and behind me Henry says, 'This ain't no place for a woman!'

I wonder why Jeremiah don't say anything, if he is ever going to say one word on my account again. His eyes are narrow like all he is seeing is Rebels, and if anyone is going to show Henry he's wrong it has got to be me.

Captain orders the first row of soldiers forward. The noise is a sharp crack and rumbling echo and then there is just the smoke from the guns drifting up and away in the wind.

Then we step forward, Jeremiah to my left and Jimmy to my right, like we've practiced. I feel the guns next to me go off before I hear them, and I pull my trigger, the rifle kicking back into my shoulder hard enough for bruising, before I turn and run to keep with Jeremiah, my ears ringing.

'Ain't no different than shooting game,' Henry says when we get back into line. 'Like we all done before. Except for maybe Ross.'

'Oh, I'm tougher than any Rebel,' I say, raising my eyebrow at Henry. 'And I shot a cow on our farm real clean once.' But Sully and Henry laugh and Jeremiah says, 'Shooting livestock ain't the same thing.'

'I've never done much shooting at home either, but I expect I'll learn quick,' Will says, and I could almost hug him.

Henry slaps me on the back and says, 'You got one more shot off than I thought you would, Roset— I mean Ross.'

Jeremiah turns away like he ain't even heard a thing.

After we've been practicing skirmishing and loading for what seems like hours, Captain stops us near his big tent and says, 'It's time you boys learned some real shooting.'

Jeremiah turns to Sully and Jimmy and Henry, the corners of his mouth turned up, and punches Sully in the shoulder like he ain't got a care in this world, like he ain't even noticed me sleeping with my back to him and not saying one word.

The first ten soldiers, Sully one of them, take their places facing ten straw bales with paper targets, and the rest of us line ourselves up behind, our rifles at our sides. Sully shifts his weight from one foot to the other, like he might not wait for orders.

Captain dangles his stopwatch from its fob and shouts, 'Fire and Load at Will!'

The air goes to humming with cartridge boxes opening, boys muttering, cartridges tearing, and ramrods ramming. The shots ring out like popping corn in Mama's skillet, first a few bursts and then a whole volley of so much noise it hurts. Mrs. Chalmers stands outside Captain's big tent, her hands over her ears, watching.

When Captain yells, 'One minute!' most the boys have shot twice. Only a few stand back from the line, Sully being one, their smug faces showing they've made the standard with their three shots.

Captain marches to inspect the targets of the men who've shot three rounds. When he turns to face the Company, he don't look best pleased.

'I would rather see you fire one carefully aimed shot in ten minutes than ten poor shots in one minute,' he says, and his words wipe the smile right off Sully's face. 'Next up!'

This time, most the boys at the front take their aim slow, even with Captain holding that watch. Jimmy fires his musket once and starts loading a second time, but then his face goes red as his hair and he steps back. Captain is down the line, standing at Jimmy's side, and soon as those rifles lower, he is yelling.

'Soldiers! Every one of you is a fresh fish, but Private O'Malley here has made a mistake I hope none of you will ever make again. What is that mistake, O'Malley?'

Jimmy slumps, his mouth moving, saying something nobody can hear.

'O'Malley,' Captain bellows, 'for those of you who can't hear, has LOST his rammer, has fired it down the field. Without your rammer, soldiers, you cannot fire. If you cannot fire, you are of NO USE to this Army and of no help to yourself. O'Malley, retrieve your rammer from the field!'

Jimmy tacks across that field, like a cowed dog hunting for scent. He searches for so long, sweeping wider and wider, until Sergeant Ames sends out four other boys to help.

'I got the blasted fucker!' Hiram Binhimer finally shouts, holding it over his head.

Jimmy snatches that rammer like he ain't the one who lost it and when he comes to our line, no one goes to joking or teasing. Instead, Henry steps out of line and comes at me fast. He grabs my arm.

'You go next,' he says.

Jeremiah says, 'Yeah, let's see if Ross can do it!' making everyone look at me. It stings to hear his doubt, like how he used to bet against me every time I joined a spitting contest.

I walk to the front of our line, making myself taller as I set my rifle in front of me, thinking of the steps, *load charge ram prime aim fire, load charge ram prime aim fire, load charge ram prime aim fire,* until I get the rhythm of it, like my body is doing things and my mind don't have to tell it. After my minute is up, there are only two holes at the edges of my target but Captain says, 'You've done some fine shooting,' as he walks past.

I don't know who he means, me or Ambrose Clark to my right, but I hear my Papa's warm, proud voice after I shot our hurt cow dead, saying, 'You done it clean on the first try, Rosetta.'

I smile right at Henry when I walk past and say, 'Let's see if you can do better.'

Will surprises everybody after we're done shooting and have eaten supper by pulling out a deck of cards. He's always reading his Bible and talking about missing church on the Sabbath, so I can't think how he's come to have that deck.

He says, 'This game is five card stud, last card in the hole.' Them other four settle themselves right down in front of our tent, near enough to the fire to keep the chill off, Sully's lantern in the middle casting flickers on their faces.

I stay put on my tree stump, watching the cards move across the overturned crate,

143

looking up at the inky sky and the stars, until the boys forget about me, until the wind changes and the tangy wood smoke starts stinging.

After a while Sully hollers, 'Hell yeah!'

Jeremiah's eyes flick over to me, a question there. It is nice, him taking an interest in me, even if he's telling me that a boy not playing cards is something queer.

'My Mama don't hold to gambling,' I call over to them, 'so I ain't learned before now. But if you boys don't mind teaching me, I aim to try my luck this game.'

Henry smirks like a wicked devil and says, 'There ain't no better way to entertain myself and make money at the same time as teaching a kid-glove soldier like yourself.'

'Well then, how can I trust you to teach me straight?' I drag my stump over to their circle, pushing between Jeremiah and Will. 'You've all got money riding on it.'

'You're going to lose your money whether we teach you straight or not,' Will says from across the circle and then blushes when all the boys laugh.

'To buy into this game,' Will adds, 'the cost is five dollars.'

'Five dollars! That's almost half a month's pay! And I ain't got paid yet,' I say. 'None of you has.'

'IOUs. What's good enough for Ole Abe is good enough for us,' Sully says. He passes me a pencil and a scrap of paper looks like it came off an envelope.

Once I push my paper signed *Ross Stone, March 4, 1862,* into the center of their little circle, right next to the lantern, Will doles out twenty matchsticks.

After the last hand, Sully's got himself a bigger pile of matchsticks than anyone else, and he is even more puffed up than usual.

'Okay. Now, we're each going to get two cards,' Will says to me, and he starts dealing cards to his left. 'One up and one down. You look at your cards and what everyone else is showing and then you make up your mind.'

'Make my mind up to what?' I ask, and Henry sighs.

None of them has touched their cards yet, but I am itching to see mine.

Sully says, 'You're deciding if you want to bet.'

'Well, how am I to know that?'

'Ain't you been watching?' Henry growls. 'This is why we oughtn't be letting no womanish paleface play.'

Jimmy elbows Henry, but that don't stop me from saying, 'You can just shut your trap, Henry O'Malley. It ain't my fault I

145

never played before!'

Jeremiah says, 'Why don't we play a hand for practice?' but Henry snorts and Sully shakes his head.

'Highest upcard bets first,' Will says, and picks up his card.

I slide mine across the slats and peer at it. There's a two of spades in my hand and a jack of hearts for all to see.

Jeremiah has got a ten of spades on his knee. He gives me a small smile but that don't make me feel one bit better, not when Jimmy with his five of diamonds has to stick up for me and throw elbows instead of my husband.

Will announces, 'Queen bets.'

Sully tosses one matchstick to the center, where it lands next to the pile of scrap paper. Henry pushes his cards facedown to the center.

'Fold,' he says, and makes a sound like growling in the back of his throat before adding, 'I can't get nothing.'

'That ain't a surprise,' I say under my breath.

Now it is my turn. I throw my free hand up. 'How do I know I should bet? It ain't teaching me if no one says a word.'

They start cawing all at once.

Jeremiah is first, saying, 'If you got a pair,

like two twos, you should bet —'

Then Will: 'The higher your pair, the better. If you've got cards in a row, then you're betting for a straight . . .'

'Course, nothing beats a royal flush. A royal flush is a straight flush to the ace . . .'

Nothing in my hand matches, but I want to get the most practice. I set my matchstick in the middle and they all look at me.

'You've got to say whether you're seeing or raising,' Jeremiah says low.

'What's seeing mean?'

'That you're betting what we all bet.'

'Well, ain't it plain if I put out the same thing as the rest of you?'

Jeremiah says, 'You've just got to say it. Maybe you ain't done betting yet. If you don't say it we don't know.'

'Fine then,' I say too loud, 'I see you all.'

Jeremiah being nice now don't make up for him never setting Henry straight. Will raises his eyebrows at me. I stare back.

Finally Will blinks and says, 'I'm out.' Then he deals the next card up.

Sully grins himself silly and throws out three matchsticks.

Jimmy sighs and folds, Henry muttering something about Irish luck. Jeremiah gives Sully a slow grin and drops three matchsticks of his own. I think hard. I ain't got a

147

card that matches and nothing in a row and I can't see my way around losing three more matchsticks.

Jeremiah leans close. 'What you got showing ain't no good.' I know he's talking about the cards, but I reach up to the back of my neck, where my short hair bristles, and wonder what he sees when he's looking at me, if there's anything he likes the look of.

'I fold.'

CHAPTER 11

In the morning, I leave Will cooking sow-belly and wait at the end of our tent row.

'I got something to say to you,' I tell Jeremiah when he comes back from the latrine.

He checks over his shoulder, but there ain't nobody close around, and those boys nearest are busy with breakfast.

'You come with me,' I say, and walk into the trees, heading back to where we were last together alone.

'Where we going?' Jeremiah asks, coming up next to me.

'Just off a ways,' I say. 'Into the woods.'

After that there is only the sound of us tripping through the underbrush and breathing cloud puffs in the cold air.

In a little clearing under a maple tree I stop to look at Jeremiah. 'You embarrassed about me?'

'What?' he says.

'Don't you care for me no more? Maybe you don't like my hair short?'

Jeremiah shakes his head. 'Rosetta, what are you talking about?'

'You're all the time acting like you don't love me, or like you don't even see how nasty Henry is to me. You never even touch me no more.'

'What do you mean?' he asks.

'When Henry called me womanish last night you didn't even say one word to him! And when I was getting ready to shoot, you made all the boys watch me, saying what you did, and acting like you didn't even think I could do it neither, same as when you bet against me in spitting contests. That ain't right!'

'I ain't treating you any different than any of the other boys,' he says, his face bland. 'This is what you wanted!'

'That's just it!' I say, stomping my foot at him throwing my words back in my face. 'You've got to treat me different sometimes! You've got to treat me like I'm still your wife sometimes.'

'How can I? How can I touch you? You ain't here like Mrs. Chalmers is. You ain't here as my wife. You're here as a soldier.'

'I'm still your wife. That's the only reason

I'm here! Ain't I still doing your cooking?'

'Didn't you think maybe we wouldn't be like at home?' he says. 'Didn't you think maybe it'd have to be different?'

'You found ways to touch me at home, before we were ever even courting.'

'What do you want me to do? Hold your hand? Kiss you in front of everyone?'

'I ain't asking you to be stupid. But maybe you ought to treat me nice sometimes. Even Jimmy sticks up for me more than you do.' I've got him at least a little bit with those words because he sighs and runs his fingers through his dirty hair.

'The boys don't like you being here,' he says.

'They ain't ever minded me coming along before.'

'This ain't the same as fishing, Rosetta. And you're my wife now. Henry don't want your blood on his hands. He keeps saying I ought not either — he says you're tagging along and flustering me —'

'I don't care what Henry thinks! You care about him more than me? Maybe Henry ain't my friend if he thinks I've only ever been in the way.'

'This ain't about who's being your friend, Rosetta! It's about how you shouldn't even be here! And you said you'd go back when it was time.'

'It ain't time,' I say. 'We ain't even fighting yet.'

'Well, I'm fighting all the time over something! I'm tired of it!'

'Oh, and you think I'm not tired? You think I like being treated like my husband don't even know me? Like I'm nothing? And all the while I've got to worry if anybody else will come to know what I am.'

'We'll be moving soon, to the Capital. Everybody says it. And then it won't be long. Once the weather turns nice, we're bound to fight. Ain't no sense in you coming any farther.'

'There's plenty sense in it! If I desert now I won't get a penny! I've got to at least stay 'til we get paid. I can't go home now! What would everyone think of me, disappearing and my husband sending me home looking like this?'

'Maybe you should have thought of that before!'

'Turns out there's a lot of things I should have thought before. But I'm here so none of that matters now.'

'It'll be harder to keep you safe,' he says, quiet. 'There'll be more people, more men to see. The boys can't always keep covering for you.'

'Covering for me?' I snort. 'Aside from maybe Jimmy, ain't none of you covered for me even once! Calling me *ma'am* and womanish and singling me out for cooking and shooting. Covering for me —' I spit the words and Jeremiah almost looks sorry. 'It'll be easier when there's more people. Ain't no one going to notice me.'

'Maybe you could be like Mrs. Chalmers. You could be a laundress or a nurse —' he says, but he don't look at me.

'How can I do that now? How can I go from being a soldier to all of a sudden being your wife in a dress? You think Hiram would leave me alone then?'

He sighs before saying, 'I heard how some Companies got a Daughter of the Regiment staying back at the fighting carrying the flag.'

'Seems like carrying a flag ain't a way to stay safe. This Daughter of the Regiment gets the same pay? Or laundresses? You think they get paid the same?'

'That I don't know.'

'Well, I ain't interested if I don't get paid. You forgetting about our farm? You even still want that farm with me?' He flinches when I say it. 'Well then, it don't matter where I'm at, in the front or at the back, long as the pay's the same and that's that!'

'I could turn you in.' He says it so slow, looking right at me, like it pains him to say the thing.

'You wouldn't,' I say, lifting my chin.

'I might. If it keeps you from being in harm's way.'

'You can't be rid of me that easy.'

'It ain't you I want to be rid of! It's just —'

That is all I need, to hear that he ain't changed toward me, and I reach out for his hand. 'Can't you find a way to still be husband to me sometimes? Ain't this time here, this being together, ain't that better than the nothing we'd have if I'd stayed home?'

He looks at me. And then he pulls me to his chest, his stubble catching at my hair as he says, 'I'm always husband to you. But —'

I don't let him finish. I kiss him full on the mouth.

'You just keep thinking that then,' I say, and turn on my heel in the slippery mud.

When Captain finally gets around to making us look like soldiers, Jeremiah takes a moment from admiring his own outfit to grab my elbow and say, 'Don't be getting ideas, Rosetta. It's just until there's orders,' like we ain't even had that talk out in the woods.

I don't let it make me sour, though. What gets me is how I thought it'd feel right nice to put on that blue coat, but the Army seems to have forgotten to notice the shape of any of us. My trousers are the most ridiculous articles I ever did put on. They hide my shoes if I don't roll them, and the brogans are the most crooked things besides, but there ain't no help for it.

Jeremiah fiddles with his coat. His uniform fits him true, and I want to grab his hands and stop them before he finishes with the buttons. He's never looked so much like something, not even on our wedding day, and his grin has a pride to it I ain't ever seen. There ain't none of that confidence coming over me, wearing these clothes. Only maybe I ain't got to be so careful now. Maybe these clothes will cover me better than the ones from home.

Jeremiah pushes his way out of the tent and I follow, my cuffs already coming unrolled and dragging in the mud. The whole Company is outside, strutting and posing in the sunny aisle, roosters with new feathers. Even Will looks like he is standing a touch taller in front of his tent, watching everyone else preening. Only Ambrose sits on his crate, always looking like he is grieved.

Sully tells everyone, 'Getting uniforms must mean we're getting our orders to the Capital any day now!'

'You got that on authority?' I ask.

'Well, no,' he says, some of the shine going out of him.

'You are about the worst gossip I ever met,' I say. 'Worse than any woman!'

That sets Sully to sputtering and the rest of the boys to laughing. Still, it don't take but a minute before they are back to fancying themselves.

I ask Jimmy, 'How long are your coat sleeves?'

He shrugs out of his coat and even though they say they are the same size, when we lay our coats next to each other, it turns out the sleeves on his come down at least an inch farther.

'You want to switch?' Jimmy asks.

Henry watches us, shaking his head, and it is a wonder how one O'Malley got to be so nice and the other so mean.

'No,' I say. 'You've got longer arms. Wouldn't make sense, us switching.'

Even if they don't fit good, all of us look dashing in our blue coats. I leave one button undone like the officers do and stand up tall and make my face serious. I put my hand in my coat the way Captain does sometimes and that brings to mind that sign back in Herkimer.

'We've got to have our likeness taken,' I say, thinking on finding a ribbon in town to send Betsy too. I almost fall over when Jeremiah and Sully and Will agree without me even trying. It takes more work to bring the O'Malleys around, but the next day being Sunday it's no trick at all to get Sergeant's permission to leave camp and go the few miles to Utica to find us a photo man.

■ ■ ■ ■

UNION

NEAR WASHINGTON, D.C.:
MARCH–JUNE 1862

■ ■ ■ ■

'Entreat me not to leave thee, or to return from following after thee.'

— *Ruth 1:16*

CHAPTER 12

FORT CORCORAN, VIRGINIA: MARCH 1862
When I was staring at Miss Riggs' big map
of all the territories, thinking outside the
tall window of the schoolhouse, past the
bone-white church with a pale blue sky
behind it, dreaming myself through Wiscon-
sin's rolling prairie, and across the wide
Mississippi River, all the way over the Rocky
Mountains and then to California where
maybe there would still be some gold left
for the taking, I never really thought my
ideas would come to much. Now here I am,
so far from home, more than three hundred
miles on the map Jeremiah gave me. Only
seeing Fort Corcoran the first time makes
me almost wish I never left.

The fort is nothing but dirt and banks and
ditches and telegraph wires strung up on
poles, jittering in the cold wind coming off
the river. We march along a tall fence looking like a row of trees with their branches

161

peeled off and through a wide gate, slipping our way through the melting snow and mud, heading to the high ground, the whole Regiment together now, all eleven Companies, more than two whole villages of people.

'We're really soldiers now,' Sully yells.

Jeremiah says, 'You got that right!' and he don't even look my way. Instead, he somehow gets the boys talking about the war.

Edward is the only one louder than Sully and the two of them next to each other make a fine pair, Edward with his tree-thick limbs and Sully with his deer legs.

'Don't mean much, being a soldier in the Army when the Navy is doing all the fighting,' Edward says. 'Those damn Greybacks keep making the Union look like a pack of fools, sinking our warships!'

'That ain't what I heard,' Sully says. 'I heard the USS *Monitor* beat the Rebs' ironclad down there in Chesapeake Bay!'

'They say there ain't even been any soldiers killed, Union or Confederate, on those ironclads,' Jimmy says quiet.

'Where you getting your news?' Edward asks. 'I like what you've been hearing!'

'Maybe we should've signed on with the Navy,' Jeremiah says.

'Ain't any grief in joining an Army that don't fight much,' I say.

162

'You don't see any grief?' Edward shouts, turning on me. 'I'd sure like to know what you're doing in an Army if you ain't keen on fighting! People are counting on us keeping those Seceshes from coming North, is what you mean. The Seceshes have got designs on our goddamn Capital, and we're here to stop them. But I guess you'd rather let those Rebs run roughshod all over us on their way to Washington?'

'I'm saying if the Union wins the war and I don't have to fight —' As soon as the words are out of my mouth, I live to regret them.

'We got people counting on us back home, is all Ross means,' Jeremiah says real quick, his hand on my elbow.

I keep on even though Edward's eyes are trained on my face, even as he's stepping closer to me, his shoulders back in a way that makes my hands go to fists. 'I'm saying there's all kinds of things I aim to do in my life —'

'And what might that be?' Edward says. 'What you got to do that's more important than winning this —'

'The Navy keeps winning, maybe we ain't ever going to get our chance to fight — or even see a battlefield!' Jeremiah steps right in front of me and shoots me a look wither-

163

ing enough to dry up a whole garden. Somehow his words are enough to get the boys talking about Rebels and when the next Union victory will be, and then no one is worrying themselves over the fool thoughts I can't keep in my head even to save myself and I am left to be secretly pleased over Jeremiah protecting me like he ought.

No one seems to mind him, but old Thomas Stakely says the thing I like best. 'All the Union needs is one good General and one good win. Then this war will be over and we'll have our country back and be home to our kin before harvest time.'

No matter what Edward or Jeremiah says, there's comfort in the idea that maybe we won't ever see Rebels up close, that maybe they will just stay where they belong, and Jeremiah will stop trying to send me home without him. We might almost be to Nebraska come Fall. All I know is, looking at dirt and dead trees ain't how I plan to spend my last days. This fort's cannons don't make me feel safe, but I sure ain't ready to be marching across a field with only my musket between me and the Rebels.

Sully is itchy to go with the millboys who keep talking war the loudest, but Jeremiah says, 'We've got to stick close — look out for each other.' It makes Sully roll his eyes and Henry mutter 'Watch out for Ross is what you mean,' but still those boys come along.

We line up in front of a rough-hewn shed with chinks left between the timbers. Captain Chalmers is standing there, the Union flag flapping behind him, a strange officer next to him, a big man with sloped shoulders and a down-turned mouth to match. The only bright thing about him is his gold tasseled sash.

'I heard that's Colonel Wheelock in front of the blockhouse,' Sully whispers.

'Men,' Colonel Wheelock booms, 'this is our home until we're ordered on campaign. I apologize there's no proper barracks, but as you've already endured tents this past month, I expect it will be no great hardship.' He points to a wagon standing off to his side, stacked with big wooden crates. 'Those are your tents there, to be pitched as soon as we have laid out the rows.'

While we wait, Sergeant Ames tells us our tents are big enough to fit four, but because we are the only Regiment at the fort, for now we only have to be two to a tent. Jeremiah winks at me. I'm thinking on the niceness of a tent to ourselves when Sully punches Jeremiah on the shoulder and says, 'I need a partner. Think Sergeant'll let me share with you?'

Will spins, a hurt look on his face, and Jeremiah don't say anything at first. There's buzzing all around us, boys saying, 'You got anybody yet?' and 'I'm bunking with you!' or 'You need a friend?'

Sully says, 'I'll help you keep Ross safe, like you said.'

There is a long moment before Sully laughs and gives me a shove.

'I got you good! Don't worry, I'm staying with Will,' he says, and Will's shoulders relax.

When we finally get to work setting up camp, white canvas tents go flapping in the wind and there's the sound of pounding and swearing up and down our Company's row. Jeremiah is all concentration, and the only words passing his lips are orders like, 'Turn it this way,' or, 'Give that here.' He is everywhere at once, hardly letting me do a thing.

Captain walks down our row, giving commands: 'Make this line straighter! Tamp that stake in more firmly!'

It can't be this way, not with Captain patrolling. I've got to do my share, but Jeremiah pounds the steel stakes to hold the edges of our tent down and won't let go of our only mallet. He aims for me to move our knapsacks inside that tent and lay out our blankets and string up our lantern so come night we've got an easy time of it. Things fit for a woman, things a wife might do.

Soon, there ain't a single boy who ain't working. Sully and Will have practically got their whole tent up, while Henry is still spreading out the canvas pieces just so, looking over each one, and Jimmy pounding in the stakes laid out neat around the edges. Henry looks at our tent barely up and me doing nothing and shakes his head. Once even Will looks at me, standing there like he can't figure me out somehow.

I sit on the wooden crate our tent came out of, feeling easier. Jeremiah sits on the ground beside me, poking at the fire with a stick. I want to curl up next to him and trace the new beard that's clinging to his jaw and flatten myself against him. I want to feel like we are home, just the two of us in our Little House with the woods around it and the smell of earth plowed up for growing things. But instead there is the golden light of the fire bright on Jeremiah's cheeks and no nice supper coming and no big bed. Instead there is the yelling and laughing and singing of the men all around us.

Jeremiah stands up and says, 'I'm going to check on Sully and the O'Malleys, maybe see if we can find some more wood for cooking supper.'

'That's fine,' I nod. 'I've got a letter to write.'

'To your folks?'

'That's right. Figure I ought to tell them where I've gone.'

'Might be good they hear it from you.'

I watch him go down our aisle and then I sit down to tell my folks all the nice parts.

March 14, 1862

Dear Mama, Papa and Betsy,
I am writing to tell you I am Gone with Jeremiah, and Safe. I am sorry for not writing you sooner, or telling you my plans, but I could not see him go to fight this War and stay Home. I am cleaving to my husband, as the Bible says I ought. I aim to help as Best I can and Earn what money I may, even if it means soldiering. I will send what I can Home for you and for the Farm and will write to tell you where we have got to.

Don't you worry none about me, I am Happy here with Friends all around, as you can see in the likeness I am sending. That Boy you don't know is named Will. We are doing nothing but Drilling and learning to Shoot and building up the fort, and I am Pleased to say I can do All of it as Well as any man here.

For Betsy I am sending this Ribbon. Don't you think it is a pretty Blue? You would be Amazed to see the Ribbons and Fine Things the ladies in Washington or even over in Utica wear.

When you write, you can direct letters to Pvt. Ross Stone, 97th Regiment, NYSV, Company H in care of Captain Chalmers via Washington D.C. The word all around camp is that we will be moving Soon now we shoot and march straight — maybe off into Virginia.

I am still,
Your Rosetta

Once I have got that letter written nice, I tuck it with the map inside my coat pocket. Putting it in Sergeant's mailbag will have to wait for morning because there is Jeremiah coming back down the aisle with an armful of wood and the rest of the boys and it is a sure thing they are all hungry.

■ ■ ■ ■

Inside our tent, while Jeremiah does up the ties on the flap, I sit on my blankets and wonder how it is we are supposed to be husband and wife here where we still ain't got real walls. Since leaving home I ain't slept outside of my clothes even once, ain't even washed, really. Not with Mama's lavender water like I sometimes used to. But then Jeremiah turns to me.

'We ain't had time like this since we were back home,' he whispers.

'You think it's okay here?'

'Why wouldn't it be?' Jeremiah asks.

All the nights we shared a tent with the O'Malleys, sometimes after Henry would get to snoring and Jimmy would start up with grinding his teeth, Jeremiah's hands would find me, would find their way to places, sometimes I would find my way to him, our mouths bearing down on each other's to keep from making sound.

'If anybody hears . . .' I say, wishing for our Little House away in the woods. 'Or if there was action and we had to get up and we weren't —' It's like we are sneaking and worrying, like before we were married.

'You think too much,' Jeremiah says, and

as he sinks down in front of me, I know he is right.

He reaches to touch my hair and I remember rinsing it in vinegar to be nice for him.

'I miss this,' he says.

'It'll grow back. When we're done soldiering.'

'Mrs. Wakefield,' Jeremiah whispers.

'Yes,' I say, thinking how he ain't had occasion to call me that since we were back home.

'It is nice being with you,' he says. 'Just you.'

I kiss him then, and I don't care about the O'Malleys or Sully and Will in the tents next to ours or what they might hear. In the dark, I tear at Jeremiah's shirt and his hands work at mine. His skin is smooth under that shirt, not like the roughness of his hands that are working to unwrap my binding and I will never get myself bound up in time if the bugles or drums call us, but then he has got the binding free and he lowers me onto our scratchy woolen blankets. I wish for our soft bed and covers to lie in, until our chests press together, so warm. Then we are pulling and kicking our way out of our trousers, our breath coming fast, and trying to keep quiet as we lie like man and wife, but I can't help myself and I call Jeremiah to me, whispering his name, whispering 'Mr. Wakefield' so I can hear him call me my rightful name again.

After what seems like hours at morning inspection, Sergeant Ames finally dismisses our work teams. We march through the palisade gate, and I shift my knapsack again, trying to ease my back. Only now there is a tightness rippling across my belly too. Relief washes over me that the aching ain't got a thing to do with the pack I'm carrying, but then a wave of worry comes. I've got to get myself a moment alone in the stand of trees we've been cutting down so the Army can keep this fort up. Much longer and there won't be a way to keep the secret of what I am.

I scurry down the rough dirt road next to Jeremiah. We ain't but a few steps when Edward pulls something out of his pocket.

'My brother sent me a carte de visite I bet you'd all pay money to see,' he says, and holds the card out on the palm of his hand. Hiram is closest and as soon as he bends over to take a look, he gets to hooting. That makes the other boys, Henry and Jimmy and young Frank Morgan, crowd around. Ambrose is the only one who keeps walking.

Frank is saying, 'I wouldn't mind poking a girl like that!' as I try to elbow my way through the clump of bodies, Jeremiah slowing in front of me.

There, in the palm of Edward's meaty hand, is a picture of a lady with no clothes on, lying on a couch for anyone to see. I've never seen such a thing.

'Oh,' I say, just before Jeremiah pushes me back out of the way. I catch Will's eyes and he drops them right to the ground.

Thomas says, 'I don't want to look at a woman of low virtue. And none of you ought to either.'

It makes the boys break up their circle and get back to walking, even though Hiram tells Thomas, 'Your wife ain't anywhere near but you are still the stodgiest man I ever fucking met!'

'Some people call it fidelity,' Thomas snaps.

I touch Jeremiah's elbow. He slows down until all our party is gone up ahead.

'Rosetta, I didn't even really look at what was on that — And anyway, while you're here you're going to have to get used to —'

'I don't care about the picture. We ain't having a baby and I've got to get myself some time away,' I whisper. Jeremiah cocks his head, confused, and I ain't ever thought

173

I'd have to explain it to someone else. 'It's my woman's time . . . my monthlies?'

'I see,' Jeremiah nods, and his smile should make me happy but it don't.

When we reach the woodlot, he and I go far enough so the sound of the boys talking and Henry swearing every time his and Jimmy's saw snags don't hardly reach us. I push my way into the low darkness of a thicket, crouching to dig through my knapsack and find the flannel strips shoved to the bottom, where anyone would have to go searching for them. I fashion a thick wad, hoping it can last, wondering about once I don't need it no more, once it is soiled.

Through the trees Jeremiah stands guard, his back to me, his weight resting on one leg.

'My Papa was always so pleased when he got a baby on my Mama, like he forgot all my brothers on the hill,' I say as I push through the brush. It is safe enough I put my arms around him.

'I can't see how he'd forget a burden like that,' Jeremiah says, 'with all the bad luck your Mama had.'

'I don't know what he was so pleased about. I ain't ever found one special thing about a baby, not even Betsy, unless more laundry and mending and coddling when there's work to be done has got something to it that I don't understand.'

'Well, there ain't no farm that don't have babies a part of it,' Jeremiah says. 'And seeing my brothers with their babies — seems the trouble might be worth it.'

We ain't ever talked about children before. For the first time I see a picture of that farm that ain't only me and Jeremiah, and hired hands come harvest. There is Jeremiah in a red barn with a dark-haired child on his shoulders, telling what makes a good cow, and the two of them poking their fingers in the dirt, sowing seeds.

'It ain't our time yet.' Jeremiah squeezes me real quick. 'But your Mama's troubles ain't got to be yours.'

Chapter 13

FORT CORCORAN, VIRGINIA: APRIL 1862
We're at mail call, and Mrs. Chalmers is there. She stands at the front of our lines, smiling at men, her skirt clean. She uses that smile of hers, gets those men's attention. I watch Jeremiah close to see if her soft skin and pretty mouth draw him too, but if they do he don't let himself get caught looking.

Instead, he leans over and says, 'Now that Captain's wife sure is a pretty thing. A nice proper wife any man would like to have. Looks nice in that dress of hers too.'

'Well, she ain't your wife and you ain't any man, seeing how you picked a different sort.' I glare back at him.

He grabs me round the neck, pulls my head toward his belly button, the sort of thing I've seen the boys do a hundred times. The sort of touching won't attract no notice.

'I got a fighting wife, that's a fact,' he says,

176

rubbing his knuckles across my scalp, knocking my kepi off.

I push him, but he just laughs.

'Don't you think if Ross here put on a calico dress, he'd look almost as pretty as Mrs. Chalmers?' Henry says loud enough for everyone around us to hear. Jeremiah stiffens. His hand on my elbow is the only thing that keeps me from turning on Henry.

It stings when Edward laughs, saying, 'I think it'd be a damn sight harder for Ross to look as sweet as that honey,' and it is a good thing Mrs. Chalmers calls his name right then to come collect a letter. He throws a wink over his shoulder at us as he goes to her, his face bright, looking like he might bend over at the waist and bow down like trampled wheat.

Edward is handsome in the way of a good workhorse, but Mrs. Chalmers don't seem to take special notice of him. I wonder what that's like, for a woman to do that to a man who ain't hers, if a plain girl like me could do that as easy as Mrs. Chalmers does if I tried. There ain't much strength in a woman who is only good at smiling, but I wonder if that is the kind of wife most men see for themselves. Still, if she knew about the dirty pictures Edward gets in his mail, I bet she wouldn't be so keen on giving him smiles or anything else neither.

When Edward has turned back, I almost jump out of my skin to hear Mrs. Chalmers read my name. I thread through the other men waiting, trying not to look at her. Still, I can't help staring as I take the square of paper from her hand, her skin silk like she's never done a bit of real work. My skin ain't never been that tender, not since I was a baby.

Mrs. Chalmers catches me staring and smiles before ducking her head. I turn away fast, snatching the thin packet out of her hand, blushing at how she must think I'm looking on her like the other men do.

Papa's thick writing is on the face of that envelope, so firm it's gone and pressed the letters into the paper and I am so hungry to read it, I almost can't wait 'til I am safe from prying eyes.

The letter is short and all in Papa's hand.

March 29, 1862

Dear Rosetta,
The Farm misses you. There is work aplenty with Planting coming on but you know Isaac Lewis is hired to help do the work and he is a good worker and strong.

The North field will be in wheat this year, and I think to plant potatoes in the rest. There's 3 new calfs just this week, one spotted.

We first thought it a Relief to get word, but the news of Your letter goes Hard with Mama and Betsy and adds to our Worries. I see how you try to do Right, but they are feeling the Stain of it on their heads, Seeing how Most Everyone here has been talking of you being gone. We wish you had Spoken to us of those plans on your last visit.

Mama says for me to tell you to Keep the Money you earn for whatever kind of Future you Hope to have.

It is a hard thing, you being Gone this way.

We Pray for you,
Your Father, Charles Edwards

My hands are shaking before I get to the end. Papa don't say it, but from the words he put on that page and the way Mama and Betsy ain't added a thing to it in their own hand, I have shamed them. I shouldn't have put what I've done before them; I shouldn't have sent that tintype. Mama don't want nothing to do with me, and Betsy ain't said even a word of thanks about the ribbon I sent. It is a long time before I stand up and push my way out of our tent. Only the campfire is still there, dying down to embers, the boys all gone. I take big strides and thrust that letter in the coals and there is no one to stop me.

The letter curls its edges in the flames and goes black and fluttery. The breeze picks up some of the flakes, blowing them down the line to where a circle of boys play cards outside Edward Stiles' tent. That must be where Jeremiah has got to.

No one notices when I walk up. Jeremiah stares at his cards, a pile of matchsticks in front of him. When he glances up at me, he wears a sly smile that tells me he is winning. It ain't the time to try talking to him. I shrug and turn away, telling myself it is better he thinks I've got things of my own to do, that I don't need attention all the time the way some girls do.

When Will sees me walking away, he calls out, 'Ross! You've got to play! I've been wanting to win something off you!' and the boys laugh.

I don't turn back, making my way through camp instead, up our Company street, past the rows of shelter tents, where clusters of men gather, finding ways to pass the time 'til dinner. I ain't ever thought I'd get to

feeling lonely, but there's all these men doing men things and no proper company for
a woman. When women gather, they are
always doing something of use, quilting to
make the work go faster for each other,
keeping company while they sew for kin,
making long days nursing babies easier,
passing gossip and family news. Here the
men sing bawdy songs and play at cards and
lose money their families need.

I find myself walking round to the other
side of the parade ground, past Sergeant's
and the other Company officers' tents, until
I get to Captain's big tent, set way off from
the rest, where the stench of the latrines
almost don't reach. At his camp, there's
signs of a woman with too much time on
her hands in the fresh-swept dooryard and
the dripping washrags even-spaced on the
line stretched between two young pines, the
water leaving little dimples in the dirt below.

I'm turning to go, my feet ruining the
broom's crosshatching lines, when the tent
flaps fly open and Mrs. Chalmers stoops to
look through, holding a lantern up, even
though it's only getting on dusk now.

'Oh! I thought I heard something out
here! You startled me! Captain Chalmers
isn't here at the moment. Perhaps I can
relay a message?'

'I — I didn't come to speak to Captain,' I say.

'You didn't? Well, then what brings you?' She hangs the lantern on the hook standing outside the tent.

Any made-up reason for coming flies clean out of my head. I ain't even sure why I've come myself. I see how it's got to be, but before I can turn to go, she ducks inside the tent and comes back with a basket and her arms full of flannel strips.

'I was rolling bandages. Please. Sit.' She points to the cleared folding table and chairs in front of the tent and sits down herself.

I look this way and that before saying, 'Mrs. Chalmers, it ain't prop—'

'There isn't a soul who pays what I do any mind,' she says, holding a strip of oatmeal-colored flannel out to me. 'And if anybody starts, well, there isn't any harm in you helping me on a hospital project to aid our wounded soldiers, is there?' She smiles at me, tucking a loose strand of auburn hair behind her ear before saying, 'There, now that's solved, what brings you here?'

'I can't — It ain't right, you being a married woman, and me being a soldier. And Captain, I don't want trouble with him.'

She don't look up from the bandage she's rolling when she says, 'That's the most

182

anybody's said to me the entire time I have been here, save my husband.'

'I've got to get back before I'm missed.' I start to push away from the table.

'Please —' she says, reaching to grab my arm, and then my heart just stops to see Captain Chalmers standing at the edge of her swept dooryard, watching the two of us. I pull free of Mrs. Chalmers, saluting her husband as I walk by, his eyes on me the whole time.

I could kick myself for getting caught talking with Captain Chalmers' wife. It is about the stupidest thing I've done in my whole life, going and ruining everything, calling attention to myself.

The boys are still playing cards, sitting there like not a thing is different, and that's because for them nothing is.

Jeremiah turns to me before going back to his cards. That sweet look don't make me feel better like it ought, it just makes me want to cry.

Edward says, 'Where you coming from, Little Soldier?'

'Nowhere,' I say. 'Moseying around.'

'You hear anything new about Yorktown?' Sully asks.

I can't even think straight, so I stare at

him until he shakes his head.

Will says, 'At Sunday services we prayed for General McClellan, that he would know how best to storm the city.'

'You think he could take Yorktown? With the soldiers he's got? I bet he'll send for more troops,' Sully says.

Henry says, 'McClellan don't ever do a thing except sit and wait and everybody knows it.'

Hiram spits, 'At least Grant fucking wins.'

'Yeah,' Edward says, 'and only thirteen thousand men killed for it at Shiloh.'

Some of the boys laugh, but Thomas is always acting the papa. 'Ain't right to laugh at so many soldiers getting killed because some General was too drunk and saw fit to drill instead of make entrenchments.'

Ambrose mutters something about a little drink never hurting anyone and there is a long silence before Jeremiah says, 'Well, McClellan can't wait forever!'

I can't wait forever either. Any minute Captain might send Sergeant to come find me, or maybe some orderly, and they will drag me off for dallying with the Captain's wife. But I can't say a thing about it. All I can do is sit like McClellan, listening to the boys talk about war like it is one big adventure, saying they can't wait to send those

Rebels home like they ain't thinking how some of the soldiers on that battlefield ain't ever going to leave it again. They talk big but there ain't one of them that does any real thinking or says even one thing that might be how they really feel. Not even Jeremiah. I don't dare say a thing about the way they're pretending to be brave, like their uniforms make them something different than just farm boys in blue coats. If I wasn't wearing this uniform, I could talk to Mrs. Chalmers any time I please.

It's like Miss Riggs standing me before the whole class, making me read, *'Lesson XXXI, On Speaking the Truth: There are many ways of being guilty of a falsehood without uttering the lie direct, in words.'* There ain't an honest thing about being in this Army, but then that ain't what I came all this way for.

When the boys finally finish their poker game and we go to our tents, I'm nothing but one big prickly feeling. I can't lie quiet, and it don't take but a minute before Jeremiah groans and rolls away from me. 'What is eating you?'

'Captain Chalmers saw me talking to his wife and maybe he's going to send me home.'

'What? When?'

'I don't know. It could be any time!'

'No,' Jeremiah says. 'When did Captain Chalmers see you talking to his wife?'

'Earlier. After I got that letter. When you were playing cards, I went and Mrs. Chalmers was there rolling bandages . . .'

'He's known all night you were talking to his wife?'

In the dark I nod.

'You're fine then,' he says, and finds my hand, squeezes it. 'Nothing's going to happen if it ain't already. Captain wouldn't sit on a thing like that if he thought anything of it.'

'You sure?'

'I'm sure.' Jeremiah wraps his arms around me and holds me close, my ear against his chest. 'You just stop thinking on it now and let us get some sleep.' And then, like it is something easy, he don't take but two minutes to start breathing slow and his arms slip away.

I ain't resting and I don't see how Jeremiah can be so sure. But there ain't any help for the way I'm feeling except one. I grope for Jeremiah, kissing him awake.

'You hold me.'

I say something of my good-byes to him, in case it comes to that, and he don't complain one bit more about getting sleep.

After roll call and battalion drill, Captain still ain't sent for me. It seems I should have stopped worrying myself last night like Jeremiah said because maybe it's true that nobody pays mind to what Mrs. Chalmers does, not even her husband. We stack our arms, fitting the bayonets together to make the rifles stand like tent poles, and settle in to rest.

'Hey, Ross! Did you hear anything from Betsy in that letter you got? It was from home, wasn't it?' Jimmy leans to ask me and I am glad for a second when Captain's aide, Josiah Price, comes running. He can't be more than fourteen, still fresh-faced and big-eyed, breathing fit to die. Sully jumps up and blurts out, 'You got orders for us?'

Josiah shakes his head. Finally, when he catches his breath, he looks round at us and says, 'Private Stone? Captain Chalmers wants to see you, right away.'

My heart about drops out of my boots.

Jeremiah stands. 'I'm coming along.'

'It's a private matter,' Josiah announces, straightening up. 'He sent me special.'

I try to smile, but inside my whole self is falling to pieces. 'Guess I better go then.'

'He said for you to bring your knapsack.'

'Couldn't last forever,' Henry says, shaking his head like he's sorry when he ain't one bit.

My eyes find Jeremiah's and we hold them together, and at least it is good he knows what might happen. 'I'll be back,' I say, but Jeremiah's shoulders slump to see me slinging my knapsack on again.

Josiah goes at such a clip I've almost got to jog to keep up with him, a sick feeling coming over me at being called out special. It can't be any good, Captain's notice falling on me. There ain't a thing I've done in drill or over the past few days to warrant this except one, and then there at Captain's tent is Mrs. Chalmers sitting at the table, her head low.

I am caught for something I ain't even done and all that's left is whether I am punished or sent home.

'Private Stone,' Captain says, starched and formal. 'It has come to my attention that you saw fit to speak to my wife last night.'

'Sir, I —' I try not to look away.

'I have not ASKED you a QUESTION!' Captain barks. 'My wife says you approached her. Is that TRUE?'

Captain ain't ever going to believe me over

188

his wife, and the lie dies right in my throat.

'It's the truth, Sir.' I hold my voice steady, swallowing as he glares at me.

'Speaking to an officer's wife is entirely INAPPROPRIATE,' he says.

'Sir, I apologize —'

'I HAVE NOT ASKED YOU A QUESTION!' he yells again, and even Mrs. Chalmers jumps.

He pauses a moment, his eyes boring into mine before he says, 'Mrs. Chalmers has told me of your proclivities and I see now that perhaps employment of a different sort might be better suited to your talents.'

He knows what I am. His wife has found me out, but still I say, 'I am quite happy soldiering, Sir.'

'To be sure, I have no intention of sacrificing any of my soldiers from their duty to our nation, when the time comes.' He glances at Mrs. Chalmers. 'However, until then perhaps your service could be of use in hospital duties. My wife has need of an escort and our wounded have need of attention.'

'Sir, I ain't got no talent for the sick and no fondness for doctors —' I can barely think, let alone talk.

'There is no need for false modesty,' Captain Chalmers says. 'My wife was quite impressed with your practical knowledge.'

My eyes fly to Mrs. Chalmers, but she don't raise her head from the table, and I wonder what it is she has told Captain. Relief floods my body and brand-hot anger gallops right on after.

'You will be expected to accompany Mrs. Chalmers to Judiciary Square Hospital and return this evening. I trust you will keep my wife safe.' He surveys me and then adds, 'I believe Mrs. Chalmers is ready to start this instant. Have you enough provisions for your own supper?'

'Yes, Sir,' I say, because she has worked it so I can't say no.

'That will be all then.' He salutes and then turns to his wife, who is beaming at him. She stands, picks up her basket full of bandages from the bench where it was resting beside her. She touches Captain's arm, her fingers drifting slow across his sleeve, and whispers, 'Thank you,' as she steps toward me, the smile still on her lips, making me think of Carrie Jewett sashaying over to Jeremiah, laying her hand on his shoulder, blinking up at him, asking if he knew where to find some nettle for her Mama's breathing.

Anyone could see Carrie didn't care one bit about nettle, but the way Jeremiah smiled it was easy to see he'd forgot all about the time at the creek when he said a girl like Carrie weren't practical for a farm wife and anyway you never could tell where the truth of her feelings lay.

It ain't fair the way some girls always get what they want with those smiles of theirs or how when a woman does the asking, I am always getting tasks I don't want.

I make my face stone and walk fast toward the tents. Mrs. Chalmers struggles to keep my pace. When we are far enough from Captain, I whirl on her, keeping my voice quiet and steady in case anybody takes notice.

'I've got to stop by my camp. Tell my people I'm coming back. I thought I was in trouble for sure.' Her hand flies to cover her mouth, her face even more pale beneath the brim of her hat. I turn away and keep marching.

'I'm sorry. I was only thinking of those poor soldiers — and it isn't possible to go on my own —' She scurries to keep pace alongside me.

Maybe I oughtn't be talking to the Captain's wife like she ain't nothing different than me, but the hot words and all my mad and worry just spit from my mouth.

'You don't need an escort! If you were of

a mind, you could go and help them any time you please.'

From the set of her mouth and the tears coming, she ain't used to being spoke to like that, and I think to apologize but we are close enough that Jeremiah sees me from the stump he is sitting on, my stump.

'Ross!' He yells for me and runs down the aisle. The relief on his face is clear as a full moon. 'What happened?' He comes as if to hug me, but I put my arms straight out to his shoulders and stop him from knocking clean into me.

'I've got orders to escort Mrs. Chalmers to Judiciary Square Hospital and help the wounded. We aim to be back after supper.'

Jeremiah stands a bit straighter when he sees Mrs. Chalmers in the aisle behind me.

'Thank the Lord,' Jeremiah breathes, and he looks at Ambrose sitting at the fire next to where we've stopped before taking my arm and leading me back to the boys at our tent, Mrs. Chalmers hanging back.

'I thought — we all thought —' Jeremiah says.

'Well, it ain't that, not yet if I can help it.'

I give Jeremiah's shoulder a pat and he says, 'You had me worried,' so low I almost think the words slipped out of his mouth without his knowing.

'I've got to go,' I say, letting my fingers trail for a moment along his arm and my eyes pull after his like they are on a string. As I turn away, Sully pokes Henry in the ribs and holds out his hand, making Henry's face go sour. That is when I know those two have taken bets on me staying or going.

CHAPTER 14

Walking with Mrs. Chalmers puts me in mind of the day Betsy came giggling out the schoolyard gate, all bound up in a knot of girls.

'We're walking home the long way,' Betsy announced.

'I got chores waiting at home, I ain't got time —' I didn't even finish when I heard Carrie's voice calling.

'Betsy! Only proper girls can promenade down Carlisle Street. If you want to come, you better not let Rosetta rub off on you!'

'I'm coming!' Betsy called over her shoulder. 'See you at home, Rosetta. Tell Mama I won't be long,' and then she was running after the girls who were already parading down the street, every girl but me, Harmony, and Ida, who were long gone and wouldn't put me in good company anyway.

I wheeled away from the schoolhouse and started walking on the road, my thoughts blacker than the shine on a beetle.

At the turn for home, I heard giggling again and when I rounded the corner there was Betsy and Tillie and Kitty.

'What are you doing here? I thought you were promenading through town,' I said, making my voice sweet.

Betsy didn't answer. She was too busy looking off at the trees lining Cadagan's fence.

I heard giggling holding itself in when Tillie said, 'We didn't think it'd be right letting you walk home alone.'

The three of them had their skirts tucked up like when I do chores, even Betsy, who was still watching the trees. There was a flash of white, and Carrie and Myra came stepping out of them trees with their skirts up too.

I put my chin up and marched past those girls, right on past Carrie, my only thought on getting home to the barn, to the cows, to Papa laughing at me making one trip with all the buckets. They fell in behind me. The line of five girls snorting, Carrie at the head, Betsy at the tail, swinging their arms wide and taking big steps in their splitting skirts. Every nice feeling I almost had for Betsy up and went clean out of my head.

I moved so fast, crashing into Carrie and knocking her flat out in the road, but she weren't the one I wanted to push down. There was roaring in my ears like underwater and I grabbed Betsy's arm and shoved her to the ground, pinning her shoulders under my knees. There was shrieking and crying and someone pulling at me but I didn't pay that any mind.

A voice yelled, 'Don't you never speak to me again, you Benedict Arnold!' and it was my voice saying, 'It's a shame you're so ugly, Betsy, when you're the only girl in the family, ain't it?'

Then I was down the road marching for home with those girls' screaming in my ears and the only thought in my head was how even Papa's belt couldn't hurt so bad.

But now I am walking a graveled path between white clapboard buildings laid out all neat behind the big main building, looking more like a courthouse than a hospital. My old hurts don't seem so bad when there's a row of horse carts waiting out front, every one of them lined with blood-stained canvas.

'Where you taking me?' I ask Mrs. Chalmers, saying the first words since we left camp. I ain't as mad as I was, but she is right to move careful around me like I might get rattled any second.

She stops in the middle of the path and takes my arm before I can pull away from her.

'Judiciary Hospital takes the worst of the wounded,' she says. 'The ones who can't make the journey any farther than this.'

Nurses and two butcher-aproned men gather round a just-drove-in horse cart and there's moaning as the men heave a boy in blue onto a waiting stretcher like he ain't nothing but a sack of feed.

'That's the surgeon's ward,' Mrs. Chalmers says. 'The ambulances drive straight there if they've got a particularly bad case.'

We walk past. Right outside the door the nurses carry that boy through there's a garbage pile big enough to fill one of them waiting carts, covered with swarming flies. The nearest horse swishes its tail, sending the flies buzzing just above, and I see it's a mound of bloody rags and parts. The parts are the worst, looking like hands I've held or arms that've wrapped around me, and that is what might happen if we ever get called to battle. I blink and something rises from my cursed weak stomach so I've got to stop and bend over, my hands on my knees.

'I don't know what foolishness you told Captain, but I had stitches once when I was twelve,' I say. 'Ain't never liked doctors and such since then.'

The sights call up Doc taking the fish-hook-looking needle out of a drawer and saying, 'Now hold still, Rosetta,' like I could stop from shaking. Jeremiah squeezed my hand, the first time he ever held it, talking like he would to a scared horse, saying 'Easy,' and 'It'll be over soon,' and 'You're doing fine, there's a brave one,' nothing but nice things. I wanted to listen, but the needle poking my skin and the thread pulling made me carry on and feel sick like throwing up.

I keep my head between my knees like Doc made me do back then, remembering how Jeremiah helped me from the table, how I wanted him to stay even after he led me to the cot.

Mrs. Chalmers' hand on my arm startles me.

'Let's keep walking,' Mrs. Chalmers says. 'Keep walking and we'll be right past. We won't go in this way.'

She pulls on me, saying I'll get used to these sights or some such nonsense. It can't look right, a soldier being sick and a lady in skirts herding him along. I swallow and straighten up, wishing Mrs. Chalmers ain't got me in this bind.

'Oh, look,' she says, and points off in the distance. 'Isn't it something?'

The Capitol rises like the sun from the trees, its unfinished dome jabbing at the sky.

It's a sight I never thought to see, but I tell Mrs. Chalmers, 'That dome don't mean a thing to me.'

Her mouth drops open, and she says, 'Oh, you can't mean that. Without the Union, what do any of us even have?'

She is trying to get my mind on something different or maybe remind me of what we soldiers are supposed to be fighting for, but I ain't having none of it.

'I don't see how it would change my farm one bit if the Confederacy is its own country or not,' I say as we make our way down the long row of buildings, gravel crunching under our feet.

'But don't you see? We're all tied up together in this. It is for the betterment of each of us if this war earns the slaves' freedom, if the evil of slavery is wiped clean from this country. And then surely no one can say women ought to be property as well and we will have our freedom next.'

'That may be,' I say, thinking how I ain't pegged her for a Quaker, 'but I don't hold with slavery either, and I can't see how freeing the slaves will change things for women one bit. I ain't waiting for anyone else to give me anything. You don't have to either.'

I am too peevish to tell Mrs. Chalmers how it ain't so easy as all that, how sometimes getting what you aimed don't feel like freedom.

Inside the ward is just as white as outside. Rows of cots with the whitest sheets since Mama's clothesline fill each side of the long hall. Most every cot has a soldier in it, only a few of them sitting up.

I stay on the strip of brown carpeting down the middle of the hall, keeping my dirty boots off the whitewashed floor. Mrs. Chalmers talks in a low voice to a man in a white uniform. He has full side whiskers standing out from his face and he nods, pointing down the ward, and she steps off, carrying her basket.

Sidewhiskers comes alongside me. 'Mrs. Chalmers tells me this is your first hospital visit?'

I nod, watching Mrs. Chalmers take the hand of a soldier before sitting on the stool next to his bed and wringing out the cloth from the metal bowl on his bedside stand. She swabs his forehead, her lips moving and his weak smile coming in return.

'Allow me to introduce myself,' Sidewhiskers says, sticking his hand out for me to grab. 'I'm Ward-Master Levi Coventry.'

I get my mind in order and take his hand and shake firm. 'Private Ross Stone,' I say. 'Ninety-seventh New York, at your service.'

There is a long silence before I think to fill it. 'Where are all the wounded outside coming from?' I ask.

'Shiloh, I expect. There were so many casualties. But tell me, are you able to write?' the Ward-Master asks.

'Course,' I say. 'I ain't got a lady's penmanship but I write plain enough.'

'Down there in bed twenty-seven is a soldier, he won't be living more than a few more days and he doesn't have use of his hands. He's been saying this morning there's folks he'd like to send word to.' The Ward-Master brings a box stamped *Sanitary Commission* down from a shelf near the door and shows how it's full of patriotic covers and papers.

I nod and take a sheaf as he presses a pen into my hand, saying, 'His name's Joseph Brown.'

Walking down that carpet, it's like I'm in

church and angels are all around. Only in church the coughs and noises ain't like the ones in this ward. Here there's ragged breathing, groaning, rustling of sheets, and somewhere someone is weeping quietly, nothing but hurt and sickness and tiredness in these boys.

The face on the pillow of bed twenty-seven is moon-pale with brown strands of hair stuck to it. The coverlet is pulled right up to the chin, where there's a hint of whiskers, and I'm checking if his chest is rising and falling when a voice rasps, 'I'm awake. Just resting.'

He turns his head to the left, his eyes still closed, his lips barely moving. 'There's a stool there. You can sit.'

I do as he says, the stool's legs scraping too loud across the floor. Before I even get a chance to open my mouth or settle my papers in my lap, he's back to talking.

'Ward-Master send you to keep watch over me?'

'I suppose you could see it like that. He said maybe I could be some service to you.'

As soon as he hears my voice, his eyes fly open and they are a dull green.

'I thought —' he starts. 'But no. You ain't her. Sound like her, though. You got a name?' he asks.

'Stone, Private Ross Stone,' I say, working to keep my voice low, my heart pounding.

'It's funny, you dressing like a soldier,' he says.

'That's what I am.'

The soldier lying in bed twenty-six looks at me from underneath the bandage across his forehead and says, 'It's the laudanum. Makes him see things. Makes him confused.'

I say, 'Oh, I see,' and try to smile before turning back to Joseph and saying, 'The Ward-Master told me you've got a letter needs writing.'

'Yes,' Joseph says. 'I've been feeling — I can't be long for this world. There's a terrible burning coming,' he says.

And then he shifts his shoulders to throw his covers back and he's got nothing but bandaged stumps for arms, stopping halfway to where his hands should be. Where the bandages ought to be white they are rust-brown and yellow.

I talk so I won't stare. 'Did you fight at Shiloh?'

'So many burning,' Joseph says. 'My arms —'

I don't know what he means. Maybe he is seeing things again. But then that other soldier in bed twenty-six speaks up. 'Joseph there, he's one of the lucky ones. Weren't so wounded he couldn't get away. You seen battle yet?'

I shake my head.

'I was a fool to have such an itch to fight,' Bed Twenty-six says. 'It ain't how I thought, having Rebel artillerymen laying their shells down in front of us. Canister. It tears right through the lines, cuts down whole Companies of men. And if it don't get you, you got to keep moving forward into it. That's bad enough. But at Shiloh the trees caught fire.'

Joseph moans and says, 'Just like a bonfire.'

'It was a sight to see. Like a halo over every tree, the way the leaves caught first. Except then the branches started falling.' Bed Twenty-six takes a deep breath and closes his eyes. 'You ever heard a hog at slaughter?'

I nod.

'That ain't nothing compared to the sound of the wounded burning to a crisp,' he says.

We sit silent and I curse Mrs. Chalmers for ever bringing me here.

Finally Joseph says, 'The letter. The letter first. Then the arms.'

It's a relief to turn away from that other soldier and tell Joseph, 'It'd be my honor to write that letter. Who do you want it written out to?'

'My Mama —' he says, his voice catching. 'Dear Mama. You tell her . . . Tell her: This letter isn't written in my own hand but these words are mine. You write that.'

I use my best penmanship to take down whatever he wants, sitting sideways so he can see. When he knows I am putting what he says, he closes his eyes but they still move beneath his lids like they are reading that letter.

'Now read it back to me,' he says when he's spent, and hearing those words is about as sad as standing round a grave.

April 12, 1862
Judiciary Square Hospital

Dear Mama,
This letter is not written in my own hand but these words are mine. I have lain in Judiciary Square Hospital in our Fair Capital almost since I have been wounded, as You have reason to know. Only this few days past, the Surgeon here, Willard Bliss, has been obliged to take from me my hands. They were, as he said, not healing as would be hoped. I have had my Surgery now and hope you can Visit me here.

Should you get this letter in good time, I shall still be here, but do not tarry. I fear I am in Dying Condition. The Surgeon says my wounds Will Heal now the worst of them are gone, but I am afraid there is no hope for me. I do so wish to see you.

If I cannot live to see your face, do not weep for me. I have died Serving this great Union. I have seen the enemy and know that God must be on Our Side, though He has yet seen fit to Reward us with Victory. I will take my place in Heaven with those who Fought before me and I will Welcome those who come after. If I do not see you before I leave this World, I will look for you on the other side. Give my love to Fannie and tell her her brother will Look Upon her from Heaven.

Most Affectionately,
Your Son, Joseph

He nods to me when I am done reading. 'It's a fair hand. You'll take it to post for me?'

'Of course,' I say, because it is the only right thing. 'Have I got an envelope here to suit your fancy?' I show him the Lady Liberty and Lincoln and McClellan.

'Oh, the Lady to be sure,' he says, and then he tells me the address he wants it directed to.

'Now the arms,' he says.

'What?'

'Burning,' he says, his mouth barely opening for the tightness of his jaw. 'Hurts something awful. Get me laudanum and some cool air on these arms. And then fresh bandages.'

'Oh, I ain't got the touch . . .'

'Just get the laudanum,' he growls.

Inside the wooden cabinet by the door are shelves of mostly identical brown bottles. The first one I grab has a paper label saying *Paregoric.* I shove it onto the shelf and the next one says *Ether* and then finally there's one that says *Laudanum,* with a rubber dropper tip.

Back at Joseph's bed, he is whimpering with his eyes closed like he don't even know the sound he's making.

There is a pitcher in a bowl on the bedside stand, and a cup next to it that I fill with water, only I don't know how many drops of laudanum he needs.

Joseph says through gritted teeth, 'The full dropper. Put all of it in.'

The sweet-smelling liquor swirls as the

laudanum clouds the water. I help him sit up and drink. As soon as the water crosses his lips he falls back into the pillows.

'Better soon,' he says, breathing that starts as a sigh and ends in a moan.

Across the aisle Mrs. Chalmers is petting a soldier's hand, singing 'Home Sweet Home' quietly, and I should've thought to sing to keep that boy easy.

'I need your help,' I say when I reach her, my voice quiet but sharp. 'He's wanting new bandages. I ain't got the knack of it.'

'It doesn't take much skill, just steady nerves and a light touch,' she says.

'You show me. I've never done doctoring except for cows and horses.'

'You'll excuse me, Lawrence?' she says to the man whose hand she's been stroking, and picks up her basket.

'Hello there,' she says when we get to Joseph, but it's like he don't even hear her. Mrs. Chalmers looks at me and says, 'Did you give him laudanum?' When I nod, she says, 'Well then, it's working,' and throws back the covers.

'Oh,' she says, like two half arms ain't what she was thinking on seeing. 'Help me hold his arm.'

She unties the spiderweb knot on the left

arm, carefully lifting his arm just enough so she can pass the roll of bandage under it.

He gets to whimpering again, but she is calm, unwinding that bandage like he ain't making a sound. The closer she gets to the end of the stub, the worse it looks with map lines of veins running in red streaks up Joseph's arm. Once the flannel is unwrapped, there is nothing but the hot red arm and a clump of rust and yellow clotted lint at the end of the stump. Mrs. Chalmers drops the flannel to the floor and picks at the edge of the lint, trying to get it loose, but it sticks fast.

She wets a cloth from her basket, gently running it down Joseph's arm, the water dripping through the lint pad and onto the floor, making a pale pink stain on the old bandage lying there. Then she wrings that cloth out into the bowl by Joseph's bed and runs it over his arm again and again. Holding his upper arm, I feel it getting cooler, but the heat still burns from deep inside and it won't be cool for long.

When the lint is wet through, it peels off easy in Mrs. Chalmers' hands. This don't seem any better than those parts by the door outside, only it's got a body attached to it. At the end of the stump the skin folds over on itself, held with a line of black horsehair stitching, smeared with thick lemon-curd-yellow pus, a sickly sweet smell coming from it.

'Don't worry,' she says, 'that's the laudable pus. The surgeon says it's a sign of healing.'

'Ward-Master says he ain't long for this world,' I whisper.

'Well, only the Good Lord knows for certain.'

Mrs. Chalmers takes the rag again and keeps wiping the end of the stump, only stopping her cleaning to squeeze the bits of softened scab and pus into the bowl. There ain't a place to look that don't make me feel something awful.

When she gets that stump cleared off, Mrs. Chalmers takes a ball of lint from her basket and a fresh roll of flannel. She presses the lint against the end of the stump with one hand and begins winding the bandage around and around it. Joseph's head moves and his eyes start to open when she touches him, but he sighs and then is still.

She catches me watching her tie the bandage knot and smiles. 'You'll do the other one.'

'No — I —'

'I'm needed elsewhere. You can do this on

your own. Unless you're a coward,' she says, as she puts a ball of lint and a roll of flannel at the foot of Joseph's bed.

'Mrs. Chalmers — please?'

'Do this one,' she says, turning her back on me, her basket on her arm. 'Then you need never do it again.'

I mutter under my breath, 'Goddamn it all to hell.'

I drag the stool round to the other side of his bed. The noise of it makes Joseph twitch, but he don't seem near to waking. I do everything just like Mrs. Chalmers did, but it takes me twice as long, flies gathering on the end of his arm each time I rinse out the cloth.

My bandage don't look so smooth and even, but I'm hoping it will still do the job when Mrs. Chalmers comes back to my side.

'I'm all out of bandages and I think it's time we get to camp. We've done some good today,' she says. 'I knew you had the knack,' she goes on, nodding at Joseph's arm.

'I ain't got the knack,' I say too loud, making Joseph shift in his stupor, and then make my voice go quiet. 'But I can do a thing that needs doing.'

We are on the edge of camp when Mrs.

Chalmers looks at me and says, 'How do you do it?'

'What do you mean?' I ask.

'Being a soldier,' she says, her skin going the same sunrise pink as the flowers dotting her dress, and I tell myself she only means about the marching and laboring.

'You grow up on a farm?' I ask her, even though anyone can tell by looking she ain't. She shakes her head.

'Well, it's like everything else,' I say, working to keep my voice low. 'It just has to be done, is all.'

'But I'm not doing it,' she says. 'I don't see another soul doing what you are.'

She touches my elbow and that is when I see she ain't talking about the drilling or working and I wonder how it is she knows the truth about me.

'I ain't got another choice in the matter,' I say to her. Then I grab her wrist and it is so birdbone tiny it might snap in my hand. 'Don't you tell a soul. I can't go back like this, not after leaving like I did.'

Her hazel eyes go big and shimmery like Betsy's sometimes do. I let her arm go.

'I won't say a word,' she whispers. 'I was only hoping . . . I get so lonely.' She sweeps her hand through the air, toward the tents, the soldiers gathering for their nightly poker

212

games, already loud with drink. And then those tears start spilling.

'It is a lonely thing sometimes. But you ain't got the same worries as me.' I shake my head. 'You ain't got to hide —'

'I won't tell a soul,' she says, her voice so firm and serious. I think on the lies she told her own husband. Then I think how gentle she was with the soldiers at the hospital.

'You've got to help me keep it secret,' I say. 'There's people back home but they don't — that letter — My husband and I, we need the money I'm earning so we can have our own place.'

'I promise,' she says, and I don't dare do a thing but believe her.

'How'd you know?'

'I don't know, little things. I had a hunch about something the day I met you on the road. And then the way you rolled bandages, so nice and neat. That's what made me stop and take notice. Your voice. And then you almost fainted when you caught sight of the hospital.'

'Captain — does he know?'

'I can't tell you how many times I've laughed at my husband when he can't find his belt, even if I tell him it's hanging on the hook in his wardrobe. Or if he's looking for his knife and it's right before him, sitting on the table.'

I ain't had much occasion to see Jeremiah do things like that, but I remember how my Mama could always find the missing bit-brace in the lean-to or the dropped gate hinge, even after Papa swore he'd looked everywhere.

'He doesn't know, that's what I mean to say. But I wonder — will you consider coming to the hospital with me again?' Mrs. Chalmers asks.

The feeling comes up in her eyes and maybe there's things about us that ain't so different, so I say, 'You asking or is Captain ordering?'

'I'm asking,' she says, her voice small.

'I can't be talking to you again. It ain't safe and I don't want no more trouble with Captain, so unless he's ordering it —'

'I understand,' she says, but I wonder how she can. 'I won't ask it of you again.'

We part ways near the tents, but first she takes my arm and says, 'My name's Jennie. And thank you.'

Only when she has left does the relief come, and when it's gone I feel how tired my whole body is.

I am past ready to drop by the time I lay myself down under our tent, but Jeremiah and me ain't had time for talking yet and he wants it. He wraps his arms, his whole arms, around me. When a shiver goes up my spine, his arms tighten.

'Rabbits running over my grave,' I say.

His lips find my neck and plant tiny kisses there, telling me what he has in his mind. I can't help it though and sink toward sleep like a bucket down the well. But what I see there in the dark makes me want to draw back, and Jeremiah's kisses are the rope pulling me up.

'You okay?' he asks, his finger tracing my jaw.

'I'm fine.'

'You're real quiet.'

'Mrs. Chalmers knows what I am,' I whisper.

Jeremiah starts. 'What?'

'She guessed it. And now she knows.'

'How does she know?' Jeremiah asks, and even if I can't see it, I can feel him looking at me.

'Because I got sick, seeing that hospital, seeing — She just knew, and I couldn't lie,' I say in a small voice.

'You told her?'

'No, not in so many words. She already knew!'

'We've got to be more careful. You can't

215

go around —'

'I know.' My voice cracks.

Jeremiah props himself up on his elbow and looks down on me. 'Was it bad, at that hospital?'

'That hospital makes Doc Cuck look gentle,' is all I can bring myself to say, when any one of those boys in that hospital could be Jeremiah, or me, how maybe Joseph is already gone, never seeing his Mama again. I think about if I will ever see my folks back home again in this world, if my Mama would come if I sent her a letter like the one Joseph sent. I hope that what Thomas Stakely says is true, that all the Union needs is one good win and this war will be over.

CHAPTER 15

FORT CORCORAN, VIRGINIA: LATE APRIL 1862

'This ain't what I signed on for, sitting here watching them Rebs, letting them get ready and we just wait! When's McClellan going to move on Yorktown? He ain't hardly even bombarded those Seceshes! We should be chasing those fools back to South Carolina! Or at least to Richmond!' Sully says, getting all worked up for his morning sermonizing about McClellan this or Rebs that, his spindly arms flapping about while we finish our breakfast and drink what passes for coffee in this Army. If he's the one coming off picket, he's even worse.

'Seems to me the farther away you get from those Rebs, the more you talk about killing them,' I say. 'You talk this big sitting out on the line in the dark? How many shots you fire last night?'

The rest of the boys, Jeremiah, Jimmy, and

Will, laugh, and that shuts Sully up for a quick moment. Then he sends me a look fit to kill a hog and says before making off for his tent, 'You got the heart of a woman and no stomach for war, so your words don't mean one thing.'

'He ain't lying,' I say. 'I like getting paid and not getting killed and still doing right by the Union.'

We sit like that for a spell, watching Jimmy rake his fingers through his ginger hair sticking up like a mad porcupine. When he's got it looking almost presentable, he asks what we've all been starting to wonder.

'Where do you think Henry got to?'

'You know Henry,' Jeremiah says. 'He's got his own time for things.'

We go back to sitting quiet and then we hear the rattling thunder of the long roll. We jump up, taking our arms and equipment.

The Regiment gathers outside Captain's headquarters tent, stacking our weapons before shifting our lines to face Captain.

Henry and bumbling Levi Blalock are there, looking like something worse than sheepish. It's been days since I last saw her about, but Jennie is off to the side, her small mouth drawn tight, her bandage basket on her thin arm like she's coming from the hospital. She is working not to look at Captain, and anybody can see she ain't happy either, even before she swipes the back of her hand across her eyes.

'Gentlemen,' Captain says. 'I have set these soldiers before you as an example, not that you might follow them, but that you might turn away from their worthless and low behavior. These two among you have done a disservice to the Army of the Potomac and this Regiment, and shall be disciplined accordingly.'

Captain stalks to stand in front of Henry. 'Henry O'Malley, do you deny falling asleep on picket duty last night and, through your irresponsible actions, putting not only your Regiment but this Army and this nation at peril?'

Henry, his face blazing even brighter, doesn't say one word, just shakes his head.

'I could have you SHOT for such conduct!' Captain yells, but Henry don't lift his head. Behind me Jimmy sucks in a long breath. Captain keeps yelling, nose to nose with Henry. 'It is a MERCY that I am assigning to you one week of picket duty strapped to a stick.

'And you, Levi Blalock, caught DESERTING last night by other members of the picket line doing their DUTY. Do you deny

219

it?' Levi's face is pale and he looks everywhere but at Captain. 'DO YOU DENY IT?' Captain yells again, and Levi hunches his shoulders, like he's expecting a blow.

'Then you shall serve one week of latrine duty AND to ensure you never forget how you have jeopardized the safety of your countrymen, endangered your fellow soldiers, and disgraced yourself, you shall be branded a deserter!'

The whole Regiment holds its breath, me along with it. That's why Jennie ain't happy with her husband and why she's got that basket on her arm, why the fire is burning hot by the tent, a poker sticking from the flames. Captain gestures to Hiram, who swaggers to the fire. He pulls that poker from the coals with a look on his face like it gives him a special pleasure to see the red-orange D glow against the charred wood. Then he and young Frank Morgan push Levi down on the ground. Hiram must be even stronger than he looks because he forces Levi's head to the right, pinning his cheek against the dirt. All the while Levi is going wild, kicking and bucking as Captain moves that poker toward him, and I knew he ain't one to ever cross.

I close my eyes, but that don't make it stop.

CHAPTER 16

*OLD CAPITOL PRISON, WASHINGTON,
D.C.: MAY 1862*

Our first real orders come a week later, the
day Henry finishes his punishment. We're to
guard Secesh prisoners kept at the Old
Capitol Prison, and even though I draw
relief with Will and Edward instead of
Jeremiah or one of the boys from home, I'm
glad to be somewhere the Rebels ain't fighting.

The three of us, me, Will, and Edward,
walk on a wide pavement, toward the four-
story brick building. Except for the arched
windows above the door, all the windows
have got curtains pulled, almost like it's a
real home but for the iron bars.

Just as we step up to the main guardhouse,
Edward elbows me. 'You know they have a
lady spy in this prison?'

'Have they now?'

'That's right,' he says, and digs his thumb

into Will's ribs. 'I'm of a mind to get a good look at her, maybe give her a good squeeze for me and my brother.'

Edward winks at the thick-shouldered warden we're reporting to, but it don't work the way he hopes because Thick-shoulders says, 'You patrol the street — I need you to keep any passersby away from the prison yard. And you other two, you'll take Mrs. Greenhow down for some air.'

'You've got to be daft!' Edward shouts. 'You think those two can even keep a sheep in line?'

Edward is still being ornery with Thick-shoulders when me and Will head up the steps into the prison. It is nicer than any house I've ever set foot in. By the wall where the floors ain't dirty and scraped, the richness of the dark wood shows. The halls are wide and plastered, and the main staircase has a carved pineapple post and a curved railing. Those stairs creak under our weight, like I am some fine person, and there is something good in that thought.

When we open the door to her room, Mrs. Greenhow jerks her hand back from the curtain at the window and then settles back into her chair at the old table there. She is a handsome woman, her nut-brown hair parted straight down the middle and swept to the back, where it is coiled and curled.

She don't even look at us, just starts scribbling something down like she can't be bothered to hurry. We stand there looking around her room, which is nothing but cracked plaster walls and boards nailed across her window, like the bars outside ain't enough. Her little girl, not more than eight or nine, sits on a pallet, slowly turning the pages of a book, watching us with a down-turned mouth.

Will clears his throat and says, 'It's time to go out to the yard, Mrs. Greenhow,' but still she don't stop what she is doing. Will looks at me, but I don't know how else we should act either, so we just wait until she folds that paper and puts it inside a book on the table. Then she turns to her daughter, saying, 'Rose, shall we?' as she stands and holds out her hands, her black netting gloves stretching up to her elbows, her black widow's dress rustling like dried cornstalks.

'You think you ought to put out that candle?' I ask. 'Wouldn't want to burn the place down, would you?'

Mrs. Greenhow gives me an eyebrow and a sharp look as she draws back the curtain, reaches through the wood slats, and blows out the candle that's guttering there in the middle of the day. She breezes past us like royalty, keeping her face looking apart from us as we head down the hall to the stairs, like we ain't good enough to speak to, like we are the traitors instead of her, and I can't help but wonder what she is about, acting the spy for our benefit.

Being that she's the only woman in the prison, Mrs. Greenhow gets time all to herself in the prisoners' yard. Me and Will stand at the gate, watching her promenade around, her skirts sashaying after her, like it is something more grand than a tall wire fence and hard-packed dirt. Some of the boys out in the courtyard watch Mrs. Greenhow as she takes her few turns, Little Rose on her arm. When a loud catcall comes, it's Hiram who's got his fingers to his lips, the boys around him hooting and slapping his shoulders, Frank Morgan laughing so much he's practically doubled over at the waist. Mrs. Greenhow, though, she don't pay it any mind, and keeps her eyes on the street just beyond the fence. She finishes her turn before sinking onto a bench, flouncing out her skirts.

Hiram can't leave her be, though. He saunters over to the fence right behind Mrs. Greenhow.

'Rebel Rose,' he calls in a singsong voice. 'I've got all kinds of secrets I'll spill, if you come upstairs with me.'

Mrs. Greenhow don't show any sign she hears him, maybe hoping he'll move on to some other amusement if she don't notice him one jot. That's what I'm hoping too, but Frank and those other boys are making eyes and snorting at his back.

'I heard you Southern ladies ain't so proper as y'all like to pretend,' Hiram drawls, 'and looks to be true, you landing here in prison and such.'

Everything about Mrs. Greenhow gets somehow thorny looking, but she still don't move.

Hiram says, 'I know you know what a man likes, but maybe you'd like to try on something Northern for a change?'

Mrs. Greenhow yelps, jumping to her feet. Somehow Hiram has worked his hand through the wire far enough to pinch the nape of her neck.

'A little nibble, that's all I'm after!' he crows, while the boys behind him roar with laughter.

'You leave off!' I shout at Hiram, and I don't care if Mrs. Greenhow is a spy or not.

'Come on now, I'm just having fun. You ain't a Rebel lover, are you?'

'You ain't to molest the prisoner!' I walk right up to the fence, and Mrs. Greenhow

scurries to where her daughter sits wide-
eyed.

'Oh, I see. You *are* a Rebel lover! I bet
she's giving you some sweetness on the side,
is that it?' Hiram leers at me, just like Eli.

'What I've got is decency, that's all. Didn't
your Mama teach you how to act right?'

'My Mama ain't here, in case you didn't
notice.'

I kick the fence where Hiram is standing.
He jumps back. 'That's right!' I yell. 'You
move along!'

'You're mighty brave on that side of the
goddamn fence! Why don't you come on
over here and we'll see if you've got any real
fight in you.' He spits at the ground, the
boys behind him silent as he glares at me. I
stay put.

'Shit, that's what I thought,' he says, and
turns to throw an arm around Frank, slapping his shoulder and laughing loud until
he's got all the others joining in.

When they walk away, I sink down onto
the bench myself, spreading my shaking
hands across my thighs.

Mrs. Greenhow lets go of her girl, pushing her back toward the hopscotch she's
drawn with a stick in the dirt. She plays
there by herself, her short dress bouncing
as she jumps. Will moves to where I am,

bumping into my shoulder.

'What got into you?' he asks, still watching Mrs. Greenhow.

'Why's he think he can act like that?' I ask. 'What right has he got?'

'I suppose he thought nobody would mind,' Will says.

Mrs. Greenhow looks calmly out at the street, but she don't fool me.

After a bit, she turns, clasps her gloved hands together like praying, and gives me a nod. Then she raises her eyebrows at me and maybe I don't fool her none either.

'Hey, Ross!' Sully yells when he comes across the prison yard for supper. 'You heard how they've got a woman prisoner here?' he says, looking right at me, and I wish Jeremiah weren't off on his guard duty.

I give him a narrow look. 'Sure did. We just guarded her.'

'What was she like?' Sully asks.

'Can't really say. She's got mourning clothes on, but she don't seem sad. She's got a clever look about her too. Acts like you'd think a Southern lady would.'

'I was guarding with Thomas Stakely and he heard she's a real saucy thing, got a mouth on her. Kind of like you,' Sully says. 'He said how she sings "Dixie" real loud so

227

the guards and anyone on the street can hear.'

'I didn't hear one peep out of her,' I say.

Sully shakes his head, 'You ever heard of taking your own child along to prison?'

'Maybe she ain't got another place to keep that child,' Will says. 'Being a widow.'

The bite of sowbelly in my mouth, the whole meal, goes sour. I wonder about Rebel Rose and why she ain't got any folks who'd take her daughter, if there is anything more alone than a widow. I wonder if Hiram is the only one to heckle her, if any of her guards have done worse. Then I think on the notes she was writing, the way she looked out on the street.

'What are they going to do with her?' I ask.

'Spying is treason,' Will says.

'Ain't that a hanging offense?' Jimmy asks, and I can't help but look over at the gallows.

'Oh, they ain't hanging no woman for this thing. She's been passing gossip, is all,' Henry says.

That gets my dander up, even if what that lady spy done is wrong, like he thinks she ain't smart enough to do more than gossip. I wonder about that candle Mrs. Greenhow had burning, her sitting there watching the

228

street. I swallow the lump of sowbelly in my mouth quick and say, 'Seems to me a lady don't get arrested for gossip if there ain't something to it.'

Will says, 'I heard sometimes those guards out on the street see her waving to people, like maybe she's still passing messages. I never would have thought —'

'You think a woman can't fight for her country?' It comes flying out of my mouth, even as I wonder if I ought to go to Captain with what I saw. Jimmy looks at me, his mouth dropped open.

'It isn't usual, that's all I mean,' Will answers, but his words are careful, like he is measuring something he don't like in my voice. 'Can you imagine after what Hiram —'

'Plenty of things that ain't usual ain't wrong,' I say.

'I heard they found some ladies in soldier's clothes in the Second Maryland,' Jimmy says, and it is my turn to look at him with my mouth gaping.

'What happened to them?' I ask.

Jimmy says, 'They drummed them out of the Regiment with their heads shaved and then they clapped them in jail.'

'How'd they get found out?' I ask. The look Mrs. Greenhow gave me flashes in my mind, and I know right then I ain't going to Captain with anything. That woman can't be trusted if she knows what I am.

'Don't know,' Jimmy says, and shrugs.

Henry looks at me and says, 'Oh, a woman couldn't stay a soldier long and not get caught. They should have made them put on dresses and go back home.'

'Being a soldier isn't a job for women,' Will says.

'Surely ain't,' Sully says, looking at me. My thoughts go dark and I wish Jeremiah were here. I take another bite of meat to keep from saying anything.

'Isn't a job for any of us, really,' Will says, and gives me a look I can't read.

CHAPTER 17

FORT CORCORAN, VIRGINIA: JUNE 1862
The relief of being back at Fort Corcoran after the week of prison guard has long since worn off with weeks of drilling when I decide I ought to send word home, even if my folks ain't ever going to write me a kind word again. With Jeremiah sitting at our fire and the water on for coffee, I pull out my papers and write:

June 8, 1862
Virginia

Dear Papa, Mama, and Betsy,
I think You don't like me to Write before now, but I thought You should Know how I fare.

I liked to hear about the Farm in your Letter. I want to know how that Spotted Calf does and if the Fields are planted and what in (Wheat or Potatoes or maybe Corn) and have you had Help to do it?

I have been Drilling and cooking for Jeremiah and the Flat Creek boys before now. We had Prison Duty and what do you think I saw there but a Lady Spy who is called Rebel Rose. She is a handsome figure and most of the boys don't think she can be a Spy, but I know better.

I can get plenty of money for myself so whatever I send, I want you should keep it. When All this is through I hope to come see You, if you will have me. My future is with Jeremiah and after we visit we will be gone to take care of ourselves out West, where no one cares how I dress or what I do.

If you write, You can direct it the same as Before, but to Virginia.

Good-bye for this Time,
Rosetta

I have only just sealed the cover when a loud cheer goes up from the boys down the way. I know in my bones that it is our orders to battle and drop down on my stump, wondering how long 'til we know for sure where we're going, if I should open that letter back up and tell my folks the whole of

232

it. Jeremiah stands to look down the aisle, his head cocked.

Edward calls over to us as he saunters up to his tent, 'You heard the news about the lady spy?'

Jeremiah shakes his head, and the gallows at Old Capitol Prison come up in my mind.

'They deported her back to Rebel country. Guess you got lucky guarding her, Little Soldier,' Edward says. 'They say she's been spying the whole damn time she's been in prison!'

'And they sent her home?' Jeremiah asks.

'Yep. Right to Richmond. Guess they figure she can't do much harm there.'

I can't help but be glad she's been sent home safe, away from the likes of Hiram, even after being caught passing messages, even if she was doing it right on my watch, like I thought. It almost serves the Army right, if they ain't taken her serious, sending her back to her own folks to live like she really is only some silly gossiping widow. Jennie Chalmers said that making slaves free will help women, but I don't know how she can be right when there's still most men who can't see the things a woman does, even when she's doing them right under his nose.

Sully comes back, all full of smiles. 'Well,

233

it ain't a battle victory, but getting rid of a Rebel traitor is something to celebrate! We ought to go for a swim, wash ourselves clean of that Rebel filth, and get the laundry done at the same time!'

None of it seems right, not Rebel Rose going free, not celebrating it like a victory, but the idea of swimming being the same as doing laundry makes me snort. Course, it ain't surprising seeing how most these boys think licking their mess plate is the same as washing it.

'No one's going anywhere 'til this coffee gets drunk,' I say.

Jeremiah and Sully are already done gulping their coffee when Will comes from down the aisle, his hands behind his back, his hair wet and fresh combed.

'Where you been so early?' Sully asks. 'You heard the news?'

'I heard,' Will says, and comes over to me at the fire. From behind his back he holds out a big cup with a lid and a handle on it.

'You want coffee?' I ask.

'No,' he says. 'I found this mucket at the sutler's. Might be better than what you have there. You want it?'

'That's all right,' I say, looking at my mess plate. 'This works.'

'I don't have much use for it,' Will says.

'And you're always cooking for me . . .'

'If you don't want it,' I shrug, wondering why he bought a mucket from the sutler in the first place, but it has a nice handle for hanging over the fire so I ain't asking any more about it.

'Here,' he says. 'You can keep it.'

I look at him sideways. 'You just trying to lighten your pack? Give me the heavy stuff?'

'Jeremiah!' Sully hollers. 'I think Will here is sweet on your cousin!'

The color comes up in Will's cheeks. 'I thought maybe you could use it.' And then he ducks his head and scurries back to his tent before I can even say a word of thanks, but not before Jeremiah gives me a sharp look and it dawns on me that Will bought that mucket as a gift.

It is just past noon when we head to the river, Jeremiah, Henry, Jimmy, Sully, and me. The four of them are like a family of skunks weaving in and out and around each other as they make their way down the hill away from our rows of tents, and I am remembering burning Summer days picking ripening seed heads from the hayfields walking to the creek with the four of them, getting our swimming and fishing in before the harvest. I rub my fingers down from my temple and the dust and sweat pills up under my fingers, almost black. I ain't ever felt so dirty in my whole life.

We have only just gotten to the path worn into the grass, when Sully slaps his knee and says, 'Damn it all! I've got to go back to camp —'

'You forget all that laundry you was aiming to do?' I ask him.

'Something like that. You all go on ahead — I'll be right back.'

Jeremiah shrugs. 'We won't go far from the trail.'

We walk through the trees edging the water to a place that slopes all gentle into the river.

Near the bank, the boys strip down to nothing but their underdrawers, dropping their trousers and shirts and shoes like cow pies along the shore. Jeremiah is the tallest and anybody would say he's the handsomest too, all muscle. Jimmy is the first one to the water, where the earth turns to hard-packed mud, his freckles standing out on his pale skin. He moves careful into the river, testing the bottom like he always does.

I leave my shoes next to Jeremiah's and roll up my trousers to my knees, trying not to see the dirt ground into my hems. I wade to where the water licks at the cuffs, the last one to get in the river flowing smooth and flat. Jeremiah is already out past Jimmy and Henry, the water lapping at his thighs, his milk-white belly sucked in tight at the cold of it, a line of grime marking his collar. I am thinking about sinking all the way into the current and swimming out to him when we hear crashing in the brushes and loud whoops.

It ain't much of a surprise when Sully bounds out of the bushes. The surprise is when Edward and Hiram and Will come chasing after him. Sully don't even stop moving to get himself undressed, kicking off his brogans in a patch of grass, stepping on the toes of his socks to pull them off and hopping out of his trousers, leaving them in one pile, his shirt in another close to the water.

Will stops at the bank, but Edward and Hiram strip and run into the water right behind Sully. Sully is the skinniest thing, all arms and legs, yelling as he leads them splashing past me, the cool water drenching me. When he gets to where Jimmy teeters, moving careful out into the river, where it is too deep to run, Sully dunks himself underwater and Hiram follows right after him, jumping in with a big splash, leaving Edward, his broad back covered with black hair, holding his arms out straight like a scarecrow's, moving slow like the water is thick.

Sully bobs up from the river, yelling, 'Feels great! Why ain't you boys in yet?' and then splashes Jimmy until all Jimmy can do is sink himself, while Hiram floats on his back, spouting water from between his teeth. Will leaves his clothes folded neat at the river's edge and starts walking out to where I am standing, and that is when I see my shirt is sticking to me, the thin white fabric showing what's underneath.

'You coming in?' he says.

I cross my arms over my chest and shake my head. 'Don't swim,' I say, and all the fun goes out of the afternoon for me.

'What you mean, you don't swim?' Henry says, turning back to look. 'We've all been swimming with you before.'

Sully stops splashing on Jimmy long enough to yell, 'Come on, Ross! You getting shy on us now?' Something about the glint in his eye when he says it gets me thinking it ain't by accident the other boys came swimming with him.

'What's the matter, Little Soldier?' Edward calls. 'You afraid of water?'

'What you ought to be afraid of is what happens to Rebel lovers,' Hiram says. 'I hear

238

they don't swim too good.'

'I ain't swimming,' I say, cutting each word short, keeping watch on Hiram. It ain't easy, not when the water is cool and clear. Not when swimming at the creek with Jeremiah is how we first got to talking about our farm in Nebraska. But I don't like the feeling dripping off these boys when they look at me.

'How did you grow up and not learn to swim?' Will asks.

'Just did.' Then I add something that is the truth, something so the lie won't feel so bad. 'My Mama worked so hard having me and my sister, she was afraid of us drowning.'

'I could show you,' he says. 'If you want to learn.'

Will stands still a moment, waiting for my answer, but Jeremiah starts yelling, 'Get out here, Will! What's the matter? You afraid of fish?'

Will raises his eyebrows and gives me a shrug before inching farther out into the water.

'I bet me and Edward could get Ross in.' Hiram grins and starts moving toward the shore. 'Teach you to swim real fast.'

Hiram is always in the fray when poker games break out into shouting, and the

239

story goes it was him who gave Edward that black eye when they first enlisted. I don't know what I was thinking, standing between him and Rebel Rose.

'Two dollars says Ross swims worse than a bag of drowned cats but puts up as much fight,' Sully laughs.

I back away like a runt pushed out of the nest, while Hiram smirks and the rest all watch, bitterness boiling up in me with each step.

'Let's see —' Hiram coils himself, making to come after me. That's when Jeremiah runs the flat of his palm along the water, sending a wall of water right into Hiram's face. Then those two yell and splash like schoolboys, until Jimmy comes to help and Hiram grabs him around the neck. He shoves him under the water and holds him there, his arms flailing and his legs kicking.

Sully yells 'Hey!' and charges through the water, punching Hiram in the jaw before Henry and Jeremiah and Edward all rush Hiram, leaving Will standing where he is. There is yelling and splashing and Jeremiah has got his arm across Hiram's throat before finally Jimmy pops up, sputtering and coughing. That don't stop the boys from throwing punches, and the difference between real fighting and playing is too close to call. I get out of that river as fast as I can, finding a place where the sun can dry out my wet clothes, keeping my arms crossed and my knees up.

Those boys keep grappling and fighting, water splashing everywhere, 'til three girls wearing bright colors come out of the trees on the other bank. Those red and green and blue dresses are a magnet to Hiram, who stops dead, and the rest of the boys, even Jeremiah, go still when they catch sight of what he is looking at.

'You ladies like what you're seeing?' Hiram yells, puffing his chest out as he stands in the river.

The girls giggle and one of them, a tall auburn-haired girl wearing wine-red, says, 'I don't know yet. I can't see much of anything!' and that gets the other two pealing with laughter.

'You lovelies ain't afraid of a big trouser serpent, are you?' Hiram calls, and starts moving through the water toward them.

'You'd be better off with me,' Edward joins in. 'His trouser serpent bit a girl back home and he had to join up or take himself a wife!'

I ain't ever heard such bald talk before, even when my Papa got to talking about bulls and cows with the men at church. The two of them, Hiram and Edward both, make me feel like I've just cracked open a rotten egg. There ain't a bone in my body that don't think they'd do something worse to me than Eli if they ever came to know the truth.

Hiram punches Edward in the shoulder like maybe they'll go to scrapping again, but that auburn-haired girl says, 'We ain't looking for husbands,' and lifts her skirt a little, showing her calf. That is when I know they are ladies of low virtue, and it ain't right but I am glad for them getting the boys' attention.

Sully and Henry trail after Hiram and Edward, leaving Jimmy and Will watching from where they stand, but Jeremiah wades back to me.

'You all right?' he asks.

'I've got to get dry,' I say.

'We should go somewhere else, upriver a bit, you and me. I don't like all them being here anyway.'

'Won't look right, just the two of us going.'

'If there's more trouble . . .' Jeremiah says, looking at Hiram coming up out of the water toward those ladies.

'Why do you think I'm sitting out here?' I say. 'You think it was an accident Sully brought those boys?'

'Sully didn't —' Jeremiah takes a sharp breath like when he's bluffing at poker, and I wonder what he's playing at. 'I mean, he wouldn't —'

'You go on. It looks like those boys have found other entertainments.'

'You could still cool off a bit more,' he says. 'Get your feet wet at least. I'll stay. I've already had enough swimming.'

'I can't get wet, Jeremiah. But don't ruin your fun on my account.'

He reaches out to put a hand on my shoulder but I am too peevish.

'You just go on,' I tell him, only when he swims out to Will and Jimmy, closer to where the rest of the boys are still courting those girls, I wish I'd asked him to stay.

Most of June is gone and it's looking like the Army don't care a thing about fighting season, when drums sound the long roll, just after supper one evening. The whole Regiment gathers on the parade ground, and there is Captain out front of his tent holding papers and Jennie Chalmers behind him, her hands twisting in her apron, looking worse than I feel.

'General Ricketts has given us our marching orders,' he finally says when we're all hushed, and my whole self goes even more

243

still to hear it.

Sully lets out a whoop like an idiot. Jimmy, hovering at Sully's side, cheers. But there are plenty who are smart enough and don't open their mouths, Will being one, and Jennie Chalmers, who walks away as soon as the cheering starts. Thomas stands quiet too, most likely picturing on his wife and children left at home. Jeremiah lays a firm hand on my arm, and I know right then what he is thinking.

When Captain can make himself heard again he says, 'We'll be leaving first thing Monday, heavy marching orders. Start getting your things in order and rest up.' He surveys the lot of us. 'You're dismissed.'

The words no sooner leave his mouth than conversation hums and clumps of men start back across the parade ground. We are walking back too when Sully turns round.

'We've got our adventure now!' he says. 'Lord knows I am sick to death of waiting!'

'Waiting is a damn sight better than getting killed,' I spit at him.

'Aw, I knew Ross was going to get cowhearted on us,' Sully says.

'I ain't getting cowhearted. I ain't the cowardly one, getting other folks to do the dirty work I ain't got the balls for.' Sully takes a step back, shrugging like he don't know what I'm about but I just keep on, madder than even I thought after all this time. 'Don't you for one second think I've forgotten what you were playing at down at the creek, setting Hiram and Edward on me. Trying to get me clapped in jail.'

'You think it was just me? You don't think I was put up to it —' Sully starts.

'Jeremiah,' Henry says real loud, 'I told you we can't keep Ross safe! If you can't go through with sending —'

'You keep your traps shut,' Jeremiah says, an edge to his voice, giving a sharp look at Henry and a sharper one to Sully. 'Both of you. Not one word. We've got packing to do and there ain't no use in wasting time with more bickering. Save it for the Rebs.'

It gets me wondering, though, what Jeremiah has said to those boys. If he has told them he aims to send me home. If there is more to what Sully tried at the creek.

Henry and Jimmy slink off in their own direction down Company B's street. Sully peels off after a few more paces, Will tagging along behind, and then it's me and Jeremiah on the main aisle, only a few groups of men ahead and behind us, too busy being excited to pay us mind.

'I've got to talk to you, Rosetta,' Jeremiah says low.

'Ain't nothing to talk about.' I make my spine a ramrod and walk fast for our tent.

'We agreed,' Jeremiah says, making his steps match mine. 'You said you'd take what pay you've a right to and go home safe —'

'I ain't entertaining no more talk about this. I've got to pack, remember?' I turn away to go down the row toward our tent, but he grabs my arm and drags me after him. I fight against him until Ambrose Clark stands up from where he was sitting outside his tent, that flask in his hand.

'Stop it, Jeremiah. People will see.'

'You come with me then,' he says, and I do.

We're silent for a good long while, so long we walk past the latrines and toward the river.

'You promised,' he says the instant we are under the trees.

'I don't want to go back there! You think they'll be proud to have me there, after what I've done?'

'It ain't so bad as all that. My Ma says she's forgiven you for leaving like you did,' Jeremiah says.

We stare at each other, neither one of us budging.

'You heard Henry. The boys — I can't keep you safe,' Jeremiah says.

246

'Captain Chalmers ain't worried about keeping his wife safe! He ain't sent her back home.'

Jeremiah don't say a thing. Maybe he knows how to tell I'm bluffing.

'I ain't sitting in church with all those people judging me. And Eli —' It is like bird wings flapping inside me, thinking on Eli, just saying his name, knowing Hiram might be worse. Jeremiah must see something in my face because he takes my hand in both of his. I lean into him.

'Ain't you nervous?' Jeremiah asks, his voice going low again.

'All the time,' I say. 'But going home ain't going to stop that. There ain't a thing for it, except do what we've got to.'

'But you don't have to do this thing!' Jeremiah says.

I think of marching to the South, to the Rebels, and of the wounded lying in hospital beds and Joseph Brown dying. I think of that last letter I wrote for him and if it were my letter instead, if it were Papa bringing it to my Mama, and what it might be for her to hear it read. But then there's Jeremiah lying alone on the battlefield. I shake my head.

'Yes,' I say, and grab for his hand. 'I do have to. My place is with you.'

■ ■ ■ ■

Jeremiah's voice in my ear wakes me.

'Rosetta,' he whispers.

It is late. I don't say anything, so he'll leave me sleeping. There is a rustling as he moves under his blanket and his arm comes around me.

'Rosetta, wake up.'

'What?'

'We've got to get up,' he says.

'Why?'

'Just get up.' He moves, getting to his feet and taking my hands to help me.

'That ain't nice,' I say, and there is the glimmer of his smile in the dark.

'You'll like it.' He drags me after him through the opening. 'Look at that moon.'

It is almost straight over our heads, shining on the tent peaks like they are snow-covered roofs, almost as light as the moment before dawn breaks, but it is still deepest night.

The fort around us is quiet, only the sound of men snoring and grinding teeth and coughing as we pad down the tent row. I don't know what Jeremiah is about, but he keeps hold of my hand.

'Where we going?' I ask.

'I ain't telling if you don't know.'

We are almost to the trees when there is a scuffling noise behind us, coming from the latrines. There ain't time to pull away from Jeremiah.

'Act sick,' he whispers. 'Like I'm helping you.'

I lean against him, dragging my feet, coughing and groaning as we scurry into the woods.

'Who was that?' I ask.

'Ain't sure. Thought I saw that white hair of Will's,' Jeremiah whispers. 'I don't think he saw us.'

We don't talk after that. He takes us down to the river. Any pickets are out guarding far off to the South.

When we come out of the trees, there is a swath of chalky moonlight cutting across that dark slate current. Jeremiah sinks down to the ground, pulling me with him.

'What are we doing here?' I ask.

'Nothing,' he says. 'Sitting.'

'You woke me up for sitting?'

'Maybe,' he says, that smile back on his face. 'Maybe not. I thought you might want a chance at swimming.'

I stare at him, and then I rest my head on his shoulder, feeling the warmth of his arm coming around me and the night air chill everywhere we ain't touching.

'It's cold,' I say.

'Not if you keep moving.'

'What if someone comes? What if Will saw
—'

'I'll keep watch,' he says. 'Besides, it's the middle of the night, no one's going to see a thing.'

'Okay,' I say, kicking off my brogans while Jeremiah's fingers draw loops across my back and raise gooseflesh on my arms. I slide out from under his hand and stand up to undo the fly of my trousers, stepping out of them and walking for the river in my drawers, my binding still tight under my shirt, thinking only of washing the sweat and dust and stink out of my underthings.

The dark water is cold on my toes. Whatever is under the surface is hidden, even my own feet in the shallows. The river rocks are slippery beneath my toes, the spaces between soft with silt. When the water is lapping at my shins, I turn back to where Jeremiah sits.

'Go on,' he says. 'I'm watching.'

I take a deep breath and push forward toward the middle of the river, letting my knees buckle until I am underwater. When I shove out into the night air I am gasping, the water cold enough to make my breath come in fits. My shirt clings to my arms and shoulders, the wet seeping through my binding, making my teeth chatter. I've got to get out or start swimming. Jeremiah is a boulder on the shore.

I swim out farther, until I ain't chilled anymore, until my feet almost don't touch bottom, swimming right into the moon's shimmering image, rippling in the lazy current. Then I float on my back, the river sound flowing in my ears, the same stars shining at home and over the land that someday is to be our farm.

A noise comes through the water. My heart goes to fluttering as I turn over. Jeremiah ain't sitting on the shore no more. I comb that bank, seeing nothing but shadows, hearing nothing.

And then there is a splash and a round shape pushing up from under the water, coming toward me. I can't help myself, I let out a yelp even as Jeremiah pops out of the water, more than halfway to me. As he comes up for air, his teeth flash, smiling as he stands in front of me.

'You scared me!' I say louder than I meant, because I am angry at him, angry at feeling scared. And then I don't care and I shove both hands forward into the river, sending a wave at Jeremiah. He is still too far away, it don't even touch him, but he lunges at me and for a moment, before his arms are around me, pulling me to him, I think maybe it isn't him. But then he is there and his cold mouth is wet against mine.

He ain't barely kissing me before I dig my toes around the rock beneath my feet and push him away.

'You scared me,' I say.

'I'm sorry,' he says, his breath coming fast. 'That ain't what I meant. Just wanted to surprise you.'

'That ain't nice,' I say, and my teeth get to chattering.

'You cold?'

I don't say anything. I don't know if I am cold or scared.

'Come here,' he says, and pushes himself through the water. His arms come around me again and he draws me forward until my feet ain't touching that rock no more.

'Don't you scare me like that again,' I say. 'I thought you were gone.'

'I'm sorry,' he says again, and this time my arms reach behind him, my fingers clinging to his bare shoulders. 'It didn't seem right, you swimming by yourself.'

And then he bends to kiss me, water dripping from his hair onto my face, his fingers tracing the front of my shirt until they find a button. I wrap my legs around his waist. He don't have a stitch of clothes on and my breath comes fast again.

'It ain't safe,' I say, thinking of Betsy's last question to me.

'It's okay, there ain't no one here,' he says, and then he kisses my neck, his fingers fumbling at those buttons and then he is peeling my wet shirt away from my shoulders and maybe it don't matter, not when he is pulling at the binding still so tight around my chest, not when he unwraps it, not when he pushes my underdrawers down from my hips and the heat of him moves through the whole of my body.

■ ■ ■ ■

BATTLE

AUGUST 21–SEPTEMBER 19, 1862

■ ■ ■ ■

'Your resolution once fixed, never lose sight
of it until it is carried out.'
— *The 1862 Army Officer's
Pocket Companion*

CHAPTER 18

RAPPAHANNOCK STATION: AUGUST 21–26, 1862

Me and Jeremiah are marching across green pastures, taking our money to get that farm. There's rolling hills and apples in Fall and fat cows and a raven-haired child gathering eggs. We work a hayfield together, the golden hay swirling in the air, going home to a cabin at night, making plans for rooms we could add if we need. But when I wake up I am curled on the hard ground, not under Mama's double wedding ring quilt, but wrapped in my wool blanket, and the only thing that is the same is Jeremiah beside me. I stare up at the lightening sky and pray we don't ever have to see one Confederate soldier, but that can't be. After more than a month of moving about the countryside all up and down the Rappahannock River, we ain't ever been closer to the enemy. I find Jeremiah's hand under the blankets, but he don't wake and it is a marvel he can sleep so solid. I lie there like that 'til most of the camp gets to stirring, 'til Jeremiah opens his eyes and smiles at me.

Breakfast is barely even a thought when news comes tripping down through the soldiers that there's Rebel pickets and artillery setting up along the river.

After that, the morning and breakfast don't ever get to being like usual. There's no jeering, no horsing around, no laughing, no storytelling. Even Sully sits quiet, chewing his lip. I force myself to swallow bits of salt pork, but when it gets to my belly it don't settle right.

It ain't clear where the notion starts but when breakfast's eaten, Jeremiah draws out his pen and papers, unfolds the sheets down onto his thighs, ironing them over and over with his hands. Soon as everyone starts seeing what's afoot, the hush gets even deeper. There ain't a human sound except the moving of the rest of the boys as they fan out, getting space for private thoughts, taking up every boulder or log that's good for sitting.

Jeremiah's pen hovers over the blank page. It goes to quivering and then he writes *My Dear Wife, Rosetta.*

I can't take none of that. I grab my things

and shove off for the trees, heaving my guts, heaving every last bit of that breakfast, heaving long past everything is clean out of my body. When I stand straight, trying to look for all the world like ain't nothing wrong, heads are still bowed, hands are still crawling across paper. I find a low flat boulder and sink down into the wet leaves and grass, digging in my pack to find the map. It is folded back to show the Capital and Virginia. From there it's easy to trace the twisting snake of the Rappahannock River, just a thin ribbon keeping us from Richmond, less than a hundred miles away, not even a five-day march.

I smooth my own letter paper over that rock 'til McClellan's grave picture stares flat out from top of the page. All the things I want to tell Jeremiah feel too big, too much to put to a piece of paper, and whatever I say won't be enough to do him a lick of good. Instead I write:

August 21, 1862
Near Rappahannock Station

Dear Mama, Papa, and Betsy,
If you are Reading these Lines, then You will already know what came of Me. I want You should know I ain't sorry do-

259

ing this thing and staying with my Husband. Sin or no, I am Proud I have been of Some Help and have done as Well as any Soldier and Better than some. I have Friends here from that neighborhood, and more besides and my Life has been Happy for having Done this Service.

I don't fear the Rebel bullets and those Cannons don't scare me None. I have Made my Peace and Forgive all who ever done a thing to me. I want You should Forgive me for all the Wrongs I done. I know I haven't always been a Right and Good daughter, or a good sister neither but I never did none of it to hurt you. I Hope you still Remember me as Your Daughter and Sister but are Proud of Your Soldier.

I am Thinking on Home and if Ever I will Come there again. I want that you lay out for the Family and the Farm what the Army sends for my part here. I will See that it is done from where I rest. I don't Aim to Die, but it gives me Comfort to know We will meet again in Heaven where there is no more Parting.

I am Always,
Your Rosetta

I seal that letter in a Liberty and Union

cover with a three-cent stamp, writing *Mr. and Mrs. Charles L. Edwards and Miss Elisabeth V. Edwards. Flat Creek Crossing, Montgomery Co., New York.* I slide it in my breast pocket and hope that when I look on it again, it's because this war is over and Jeremiah and I are packing for one last visit home.

Across camp, away from the boys writing letters, the Chalmerses hug like they ain't ever going to see each other again. Captain hands Jennie into a wagon, kissing that same hand. When he lets go, her shoulders hunch like she is crying, and she keeps herself turned around, her eyes on her husband as that wagon drives her back the way we've come. Watching her fade into the trees pulls at something inside me, seeing her for maybe the last time. I could be just like her, saying good-bye to my man, going away alone.

I hurry to Jeremiah. All around, men who ain't writing letters sit, housewife kits on their knees, coats in their laps, needles in their hands, stitching their names across the collars, like it is nothing to think on being so torn up a person wouldn't know a body, or being shot down with the whole Company.

I sit myself silent beside Jeremiah. He

looks at me once, his eyes full. From my own housewife kit I unspool some coarse thread, break it between my teeth, and lick the frayed edge. Holding the needle up to the sun, I push the wet thread through and shiver off my jacket.

'Give me yours too,' I say soft, and start sewing.

'We're to hold here,' Captain says, 'and protect the railway in the town if the Rebels break through the Pennsylvania Regiment guarding the bridge.'

The town below the knoll where we've stopped ain't much, a few brick buildings and the train station, its tracks running over the muddy brown river, trees growing all around and hills sloping away. Without those trains running we can't get provisions and munitions and reinforcements. It don't matter how pretty the rolling grassland is, or how tall the corn grows in the rich soil around this town, there ain't none among us wants to be traipsing about in the countryside looking for farms with cows we can give vouchers for, not when the whole place is crawling with Seceshes.

Down beyond the town, too far off to make out much more than the blue of their uniforms, those Pennsylvania men line up in a trench on the other side of the bridge, a dog weaving through their lines, barking at the trees where Confederates are firing, maybe Jackson's whole Corps.

'This ain't good luck,' I say as we file through the tombstones littering the hill, trying not to think on the souls beneath as we hunker down and kneel for cover. Me and Jeremiah have got the best hiding place with oxeye daisies growing at the foot of a headstone so old it's got soft edges, the bones beneath us waiting for Kingdom Come a long time now.

'Plenty of things ain't good luck.' Sully shakes his head and sends me a look. 'At least maybe the Rebels won't be looking for us here.'

But those Rebels send a thunder of artillery fire right over the railroad bridge, over the Pennsylvanians' heads, right toward us, making me cower. Puffs of white smoke rise and hover over the box elders and poplars, smelling like sulfur.

The heights behind us are lined with our Division's artillery, hidden among the skinny tree trunks. Beyond them is Colonel Wheelock and the rest of the high-up officers.

Sometimes we can hear more artillery echoing from upriver and that's when this river ain't big or wide enough, not even the Potomac River would be enough.

'We ain't winning,' Jeremiah says.

'What?' I ask, even though I can hear him plain. 'How do you know?'

'If we were, those'd be the first words out of Sergeant's lips, how them Rebels are falling back,' Jeremiah says.

Sergeant paces at the end of our row of gravestones, looking like he's counting us, like he's measuring our chances. Jeremiah must be right.

I trace the letters carved on our gravestone, the shadow of a furrow, spelling out *Deliverance Lockhart, dau. of Samuel & Mary, My peace I give unto thee.* I flatten myself against Jeremiah and imagine sinking down into the earth, down to the bones below us.

Jeremiah bumps into me, his thigh long against mine, his head tilted so he can see around our tombstone. 'Any Rebels come across that bridge and we start seeing action,' he says, 'you slip back.'

'I ain't going nowhere but with you,' I say.

'Ain't no sin in falling back,' Jeremiah says. 'Helping those that need it when the time comes.'

There is comfort in those words. Especially with the sick feeling that's settled in my belly. But I signed on for this and there ain't a thing I have ever been made to feel proud of in my life but the doing of a job that needs doing.

All night we are pelted with warm needle-sharp rain. Horses hunched and huddled in a stormy field never felt so miserable and I get to cursing myself for leaving my rubber-backed canvas by the side of the road, way back when we started marching. The kepis the Army gave us don't hardly have a brim and they don't do a thing to keep the rain out of our faces or from going down our collars. I am soaked through to the skin before it is even close to morning. Sometimes I drop off to sleep for a bit, leaning on Jeremiah's shoulder, only to jerk awake as often as a horse twitches at flies. But mostly we are awake and staring, nervous for Rebels to come out of the weather.

At first light Sergeant comes along our row of graves. He crouches down next to Thomas Stakely before moving on past. Thomas crawls to where Ambrose is hunched at the next headstone and that is how Sergeant's orders to march come whispering from mouth to mouth down the line. Will brings the orders to us.

'The enemy is moving, looking for another way across. We're marching off to some ford, to keep them getting through,' he says, and pats Jeremiah on the shoulder, sending him past me, crawling to the next grave, where the O'Malleys wait.

'You ready?' Will whispers to me once Jeremiah is gone.

'Course,' I tell him. 'It'll almost be a relief, leaving here.'

'Sully says we might see some real action today. You think you might say a prayer with me?' Will asks.

'I don't mind praying,' I say, and the words are barely out of my mouth before Will takes up my hand in his clammy one.

'Dear Lord, give us the strength,' Will says. 'Give unto us your whole armor, that you may help us withstand the evil day. Hide us under your shield of protection, that our enemy will not find us. Amen.' He squeezes my hand before opening his eyes. 'Thank you,' he says, and crawls off the way he came, and I wonder if his prayer made a lick of difference.

'What's Will want with you all the time?' Jeremiah asks when he scuttles back from telling Henry the orders.

'We were just praying,' I say. 'Ain't nothing wrong with that, is there?'

'No,' Jeremiah says. 'I don't like him taking such an interest, is all.'

'He ain't taking interest. He's just lonesome and looking for a friend. You got something against me having friends?'

Jeremiah shakes his head, and I wonder what he is about until Sergeant comes before us.

'We've gotten word from Brigadier General Ricketts, down from General McDowell himself, that our Division is to stop the Confederates from finding another way across the river,' Sergeant says, sweat dripping down the lines in his face, the day so humid already after the Summer storm.

'We've got Rebels hitting us with shells right over there!' Sully says, loud enough for Sergeant to hear, but it don't do no good.

We march off quiet, if hundreds of men can be quiet. There ain't no singing, no wandering in our lines, nothing except the clinking of bayonets on canteens, boots tramping through reddish mud that splatters on our wet trousers, nothing except the way-off sounds of cannonball blasts echoing everywhere. Dying ain't never felt so real before, and I ain't ready, not like I told Will. I march closer to Jeremiah. He turns to look at me and gives me something like a smile, something meant to make me feel better, I think, but it don't.

■ ■ ■ ■

We are still tramping on the turnpike four days later, our orders having blown us about like a weathervane, sending us every which way trying to find the Rebels. Now we are marching away from the river, headed for a gap in the mountains. Will swings his pack around to the front and digs through it. He don't look around while he pulls out his deck of cards. He holds them in his hand and looks down at them, his lips moving. Will has been wearing his serious face all the time since we started marching, but he looks almost relaxed as he drops those cards into the grass alongside the road.

'What'd you do that for?' I ask him.

He gawks at me. 'Do what?'

'Your cards. You dropped them.'

'I left them back there,' he says, and the boys' attention snaps to him, like a bunch of hens all seeing the same bug at once.

'You dropped your cards?' Henry asks, turning to us.

'I did,' Will says, and straightens himself like boys do sometimes before a fight.

'What for?' Jimmy asks.

Will says, 'I'm not dying with gambling on my head.'

'You ain't playing poker no more?' I ask.

'Why didn't you give one of us those cards?' Henry tries not to yell.

'It's a sin,' Will says.

'What's a sin,' Sully says, 'is keeping us from the one enjoyment we've got. Now how are we going to entertain ourselves?'

'Read the Bible?' Jeremiah says. 'You didn't drop that, now did you, Chaplain Eberhart?'

That strikes all those boys as funny and they laugh so hard Will don't have a chance to answer. Seeing them gets me laughing too, even though Will's face turns red, even though there's artillery banging off in the distance.

We make a bivouac under the trees hanging over the road, hoping the shade will help, but it don't much. My clothes are wet with sweat and stuck to my skin.

'Ross, please tell me you didn't throw out your map like Chaplain over there,' Sully says, about the time Will maybe got to thinking those boys had forgotten what he's done with his cards. All the boys get to laughing again, even though Will's cheeks blaze.

'Heck, no,' I say, and feel bad for laughing when I know what it is to be teased.

'Well then, have you got any idea how far it is to that gap?' Sully asks.

I pull out my map, stare at the turnpike taking us away from Richmond.

'If that last town really was Warrenton,' I say, picturing the white church steeple, stabbing at the clouds with its spire and the unfriendly feeling coming off the deserted streets, 'the closest gap is something like thirty miles. Maybe more,' I tell him.

'We ain't ever going to stop those Rebs at this rate!' Sully says, and flops onto his back.

My stomach rumbles and complains. I lean over to Jeremiah.

'You got any rations left?' I ask.

'No. I ate my crumbs for breakfast.'

'I ain't tried that,' I say, and I turn my haversack upside down over my palm. Only a few stale bits of cracker fall out.

Jimmy overhears me and says, 'I got some salt pork, if you want it. But it's gone funny, made me sick to eat it.'

'I don't need anything else making my stomach upset,' I say.

Turns out not a one of us has got any rations left to speak of, but Sully and Henry and Edward and Hiram have energy enough to start chanting, 'Crackers! Crackers!'

Soon the whole Regiment is chanting, even Chaplain Will. That is when Captain finds it in himself to let Sergeant Ames give us some of the rations left in the wagons that ain't broken down, that we ain't had to burn.

'I see how these crackers got the name teethdullers,' Henry says as he smashes his against a rock with his rifle butt. I try the same and break my cracker into four pieces, washing them down with water.

Henry sits himself right down beside Jimmy, and it don't take but a minute before he droops over onto Jimmy's shoulder, his mouth hanging open. He is the only one of us who can sleep and Jimmy never shoves him off. He just sits there quiet and lets Henry doze.

Jeremiah pokes me. 'You want a fancy place like that house back there?' he asks, and I know just which one he means, the white one with sprawling lawns and fancy flowers planted everywhere.

'It don't got no farm around it,' I say. 'All those flowers are just taking up good soil a kitchen garden could grow in. And, you ask me, fancy buildings don't make up for the feeling of a place.'

'You ain't ever seen a town you liked, have you?' Jeremiah lies back on the grass.

'I ain't got use for a town. But I bet there's good planting to be done around here.'

Jeremiah closes his eyes, leaving me with thoughts of Nebraska, and if it really is good farming, and how soon we might get ourselves clear of this Army. But then Joseph's face comes up in my mind, how pale he was against that hospital pillow. There are things it would be fitting for Jeremiah to read if it comes to that, so I sit with my back to an ash tree right near Jeremiah and let my thoughts spread like the branches shading me.

August 26, 1862

My Dear Jeremiah,
I don't want to sit and write these Words to you. I have been thinking on Us living through this War. I have been feeling it to be True, this fact of Us together. But now I have tasted War. I see how Dreaming on a thing don't make it so. It has got me thinking on things I would have you know.

I'm not sorry for this Thing we've done. You did Right by letting me stay. There ain't a thing to make me take back These Days with You. You gave me friendship and then Love and Freedom to live a different Life. There ain't a person else in this World who gave me

More, and you should know it. I know I never wanted the things I should or been a proper Wife, but you don't ever make me Feel it too much.

If we see this War to its End, if we can live Free on our own Place, the two of Us, I want you should know I will give you all that is left of my Life. It is all I want to work that Land with you and see those crops come up and if God is Willing, what children we may raise up alongside the farm we build. It will make this all Worth it if we can have our Place.

And that is what I would Give to you. I would Give you my Love. I would give you our Dream. Even if I am only watching from the Other side, I give you these things.

Your wife,
Rosetta

CHAPTER 19

WARRENTON TURNPIKE: AUGUST 28, 1862

We march past a hayfield, bigger than any of Papa's, fine-stemmed grass pushing up new seed heads and rolling away from us toward the trees, where a white clapboard farmhouse stands. The sweet smell of curing hay comes to us on the breeze, the first cutting most likely done not even a month ago. It makes me wish for home, to hear Mama singing hymns to the horses from where she sits up in the hayrick, me and Papa a mirror image dance of scooping forks, twisting trunks, and throwing arms to get that hay put up. For a moment I pretend Sully yelling at us to hurry as he jogs ahead is Papa hollering, 'Step up, gleaning girl!' to Betsy raking the least little bits behind us.

But it ain't Papa marching up ahead. It's Thomas, the circles under his eyes getting darker every day and his griping to old John

Morgan getting louder too.

'My wife is asking every letter when I am coming home,' he says, looking out over the hayfield. 'Says she and the girls ain't up to the task of harvest on their own.'

'I bet all those ladies need is a good poking,' Hiram says, and that gets Thomas' Adam's apple bobbing, but no one wants to say a thing where Hiram is concerned.

John acts like he ain't heard and says, 'At this rate you and me and Frank and half the Army will need furloughs just to keep our farms going.'

'Maybe Pope means to march us to death,' Henry says, and something about the way we all feel it stops Hiram's laugh cold.

'At least we'll see the countryside before we die,' Jeremiah says with a bitterness I ain't never heard out of him. It scares me more than anything, seeing his face hard and closed.

'We'll be fighting for sure,' Sully says, all breathless from weaving up and down the column to get what particulars he can from Sergeant. 'Lee has got Jackson on the move! Maybe twenty thousand men! The Pennsylvania Regiment up there is seeing Rebel pickets ahead guarding at least a Brigade of Rebels.'

'We don't want to meet Stonewall Jackson

if we can help it,' Thomas says. 'He made that name for himself right around here. My brother-in-law saw firsthand at Bull Run how Jackson don't back down.'

But Sully just keeps on running his mouth, 'Those damn Seceshes got our supply trains at Manassas Junction and they broke up the rail line. We ain't getting even a taste of those crackers and candy and oranges that were on that train.'

'This fool Army!' Henry says. 'We ain't doing a thing out here but marching ourselves into the ground!'

'It's no use thinking on what we ain't getting,' Jeremiah says, but I still feel myself getting saucy too, my legs aching and my stomach warbling at the thought of candy and oranges.

'Maybe the Rebels needed it more than we do,' Will says, all quiet-like.

'What?' Sully says. 'Chaplain, you've got to be kidding! You feel sorry for those Rebs?'

Will don't flinch or back down like I think he might. He just says, 'Those boys used to be our countrymen. Maybe they needed it more than we do. "Therefore if thine enemy hunger, feed him; if he thirst, give him drink: for in so doing thou shalt heap coals of fire on his head." That's in Romans.'

Sully comes to a full stop and dams up

276

the middle of the road, making Henry bump into him and blocking the rest of us. The soldiers drawing up behind us have to split to get around.

Hiram turns, pulling Edward around with him, and says, 'We got a fucking Rebel lover here?'

Sully stares at Will, and Henry takes up a spot next to him. Jimmy and I look back and forth between them.

'Will just wants those Rebels fed up good so no one can say it ain't a fair fight, ain't that right, Will?' I say, and then Jeremiah slaps Will on the back, making him stumble.

'You've got the most grave face, Chaplain, I almost believed you was serious!' Jeremiah says, and then he laughs and pushes Will forward so we are all moving again.

It ain't Jeremiah's real laugh, it don't roll out of him, but the other boys get to chuckling. It don't make me chuckle seeing the boys' bad tempers, or having to protect Will and keep us all getting along, me and Jeremiah taking a stand for the right thing without anybody knowing we're doing it. I wish I could fold his hand into mine without getting noticed, but that is when the call to arms comes echoing.

I shoulder my rifle like I ought, but then I

277

have to step out of our line to heave up mostly nothing into the yellow yarrow along the edge of the turnpike, cursing my nerves. Jeremiah stops too, waiting for me. He don't say a thing, not until we get back into the column winding its way down the road. Then he puts his hand on my shoulder as we walk, like a butterfly landing on a blue-bell.

'We'll be fine,' he says.

And that is what I tell myself over and over, letting my mouth move with the words so it somehow seems like they are more real. The air all around is hot and tight with nerves and excitement and everyone is hushed, listening and looking for what's to come, wondering how many Confederates are behind the soldiers making up the picket line stretched across the woods, how big that Brigade is.

Way across that hayfield, a horseman looks down on us from a rounded grassy hill ahead, a dark shape moving just at the edge of the trees. When he comes out into the sun, he is wearing a gray coat and a gray brimmed hat.

I suck in a breath and hear Will beside me murmur, 'That's Rebel cavalry!'

'Thomas! Is that your goddamned Stone-wall Jackson?' Hiram yells ahead.

'Naw,' Edward says. 'I've seen pictures in the papers. Jackson don't wear a stag hat like that.'

Then an officer from one of the Regiments in our column gallops across that hayfield toward the Confederates. Everyone goes quiet watching as he brings those Rebels' attention to himself.

He don't hardly get to the top of the knoll before white smoke puffs up out of the trees by that farmhouse and then shells hail down on us. The earth heaves and smoke swirls into the air.

We are out in the open, plain as day on the road. The men in front of me keep moving, the lines staying true somehow. I clutch my rifle tighter, hunch my shoulders, and follow.

Another shell blast sounds. Dirt and grass shower down over us and then a shell explodes right in the ranks of the Regiment ahead of us. It is more than dirt that flies up this time and everywhere turns to screaming, everything happening at once.

A space clears and two boys lie there, twisted and tangled like no man in life, one's foot still twitching, both of them looking young enough to be boys from home, their blood already soaking into the dust. And then there are more shells, pounding down after Captain Chalmers and Colonel Wheelock as they kick their horses into a race off the road and across another field, away from the artillery fire, headed for an apple orchard, leaving us there in the road.

All around me our Regiment is like a line of ants gone to swarming. I stand there, staring, until a hand yanks on my arm. It is Jeremiah and he is yelling something, but I can't hear it for all the noise and there is someone pushing me from behind and I am swept along too.

Jeremiah drags me down to my belly beside him in the grass along the turnpike. Boys fall to the ground around us, getting down flat and taking cover.

'What were you doing standing there?' Jeremiah yells.

I don't have no answer.

Galloping horses clatter, bringing cannons and caissons up the turnpike. One team of horses stops near us, the shine of sweat darkening their necks and their heaving flanks, the pink flashing of their nostrils flaring, their tails clamped. The riders jump off the lead horses and unlimber the cannons faster than Papa ever unhitched a horse in his life. When those horses have been trotted away to safety, the cannoneers aim their pieces at that hill, thundering shells down on the farmhouse there, covering our Pennsylvania Regiment as they move out into the grass. There is so much noise, shells tearing up the hayfields, rifles scaring off whatever livestock might be left. All I can think is that farm and how there ain't a thing you can do to stop this war ripping right through your home, right through your whole life, and the roaring is so loud my ears go to ringing even after I press my hands to them.

Chapter 20

THOROUGHFARE GAP: AUGUST 28, 1862
The attack don't last long, our bugles blaring to signal the Rebels' retreat. Sergeant Ames gathers us together, finding some shade away from the bodies of those two boys. He stands along the edge of the road, the sun beating down on him, his face red and beaded with sweat.

'We've gotten reports the Rebels have already been seen coming through the Thoroughfare Gap, and we've got to beat the rest before we're overrun.'

Just like that we are back on the march as the crow flies, scrambling through chokecherry and brambles to get to the Gap, no time for proper roads. Every step is its own battle and every time I lose footing, it jolts my knapsack and makes its straps dig into my shoulders. Jeremiah looks back at me each rail fence we have to climb, and sometimes he starts to reach a hand out to help me across. I get to wishing I could take it, but even just the offering of it pulls me along.

Sully marches in front of us and sees how we ain't keeping up as we should.

'Keep coming!' he says. 'We've got to beat those Rebels. Get to that Gap.'

We finally halt where a creek trickles through the trees. Captain don't have orders for us, not even dressing right and stacking arms. 'All right, boys. Fill your canteens and get what rest you can. We won't stop here long.'

I sink to the ground with the others, tiredness going through me like a taproot, sinking deeper and deeper. We ain't even settled when Sergeant comes round and takes a few boys out for picket duty. Sully gets to squirming that he ain't one chosen.

Jeremiah turns to me, saying, 'Give me your canteen. I'll go fill it and you rest.'

Before, I might've made a fuss, but this is a thing Jeremiah can do, a way he can be husband to me, even here, and so I take my canteen over my head and give it to him. Sully gets himself up off the ground and takes Will's and the O'Malleys' canteens off them. Jeremiah goes to ask Thomas and Ambrose. Ambrose holds up his flask, says, 'I've got fluid enough.' Then Jeremiah and

Sully go together, taking all our canteens along.

Will sits, digging through his pack, tossing out his rubber blanket, extra rounds of ammunition, his half of a shelter tent. Finally he pulls out his Bible, a daguerreotype tucked inside for safekeeping.

'I never thought I'd come to this,' he says, looking close at the brown leather binding, and then setting it down on the grass, like a mama putting a baby down to nap.

'Come to what?' I ask.

'I can't carry it all anymore,' he says. 'My pack. It weighs too dang much.'

It's the closest Will's ever come to swearing, and I'm surprised he even says what he does with his Bible there to witness. I think of the mucket he gave me, but I ain't so tired yet to leave it by the roadside. Will slips the daguerreotype out and carefully slides it into his chest pocket, but not before I see it's of a man and woman.

'That your Mama and Pa?' I ask.

'It is,' he says.

'Close to your heart, that's a better place for them anyway. And you got lots of verses by heart, don't you?'

Will nods but his face crumples, so I say, 'Then you're already carrying what you need. You could bury it under a tree or something and when we come on back you can find it. I've got some flannel you can wrap it up nice in. Keep it clean.'

I hand him one of the rags I pinched from Jennie, thinking how lucky it is I ain't needed it before now. He takes the flannel from me, his hand brushing mine. 'Thank you. That'll do real nice.'

We both know it ain't no use coming back for that Bible but it makes him feel better, wrapping that book like a gift.

'You want help digging a hole for it?' I ask, even though sitting feels good.

'That'd be nice,' Will says as he gets up. I follow him away from the resting boys, down toward the creek. I think we might run into Jeremiah and Sully coming back with our canteens, but Will veers off once we are in the trees. Before long he drops to his knees under a dogwood.

'This is a good spot,' he says.

Using our bayonets, we scratch out a shallow grave, Will all the time checking over his shoulder like he is nervous Rebels might find us. Finally he lays the Bible inside the hole, placing it just so before standing up.

'I'd like to get some stones for a marker,' he says, putting a hand on my shoulder. 'If you don't mind.'

I shrug out from under his hand. 'I'm

happy to.'

We make our way to the creek, and while Will is picking out a few round rocks, I look up and downstream for Jeremiah. There is no one.

Back at the hole, Will scatters handfuls of dirt over the Bible before placing the first rock. Right as I am squatting down to add my rock to the mound, Will stops my hand.

'Thank you for this,' he says, still holding on to me. 'And for your friendship.'

'It ain't nothing,' I say, drawing back.

He don't let go.

'Ross — I don't know how —' he says. 'I've been fighting with my — There's something I want, something I've been wanting to ask —' He leans closer, his hand still on mine, and that is when I see what he is about.

I yank my hand away and scramble to my feet. He jumps up too.

'What are you doing?' I yell, but I ain't the same kind of scared like when Eli came at me.

'I didn't mean —You've been so kind — I thought —'

'Don't you tell a soul!' I say. 'I ain't leaving this Army on account of nobody.'

'Ross — I wasn't —'

'You say one word to Captain and you'll

have Jeremiah to answer to. He ain't my cousin,' I say.

'Jeremiah? Your cousin? I saw the two of you, at the river —'

'He's my husband, so you just get those thoughts out of your head,' I say. 'And if you think he's just going to let you —'

'Your husband? What are you —' Will gapes at me. 'I thought —'

And then I don't know what Will is about. 'What did you think?' I ask.

Will stands there, his mouth open, studying me like he ain't ever really seen me before.

Real slow he says, 'All this time, I thought you were — You aren't a man? You've been lying.'

'It ain't a lie,' I say. 'This is who I am. There ain't a thing different about me.'

'You're not a man! That's a real big thing, from my way of looking. Knowing, it changes — I shouldn't be here with you. This is unseemly,' he says, and walks away.

'I ain't no different. It don't have to change a thing —' I'm saying when suddenly I am back home, seeing Horace Greaves mourning at Albert Nofrey's grave. I think on the two of them living on that farm together all those years, old bachelors 'til the last, and how after Albert died it

287

wasn't long before Horace was buried right beside him. I clap my hand over my mouth and let Will stomp off through the trees.

I can't quit worrying over Will. I can't even look at him. Not once I am back along the road, resting with Jeremiah. Not when Sergeant gets our lines moving again. Not an hour later when we stop at a white clapboard church. I can't think what to even tell Jeremiah, not after he was right about Will taking an interest in me. I keep seeing Will leaning toward me and the surprise on his face when I told him Jeremiah was my husband, when he said I'd been lying. I keep thinking of all the nice things he's ever done for me and seeing each of them different, how Sully called him out for being sweet on me.

But Sergeant is before us saying, 'Men, we'll leave our knapsacks here. You can trust we will return to get them once we beat back those Rebels.'

Those words get me thinking on worse things than Will or being found out. I shrug free from my pack, thinking how my load is heavier now than it ever was, and Will lightened his load too soon.

We hide among the craggy mountains, slabs

of rock thrown every which way, a scattering of gray-green pitch pines looking like the lace edging of Mama's church-best petticoat against the blue of the sky, land that ain't good for a thing except getting through it. Beyond we can see the skinny Gap, barely wide enough for the train tracks and the turnpike.

On either side of us, the slope rises steep and if those Confederates are up on the mountainsides we ain't got a chance of getting them out.

Will quotes Scripture from where he marches with Thomas, saying, 'Yea, though I walk through the valley of the shadow of death, I will fear no evil: for thou art with me . . .'

I pull my rifle to the front, my hands wrapped tight around the stock, telling myself I ain't afraid of battle, feeling how there ain't no Rebel bullet meant for me yet. Behind us, the artillery Brigade sets those cannons to work before the horses have even been moved away.

'Been thinking,' Jeremiah says, leaning over to me.

'Uh-oh,' I tease.

'Stop it,' he says, but he smiles, even here he is smiling. 'A man can think sometimes, can't he?'

'Oh, I suppose he can any time he wants,' I say, and wonder if I should say a thing to him about Will.

He starts again all quiet. 'When we get out of this war we ought to get ourselves a place with a piece of nice woods like this.'

'Woods? What do we need to be hiding from on our own place? After this war is done I don't ever want to hide again.'

'Not for hiding.' He chuckles. 'Well, maybe for hiding. For when you get your dander up. Or for when we want to be alone, away from the children.'

Just for a moment I see myself holding Jeremiah's baby, laying that child in a crib Jeremiah made, like our papas before him.

'You've been aiming to have a farm that don't got any trees? Or you just like the looks of these rocks now that you're standing on them?' I look around, making sure no one's listening. Only Will is close enough and it don't matter what he hears now.

'No,' he goes on, 'but they're nice for admiring.'

'You mean I married a man ain't never thought on having a woodlot on his farm before now? And now that he does think on it, he only wants trees for admiring instead of building and burning? You want some boulders for admiring too?'

'Just woods.' Jeremiah says. 'No rocks. They ain't good for much besides fireplaces. Trees, now they're good for lots of things. Hiding . . .' he says, but he don't finish because we finally catch sight of what we've been waiting for. Coming down the slope of the mountain to the East, there's flashes of gray through the trees, quick enough I almost ain't sure what I'm seeing, but the buzz going through the boys is answer enough.

Down the line from us, Hiram yells, 'Secesh sons of bitches! Goddamned traitors!'

I wonder what is going through Hiram's mind, drawing the Rebs' attention and maybe their fire, but then he yells real loud, 'Suck my ass, skunk eaters!' and sets us all to laughing.

The laughter don't last, though. We watch those Confederates move down from the mountain until they are as close as a privy to the house — close enough to see, but not to smell. In the splashes of the last light through the trees, their rifles look the same as ours. They look nothing like what I expected of plantation owners' sons and slaveholders and such, not a one of them wearing a matching uniform. They look like any farmer from home and except for the gray they're wearing it is almost like we are coming out of the trees to kill ourselves, coming for our hill, flanking our own rifles.

Jeremiah shakes his arm. 'Rosetta, let go! We've got orders!'

He fires, the roar loud and fast, and he don't look at me once after that, too busy watching the Rebels running for cover behind trees or moving back away from our skirmish line, loading his rifle without needing to look at what he's doing. He aims his rifle again and when the crack of his firing sounds, I don't even aim, I just close my eyes and pull my trigger and try not to think where those bullets go.

It is full dark when the gunfire dies down. Sergeant musters our Company back together.

'Boys,' he says, 'we're falling back to Haymarket —'

There are a few cheers, and I can't help looking back at Will. He keeps his head down.

'— and then we'll be joining the rest of the Army at Manassas. There's more fighting to be had tomorrow.'

'We've been sent on a fool's errand,' Edward says low. 'Should've saved our energies.'

'All we do is fucking retreat when the

damn Rebels come! I didn't sign on for god-damned running,' Hiram says.

'Those Rebels were running for cover,' Sully says, 'running from shots I was making!' and it gets me thinking about Will running away from me back in the woods and what all he was taking cover from.

'Our duty is doing what we're told,' Thomas says, shaking his head and making all the boys go quiet. 'Even if we're too late to do a thing worthwhile.'

CHAPTER 21

BULL RUN: AUGUST 29, 1862
All night, marching back the way we've come, the picture of Preacher posting the casualty list that brought this war right to us keeps playing in my head. He stood there next to the church door, silent and somber, waiting as Mrs. Waite hefted herself up the steps, her round belly bulging beneath her dress, Alice Wakefield holding her arm. And then, after what seemed forever, Mrs. Waite just dropped to the ground, too heavy for Alice to catch her, too fast for Preacher to grab her arm. Papa and Jeremiah's Pa carried her inside, the churchladies hovering and fanning, but I went to that list, read where it said *Killed at Bull Run, July 21, 1861, Clarence Waite,* killed at the same field we are marching for.

In the blush of morning, the road before us teems with Union troops massing, a tangle

294

of lines marching and horses galloping and flags waving and thousands of men. In the light, Jeremiah's hands are black from shooting, and Jimmy's face too. The only boy who ain't got smears of sooty gunpowder all over him is Will, though he looks almost as tired as Thomas Stakely, who is more than twice his age. It must be fear of battle that made him forget himself under that dogwood.

There is a seriousness to all our boys, and the men we pass on the road look even worse. One man sits on the grass, his head on his knees, his shoulders shaking. The man beside him stares off at nothing.

Another soldier, his face black, his jacket sleeve stained with what looks like blood, stands at the edge of the turnpike. As we come to him, he says, 'Charles Combs? Have you seen Charles Combs?' His voice is dull like he's been asking so long he don't even know he's still at it. Off behind him, a Company rallies around their flag. We march past officers yelling out orders from all over that field: 'Forward, March!' and 'Left Flank!' and bugles calling and I don't know how anybody can keep straight which ones to listen to or where they are meant to go.

We stop at the top of a hill with a little

creek cutting across the base of it. Beyond is noise and men and horses and smoke covering most of those meadows. The earth shakes with the bang of our artillery and the Rebs' answer. In the space between are sounds like screaming and moaning and yelling and that is when I really see the field below us. What I first took to be shadows in the grass are Union boys. Scattered all across the spread of the land. Most of them lie still, but if I watch some long enough, parts of them move: arms, legs, bodies, more than I can even count.

'I can't stay sitting here,' I say to Jeremiah.

'You can't go home now,' he says, and his arm comes around my shoulder. 'We can't.'

'I ain't talking about going home. I'm talking about those hurt boys out there. We've got to do something for them,' I say, my voice loud to be heard over the noise. I catch Will's eyes darting away from me.

'Like what? You can't go out there. We've got orders to wait.'

'Maybe there's other things I could do, if I've a mind to,' I tell him.

'It don't matter what you've got a mind to do. We've got orders.'

I stand up and say, 'Waiting here and seeing that down there don't sit right with me. I'm going to ask Sergeant to let me go help those boys.'

Jeremiah doesn't move.

'You coming?' I ask.

He doesn't say anything at first and then he says, 'I don't know a thing about nursing.'

Jennie Chalmers' pale face flashes in my mind before I say, 'It ain't difficult and you're more than able. You don't want to, that's another thing altogether.'

I memorize the high set of his cheekbones and the straight line of his nose, the blue of his eyes, the shock of hair falling across his forehead, thinking on if it was him out there in that tall grass. He must see something in my stare because he says, 'You get your answer from Sergeant and come back here.'

I work my way through the resting boys under the trees, nodding to Thomas and Ambrose. Edward is dozing and Hiram is busy carving on something with his bayonet. Near our Regimental flag, Sergeant Ames rests with Sergeant Fitzpatrick from Company G. When he sees me coming, he excuses himself and stands, and I wish Jeremiah were here beside me doing the talking.

'Private Stone,' he says.

'Sir, I know we got orders to stay put, but I'd like to take water to those wounded boys on the field.'

Sergeant Ames has got a kind face but that ain't why he got voted Sergeant. What got him voted is how he listens and stops to think on it, and then tells me the truth even when it ain't what I want to hear.

'Soon as night settles,' he says. 'Come dusk, soon as the shooting stops, you can go out to those soldiers. It's a good thing you want to do, but it isn't the time now. You've got to get some rest while you can.'

Then he points North, up the road to a two-story box of a house, all rust-red fieldstone against the gold-tipped green fields. 'You see that stone house there?'

I nod.

'That house is serving as hospital, and Pope's headquarters are off behind it. We'll want to get the wounded there.'

After Sergeant tells me the countersign for crossing through the picket line, I come back to Jeremiah. He has already dozed off so I just settle in quiet next to him, our backs against a tree trunk, our sides pressed against each other, the rest of our Company spread out to either side. He murmurs something, his arm shifting behind me and reaching around to hold me. I get to wondering what someone watching, Will maybe, would see between me and Jeremiah, what seeing two men like that might make him think, how Will has been thinking it all this time. But it don't matter if anyone sees me and Jeremiah, not when we've got battle all around us and the screams of the shells and the dying mixing together. I've got to have this moment here with my man and anybody thinks it strange, I am past caring.

When the shadows get long, Jeremiah and I take our rifles and canteens. We go careful through the trees to a branch of what must be the same creek running at the bottom of the hill. It's nothing more than two or three steps across, running in a slow trickle behind the line of our boys along the road, this branch maybe flowing to water one of the farms near here, the boggy grass at its edges a deeper green. Jeremiah crouches at the bank, pushing both our canteens down into the water, careful so he don't stir up any silt. Once they are full, he holds on to them. Both of them.

'I don't want you going out on that field. It ain't safe,' Jeremiah says, staring into the creek.

'It ain't dangerous now,' I say, ignoring the sounds of battle way off to our West.

'It's a battlefield, Rosetta,' he says. 'Ain't nothing safe about a battlefield.'

'I've just got to, that's all. I've got to do something good. I'd feel better, having you with me.' I touch his shoulder, smiling like Jennie does, like I've seen Mama do. 'You could do those men a kindness,' I add, even though giving water ain't going to help, not really.

'I ain't got that much kindness in me, Rosetta.'

'That ain't true. You've got plenty.'

Jeremiah scoops both hands under the water and splashes his face. I squat next to him and do the same, washing the road grime and sweat stick off my face, the cool water running down into my collar. When I open my eyes, he is watching me.

'That may be, but we ain't here to do kindnesses,' he says. 'It ain't going to help us when the fighting comes. I want brave ideas in my head tomorrow.' He looks quickly back from where we came and then turns to me again, steadying himself with a hand on my knee before kissing me.

'You shouldn't go,' he says. 'It's what I've decided.'

'It's what you've decided? You want to be the kind of man that bosses his wife? You want me to always be asking your permission for everything I do?'

'Why can't you do what I say, one time?

Just once!'

'Maybe when you stop asking me to go against what's in my heart. Maybe when you stop treating me like I can't do the things I want!'

'When have I ever — ? Ain't you here? You think any other man would let his wife — ?' He shoves both canteens at me. Then he stands up and stalks his way through the trees. I sling the canteens across my chest and then my rifle, watching his back, the slouch of his shoulders showing a tiredness he didn't use to have even though his steps are quick and angry. A sorry feeling drips through me slow. But I ain't asking for anything more than what Jeremiah might.

'Anybody want to come with me, give water to those boys out there?' I ask when I get up amid the boys, acting like there ain't a thing wrong between me and Jeremiah. He don't even look at me, his face closed off.

Jimmy opens his mouth to talk, but Henry pinches his elbow and says, 'We ain't rested yet,' and that closes Jimmy's mouth right up.

Sully says, 'That ain't the kind of action I want.'

Will stands up and slings his rifle across his back. 'I'll go,' he says, and I can't help

301

but wonder why. I don't want to talk to him. I don't know what there is to say. To him or Jeremiah.

'Look who ain't no parlor soldier,' Sully says, but Will don't pay him any mind.

'Let's go,' he says.

'You got water?' I ask, and Will nods.

'We'll be back,' I say, mostly for Jeremiah, daring him to put a hand out to stop me. He stands, and I get ready.

'I'm coming,' he says. 'But I ain't doing no nursing.'

The three of us make our way through the trees along the creek. There ain't no animal sounds, no crickets, no owls. We are silent too, the three of us walking single file, Jeremiah in back and Will in front. There is just our boots squishing in the mud, the trickling water, the moans and cries of the wounded floating over everything.

The weight of it all drags me forward, keeps me from turning back.

'I'll stay here,' Jeremiah says, nodding to the small fires off in the distance, Rebel campfires. Hiding in the gloom there are soldiers living and dying, maybe sharpshooters waiting to pick us off.

'Be quick about it, Ross. That shooting ain't far off.'

302

'You ain't got to worry. We won't be long,' I say, and that's the most tenderness I can muster. I open my mouth but no words come that might make things right with Jeremiah. Not when he is always acting like he don't trust me to do this, like he don't think I can.

I catch up to Will and for a minute I am glad I ain't added the truth of what's passed between me and Will to Jeremiah's tally against me. Will's face is shadowed as he parts the tall grass, but his steps beside me don't falter. The silence between us feels like a sheet of window glass and it ain't something I know how to break. And I'm too tired to fix it if I do.

We pass swollen bellies of horses sprawling out, looking big and pregnant when they ain't. The moans and cries of the wounded get louder, telling us where to go, worse than any crying my Mama ever did losing her babies, worse than any of the mamas who struggled to birth these men lying out on this field. My heart breaks just to hear it, and I give myself over to the soldiers splayed out before me. Nothing in that hospital made me hard enough to see the boys lying on that field, boys long past saving. I can't help thinking about it being Jeremiah lying there, about a wife waiting at home, like Mrs. Waite carrying her soldier's baby, or Jennie Chalmers. It makes me want to do what little I can.

We pick our way around those boys. There ain't a thing to be scared of with a body, it's the ones still living to be worried about. Near a young boy, my foot slides in something. I fall to my knees and it is all I can do not to lose my whole stomach, sickness rippling through me to see the curdled blood I am kneeling in. That Bible story about how Abel's blood soaked into the ground ain't right.

Will reaches down to help me; his hand is cool and moist, and I am surprised by his grip. He peers at me.

'I won't tell anyone, if you'll do the same,' Will says.

'I ain't breathing a word about it. We can still go on being friends,' I tell him. 'To my way of thinking, you ain't any different now than you ever was.'

Will gives me something like a smile and then he hauls me up out of the wet.

I turn to Jeremiah, just the dark shape of him, holding his rifle ready. I don't know why I've always got to push so hard. I raise my hand to show him I ain't hurt, hoping it is enough.

■ ■ ■ ■

The first boy I bend low over don't move
but a wheezing comes from him. Crouching
down, I make believe his chest ain't all
caved in, and that those are something
besides ribs glistening in what little light
there is. I can't think of a thing to say and I
don't know if it is right to lay a hand on a
boy so hurt as this.

'Kill me, please,' his hoarse voice comes.

'You ain't dying.'

'You've got to kill me. I can't stand it!'

'You've got to stand it. There's stretcher
bearers coming,' I say, but I don't know a
thing about it being true. 'You've got to
stand it a bit longer. I've got water if you
want it.'

'Want to die!' He forces the words out.
'Please!'

There ain't a thing to do for that boy, not
a thing but what he is asking. I look for
Jeremiah, but he is back where the line of
bodies begins, his rifle raised and pointed at
those Rebel fires. I don't know what words
a man ought to say before dying, and Will is
swallowed up in the night. My musket is
cold in my hands and it is good it is already
loaded because my hands go to shaking.

'You've got your soul right with God?' I ask, but that boy just keeps saying 'Please!' over and over.

I see Papa putting his rifle in my hands and saying, 'It's loaded. You aim right here,' and tapping the cow's broad forehead.

I lower the barrel, right to the boy's temple, telling myself it's a mercy and still he begs and moans like he don't even see what I've done. There's the rattle of shots off in the distance. Answering this boy's prayers will bring those Rebels' attention this way, closer to me, to Jeremiah. I can't do that. I can't do even this one thing for that boy lying there; all I can do is give him water that won't help none. I thought my heart had already broken, but now it is gone to pieces.

'I'll be back,' I say, tears running down my face. 'There's stretchers coming.'

I've got to move on, is what I'm thinking. I've got to do something more than standing there and saying no to the only thing that boy wants. The wounded and dead lie all around in rows like they are still in line of battle, making it easy to see how the fighting went across the field. There ain't one stretcher but there are other shapes down the line, bending over the bodies, and I hope they are helping. I move away, trying

not to hear the man behind me go to shrieking, 'Please please kill me' over and over,
trying not to think what the greater kindness would be.

There's so many more boys, all of them
gone, no rising of a chest or anything telling
me there's still a soul there. Maybe all the
boys with lives to be saved are already gone,
taken by their Companies or dragged off by
themselves. There's nothing to be done for
these boys, not in truth, but a voice calls for
water, so I keep moving 'til I find a man old
enough to be my Papa. With my hand under
his head, I lift him up a bit before fumbling
with my canteen and pouring a sip for him.

'More,' he says, so I give it to him and
then he don't say anything else. There's a
warm stickiness on my hand and a wetness
seeping through the knees of my trousers.
He's bleeding in slow pulses from his side,
his breath gasping.

The minutes are long before there ain't
no life left. I sit with him, with his body,
waiting for his spirit to go. That is the least
I can do for this stranger, the smallest thing
he is owed. It takes a long time, watching
the last life go, the little tremors and tics,
making sure. I think on Papa and if I will
ever meet him again.

This man has still got a haversack slung

across his chest. It ain't much inside, a cracker and some salt pork, and I feel like a thief, but with boys hungry behind our lines there's no use in leaving good rations on the field so I put what's there into my pockets.

When I straighten up, there's a shadow bending over a body back from where I came, back where that boy begged for me to take his life. I don't want to see him again, but Jeremiah must be over there and maybe Will, so I hurry that way.

'Will!' I call low as I get close enough. 'That you?'

The boy don't answer. He is working at that body's feet.

'Jeremiah?' I try again, but still he don't turn my way or even move.

This boy is rail thin; his pale bare feet stick out from pants too short. When he stands up straight and spins around fast, his rifle pointed right at me, it's for sure he ain't Jeremiah or Will at all.

'Get back,' he says.

The whole world stops. Jeremiah is by the edge of the battlefield. I remember those shots off in the distance. I wonder how fast I can run as I reach for the rifle from across my back.

'Don't!' the boy yells. 'Don't you think it!'

'I don't want trouble. You can just let me pass on by,' I say, the words so calm and slow even though I am thinking whether I can get to my rifle before he shoots his.

'What makes you think I can trust a Federal?' the boy asks, and cocks his gun.

'I ain't done one thing to you,' I say. 'I only thought you were my —'

There is a flash of fire off to my left and a blast. I throw myself to the ground as that boy drops right where he was standing.

'Rosetta?' Jeremiah yells, scrabbling through the grass. He hunkers at my side, talking so fast, saying, 'You all right? You hurt?'

'No,' I say. 'Where is he? What happened?'

'I was afraid — I shot him,' Jeremiah says, and shakes his head. 'I shot him.'

Jeremiah wrenches me to sitting, searching my face. Then he is gone, taking his rifle to where that boy has fallen, where there's awful strangling sounds and then a rammer scraping and I crawl after, my legs too shaky for standing.

'No, Jeremiah! You can't —'

'Rosetta — don't —' is all Jeremiah says. And then he fires again, right into that boy.

Will comes running, calling, 'What was that?' and I am waiting for the flash and bang of other guns firing.

I don't know why I tell Will, 'A Rebel sharpshooter,' when that boy was no such thing, when now I see the shoes he was taking off the Union dead, when that pair of shoes is all he died for.

I am lying curled on my side, Jeremiah's warmth at my back like always. I almost forget until I open my eyes and in the first light of morning, see the knees of my pants, rust-brown and stiff with blood.

I scramble to sit, my mouth watering as my stomach turns. Jeremiah is already awake, clutching his knees, staring at the ground. The blank look on his face makes me swallow back the sick.

We are the first ones stirring so I touch his shoulder.

'I never meant for you to have to do a thing like that. Not on my account,' I say, taking Jeremiah's hand and tracing the Winter trees of veins there, imagining I can feel the blood flowing strong.

A strange flat voice comes out of Jeremiah when he says, 'This ain't a good place,' and after that I put what he's done down with all the other things I won't ever say another word about.

CHAPTER 22

BULL RUN: AUGUST 30, 1862

When I wake again, it ain't because I'm rested. It's because the sun is full up and Jeremiah's hand is shaking my shoulder.

'What?' I say, and then I see Captain standing stiff before us. I bolt upright.

'Your efforts last night have not gone unnoticed. I want to express the gratitude of the Union Army for your assistance above and beyond your duty.'

Captain's gaze is piercing. Jeremiah nudges me.

'Thank you, Sir,' I say. 'But there wasn't much we could —'

'Your efforts have not been in vain,' he says, turning to go. 'This Army is proud to have soldiers like you.'

As soon as Captain leaves, Sully starts whispering to Jeremiah with so much excitement he might as well be yelling.

'Before Captain decided to get all lovey

311

with Ross here, he told me they've got reports those Rebs are retreating! Maybe they're licked already!'

Jeremiah looks out toward the field, past where Will is kneeling, his hands clasped.

'What I hear out on that field,' Jeremiah says, 'don't know how we could be winning.'

'Must be mostly Rebs dying out there,' Sully says.

It ain't worth stirring myself to tell him any different and risk bringing up feelings no one else needs now. Especially when Jeremiah's face has already got a look I can't stand, something bleak that weren't ever there before.

It ain't long before Sergeant comes, saying, 'Two Regiments in the Brigade are staying in reserve to guard the stone house, but our Regiment has been ordered forward. We're to relieve Kearny's men, who have been stretched thin holding the Army's right flank.'

My Mama lays baby's breath and yarrow at my brothers' graves to mark each year, and cries over every letter her sister sends, and now I am marching into battle. Why ain't I said a proper good-bye to her and Papa?

Let us live let us live let us live. The words swell up in my heart until Jeremiah says the first thing to me since we woke.

'Don't you think about last night. It ain't our time yet,' and he rests a hand on my shoulder.

Our bugles sound and voices roar as we march past the stone house and up a steep hill. Our blue Company flag waves ahead of the officers on their horses and the drums roll and my feet move without me even willing them. The air around us is tight like before lightning, and I think of Mama's pregnant belly stretched taut.

Captain yells, 'Left Flank!' and we turn from the road, through a strip of meadow, to a swath of trees where a ghost smoke rises. Double quick our lines braid themselves through trees. I watch for rocks and branches but the boots and legs in front of me are moving moving moving and then out from under Jeremiah's foot, a wild violet still blooming, its purple flowers rising up from being crushed.

Firing rumbles in front of us now, the musket volleys coming closer, louder. Artillery roars off to our left, shells hail down around us, and this is what is meant by hellfire. Our lines go to wavering and breaking and it is all I can do to keep pushing forward. I want to throw myself down into the ground, anything just to stay living, but Jeremiah is there ahead of me and so I bring my rifle to my shoulder like everyone else.

The bullets keep coming and the whole Company wheels to the right, a herd of horses bolting, and then there is a steep bank rising up before us, maybe a hundred paces away, taller than any man, and so clear it ain't natural. That bank stretches to the left and right as far as the eye can go, giving the Rebels cover to run behind for miles.

Our flag flutters up ahead, its gold fringe catching flashes of light coming through the trees, and there ain't no orders to be heard but the boys move after it.

I stay on Jeremiah's heel, branches snapping across my face and arms. *Let us live let us live let us live.* Gray boys move, flashing in and out between the trees in front of the bank, Rebel skirmishers set out to stop us from getting near to what must be at least a full Brigade hiding behind that embankment. We can never get up to those Rebs and still be living and I want to grab Jeremiah's arm and run back the way we came, back through the trees with him in tow.

Beside me Sully yells, 'C'mon! Keep coming!' and I don't know if he's talking to us or to the Rebels.

The Company in front of us rushes and runs across that ground to the mound, leaving us open. A panic races through me as they go, when we are left open. There is a volley of fire and smoke and the *thug* of bullets hitting bodies, the tang of gunpowder mixing with blood, only a few of that Company even getting to the base of the embankment. Most of them fall and we are next and we've got to get to that mound. I push into a run, Henry and Jimmy off to my right side, Will on my left, Sully with Jeremiah in front.

'Stay back!' Jeremiah yells, and shoves me with his elbow when I try coming up alongside him.

The cries of wounded men pierce through everything else and then, from behind that embankment, the shriek of the dead comes, a sound that is wolf howl and rabbit scream mixed together, raising gooseflesh on my arms, coming, coming not twenty yards away and they are coming and everything inside me goes to pounding and shaking.

Jeremiah lags 'til he's beside me, reaching his left hand out and grabbing for me, yelling, 'Stay down!' and then I'm on the ground with the wounded, lying flat on my stomach, the blood pumping in my ears the only sound. Jeremiah's touch is gone, he has pushed me down, he is nowhere near.

And then there he is, running in a crouch, running at the Rebels and I get my rifle right. I aim toward the Seceshes coming through the smoke, toward the soldiers moving along the top of that embankment. Rifles blast and waves of men run and hunch and bend down like oats heavy with seed. Only some of them rise and rush forward, Jeremiah with them. Some falter and fall and there's a swell coming from behind me as more move up to plug the gaps, each one a boy we've lost.

Sergeant bellows, 'Fire at will!' through the noise, but all I can do is keep low.

Boys from my Company are cut down. Young Frank Morgan falls, rolling and writhing, his Papa dropping beside him, but before I see if they get back up more soldiers rush forward and everything is moving. I don't know where any of my boys are, but I have got to do this thing. I get to my knees and then *it is time it is time it is time* to make my run across moldering logs and branches and dead leaves and men.

Almost at the base of the bank, I fling myself to my belly again as the rifles roar and crawl for the next closest tree to take shelter, my fingers clawing at its bark. At the top of the mound, blood sprays from a horse shot out from under his Rebel officer, the officer still waving his arm to those men behind him even as the horse goes down, its legs crumpling. It somersaults and somehow rights itself and the officer is gone, a shadow in the trees. That horse stands on three legs, its one foreleg flapping like Mama's stockings on the line. It ain't got a chance at living anything except pain. I aim my rifle and fire. The horse buckles and goes down again, goes down clean. But I ain't here for shooting horses.

My eyes burn in the smoke until I find Jeremiah behind a tree just ahead. He is whole and a coolness flows through my veins.

I stay kneeling close to that tree and load charge ram prime and get ready to shoot again but the firing is coming off to our right now, shells landing everywhere, leaves and branches and dirt flying, mixed with I don't know what else and smoke hiding everything. The Rebs ain't looking for mercy and they sure ain't planning on giving none, any one of them aiming to kill Jeremiah or me or one of my boys, like that soldier last night.

'Ross!' Will comes from nowhere, grabbing my arm, scaring me. He points at the embankment and there is Jeremiah with the

Union boys, his long legs striding, running up out of the trees to that embankment, trying to break through and a Secesh right above him on that mound, raising his musket. It ain't a thought, it is just a thing I do, leveling my own rifle and pulling the trigger quick, and the Secesh is gone.

But there are more Rebs coming for Jeremiah. There ain't time to reload, not when that line goes to swarming gray and grappling blue and all of them clubbing with muskets.

'You cover me!' I yell at Will, his rifle sloppy in his hands, and then I charge, thinking how nice my bayonet stabs.

Before I get to Jeremiah, to the fray, before the ground even starts rising, there is a bugle call mixed in with the fighting and screaming and our flag moves off to my side, away from the embankment, back through the trees. The flood of our blue boys comes back, swirling Jeremiah up in it and coming all around me, elbows and hands and knees jabbing at me, pushing me around and then we are running. There are bodies strewn under the trees and I don't know how I get over or through without stepping on them or tripping and falling, or maybe I do and don't know it, I am running so fast to get back through the trees, away from the embankment and that firing, hoping Jeremiah is running too.

Jeremiah stands stock-still like a dog pointing. Next to him Sully paces. Both of them watch the men coming back from those trees across the slip of clearing, flowing like blood from a fresh cut, fast at first and then slower and slower. The two of them stare at the men that come, working to see who can put a name to each one and how quick. Company K's skirmishers slap the backs of the boys coming past, the ones that ain't bleeding or hobbling.

I don't know a thing except for the ringing in my ears, sitting on the ground on top of dead leaves, looking at my blackened hands and waiting. Waiting for something important. There's a wetness down my side and my hands go flying to it quick and jittery and I can't look at myself. It ain't sticky, it is my canteen with a hole shot through it and not a drop of water left inside. I take the canteen from around my chest and hold it in my hands, a thin, high laugh coming out of me. Jeremiah reaches his hand down and squeezes my shoulder 'til it hurts. When I snatch at his hand it has got blood on it. Seeing that, I come back to myself a bit, like waking up and not knowing where I am.

'What's this?' I ask.

He twists away, says, 'It ain't but a graze.'

'You ought to wash it out,' I say.

'It's nothing,' is all Jeremiah says.

'Let me bandage it,' I say, but Jeremiah don't want nursing and shakes his head.

I get my mind in order. Edward and Thomas stand off to Jeremiah's side. Sully is working a path into the ground with his pacing. Levi Blalock, the brand still red on his face, drags Andrew Bile who I only know from work duty through the line of skirmishers. There is old John Morgan and Thomas Stakely with Frank's arms draped over their shoulders, his head lolling and feet dragging, the hoarse rasping of John Morgan weeping making my hands bunch up the wool of my trousers. The O'Malleys ain't back yet.

Will kneels at my side, muttering over and over. 'I couldn't do it,' he says, gripping his rifle. 'I just couldn't do it.'

I've got to do something, to pull myself back to this place, to keep from thinking on where the O'Malleys might be. I say to Will, 'What are you talking about?'

He starts like I jumped out from behind a doorway at him, but he says, 'I couldn't shoot. Not with God watching. How could

I shoot those men? I couldn't. Not to cover you, not even to save my own self.'

I know something of what he is feeling, but he looks like he don't understand it himself. I don't know what to say to him and he turns back to his rifle and cleans it out. Three Minie balls come from out of that muzzle. He oughtn't be doing such a thing in plain view, he oughtn't let anyone see he ain't shot according to regulation, but then maybe it don't matter so much for him to act right as it does for me.

'You ain't got to aim at no one. You just shoot and it don't matter what you don't hit,' I tell him low so no one hears, not even Jeremiah.

Jeremiah stands rigid, his eyes gone somewhere else, same as when he was leaning over that boy last night, his throat already shot through, that rifle echoing again. He takes off at a run, darting in and out of the trees as he goes to the clearing, heading back to where the fighting was, like he has lost his head entirely, his legs scissoring so fast past the skirmish line, Sully charging after.

And then I see why he is running. Stumbling across the clearing is a humpbacked man and it is Henry and I know what he's got on his back. Henry gently lays that body down so the tall grass swallows it up. Then he and Jeremiah swoop low like gathering chaff to carry the load between them and the tears running down my face burn.

Sully jogs ahead and where Jeremiah and Henry walk, the skirmishers step aside, parting to let them pass, a few of them looking to see if it is anyone they know before turning right back to the trees where those Rebels might be coming. Jeremiah and Henry and Sully bring that body to us and lay it down on the damp leaf-covered ground.

Seeing death last night and seeing death when it's a boy I've known my whole life ain't the same thing, and I want to think Jimmy ain't dead but it is plain from the condition of his head, part of it gone, that he can't be living and then there is the smell of him, burnt flesh and blood and shit mixing with the wet, warm moldering smell of the leaves that our feet are mussing up. Will mutters what sounds like the Lord's Prayer and then I say, 'We've got to have him buried.'

Those words don't but leave my mouth before Henry sinks to the ground next to his brother and I don't know why I said it so soon.

'You can sit with him as long as you like,'

Will says, and it is the right thing. 'Long as you like.'

We make a little knot. All up and down the length of cord that is our Brigade weaving through the woods there is a smattering of knots and no one even cares that there is still fighting going on behind that embankment.

Henry sits a long time, just looking. Sully kneels beside him, his hand on Jimmy's knee, like he's got to touch him to know for sure. The rest of us stand silent until Henry takes a long breath.

He sighs it out and says, 'He's gone,' like he's been waiting for some kind of feeling, like Jimmy's spirit has up and flown. He opens Jimmy's jacket and inside is Jimmy's name written in his own hand. So careful Henry unpins that name tag and then takes a letter from inside Jimmy's jacket. When he is holding that letter, he goes to gasping, big wracking sobs, and it is the first time I've ever seen one of these boys cry.

'You want us to find him a place —' Jeremiah asks.

'No!' Henry shouts. 'I've got to bury him! I've got to see it with my own eyes so I know where to find him after.'

And then Henry finds me. 'You!' he yells.

'It's your fault! If you ain't come with us, this never would've happened!'

He comes at me, shoving me square in the chest hard enough I fall. There is scuffling and grunting and when I get my feet under myself, Jeremiah is holding Henry back, Sully is looking like he don't know where to stand, and Will is gaping.

'Simmer down!' Jeremiah yells. 'I ain't having this!'

'This ain't about me,' I say. 'Jimmy lying there ain't got a thing to do with me.'

'It's got everything to do with you!' Henry pushes past Jeremiah. 'If you weren't here, we could've been looking out for him! Instead of always keeping watch on you!'

Jeremiah shoves Henry and he crashes into Sully, who puts his hands out and pushes him upright. Henry knocks into Jeremiah, sending Jeremiah reeling, and then Henry barrels at me but my fists are up and I aim straight for his nose.

My fist smashes into it, shock blooming across his face as he falls backward.

'I can take care of myself! I don't need no one keeping watch over me and I never asked for it neither!' I bellow, and clench both my fists, ready. 'If you've got a problem with me, then we settle this right now 'cause I ain't going anywhere! You want to blame someone for Jimmy dying, you blame those Rebels! There ain't one of us here who could have done a thing different to save Jimmy and there ain't one of us who wants to leave him here in this ground!'

My breath comes fast and blood pours from Henry's nose, down his face. Jeremiah gives Henry a shove and Will grabs me, his hand tightening on my arm and my knuckles aching, but I just keep talking so I don't get to crying and I don't care who might hear what I've got to say.

'You know why I came here, and I ain't asked for one thing different or special, and I ain't going back, so if you've got something to say, you say it right now and be done with this thing.'

Not one of them says a single word. Will's hands loosen on my arms and he steps to the side of me. His mouth works but he don't make a sound.

'You got anything else needs saying?' Jeremiah yells at Henry.

Henry sinks down on the dirt. 'I just want — I can't —'

And as soon as that fight started, it is over and I don't know what is different, but we all settle back to the ground like leaves falling. Jeremiah looks at me like I am a ghost or some frightening thing he doesn't understand, like he is seeing me from some other place. I look away from him, scared this war has changed everything.

There's only one thing for the aching after Jimmy's buried and that's to keep busy, even if the orders are to wait.

'Let me have your canteen,' I say to Jeremiah.

He holds his out to me. 'There ain't much water left,' he says

'Give me that hand of yours, too. I won't take no for an answer.'

He sighs then, saying, 'It's barely more than a scratch,' but he sits down next to me.

I dig for the flannel cloths in my knapsack. At this rate I won't have enough if I ever need them for myself.

And then it hits me. All my sick feeling days. The tiredness sinking into my bones. I count back to when I last had my woman's time. It ain't come as regular since we up and joined, but it ain't come even once since being at Fort Corcoran, since before marching to Bull Run. I can't be certain, but it can't be, not like this, not when it ain't what I planned, when we ain't settled on our farm yet.

'Ross?' Jeremiah says.

326

'I've just got to get this wet,' I say, keeping my head down while I make my face go blank. There's no reason to go telling Jeremiah something that'll make him think different on me being here, especially when it mightn't be true, especially when I just took Henry on. There's no way to tell him, not now, when it's not a welcome thing.

Then I take up his hand, laying it across my lap, and put my mind to the gash across the back, almost as wide as my fattest finger. The edges are black and maybe it is gunpowder or burnt but it don't come away when I dab it gentle, Jeremiah hissing at the first touch.

It gets to bleeding, and I look up at Jeremiah. 'I'm sorry,' I say, remembering his smile all those weeks ago when I told him we weren't having a baby. If this thing is true, I am sorry for so much more than his hand. All I can think is the worry a baby will bring and the fight I will have to keep Jeremiah from sending me home and I don't want none of it.

'It don't hurt much,' he says, but I can already see the bruise darkening his palm.

I get that hand as clean as I can and wrap a fresh cloth around it, thinking it needs some of Mama's comfrey salve. When I'm finished, Jeremiah takes my hand, looks at the blush across my knuckles.

'I'm sorry I didn't see that coming,' he says.

'Ain't no way to see a thing like that,' I shrug. 'Maybe it's a good thing you got a fighting wife.'

I am tying the knot on Jeremiah's wrap when a man with light hair and eyes, maybe the age of Jeremiah's oldest brother, comes to me.

'You think you could help me with this?' he says, and shows me where his trousers are torn almost from knee to ankle.

I ain't ever spoke to him before, but I squat down and fold back the flaps of wool. There is a deep tear running down the back of his calf.

'I've got to touch it a bit,' I say, looking up at him.

'It's okay,' he says, squaring his shoulders. 'I can stand it. Name's Milo Keller, by the by.'

The way the skin pulls apart makes me think on Doc Cuck's curved needle.

'It needs stitches,' I tell Milo, and when he grits his teeth I keep going. 'I ain't got the skill or the tools for it, but I can wrap it. You got any clean rags?'

He shakes his head and then I am digging

328

through my pack again.

'Jeremiah,' I say. 'You go get Ambrose's flask, unless you got any pop skull, Milo?'

Henry says, 'Goddamn it!' and moves off away and I don't know what I've done 'til Jeremiah growls, 'Watch what you call things, Ross,' and goes after Henry, leaving me with Milo and the picture of Jimmy's busted head coming up in my mind.

'I'll go see about Ambrose,' Will says, and when he comes back he says, 'Got this from Edward,' and then he starts talking to Milo and holding my rags the whole time I fix up that leg.

Captain is taking another pass through the troops when I am tying off Milo's wrap. He stops near me but I keep about my work.

'Private Stone,' Captain says.

'Yes, Sir?' I say, and stand up.

'There's others with wounds throughout this Regiment. May I send them to you? The Brigade surgeon has his hands full with more serious cases.'

I stand there with my mouth hanging open. It is Will who talks.

'Sir, we'd be happy to help any way we can. But we don't have any supplies.'

'I'll see what I can muster,' Captain says. 'You're doing good work.'

After that, other boys bring us their hurts,

and Sergeant Ames brings us a few flasks of liquor and some cloth that Will tears into strips.

I watch Jeremiah pacing with Henry, wondering if keeping busy will drown out the artillery banging and rifle volleys and horses screaming and lives being taken. Nothing stops my thoughts. The blood and rags just keep me counting the weeks, nine of them back to June, and I will my courses to come and the sick feeling to go.

It is afternoon when Captain comes back again.

'Men, we've orders to advance forward in pursuit of the enemy,' he says, and there is something in the way his voice is dropped that lets me know it ain't an order he likes.

'It is madness, trying what we already tried this morning,' Thomas Stakely shouts from where he stands next to old John Morgan with tear tracks through the soot on his face. 'Those Rebels that fired on us ain't gone anywhere. We've got enough dead!'

'Now we can get those bastards who got Jimmy,' Sully yells back. 'And Frank too!'

'Ain't letting them take you, Jimmy,' Henry says like he is somewhere else, like those black feelings are the only thing keeping him from losing his head.

There ain't no more grumbling about the orders after that, even though me and Thomas can't be the only ones who ain't keen on going back at that embankment again, but baby or no, I have got a duty to do.

We all start checking our weapons and moving into line of battle as best we can between the trees. Jeremiah is to my left and Will to my right, Sully and Henry behind, plugging the gap where Jimmy should be.

'The time comes,' I say to Jeremiah, 'you don't give me a thought. You just do what you've got to. You don't have to watch over me.'

Jeremiah stares, and it is the look he gets going into a battle, cold and far away. Then he says, 'Don't you for a minute think I can stop from keeping you in my sights and wanting you safe.'

He is schooling me, telling me something of his heart. It is a sweet thing, but that don't keep me from saying the only truth I'll let him believe.

'I don't need protecting. I can do this job as good as any.'

'It ain't about you doing the job. It ain't never been about that,' he says.

'Then why — This whole time I've been trying to prove —'

'I can't remember a time you didn't do whatever you lit onto, like it was just natural. I thought all I wanted was to keep you safe, protect you from this — but I wouldn't change it for anything, you being so stone-headed, coming here, giving us this time.'

'I lit onto you,' I say as the Companies before us file out of the trees, 'and the way opened up before me.'

As soon as those boys march into the clearing, a storm of shells hails down all around them, blasting the tender thoughts out of my head. Those Rebel batteries keep up the fire so steady the Regiment can't even advance a hundred yards to the trees on the other side of that grassy strip and our line can't do a thing but move back to where we started.

When Henry don't get none of his revenge, he is all over, pacing and sitting and then standing. It is plain he's got too much feeling and nowhere to put it.

Ambrose comes to Henry's side, taking hold of his shoulder and offering up that flask of his, saying, 'I'm only trying to help. You can bear up better under it if you dull the pain a bit.' But Henry don't look at Ambrose and he don't take that flask, even when Hiram shouts, 'Do us all a favor and take the fucking drink, man!'

Finally Will goes to Henry, puts a hand on his arm, and says, 'You want to write a letter home, or you want one of us to?'

That gets Henry sinking down to the ground, his head in his hands and his shoulders shaking. I ain't ever been able to keep from crying when a person's grieving, and I've got my own mourning to do for Jimmy. Jeremiah stands there, his face pinched, too proud to cry. Sully moves off a bit, looking away. But Will stays beside Henry until he takes out his papers, and there is one more thing in this world I wouldn't know how to tell.

The sun is low in the sky when the Rebels come away from the embankment to test our lines. Directly before us, not two hundred paces across the small clearing, shadows start moving in the trees. There ain't a single boy of ours that ain't ready with his musket primed, and Sully wipes his cheeks with the backs of his hands, saying, 'Come on, you goddamn Greybacks!'

It don't take more than Sergeant saying, 'Boys, I think they are Rebs! Fire on them!'

In the tiny space between Sergeant's order and the hell blast of muskets, Henry yells, 'For Jimmy!'

I aim careful in the dying light and fire two rounds and I can do it if I think on Jimmy, if I let myself think on what I've got to protect, not just me and Jeremiah, but all of our future balled up inside me. The first don't hit a thing, but the second shot makes a space in the line advancing. Something heavy settles into my belly when the stain blooms on that soldier's chest, the hole in the line, the tear in the fabric of some other family.

Yells of, 'Cease Fire! Cease Fire!' come down the line. 'Those are our own men!'

It is a worse sick panic, thinking I've shot one of our own, but the men across the field keep coming. Only our artillery fires and still they are coming and they let out the same shrill howl we heard at the embankment and charge into the flank of the Companies to the right of us. Then men are running everywhere and bullets are hitting bodies again and all through the ranks is confusion and yelling, and it ain't right, but in that moment a small bit of peace comes over me that at least it weren't someone friendly I shot down, that at least I kept some of those bullets from ever coming this way.

It ain't long before that peaceful feeling is

gone. Men start bellowing 'Retreat!' and our flag streams off into the trees. I yank Jeremiah's sleeve and run.

We run until we put a low hill between us and them, until Captain reins his horse to a stop before us, nothing about him looking so sharp as the first time I saw him.

'Boys,' he says, his horse jigging back and forth in front of us, its breath as labored as ours, its eyes as white, 'I know we've had losses and we have scores that want settling. But you have seen — we cannot move forward. We cannot fight this ground and win. For the protection of our Capital and for the continuance of this Army, we're falling back to Centreville to resupply.'

After he says those words, he wheels his horse around and trots away, so he don't hear the grumbling. Maybe I am the only one wanting to leave this place, wanting to be somewhere safe.

'This ain't how to end a war,' Thomas says, shaking his head. 'I never should've told my wife it'd be over by Christmas.'

'The womenfolk knew. My wife knew none of it would come to good. She tried to keep Frank home — but I was supposed to look after —' John Morgan says, his eyes glassy.

'All this Army does is retreat!' Sully says.

Henry sits on the ground, refusing to move. 'All for nothing,' he says. 'All of it for nothing.'

'It's not for nothing,' Will says.

'How ain't it?' Henry goes almost to yelling. 'How ain't it for nothing when my brother is buried in that field and we ain't a step closer to beating that enemy out there? What thing did he die for? He ain't even got all the money we was promised.'

'We're still fighting for our country,' Will says, 'even if we don't win. We've still got the idea of it, the idea a Republic can work. We can still fight, even if we lose, and that doesn't make it a thing unworthy of the fight.'

'He never was fighting for his country,' Henry spits.

He don't say what we all know, that Jimmy was only here because of Henry. I have been fighting for my place by Jeremiah's side, for a place to put my dreams, and maybe that is something like what Will is saying, maybe that is part of what Will was trying under that dogwood tree. Maybe he and Jennie and people like them who feel the principle behind this war are fighting for a place they want to live, for a country where they can do what feels right to them, a country they can feel good calling home. But what good is that place if there ain't none of our friends left to share in it?

Night falls, the sky clouded so thick there ain't a single star shining through. It's only fitting when the drizzling starts and the whole of us, already low spirited, get rained on too.

There ain't no talking as we march. Someone, Will probably, or else Thomas, starts humming the 'Battle Hymn of the Republic,' but no one catches hold of the tune. I keep my feelings to myself, everyone does, and as we get farther away from the field, the only talking is lone men, calling for their Regiments by number, Second Michigan or Nineteenth Indiana or Fifty-sixth Pennsylvania, their voices coming out of the gloom like lost souls. Only when volleys of firing come from behind us does my heart get to pumping, but there is only a few rounds and then it is quiet again, except for the tramp of feet and the rattle of the artillery caissons over the rough road.

It's pitch-black and I can only keep my way by holding on to Jeremiah's shirt, him with his arms stretched out to keep from walking into something or to keep hold of the boy marching in front of him, I can't be sure which.

I only know we're crossing a bridge because there's the sound of water running under us. The rounded edges of stones press against the thin soles of my shoes and there ain't a blade of grass to brush across my trousers anymore. Jeremiah bumps into an overturned wagon left on the road, already picked clean by the soldiers gone before us. Those parts of me that have got to move, keep on, but all the rest of me is frozen still, like I am lying next to an ice block in the hot Summer.

Sometime in the night we get to a town, or leastways I think it is a town from the dogs barking and the sharp tang of cows closed in. Ahead we hear men shouting and once I get over fearing they might be Rebels, I think it must be townspeople, waking late to cheer us as we come back. But then I hear their words.

'We hoped you'd lose!' a voice calls loudly out of the murk.

'You only hoped? Hell, I knew Pope couldn't win, that arrogant bastard!' another voice answers, and then others laugh along with him.

Of course Sully is stung and from off to Jeremiah's right he yells, 'Who are you sons of bitches, to be laughing at us?'

'We're Franklin's Corps, Army of the Potomac. And we're damn pleased to be fighting for a General that knows something, instead of that fool Pope.'

Hiram yells back at them, 'I don't care if you're fucking Jesus' Army! Here I thought we was all fighting for the Union, but you must be some kind of special jackasses to be cheering for the goddamned Seceshes.'

It don't do a lick of good. Even after we pass they keep jeering, making us feel low, and I hope Henry ain't hearing the things they are saying. If I ever had any thought of us all fighting for the same thing, it is gone now, left on the road just like Jimmy on that battlefield, just like Will's Bible wrapped up in that flannel.

Our line stops. All around me boys drop to the ground with groans and sighs. I stare into the night, trying to make out shapes, when someone moves in close to me. He don't have to say a word. I know it is Jeremiah from the warm-earth smell coming from him, coming even when there's other smells mixed in: blood, sweat, fear.

His arms pull me tight against his chest and I bury my face in his shoulder. He shakes and it is dark enough I can still say I ain't ever seen him cry. My heart goes to cracking wide open, but at least I am alive to feel it. I am a different kind of woman now, a wife who knows what this war really is. At least I am part of this war, part of the things Jeremiah's done here, things that will always be hiding somewhere in his heart.

Jeremiah holds me a long time and my breathing comes as ragged as his, but the two of us made it. Our dream is still shining off there in the distance, and that is enough of a star to pull me through this black night, as long as I don't count the cost of it.

CHAPTER 23

CENTREVILLE, VIRGINIA: AUGUST 31, 1862
'We might've guessed at it, is all. Henry never was cut out to wade through any kind of grieving,' I say to Jeremiah and Sully. 'He ain't got the determination.'

It's the honest truth but I don't say the whole of it, how Jimmy shouldn't have been here neither, how he was too nice for a soldier. It ain't the thing they want to hear. They want all cream-and-sugar words.

But we've been waiting for near to an hour, long after the fresh ration of sowbelly went cold, for Henry to come trudging out of the trees or from between the brick and clapboard houses, all sheepish and gruff at how we got ourselves riled up. Only it don't happen like that because he never comes. At roll call Sully tells Sergeant that Henry must be lagging and even after Jeremiah opens his knapsack and finds Henry's letter home stuffed in it and Will has already gone

341

down the road looking, the boys can't find their way to seeing that Henry ain't coming back any more than Jimmy is.

'Henry should've told me so I didn't waste my time this morning,' I say when Will goes to report him missing. 'I could've given his ration to someone who'd maybe appreciate eating something warm. It sure ain't my idea of fun cooking in the rain for people without the decency to show up for breakfast.' I don't say how seeing that bit of salt pork burning in the pan was almost more than my stomach could stand.

None of my jokes is any good, but it's either laugh or cry. It's plain there ain't a thing I can say to make it better, and I am just pretending it don't touch me to have two of our boys gone. All of us lost ourselves in the haze yesterday, and there wasn't one of us keeping close watch on each other. Not like we should. All we know is that Henry was with us when we bivouacked for the night and when we started stirring he wasn't. Now he and his pack and his rifle are gone.

My throat closes and tears start coming so I try saying, 'Cooking's less of a chore now, I guess,' but my fire with the mucket hanging over it, working on boiling water for coffee, almost does me in.

Jeremiah lifts his head up. 'You ain't help-ing, Rosetta. 'Specially not when we all know there ain't any lost love between you and Henry these days.'

I ought to be yelling for his forgetting himself and using my old name, but every-one is too busy huddling under their pon-chos and rubber blankets to be listening to a thing we're saying. Staying dry and chew-ing on hardtack is already too much trouble.

'How could he do it?' Jeremiah asks. 'How could he leave like that? Without saying a word? What if he ain't all right?'

There ain't an answer to those questions, and we go silent after that. What was Henry thinking when he knew the facts as well as any of us, when we all saw Levi Blalock cursing and fighting against Hiram and Young Frank, that glowing D searing through the stubble and into the skin on his cheek? A punishment like that ain't easy to push aside, and even with the heavy burden Henry is carrying, to up and leave, risking such a thing? If he were smart, he'd at least have taken my map. But when I open my pack, it is still there on top and it is clear he ain't thought the thing through to its end. Course, none of us thought this soldiering through to the end. I still can't. Especially when I don't know what my body is playing at and every day that passes I've got more to worry over.

There is a rumbling clatter as a wagon carrying more wounded soldiers drives up the road, and Jeremiah and Sully's attention snaps to it. The wagon bumps to a stop in the ruts outside the gate of one of the plain houses across the way where piles of the surgeons' handiwork grow outside the windows. The bay cavalry horse tied to the paling fence in front rests the toe of his hind leg on the ground. The warm rain drips down his belly and he's too tired to even try for the short grass that's nibbled down around the post, too tired to even flick an ear. The driver jumps down and another man runs up and opens the door to the house, calling inside before coming back to help lift soldiers out of the wagon. None of them is Henry.

Just when I can maybe wipe my mind clean as a slate, Will comes back from reporting to Sergeant. He slows to help another soldier stumbling up the road, stooped and filthy like every single one of us, stained with blood and dirt and gunpowder and who knows what else.

Will ain't long hefting that man up the steps into one of the houses and then he is before me.

'You think you might want to help at one of the hospitals?' he asks. 'Pretty near every building in this town has got wounded in it.'

I think of new casualty lists posted in every town in this whole country, of Jennie Chalmers keeping her worries at bay nursing over a new stream of boys at the Judiciary Square Hospital. There is sadness everywhere now.

I shake my head and tell Will, 'I can't muster up the energy just now,' but really I can't touch those wounded and not think on Jimmy, not think on John Morgan holding his dead son's hand, cradling his face, or that soldier I aimed at so careful.

Will looks at me through narrowed eyes before shrugging. 'I'll be checking on how Thomas is, ministering to John, and then I'll be over at that house, if anybody needs me,' he says.

I nod. Across the way, the bloody hands and feet and legs and arms keep spewing through the front window. Those parts land in a big heap, and bodies lie out in the front yard and we watch like steers waiting our turn for slaughter, listening to the crying and groaning while the surgeons carve our boys up into cuts of meat, hoping that ain't what's coming for us.

CHAPTER 24

Fort Corcoran ain't much to look at and I never thought it'd feel at all nice to see those dirt piles and telegraph wires. But after days of rain and mud and mourning, anything meaning shelter and rest where we can pitch tents and live almost civilized makes me feel a tiny bit better. We don't know how long we'll stay here, and I know it ain't anything worrying on can fix, but that don't stop me.

Now we've seen action, Captain's lost his keenness for drilling all the time and that is just fine by me, except away from the battlefield, my mind won't stay easy. I wake before morning, remembering dreams of mouths filling with dirt, of blood wrung from soiled cloths, of embroidered names I can't read, of Papa burning bloody sheets. I reach for Jeremiah, thinking to hold his hand, but we are spread as far apart as can be. He twitches and grinds his teeth until they squeak.

He takes a sharp breath, and then he is bolting straight up, looking all around with eyes that ain't focused on anything, saying, 'You're here?'

When I say, 'Course I am,' he lies right back down and is sleeping so fast that he must not have ever been full awake. After that, my mind is working 'til dawn, wondering how long before I have to tell Jeremiah my fears, how long before I'll know for sure. I am glad when Jeremiah wakes up proper except for the circles under his eyes.

Outside in the shade of our tent, Jeremiah sits, tight and drawn. I look sidelong at him, thinking on how his face was always easy and peaceful back at home in our Little House, wondering if a baby would be a thing for him to be happy on again when Sully comes walking fast down the aisle, carrying a newspaper.

'You heard the rumors about General Lee?' he says, and thrusts the paper at Jeremiah.

'Can't say we have,' Jeremiah says, his voice flat even as he reaches for Sully's paper.

'Everybody says he's moving his Confederates into Maryland.' Sully talks loud, and

Hiram from the next tent over looks up from whatever he's carving.

'I got that paper from Thomas Stakely and it says Lincoln's fired Pope,' Sully keeps on.

'Course Lincoln ought to fire him,' Edward yells from where he sits by Hiram. 'They brought him from out West to win and all he did was lose the biggest battle since the first Bull Run!'

'What's this mean for us?' I ask Sully.

'What it means is McClellan's in command of our Army now.'

'What it means is we might be leaving for Maryland any day,' Jeremiah says, looking up from the paper as Sully snatches it away, my heart sinking at the words.

Hiram calls over, 'McClellan is damn slow moving, but his soldiers like him real fine.'

Edward says, 'That's because he keeps them in supplies. And he don't get them killed. Look at how many we lost — Jimmy, Frank, Henry — and we didn't even see an hour of action.'

Hearing those names rattled off don't make me want to go to Maryland and chase after General Lee. Jeremiah is already pulling inside himself, and if we are moving soon, I can't add new worry to the weight of all that.

'Henry ain't dead,' Jeremiah says. 'He's

still out there.'

'Sure he is,' Edward says. 'Bet he'll be joining us any day now.'

I let myself think on deserting. Only instead of going to keep watch over Jimmy's grave like Henry must've done, there's me and Jeremiah walking through the dusty yard, pushing open the door to our Little House, sitting down at Mama and Papa's table to tell them the news about a grandbaby on the way. But I get that far and my brain says *no no no no.* Neither of us is going to live easy if we put aside this duty we signed on for, if the red-hot branding iron is always burning in the back of our minds. There's no going back and pretending we never left, and I ain't going home to nothing but waiting when all I've got is a sick feeling. Maybe that feeling ain't nothing but nerves.

Will comes shambling over, and Sully turns his back on Edward when he says, 'Chaplain Will! Now we might be going off to Maryland, guess I'll wait a few more days and ask the Good Lord for forgiveness right before I die. What do you think about that?'

'You're not worried you won't get that chance?' Will asks him.

'Well, see now, I'm worried about other things I mightn't get the chance for —

liquor and gambling and women. Mostly women,' Sully says, and I wonder how he can be poking fun, after everything.

'Aren't you worried about your future self?' Will asks. 'How do you expect to ever find yourself a wife of noble character, if you aren't virtuous yourself?'

'Aw, Chaplain! Stop quoting the Bible at me! Any wife I find won't have to know a thing about my sins, and God knows I've got the best intentions. He's hearing me right now, saying I aim to be good and sorry for doing the things I ain't done yet. And if I can get all the benefits of a wife for a few bits, well, the Good Lord wants us to be happy, now don't he?'

'That's not how salvation works,' Will says, and then he is looking at me. 'You've got to be penitent. You've got to regret those things you've done, and struggle against that sin in your heart. What you're talking about doesn't sound like turning away from sin.'

'This mean you ain't getting a new deck of cards?' I ask, wondering if Will is talking about what he tried with me in the woods.

Sully don't give him a chance to answer.

'Ain't none of us playing poker, not with Henry and Jimmy gone,' Sully says, his voice gravelly with feeling. 'Ain't the same. But no. I ain't turning away from sin. I don't care what Chaplain Will here says. I'm running right into it. God knows if he gave me time to find a wife, then I wouldn't be in this position.'

Jeremiah says, 'My soul ain't the only thing thanking the Lord I already found a wife of noble character, and I didn't even spend a single ruby neither.'

I blush at Jeremiah talking bawdy like that about me, about things we've done. I ain't ever heard joking like that from him before. Sully laughs and winks at me, making my face go so hot I've got to turn away, especially thinking how *noble* is the last word Jeremiah might call me if he knew the secret I ain't found a way to tell him yet.

'It isn't right, blaming God for your sins,' Will says, like he can't see how Sully's already made up his mind.

'I don't blame God so much as the Union Army,' Jeremiah says, so quiet I almost don't hear it.

'I ain't saying my sinning is God's fault,' Sully says. 'What I'm saying is I ain't willing to risk dying and never tasting horizontal refreshments, pardon my frankness. Not if God is going to let so many good boys die out there. Now, I've got some idea Captain ain't going to turn down a request or two for passes to the Capital, so you want to join me for a night on the town, Will? Or you going to stay here and deny how hungry you are?'

'I'm all full up,' I say.

Sully snorts and then Jeremiah and he both get to laughing for the first time since we marched on the Warrenton Turnpike.

Finally Jeremiah stops and then he looks at me and says, 'I ain't hungry neither.'

That almost sets them off again, but then Sully's face goes sullen.

'You mean, there ain't no one to come with me?' He says it like the idea is a toy that just broke and lost all its sheen.

Hiram walks over from where he's been sitting and slaps Sully's back, holding up what he's been carving, a coarse white ring.

'You know what this is?' he asks.

All of us stare at him, at that thick circle of some boy's backbone resting on his palm. There's worse things than the pulling inside Jeremiah's been doing.

'It's a little something I found at Bull Run,' he says. 'I'm sending this ring to a gal I like to play stink-finger with sometimes, to keep her thinking about my finer qualities. But have I ever got a treat for you! I'll show you a good fucking establishment or two.'

All I can think is how if Henry hadn't left and Jimmy weren't gone, Sully wouldn't have to go anywhere with the likes of Hiram. But Sully steps off with Hiram, something like a smile pasted to his face, a hollow laugh coming out of him when Hiram says, 'You and me can give those old whores fits!'

We have almost given Sully up for the night when the sound of a fiddle comes reeling through the tents.

'You think that's them?' Will asks.

'Even if it ain't, it's worth taking a look-see,' Jeremiah says, and with that the three of us are up and moving toward the sound.

There is already a crowd when we get to the parade ground. In the center is a woman, her foot resting on a stump, her red dress hoisted up to show her whole calf, an upturned kepi in her hand. Behind her another woman dances with Edward, while Sergeant Fitzpatrick plays the fiddle.

Sully sits on the ground, three jugs at his feet, a tin cup in his hand, a silly grin on his face.

'We brought you fellas a dance!' Hiram shouts, and points at Sully. 'The whiskey is thanks to all the poker we've been winning, but if you want to dance with a real lady you'd better bring some greenbacks of your own!'

That sends some of the boys running back for their tents, whooping and shouting like they've never seen a battlefield.

'I like the view I'm getting for free just fine,' Ambrose says, and makes his way over to the line starting up by Sully. Me and Jeremiah and Will stay put. I don't know where to look, at those ladies doing things that don't belong in public, or at the boys making fools of themselves over it. Still, it ain't long before Jeremiah's foot gets to tapping. Some of the younger ones, like Josiah Price and Levi Blalock, get to hopping around Edward, who is still dancing with that woman of low virtue.

'Let's dance, Rosetta,' Jeremiah whispers, his breath hot in my ear.

'We can't!'

'I don't see why not. There ain't enough women to go around, and with those two ladies, you and me ain't going to attract no notice. I for one am not letting this chance go to waste,' he says, and tugs on my arm.

As we push past the crowd around Sully, he yells, 'Come on, Chaplain! When are you ever going to live a little?'

Not two seconds later, a cheer goes up and that is the moment Jeremiah puts his arm around my waist, saying, 'Not a single one of them is going to remember this night, but us.'

That is all that needs saying and then we are waltzing through the dark, covering ground across the open space, moving farther away from the ruckus. Jeremiah's steps are long and sure, his hand cupping my shoulder blade, telling me where to go. He lifts his arm and pushes me under to make a turn, and as I spin, I catch sight of Jennie Chalmers and her billowing skirts, dancing at the other end of the parade ground with Captain, the fiddle washing over all of us, everything else fading into the night.

I don't know how long we dance like that when a yell goes up and all kinds of laughing. Jeremiah and me turn as one to see about the fuss. Someone has built a bonfire at the edge of the parade ground, and in the light, other pairs of boys dance and Hiram's two whores put on a show to make any decent person blush. But that ain't where the hooting is coming from.

Will is hanging on that boy with the torn-up leg, Milo, and Edward and Hiram and a few others there watch, the fire playing on their faces.

I don't even try explaining to Jeremiah. I scurry to where Will is leaning to kiss that boy on the mouth, making the others gathered around hoot and slap their knees all over again.

'Will!' I holler as I get close, and he turns lazily toward me, loose-limbed from drink.

Hiram jeers, 'Aw now, Ross, don't spoil our fun! It ain't every day we get to watch a real gal-boy in action!'

'I ain't spoiling nothing,' I say. 'I'm just aiming to get myself a word with the finest dancing Chaplain you ever saw.'

'Oh, hi there, Ross,' Will slurs, nearly falling as I take up his free hand, leaving Milo standing there looking so confused the other boys start laughing again.

'You got cut in on by a real lady!' Sully laughs, and I pray Jeremiah is right that none of these boys will remember a thing come morning.

'Being a Chaplain must get powerful lonely, is all I got to say,' Edward calls.

'You come on with me,' I say, and when he leans his head on my shoulder it is a dead weight, the vapor coming off him thick.

I practically drag Will to the edge of the field. Jeremiah is standing where I left him, but when we get away from the light of the bonfire and the other boys, he comes to help me get Will off the field.

'What were you doing, Rosetta?' he hisses as he takes up Will's other arm.

356

'That's a pretty name,' Will says. 'So pretty . . .'

'I ain't the only one that's got secrets,' I tell Jeremiah.

In the morning, I can't even finish washing myself. I stand up and stride back to the fort, past our tent. There's a few boys stirring, all of them looking sick as dogs. I nod to Thomas Stakely working on a fire, Ambrose sitting next to it, holding his head, but I don't stop as I go past on my way straight for Captain's tent and the company of Jennie Chalmers.

She is there, bending low feeding kindling to the fire, a kettle hanging over the flames. I don't say a thing, just stand there watching. When she straightens and turns, she lets out a little yip. I look around, making sure there ain't a body around who might see me talking to the Captain's wife.

'I apologize,' I say. 'I wasn't meaning to scare you.'

'Ross! I'm so glad you've come! I thought I saw you dancing last night, but then I wasn't sure . . .' She smiles, but there is a new narrowness to her face.

'Are you well?' she asks, coming closer and touching my elbow.

'Mostly.' It is true, seeing as how I am still

living. 'And you?' I ask.

'Likewise. But how have you been?' she asks, her voice dipping down low, searching my face.

There's things I can't tell anyone, so I say what's easiest. 'I've been fine,' I say, and then I can't stop myself from adding, 'One of the boys from home, he ain't come back with us, and another one passed on.'

'Oh! Oh, I'm so sorry,' Jennie says.

'You've been visiting the hospital?'

'I go every day. There's so many —' She shakes her head. 'Were you thinking of coming?'

'No, I don't think I can now,' I say. 'I tried nursing some at Bull Run, but I —'

'My husband says you were an excellent battlefield nurse.' Jennie checks her kettle and then moves to add more kindling to the fire. 'Would you like coffee?'

'No,' I say. 'I've got something that needs asking. Is Captain . . . ?'

'He's gone to a meeting. Would you care to sit?'

I nod and we move to the folding wooden chairs by the table. I don't know how else but to come right out with it.

'You ever heard of a woman missing her time and not having a child on her?' I ask.

Jennie's hands fly to her mouth, making a

little prayer-tent shape there in front of her lips. Finally she takes her hands away.

'You think you're with child?' she whispers.

'Not really. Just ain't had my time since before we went marching,' I say, thinking how my belly don't feel any different when I lay my hands across it, how if anything, it is smaller.

'I don't know,' she says. 'I could ask one of the ladies, or maybe the surgeon —'

'No,' I say. 'I don't want no one else knowing. And it can't look right, you asking a thing like that.'

'What are you going to do?' she asks.

'I don't know,' I say. 'This ain't what I planned.'

She reaches across the table and squeezes my hand. 'You have to keep safe,' she says. 'In case. Have you thought about going home?'

'I don't want to go home,' I say, my voice edging above the whisper we been keeping ourselves to. 'Not without Jeremiah. A baby needs a father.'

I look at her hard to see if telling is crossing her mind, but there's not a thing except worry in her eyes.

'Of course,' she says, and it is honey to hear her agree with me.

There is a long silence. I can't think of a thing to say.

'Oh! That reminds me!' Jennie jumps up from her seat and goes to a large chest that must be serving as Captain's desk. She takes a canvas bag from inside and rummages about. 'Here it is!' she finally says, holding up an envelope. 'I've been holding on to this for safekeeping. It was waiting here when I got back from Virginia.'

She holds the letter out to me, and I know it is from Papa before I even see his writing on the front, just from the way he's folded the paper so neat and square.

I slide it right into my pocket, trying not to think on what Papa might have written. When I am done she is peering at me.

'You really think you're expecting? Do you feel like you are?'

'I don't feel much different,' I say. 'Except on the march, I couldn't keep a thing down.'

It don't matter that she don't have answers and she can't help me, that her only advice is going home. It just feels good to tell my worries to her and put those thoughts with someone else for a bit.

I stop near the parade ground where I can be alone and take Papa's letter out, peel it open carefully, unfold it slowly. I let my eyes relax, let the sparse words blur for just a moment. Then I steady myself to see what Papa has written.

August 3, 1862

Dear Rosetta,
We are always Glad of Word from you — there is almost no News otherwise, with you Gone so Far.

As you must know, it has been Busy here with haying. The Wheat is good this year, and what Potatoes the gophers haven't got. That spotted calf you asked after is weaned and sold to Nilsson as we cannot take on more now.

We Hope to see you before Too Long. Your Mother says to tell you Come Home and we'll not speak of it again.

We Pray for you,
Your Father, Charles Edwards

I crumple that letter, stuff it in my pocket. It don't go so hard this time, feeling their shame, but even if she was right, Mama never did know the words to make me do what she wanted.

Even feeling sick as they do, the boys still spend the morning passing rumors we might be leaving any day, telling each other they can't wait to be marching on those Rebels. I'm thinking on my own worries, about how it don't seem right, Jennie Chalmers knowing something Jeremiah don't, when Will sits himself down beside me.

'I wanted to thank you for what you did last night,' he says.

'It ain't nothing,' I shrug. 'Anybody would've done the same.'

'That isn't so,' he says, and then he leaves me to wonder if I were a noble wife like Jeremiah said, if I ought to talk to him before we get to marching again.

I wait 'til night, 'til we are lying under our tent, Jeremiah's body curled around mine, his arm over my shoulder, his hand in mine.

'I've got to talk to you.' It comes out quiet.

Jeremiah's body goes still as a deer listening to the wind.

'Okay,' he says, and turns so he's flat on his back. I can just make out his face. It looks blank so I know I ain't kept my voice calm.

Under my hand his heart beats faster as he waits for me to talk. Everybody is sleeping in their tents and someone's snoring mixes in with the frogs and the lonely screech of an owl hunting. I reach across and pull him close, sliding my hand down his side, bumping along his ribs. He's dropped weight from marching with no rations.

'What's this about?' he asks, his fingers closing on my hand. 'You've got a seriousness to you I ain't —'

I open my mouth, but nothing comes out. My Mama has announced a thing like this more than once, but there ain't a way for me to say it all warm with love. There ain't nothing but fear gripping my belly.

'It ain't nothing,' I say. 'It's just I've been thinking if there'll be more fighting for us to do.'

'Seems likely.'

'You think we can stand it?'

'Ain't got a choice, unless you're wanting to go on home.'

'Not without you,' I say, tears pricking my eyes.

I turn my back on him, my heart pounding.

He don't say anything for a good long minute. I let those hot tears run. He slides back down next to me and puts his arm around me.

'Rosetta,' he whispers. 'I'm sorry. I thought this war would be over quick. I thought we'd have our farm and be wintering over somewhere while we waited to get our house built and put in our own crops. Lord knows I'm glad you came — but if you're scared, you ain't got to stay on my account — I can find a way to stand you being gone home if I know you're safe.'

I let those words sink through me. Neither of us says a thing. I want to be here with Jeremiah, and I want to be living that life we dreamed. Instead I kiss his hand, where the bullet graze is fresh healed. I tell him something for both ways.

'I'm safest where you are,' I say, and hope it is true.

It is late in the day when Jennie comes to our fire, her chin up even as she's casting about like a spooky horse.

'I came to talk to Private Stone,' she says from where she stands at the aisle's edge. 'Alone.'

From across the way Edward lets out a low whistle, and she wraps her arms tighter across her chest.

I jump up from where I am sitting, following her down the row, her swirling skirt drawing the attention of every boy we pass, even when they all saw so much more the night before.

'What are you doing?' I ask when we get clear to the parade ground.

She stops and looks around before meeting my eye.

'I found someone for you,' she says, and leans close. 'A woman. It isn't cheap, but she — she knows the herbs to — she says she can purge your womb.'

My mouth drops right open. 'Oh.'

Jennie presses a slip of paper into my hand. 'The address is there. If you want to go — I can ask Captain for an escort to the hospital again.'

'I don't know — I've got to think —'

'Of course,' she nods. 'You let me know if —' And she turns on her heel, her calico skirt billowing like sheets on the line as she moves away through the gathering twilight.

I walk slow back to our tent.

'Oooh, boy!' Hiram stands and claps as I go by. 'You got balls to be diddling with the Captain's wife!'

The boys have all got questions on their faces when I move into their circle around the fire.

'News from the hospital,' I say. 'One of the soldiers I saw there — he's gone.'

No one bothers with me after that. The smoke twists into the night just like when Papa's burning sheets, my Mama sobbing

365

behind her closed door. I look across at Jeremiah, picturing Papa's hands cradling Betsy, and then I open my hand, letting that slip of paper flutter down into the flames.

CHAPTER 25

MARYLAND: SEPTEMBER 9–16, 1862

It turns out McClellan ain't so slow as Hiram says, and it is only a few days before orders come for us to march into Maryland. I push my worries out of my mind, and the first town we march through makes it easier to think I am doing the right thing. It is a sight to see. Stretched along the road, the whole town, all their women and children, is out to meet us. The young girls wave white kerchiefs and some of the children have brought flags too. At a brick storefront, a girl looking to be Betsy's age stands, a glass jug of lemonade resting on the railing beside her. Sully stops right there in front of her, and she lowers a dipperful down to him. He tips his kepi all gentleman-like when he is done, and a smile lights that girl's face. At the upper end of the street, two young ladies run out to meet us. They come alongside Will and the older one, a plain girl with a long straight nose, asks, 'Would you care to join us for a hot supper?'

Will's face goes red but he says, 'I would be pleased to some other time, but we have to keep moving.'

The other girl, chestnut-haired and scrawny, smiles, looking up at me through her lashes. When I nod, she blushes, like the only thing she sees is a soldier belonging to this Army, but she don't even think about the things I might've done. I thought only Jeremiah would ever look at me like I was something worth wanting, but now those girls even get me feeling brave and handsome, like I really am part of this Army. It's enough to make anybody feel like Independence Day, but it is a strange thing to think she wouldn't be so admiring if she knew everything I am hiding.

The two girls stay standing in the street, and when Edward passes he calls out to them, 'We'll be back, Miss! You save some of that sweet, hot supper for me!'

Hiram steps out of line, saying, 'We have need of a good cook here in this Army and I would be pleased to take both of you ladies on my staff!' and then he thrusts his hips at them.

Those girls' mouths drop, making Hiram laugh and every boy around him too, and then he shoves Will, saying, 'I have got to take you for a good diddling when we get back to the fort so you won't be so fucking shy when your chance comes.'

Will don't join in the laughing, but his face turns an even deeper red.

After we leave that town, we still pass houses here and there flying Union flags, and then the drums and fifes and even the bugles start blaring marches. It gets us stirred up and cheering and almost forgetting what it is we're going to do. Sometimes the noise brings children running from the houses, some with little offerings. A red-haired boy comes bursting from a plain clapboard house, his mother running after him. He comes right to us, holding out two slices of thick wheat bread, and I thank the Lord I ain't so sick or nervous now that I can't stomach the tidbits, that maybe my worries are nothing more.

Jeremiah kneels to take the fresh bread, his face gentled by the niceness of the offering. That boy smiles so wide when Jeremiah says, 'Why thank you, Sir,' and it is tender seeing how he might look on his own child.

We wake to the crack of gunfire and the roar of artillery echoing through steep ravines growing oaks and pines and tangles of mountain laurel. From my map I know we are marching on the National Road, heading for a place called Turner's Gap.

The louder that artillery gets, the closer Jeremiah stays to my heel. When I catch him watching me one too many times, I give him a sharp look.

'You stop worrying,' I say, for both of us really, but Jeremiah starts taking slower, smaller steps like that is enough to keep us safe. A look passes between Jeremiah and Sully, and then Sully starts to the front.

'You feeling all right?' Jeremiah asks.

'Just fine,' I say.

'You been sleeping more than I've ever known you to,' he says. 'Can't even stay awake to eat half the time.'

'I'm just getting what rest I can. Besides, hardtack ain't worth staying awake for anyway.' I don't tell him how the sight of it, especially when there's weevils making tunnels through it, gets my whole stomach wanting to empty itself, not when he's already finding things to ask questions about, when I can't stop the tiredness from just overtaking me.

Sully shakes his head at Jeremiah when he gets back, saying, 'There's no word.' We know from the sound it ain't peace. Down at the road, the lead Regiment lets out a loud cheer that ripples through the five Regiments ahead of us, far off at first but getting louder and louder as we march. And then all the boys and Sully and Jeremiah beside me join the noise.

There, sitting on the blackest horse I ever saw, overlooking the road and the mountain, is General McClellan. He is something spectacular, like a king, his mustache trimmed and a straw-colored sash about his waist with his sword hanging from it. As the men keep cheering, wave after wave, McClellan flings his arm toward the top of the mountain we're climbing, pointing to where a crown of smoke rests above the trees. He don't say a word, only moves his arm to point again, and everyone cheers again.

Our enemy is coming closer all the time, and there ain't no way to escape the fighting if they keep bringing it North to us, maybe not even if I were back home. That's what I tell myself. Our Army ought to be winning, that's what everyone says, and if those Rebels keep beating us, we'll end up with nothing. Thinking that gets me to yelling too, and just for a bit I don't even feel the weight of the rifle on my shoulder or the heaviness in my belly.

It is late afternoon when we turn off the

National Road and follow a little farm road to a pasture filled with smoke and noise and crawling with soldiers. Sergeant yells, 'Get down!' and we kneel, our rifles ready, our breath coming in gasps that don't allow for talking. Before us is a rough zigzag fence and a small, scraggly cornfield cleared of trees and scratched out from rock, the work of farming land like that barely even worth the harvest. Union men from another Regiment mash themselves against the near side of those rails, hunkering down and keeping their heads low because there are lines of Rebels, maybe a whole Brigade of them, snaking through that cornfield. The fence must give more shelter than I'd guess because the soldiers there are pushing those Rebels back, leaving the silent dead and hollering wounded, Union and Rebel, so close the men at the fence line could reach through and stab them quiet or haul them to safety without leaving their post.

We wait in reserve, seeing everything and doing nothing. The men load and fire as one and I can't help grabbing Jeremiah's elbow, just to make him give me an almost-smile before he goes back to watching the field, to remind me this is where I ought to be, that we are safe here so far behind the fence. The crack of the rifles echoes back off the hills and a line of Rebels is cut down and there is more crying out before the next roar of artillery. I think on that cheering when we passed McClellan and there's none of that Glory and Courage now, with the madness all around.

When the sun drops behind the mountains and shadows creep over us, the chill comes with it. After a time the shooting dies down and there is only the cries of the wounded. It is too dark for there to be any use in fighting anymore, but those Rebels ain't gone from the trees, so we've got orders to stay put and sleep on our arms. I can't see how any of us can rest like that but still, with Jeremiah on my left and Sully to the front and Will along my right side, it is almost morning when I startle and see I've slept as deep as ever and dropped my musket too.

Most everyone is stirring. Captain Chalmers is talking to Sergeant Ames back behind the last rows of our Regiment and before long Sergeant comes to us and says, 'Seems the Rebels left in the night. We've got the high ground now, and we've got to bury our dead before we press on.'

'Must be nice, sitting up there in fancy deerskin gloves, watching us be the reapers,' Ambrose says, frowning even more than usual at Colonel Wheelock on his horse at the edge of the trees.

'Dirty work or not, it isn't right leaving those men out on open ground,' Will says, and no one can argue with a thing like that.

My feet are leaden as we go straight out to that fence line with bodies still draped across it, not fifty paces from where we slept. Some of the boys push the bodies away and clamber on over, but Jeremiah goes to a place where there's nobody to move off the fence and that's where we climb. On the field all manner of dead lie among the cornstalks bent and broken. One man lays with his hands like claws and blood clotting his beard and no shoes on his feet. Standing next to another body, licking at the blood jellied where that man's head should be, is a skinny-looking farm dog.

'Get home!' I yell, gagging to watch that dog doing what only comes natural. 'Go on! Get!' I yell until that dog slinks away, but I know it will come back as soon as we're gone. I can't stand the faces of those men lying there, some still looking like the terror is on them, some looking like sleeping except for the trickles of dried blood coming from their mouths or noses or ears.

Jeremiah stoops low over a body and when he straightens and turns it is almost a marvel to see him moving, to see him whole and strong. He don't notice me and from the look of his eyes he is thinking on Jimmy again, or maybe wondering about the men staining his soul. When he finally feels me staring, his face brightens for a moment. Then I stop thinking about the bodies and smelling everything that comes from them and only look close enough to know which need burying and which are still cursing and crying.

'Ross!' Jeremiah calls from where he is kneeling, his hand on a boy's shoulder. 'I need your help.'

'I'm coming,' I say, taking my fingers away from the cold neck of a soldier, picking my way through more bodies to Jeremiah.

'You've got to help me get this soldier to the wagons,' he says like he might come apart. 'Maybe they can get a surgeon.'

'We ain't got a stretcher,' I say.

'Don't matter. We can't leave this one.'

He's crouched down beside a boy curled up on his side, crying and holding his stomach.

'We've got to get you to the doctor,' he says.

That boy wails 'Noooooo,' to Jeremiah or to the way he's feeling or maybe both.

'We can call the band to come get him,' I

say. 'We ain't here for the living, Jeremiah.'

'No. It's got to be us,' Jeremiah says softly. 'Come here.'

Squatting at that boy's side, seeing his face, I gasp. Beneath the dirt and blood and tears that face is smooth with a narrow jaw and not a single whisker, and it almost makes me start crying.

I ain't the only one. A rush of words spills into my mouth, things I want to ask, but I catch most of them.

'What's your name?' I ask that girl, but she don't answer for all the crying she's doing.

'Rosetta!' Jeremiah says quiet, but firm. 'We've got to get her off the field!'

That girl's eyes lock on mine.

'I'm Rosetta Wakefield. This is my man.'

And then her voice comes, all ragged. 'Emma Davidson,' she says before she is moaning again.

'You got kin?' I ask.

She says 'Nooooooo' again, but maybe she is just crying. The best thing we can do for her is find her people if she has got any here. I look all around, wondering if one of the bodies sprawled here is her man, but not a soul is stirring. If she's got anybody looking for her, hopefully they've got ideas where she might be. I wonder how Jeremiah would ever find me, if the worst happened.

'You got kin here?' I ask over.

'That ain't what matters!' Jeremiah says, grabbing her feet, but he is wrong, he is only thinking about this moment and not what comes after.

That girl don't answer, though, and there's no sense in waiting. I hoist her from under her shoulders, listening to her shriek and seeing the shimmering of blood, her torn clothes showing gashes like small mouths gaping. With wounds like that, she ain't keeping her secret if she gets to a hospital.

We bump back over the field, over the fence, our every stumble making her wail, and it is the hardest thing I've ever done carrying that girl screaming from the field until the moment when her crying stops.

Maybe the pain has got to her and she has fainted.

'Jeremiah! Jeremiah. We ought to check.'

Jeremiah stops. 'Okay.'

We lay her down gentle in the dirt and rocks sloping away from the battlefield. Jeremiah comes to her shoulders and I lean over her. Her eyes are wide open and when I put my ear to her mouth there's no breath against my cheek. My fingers scrabble under her collar, feeling for a pulse, but there is nothing.

'She ain't breathing,' I say. 'Maybe —' But then Jeremiah is on his knees, doing all the things I just did like he ain't even heard and then he just sits back on his heels, his chest heaving.

There is only one thing else we can do, and so I open up her coat. Inside the breast pocket is a thin strip of paper, the name *David Galloway* printed neat across it. Jeremiah clutches that paper when I give it to him. There ain't a single letter for anybody back home. Emma Davidson was thinking she was being smart, keeping her name safe, keeping her people from being shamed. But we ain't ever going to find out another thing about her.

'We can't leave her here,' I say, and prod at him, but he don't move.

I take up Emma's body again and try dragging her back to where some of the boys are digging shallow graves but she is cumbersome, her arms flopping like they are loose-hinged and her legs trailing, leaving marks in the dirt.

Seeing me struggling is what gets Jeremiah up. 'You oughtn't be doing this,' he says.

I slowly lower Emma, laying her hands across her chest. 'What else should I be doing then?' I ask, only I ain't sure I want to hear his answer. Maybe he knows something of my fears.

'Not this,' Jeremiah grumbles.

'You help me then, if you're so worried about it.'

Jeremiah looks at me and heaves a big sigh.

'You get the arms,' he says. 'I'll take the legs.'

We don't get but a few steps when my grip starts slipping on her wet sleeve, and already there is a cold dampness to Emma's body that makes me want to pull my hand away fast like touching Mama's stove, that brings my sick feelings back. Jeremiah keeps walking over the rough ground while the body between us tips and swings.

'You've got to slow down,' I say.

'What?'

'Slow. Down. I've got no grip —' I stumble and Emma's right arm slides clean out of my hand. Her whole body sways and then my other hand slips and I ain't never seen a thing so disrespectful as dropping that body, her head banging into the ground with a thud and then the whole motion of it making Jeremiah lose hold on those feet too.

'Damn it, Rosetta!' Jeremiah says, straightening up and acting more mad than he has a right to.

'Don't you speak to me like that,' I yell back at him. 'You're walking too fast!'

'You can't be dropping people! It ain't right, forgetting — None of this is right.' He don't yell, but he is working to make his voice stay quiet.

'If you just keep your ears open, and listen when I ask you to slow down — or maybe if you take the heavy end, like you ought to —'

'Like I ought to?' he says. 'Like you always do what you ought to? Is that what you're thinking?'

We ain't arguing about the same thing as we started. We've got ourselves into something else, only there's boys around now so I don't want to do this. I don't want Jeremiah getting me so riled I tell him something I'm not ready for him to know, especially after seeing what happened to this girl.

'I ain't been thinking anything like that, except right now with moving bodies,' I say. 'I've got blood and stuff up here making me sick, and a face looking at me and you've just got to slow down is all. I ain't talking about a thing else.'

Jeremiah looks at me for a long minute. Then he sighs and it ain't a nice sigh like he is giving in, it is a sigh like he ain't going to bother with me.

'You got something else you want to say?'

When he don't answer right off I stoop

down and make myself touch that dead body again.

'Switch places,' Jeremiah says, and he is already halfway to me, with a look that says he means it, so we do.

When we lay that girl's body down in the trench Edward and Hiram are digging, Jeremiah's face has got too much sadness on it, and I can't stop hearing that girl's shrieks.

'You put any soldiers named Davidson down there already?' I ask.

Hiram shrugs, 'Might've done.'

'What about Galloway?'

'Like I said, might've done.' Hiram glares up at me.

'Ain't you checking for names?' Jeremiah asks.

'It's Pennsylvania men in here. Knowing beyond that is officer's work, you ask me,' Hiram says. 'But if the two of you got such a keen interest, I'd be happy to give up this shovel. Edward too, I bet.'

I am halfway to grabbing it from Hiram when Jeremiah puts his hand on me.

'Let's get back to work,' he says, and with his hand pinching my shoulder he steers me back out to the field, back to where we found Emma. I crouch at the first body I find, and as I unbutton that soldier's coat,

Jeremiah gives my arm a squeeze before moving off a few paces.

This soldier don't have a scrap of paper pinned inside. But neither one of the names Emma gave might mean a thing to finding her kin. Maybe when I get clear of this Army I will find some way to get word of Emma back to her people, but I don't know how and anyway that ain't enough. Without the letter in my breast pocket, anyone reading the name *Ross Stone* stitched in my coat wouldn't have a way to tie me to *Jeremiah Wakefield.*

My hands hover over the buttons of that soldier's coat. Emma's blood is drying into the cracks of my skin and my mind won't ever be easy or let me get a moment of peace again. I don't know how I can ever get clean. It makes me retch and gag again thinking on other people's blood on me, of myself in Emma's stead, Jeremiah's baby gone with me.

It is all I can do to keep from shaking my hands and running down to find the first creek. I just want to walk into that water, any water, and wash myself clean, my clothes, the lot of it, letting the blood and everything swirl away.

'I've got to wash,' I tell Jeremiah as we

march along the National Road, with nothing but heat and dust and sweat, and trees closing out the sky, the patchy light of late afternoon coming down through gathering clouds. Past a big old stone mill, four stories high and clinging on the edge of a twisting creek, I shove off the graveled road, not caring how it looks to anyone else. Artillery pounds from somewhere ahead of us but I make my way down to a wide crossing, water running in small ripples under a stone bridge with two arches. The creek bank is overgrown with tall grass and too steep to walk down to the water. I shrug out of my knapsack and my coat and crouch to slide down the last little bit, through the brambles snatching at my clothes and pricking at my hands. My feet land straight in the creek, cold water splashing up onto me and seeping into my boots, cold enough that I ought to be sucking in my breath, but I don't. The green of the grass, the trees just thinking on turning, the rocks making up that bridge, all of it shows in the creek. Horses' hooves shod in steel clatter on stone as Colonel Wheelock and Captain Chalmers lead our Regiment over the creek. Soldiers' feet tramp across the bridge and on the road, hundreds of tin cups hit against belts and rifles, almost drowning out any of the boys' voices. Little fingerling fish dart away from rocks along the creek bed and a water skeeter dances across the surface. I don't care about none of that. I don't care that my boots are soaked through. They've been soaked with worse things.

'What are you doing?' Jeremiah asks, pushing through the brush, coming down to the water. He teeters at the edge, his canteen in his left hand, his right hand unscrewing and screwing the cap. 'We ain't got time for you to bathe.'

'I can't keep on with all this death on me,' I say, scrubbing my hands and arms. 'I ain't going one more step until I've got my fingernails clean, at least.'

'Rosetta,' he says, his voice low but creeping toward warning. 'You okay?'

I nod.

'Well then,' he says, 'this bathing, it's womanish.'

'I don't care if it is.' My voice wobbles. I shove my hands back down into the water and I don't know where the words come from but they won't stop. 'I ain't going to my death unclean like this!'

'You've got things to ask forgiveness for?' Jeremiah asks.

'Course I do! How could any of us not?' I cry, rubbing at my dirty sleeve hems. 'I've got more sin than most, what with the lie I keep living, the same lie as that girl we left buried on the mountain.'

Jeremiah is silent, but barely two breaths later he wades into the water upstream from me, pushing his canteen under the lazy current. Seeing him in the water beside me puts a warmth in my chest and foolishness spreads across my cheeks because the lie ain't the part I regret. Maybe it's the truth I've been hiding from him that's hardest to bear.

'I'm okay. I don't have to do this now. It's just — We've got to have a plan,' I tell Jeremiah.

'What are you talking about?' Jeremiah asks. 'We have a plan.'

'I ain't talking about the farm,' I say. 'I'm talking about if we get to another battle.'

Jeremiah looks off in the distance, like he ain't heard.

'I don't like getting separated,' I say. 'What if one of us gets hurt?'

'That ain't going to happen.' Jeremiah shakes his head.

'There ain't no way to tell a thing like that. You know it. You've seen how it is when the shooting starts. That girl —'

'I don't want to think about that!' Jeremiah says, his voice getting louder. 'I don't want to think about any of it!'

'Well, we've got to. We ain't got a choice. If you push me down like you did at Bull —'

Jeremiah cuts me off. 'We can't ever go back home after all this,' he says low. 'It won't ever be the same, not after — not without Jimmy and Henry.'

'I thought we weren't planning on more than visiting,' I say real quiet, trying to look him in the face, but he keeps watching the current.

'It ain't only the one soldier, Rosetta. On the field — He was just like Jimmy — Our families, how can I tell the folks back home?' He looks at me then, his hands up in the air.

'That's why I'm here,' I tell him. 'So we ain't got to tell anyone. I've done the same as you. We all have.'

'I never thought it'd be like this,' Jeremiah says.

'We're too far into all of it. Ain't a bit of it that can be undone now, so we've just got to do accordingly,' I say — for myself, too. 'I want to be with you when things happen. That girl we found — I don't want to be like that.'

'That won't be you,' Jeremiah says. 'And there'll be time for bathing after.'

I don't have to ask what he means by *after*.
I clamber out of that creek, slipping in the
mud and wet grass, and sling my knapsack
and coat across my back. Jeremiah hauls
himself up out of the water and rests his
hands on my shoulders. The look that
comes over his face ain't peaceful, but it
ain't the same drawn look he had before,
and that is something.

'We'll make ourselves a good life,' he says,
leaning toward me, his eyes open, his lips
brushing mine, and then he moves past me
and we make our way to the road. My heart
aches, thinking how the life we dreamed on
is already something different than what we
started with, how there is already more to it
than he knows and he won't ever forgive
himself for not sending me back if something happens, how maybe I won't either.

CHAPTER 26

NEAR ANTIETAM CREEK, MARYLAND:
SEPTEMBER 16–17, 1862

We make our bivouac on a treed ridge, the rattle and bang of skirmishing echoing below us. Me and Jeremiah walk off a little piece from the rest of the boys, looking for a place for our tent. We find a sheltered grassy spot under a poplar where the boys' hushed talking almost doesn't reach us, and Jeremiah stares down at the valley of farms spread out below. The closest one is a farm so pretty it makes my heart ache. I know Jeremiah feels it too from the way he stares at the cluster of whitewashed barns with their stone foundations and plank sides. I dream how many cows and how much hay will fit, anything nice.

'You ever think what we'd be doing if we ain't left Flat Creek?' I ask.

'There ain't no way around the war.'

'Maybe,' I say, even though he is right. 'I

just wish we could have seen this country-side without the war being the cause of it.'

Nothing takes my mind off the jittering coming from the boys all around us, not even when we busy ourselves with setting up our tent. My hands shake as we unfold the canvas pieces of our tent and snap them together in the gentle rain that's started up. We're stringing the canvas across two poles when Sergeant comes round.

'There are to be no fires tonight,' he says. 'Not with the enemy so near.'

There's some groans from the boys about a cold supper of teethdullers and coffee grounds, but the words alone get my stom-ach riled up, thinking of carrying a baby into battle or leaving Jeremiah's side. It is too much to ask, judging the worth of one for the other.

We settle on our blankets, the long night stretched out before us, listening through the patter of rain on canvas to make out the sounds of Rebels coming, counting how long between the rolling thunder of artillery firing. When Jeremiah talks it ain't like he's keeping me from sleep.

'How you feeling?' he asks.

'I feel like myself,' I say, thinking he means after washing.

'We're fighting hard tomorrow for sure,' he says.

He's thinking of me standing in the creek washing away that dead girl, so I say, 'My place is with you.'

Jeremiah leans over me. 'Lord knows I love you. But if anything happens to you . . .'

And then he kisses me and clasps me to him tight and my heart grows so it might burst right through my rib cage.

'I love you more than anything,' I say, and there is my answer. More than anything.

'If we don't fight, our plans, our farm . . . I don't know what will come of it,' Jeremiah says in the quietest whisper, and it's the truth.

'I don't know what will come of our lives either way, if we fight or if we don't. But when this war is over, we don't have to say one word or think one thing about it ever again if we don't want. You heard Will. God will forgive us what we got regrets for, even if we ain't the same new husband and wife that started away from home.'

'There's some things ain't changed,' Jeremiah says, and then his mouth is on mine again, his hands roving across my back, kissing down my neck. When he un-clasps my belt, his hands hover over my belly, like he is feeling something different

390

about my person. But I find the buckle on his belt and work his trousers open too and that is the end of it. Then we are crashing together and I have to clamp my mouth against his until the next roar of artillery comes.

Before the first light even hits my face, battering artillery echoes through the valley and into my bones. I roll over to see Jeremiah gazing on me, his mouth starting on a smile, but there is another bang of the cannons and that smile fades as he reaches to hold my hand. We ain't got words for each other and we just stay like that, alone for a little while, our eyes saying what needs to be told before the Company gets to rustling itself together for reveille. When we drag ourselves out of our blankets there's patches of fog hovering like ghosts over graves. Rising above the low woods to the South is a twisting line of black smoke, thick enough that it ain't coming from a campfire or stove.

The Company is scattered under the broad-leafed trees, hardly a soul talking. Me and Jeremiah make our way to Will and Sully. Sully sits quiet on the ground, his eyes dull and hard, and he ain't a dog straining at his tether no more. Seeing him so still gets me wondering what changes the boys might see in me, if they're even looking. We've all seen things we never hoped or dreamed, done things we ain't planned. My life back home weren't near so bad as I thought.

As soon as me and Jeremiah sit down, Will says, 'There's something on my heart, making me think of how, before the Battle of Jericho, the Lord told Joshua: "Be strong and of a good courage; be not afraid, neither be thou dismayed: for the Lord thy God is with thee whithersoever thou goest." I feel the Lord in this day.'

'I don't know about the Lord,' Ambrose says. 'I've found it more expedient getting my strength elsewhere,' and he pats the pocket where he keeps his flask.

Will's words don't make me feel better either. Especially not once we get our orders before it's even past milking time and my only hope is that they keep us in reserve again this time. We shoulder our muskets and get into formation, our Company blending in with the lines of all the others, rows and rows of blue soldiers. Our Regiment and two others march across a ragged field, moving toward the woods ahead. The horns of the Regimental band out in front float back to us through the fog, through the noise of cannonading, but what I listen for is the swish of our legs through tall grass. Then the swish is gone and we are marching through plowed farmland, our feet quilting new lines in the harrowed soil. The sound of artillery gets louder and our own batteries blast over our heads. It is too much to think we ain't going to battle now when they are working to clear the way for us. My heart pounds and my mouth is so dry but I've got to keep moving, and anyhow my feet wouldn't stop now even if I told them to, they've got to keep themselves lined up right next to Jeremiah's; as long as I am with him, it will be all right. It has always been all right.

At a field of corn grown up taller than any of us, the ears ripe with browning and drying tassels, Sergeant orders us into line of battle, and we stand like our own crop, waiting, wondering who is going to be picked off.

Up and down the rows of corn, men check their rifles, making sure they've got them loaded, and I do the same. Every swallow turns to a gag. Jeremiah's face, drawn and more pale than ever, brings sorrow crashing through me. I look straight up to the sky and hope Will is right.

Then Sergeant yells, 'Forward, March!' as we watch that first line of men disappear into the corn, the rows scarcely wider than their shoulders, the leaves swallowing them as soon as they are two steps in. We are not in reserve. We are being put forward, but there is nothing to do now because the next line steps forward and we do too and it is like I can feel the throbbing of every heart in the line stretching to my left and right.

'Ross!' Jeremiah yells, and I turn to him. 'You're sure?'

Something makes me think he knows what I've been hiding, but I just put my left hand on my heart and nod and then we step forward into the corn. In between the musket volleys and shelling, a dry rustling is all around me as every one of us pushes through the stalks. I can't see Jeremiah and my heart goes to hammering in my ears so I keep my mind on that. With each step the air changes, the light growing brighter. A new crack of muskets tells me our first boys are through the corn and that is waiting for us too.

And then there's the last of the corn and volleys of gunshots come, but I step forward. Already there are boys lying on the ground screaming, a haze of smoke mixing with the fog still hanging over the ground, the smell of gunpowder thick in the air, mixing with shit and the rusty smell of blood. I've got to see Jeremiah, I've got to know he is there so I press forward, stepping fast over Union and Confederate boys lying on the ground toward the line of Rebels hiding behind the snake-rail fence. And then everything around me slows down and I can see it so clear. A dark shape moves and I aim. My rifle fires loud in my ear but there's no way to tell if that bullet hits its mark. I look to my right but Jeremiah and Sully ain't there. On my left, Will is hunched down next to me. I slap him on the shoulder, startling him into a run as more yelling boys crowd up from behind us. All I can think is to find Jeremiah. I fumble with my cartridge box and rammer and then I get the feel of it and load charge ram prime fire again and again. Bodies are falling around me — no, not falling, not dropping — they are knocked right out of the lines, men and things flying through the air.

We stand there plain as day for those Rebels to fire volleys into, them safe behind that fence, not three hundred paces away. As soon as that thought goes through my mind, I get myself low, crouching and firing, and then, moving through the smoke is Jeremiah, just up ahead.

There is a loud crack right in front of me and a wrenching in my hands and my musket spins away from me. My hands sting and burn but they look whole and then I get smart and throw myself flat on the ground, looking for my rifle. It ain't anywhere but there's a boy lying curled like he is a baby sleeping and I crawl to him on my belly. I yank his rifle away from him and he don't even wake, and then I see that D brand on his face. At least dying like this means Levi's family will never know what he done, and there ain't time to wonder if that is better.

I stay low, my head almost against Levi's belly, hiding behind him as best I can, keeping myself safe. His rifle is still loaded so I prop myself up, firing over Levi into that fence line of Rebels and I load charge ram prime again faster than ever, the whole time wondering where Jeremiah has got to now. Everywhere are running boys and galloping horses and smoke and noise and the bullets coming fast like a hailstorm. They don't even scare me no more, those bullets buzzing all around. You've just got to move as fast as you can and not let yourself think on them, not let yourself think on anything, and that is what I do.

I keep firing. I can't quit working my rifle. Not even when an artillery horse gets to screaming and galloping across the field, dragging its harness and traces, but then I see I'm wrong and it is tangles of innards. Not even when a line of our men moves forward and every one of them gets cut down by those Reb artillerymen laying canister right in front of them. Not even when the shrapnel flies up into the lines behind them, tearing them to pieces, a whole arm flying up like a bird taking flight only to come flopping right back down.

I fire until my hands burn, the barrel of that rifle is so hot, and then make my way toward the fence, stumbling over the wounded and dead lying there, and maybe it is a marvel I ain't been shot yet myself. Some of the bodies still have cartridge boxes and using what is there for the taking, I don't know how many times I shoot. But then jeering starts up from those firing Rebels and our troops are falling back.

The panic hits me that I don't know where anyone is or even where we came through that corn.

I yell, 'Jeremiah! Jeremiah!' and scramble back looking at each boy, only none of them are him. It don't make any sense how that cornfield got so far away but I can't even find it now and then I am tripping over the stalks, the cornfield stripped down to nothing. Jeremiah ain't anywhere. All the worst thoughts spill into my head, but maybe it is just he has already quit the field.

A row of boys lie in the stubble, laid out by canister, their bodies twisted and torn. And then a lightning bolt goes through me. There, sprawled on the ground, is a lanky body, his kepi gone and that shock of hair I would know anywhere.

CHAPTER 27

ANTIETAM: SEPTEMBER 17, 1862
'Rosetta,' is all he says when I kneel by him.

'I am here,' I say, 'and you are okay.'

His hand scrabbles across the dirt and I grab it in mine.

'You are going to be okay,' I hear myself tell him. 'You have to be.'

The way I say it must catch his attention because his eyes find mine and they are so blue, bluer than any bluebell.

And then I say the one thing left to be telling, 'There's a baby coming and you have to be here. You have to see it.'

His look is raw then, and his breathing goes wrong.

'Home,' he says. 'Home.'

I tell him hush and he don't say a thing more. I press my ear to his chest, listening for him, for his heart, for his breath but the thundering coming from every direction is too loud. I don't worry about the blurs of soldiers running past, there is only him, his face, his coat ripped open, his shirt stained with seeping blood, his knapsack and rifle gone. I grab him under the arms and drag him backward, keeping myself bent low, watching his feet bump over the ground. It should be hard, he should be heavy, but he ain't. The firing boxes us in, and men too, but I don't care for a thing but getting Jeremiah out of the battle, to where we can't be seen, to a hospital. I stumble over a body or a hole in the ground or the bent and flattened cornstalks, I don't even know what because there is Jeremiah's head bouncing against my knees as we fall.

I get myself right up and out from under him. We are near trees, not in the field we came through, some other place. I shove my arms back under his and now he is like lead and so still but he is just hurt and he is still bleeding, there's lots of blood seeping from his belly and I've got to get us safe. The ground around us shudders as shells land. It is so loud, the whole world going to pieces and hell swallowing us up and hauling us down. I look for the safest thing and drag us behind a rotting log. There is some grass there and dead leaves to make a bed for him. We are clinging to the edge of the woods and maybe the trees will hide us.

I lean into Jeremiah. I try to hear him breathing, to feel it and I can't but he is all right, this ain't nothing but Doc Cuck could fix. I pray harder than I've ever prayed in my life for it to be safe to try for the hospital or for a stretcher bearer to come find us, but we are too far from our lines and too close to the Rebs for that.

I lie like that a long time, by that log in the dead leaves, Jeremiah's head pulled against my chest. His dark hair slicked back like on our wedding day, but with sweat this time. I pet his hair like he is a small animal. I rock him. When the fighting swirls back around us, I hug him tight and pray until it swirls away again. And then I say all the nicest things to Jeremiah. I tell him about the size of my love for him and about our farm and everything we promised each other, the woods and cows we'll have and the fields growing. I tell him about the baby growing inside me, how my pants don't fit right no more. I trace the muscle in his neck that flutters and tremors. It is a long time before I see that his eyes are open wide, their bright blue turned to dull ice. There are drops on his shirt, and it is not raining so I know they are from me.

I work myself up to sitting when the field goes almost quiet, his head in my lap. The

401

trees crowd out the sky or the sky has gone dark, I don't know which. The ground is quaggy with leaves, mud, manure, blood. Sometimes other men move past us, hobbling farther into the woods. We are there so long, the cannonading has stopped. The rifles have stopped except for way off in the distance. Only the screaming is like before. It has turned to a field of the wounded and the dead and ain't none of them quiet. The wounded shriek and cry, and the dead hiss and pop. Except for Jeremiah. He is quiet because I said so, because I said *hush.*

I sit so long we get stiff. I try not to look. His face. I look at his face. The drops on his shirt, I try to rub them out. I rock him.

When he sighs I think *Maybe* but some part of me is smart and knows he ain't Lazarus raised from the dead, and he sure ain't Jesus. It is just his body doing what his mouth already done and saying its last words.

Someone close is making noise. Lots of noise and I am rocking and saying *hush.* It is not raining but there are too many drops on his shirt to count and my face is wet with something, blood or sweat or tears.

His belly is all wrong. It is all wrong and twisted into something else altogether and I will fix it. I must make it better but I don't know what to do. His jacket is open. His shirt is ripped and his body underneath is so awful — torn, with inside things pressing their way out.

I don't want to see it anymore, I want it to go away, I want him to be right. I try to fit his jacket around him, to button it, to make him how he was in the likeness I sent to Mama and Papa. But he is stiff and I don't want to hurt his head, I don't want to leave his face, I don't want to see him like that. I almost can't do it. He is so heavy, heavier than when he is sleeping, but I make his jacket right. Then I lie next to him and hold him, my head on his shoulder as he lays like we used to in the big bed at home. He is cold and he looks up to see the stars like we did before. I look too and between the black reaching fingers of tree branches there is the Big Dipper and the Seven Sisters and we just look and look. All night long we look until we are both so cold.

I am sitting on the church steps at the ice cream social, churchladies and their families dotting the yard. The door behind me pushes open and someone comes down the stairs. I don't pay any mind until the footsteps stop right beside me but I don't look to see who it is. I already know. He don't

403

wait there long before he gets tired of it. He clears his throat and I think maybe he will leave, and I want to grab him and stop him, tell him that he can't, but then he holds out a Jacob's ladder, purple-blue and bell-shaped.

'For you,' he says.

Ain't no one given me a flower before but I don't touch it at first. I wait until a look of worry comes over him, and then I'm done teasing and I take it from his hand and his smile back is the sweetest thing. That flower is still pressed at home in the Bible at the bottom of my hope chest so I could keep it always and now it ain't right that the only flower he ever gave me was that one, how there ain't no flower in the whole world that makes what's happened right. And then his footsteps take him away, and I want to call out to him, to stop him, but it is too late. He is gone and I am left in a forever I ain't ever dreamed.

Something pokes me. Shoves again, hard. Union soldiers, with dirt and blood and stains on them. They are checking the dead, they must be. That is how I remember.

'We're going to take him now,' says the one closest to me, his rifle butt low to the ground, the one who's been poking.

'No,' I say, real low.

'You ain't got a choice. You want him left out here?'

'No! He can't. This ain't where — He don't belong here!'

Riflebutt talks quiet. 'No one belongs here. That ain't him here no more, that's just his earthly body.'

'He belongs back home. He can't stay here.'

The others start reaching for Jeremiah's feet.

'You stay back!' I yell loud and strike out, scaring myself.

Riflebutt talks again, 'Either you let us take him now and he gets a decent Christian burial, or he stays here by this log.'

'No! You've got to send him home. Send him where I can find him! He can't be here! He's got no people here. His Ma and Pa . . .'

'He your kin?' Riflebutt asks.

All I can do is nod.

'He won't hold long enough to get home. You've got to let us take him now.' Riflebutt squats down, lays his musket on the ground.

'You got anything you want to take off him before we move him?' he says.

I look at Jeremiah. His face. His eyes. He ain't there no more.

'Letters,' I say. 'He's got letters. I can't —'

Riflebutt unbuttons Jeremiah's coat. I drop my head into my hands. Tears leak out. The featherweight of letters lands in my lap.

Wrinkled and smeared envelopes. One says my name, *Mrs. Jeremiah Wakefield.* My face streams. My hand shakes holding those letters. The soldiers grab Jeremiah's feet, his arms. His jacket ain't buttoned nice no more.

'His jacket!' I cry. 'His jacket!'

And then I think of my letter for him. It should be with him.

Crawl to him. Take the letter from my pocket, push it inside his jacket so it will be with him always. Pull those buttons through. Make him look right, my hands to his chest, remembering the feel of him. Trying to make it be enough.

'You've got to get up,' Riflebutt says, rips my arm away, uproots me. They lift him. Every part of my body strains for him, his bones calling to mine. It is all I can do to let go, to follow where they take him, to the tree where I kneel and watch his eyes disappear under the dirt, my mouth clamped shut against the screaming. It is all I can do not to throw myself down into the hole where they bury everything I ever had.

■ ■ ■ ■

WOUND

NEAR SHARPSBURG, MARYLAND: SEPTEMBER 19–OCTOBER 6, 1862

■ ■ ■ ■

'We are now but a handful.'
— *Corporal Thomas Galwey, Eighth Ohio Infantry, after Antietam*

CHAPTER 28

Don't feel a thing. Don't think. Legs move. Legs just up and walk themselves. Soldiers straggling. Dragging. Hobbling. Leaning against each other. Holding themselves together with arms tight.

Walk. Follow after them. Follow. Hold those letters, hold the only other thing.

I ain't dead. Something worse.

Go up the low ridge. Pass that farm. Find our colors. Find the boys, what's left of them. Every last one ragged and torn. No one fit for more fighting. Our flag in strips of blue and white.

Feet stop. Legs buckle. Sink to the ground. The Company a circle around the flag.

But not a face means a thing to me.

CHAPTER 29

Dull and blurred, like a photograph of everything moving. Smoke. Black specks moving across the fields. Patchworked fields that ought to be green. That pretty farm. Legs of men passing, then gone. Long earthen mounds. My breath rasping.

Someone says 'Ross' over and over. Far away. A dark blue shape in front of me, blocking the field.

Can't see the field. Can't move. Don't ever want to move again. Something lands on my shoulder. Shrug but it won't go. It squeezes tight, shakes me. A hand waves in front of me.

'Ross!'

A voice I know. A kind face, a worried slant to the eyebrows.

'Ross!'

Blink. Blink hard. Make myself see the face. I know that face.

'Ross! You okay?'

No words come to say what there is to be telling. Shake my head.

'You hurt?'

I only shake my head.

'Where's Sully?' the voice asks. It is Will. Will is still here.

Shake my head.

'Have you seen Jeremiah?'

Hold out my hand. Hold them out. Those letters.

Will sinks in front of me, his hand still on my shoulder.

'No one,' my voice croaks. 'Not a soul but you.'

CHAPTER 30

Dusk falls. What's left of our Company huddles close around a few small fires, not even half the boys from two days ago. But I can't think on Jeremiah. Sully neither.

Hiram's voice comes out of the night, louder than the rest. 'We licked those goddamn Rebs! Got ourselves a fucking Union victory!'

Edward says, 'Sergeant's got word those Seceshes are turning tail and crossing the river, going back South where they belong.'

There's low cheers. Someone laughs.

I drag myself away, feeling torn apart and empty. I lie in the open, away from the campfire, because I can't think about being under a tent, talking, lying with Jeremiah. I stare up at those stars and try telling Jeremiah I am sorry we ain't done all the things we said, how I wasn't at his side when it mattered, how I didn't keep him from getting hurt like I meant. I try telling him how it feels being left here, lying on this ridge, strange trees hanging their broad leaves over me and those fields below. I look toward the edge of the woods down there with him underground, but it calls up things in my head I don't want to be seeing.

My heart just rips open.

This ain't the life I ever wanted. This ain't my life at all.

And the tears come running down my face, into my ears, drowning out almost everything.

CHAPTER 31

It ain't even dawn. I can't sleep, my eyes on stars disappearing one by one. I can't stop thinking on Mama losing every one of her babies but for me and Betsy. Mrs. Waite seeing her husband's name on that first casualty list, her baby close to being born. Joseph Brown dying in that hospital, his Mama reading his last letter. Henry laying his brother in the ground, Jimmy blanketed with dirt. And Jeremiah. Always Jeremiah.

I am still wearing my coat, sleeping in it because of the chill. Because Fall is coming on now. I reach inside my breast pocket and take Jeremiah's letters from it. The one for his Ma and Pa and brothers on top, his coarse scrawl across the envelope. My hands shake putting that letter back in my pocket before I get to staining it. The other letter, the one saying *Mrs. Jeremiah Wakefield,* has got his family's address on it like he is still trying to tell me what he wants. I wipe the tears away with the back of my hand so I don't spatter any of them on the writing.

The sky gets lighter. There's only a little more time before the sleeping boys start stirring, humped shapes rising out of the grass in broken lines, like the dead scattering the fields below.

Thinking don't do me no good. The tears roll too fast and my nose runs. I've got to get hold of myself and keep quiet so no one wakes.

I wipe my nose across my sleeve, turn that envelope over. Jeremiah's hands touched that paper and then I am crying again and smoothing his letter like maybe something of him is still there, my fingers slow and careful on the seal.

CHAPTER 32

I get hold of myself, will myself to do this thing, to open that letter, see these last words from Jeremiah, the last there is of his voice.

Mrs. Jeremiah Wakefield

Just the writing there, my name in his schoolboy's hand, makes my eyes swim. My voice whispers, 'I can't.' I can't read any of that letter, what Jeremiah said. I can't think about the things he might have put in those lines, not for a long time. Tears stream down my face. My knuckles go white from holding on to that envelope, ruining it, ruining the only thing left of Jeremiah except — But I can't think about that now. It is too much. I look up into the sky to stop those tears only it don't work, not with God and Heaven and Jeremiah there already looking down.

Choking back sobs, my throat closed up and aching, I pull my knees to my chest and rock myself, the paper crumpling against me. I've got to stop this, I've got to get hold again. But there ain't a thing to fill that lonesome wildness, that empty ache inside.

The sun is peeking over the low ring of mountains and I take that letter, clutching it. It is damp and the edges are going pulpy so I put it straight inside my pocket, over my heart. It is so light, like it ain't even there. Like the other bit of him I carry.

I ain't ever felt so alone. Will is just a little ways off, curled under his blanket.

'Will!' I whisper. 'Will!'

He bolts straight up.

'What is it? You need something?' he asks, rubbing his hands down his face.

That letter is somehow back out of my pocket, and holding it out for Will to see gets my eyes filling again.

Will looks at that letter addressed to Jeremiah's wife and then at me, but he don't say a thing, he just waits.

He's the only soul left in this Army knows my name, besides Sully who is missing and Jennie Chalmers who ain't near, who I probably ain't ever seeing again neither.

I can't talk. I can't stop with the crying. Will puts a hand on my shoulder and the heat of it makes me feel like a burnt-out empty shell.

His hand stays put. 'You want company or you want to be alone?'

'Company.'

He stands there next to me, his hand on my shoulder. It gets me tearing up again.

'I've got to see him,' I say.

Will looks at me. 'See who?' he asks.

'Jeremiah. The place where he is.'

'You want me to come along?' he asks.

The sky is going pink but no birds sing. We ain't got time before reveille.

I say, 'If you can.'

'I can.'

We march back on that field, just days since I dragged Jeremiah from it. My whole life. My dreams gone. Tumbled over. Passed. Like I already lived them in my head and now I've got to live another life without him only I don't see how I can.

Our legs thresh the grass. Over torn ground, rocks, holes. There are ruined fields and ugliness everywhere. A magnet draws me to that place, to the tree where he is buried, where something of me went and now I've got to get it back.

Will keeps pace. We don't talk, don't stop, don't look at what we pass. We don't watch the burial details working their shovels into the earth, burying the Rebel soldiers still left all across the battlefield. Looking don't

418

serve no purpose but making me mourn even harder. The cornfield is gone. Nothing left but broken stubble and stalks like a scythe has been taken to it. I don't know how any of us walked out of there with our lives.

The field. The woods. The log. The place where we were last together. Empty like he was never there.

I squat down, press my hand to the leaves where we laid, claw my hands into the earth, but all I feel is hollow, even though that can't be. Will stands there on the other side of that log. I look around and it is the first time I even see where we hid, the bodies scattered like boulders around this place. There ain't nothing but Rebel soldiers left here for days and the tree where Riflebutt took my whole life. The tree witnessing over the battle and over Jeremiah, keeping his body sheltered.

His mound ain't far, at the edge of the woods, his place marked with a slat of wood carved with *JW* and *97NY* on it.

I kneel and wait to feel something, something to ease the bayonet through my heart.

I wait to feel Jeremiah, something of him still here, still with me in this world. Will kneels with me and he puts an arm around my shoulders. It is nice whether he means it in friendship or something different, but it ain't the arm I want. We sit like that a long time, not a sound passing between us besides the wind rustling the leaves. Quiet. Not even a bird. Nothing but flies buzzing.

'You want to say a prayer?' Will asks after a while.

'No. Past time for that.'

We sit some more. I don't see God in this thing, I just wait to feel Jeremiah's spirit touching mine.

Jeremiah. His blue eyes. The heat coming off him when he stands next to me, not even touching me. His voice whispering *Rosetta*. His body saying all the things he can't.

I want to shriek. Cry. Throw myself on that grave like I've seen Mama do. But I spool my nerves in tight because that ain't who I'm supposed to be. I can't even be Jeremiah's wife in secret now.

Bugles call. The field echoes with reveille. But I can't move, I can't think of leaving this place. The woods are quiet. The grave is still and I have to turn away from Jeremiah laying buried under that tree spreading its branches to the sky, without even the company of crows.

CHAPTER 33

We line up for roll call in front of Captain's tent, facing our flags flapping in the wind. We draw together to fill the holes in the ranks. There are all these men around me, but none of my boys hemming me in, keeping me safe, holding on to my secrets. There is Will to my right and Thomas on my left and they don't even know what it is like where I come from. They didn't see how my Mama smiled on my wedding day or the pride my Papa takes in bringing in the nicest hay in the whole county or the way my sister used to hold my hand walking up the schoolhouse steps. They don't know none of those things about me. My eyes sting. I've got to keep myself from crying.

The list don't take even half as long now when Captain don't speak the names of the missing, the names I want to hear. I bite my lip, keep the tears from spilling over. My fingers clench onto my trousers. Hiram grumbles to Edward about McClellan only sending Porter's men across the river to chase after the Rebs and how General Lee sent Porter running right back. If Sully were with us, he'd be saying the same. Even with all our dead, he'd be wanting revenge. But I don't see how there is anything to make right what's been taken from us.

Captain don't pay no mind to those men grumbling, tells how General McClellan aims to get us fed and rested and supplied before we set foot chasing those Rebs, and after dress parade each morning, we won't worry about drilling and such so long as we keep our rifles in working order.

'Besides,' Captain says, 'Colonel Wheelock says we'll be marching again in no time.'

A ripple of feeling, of excitement, goes through the whole Company, and I don't understand it one bit. How they ain't gagging at the soured milk and rotting meat smells coming off that field and knowing it is our own boys out there.

'Some of the Regiments will be moving closer to the river, to the Potomac,' Captain says.

My arms wrap themselves around my chest and my heart flies to bits just thinking on leaving Jeremiah. Will looks my way, silent. Jeremiah would tell me I am acting womanish. My arms fall but my fingers go back to gripping my trousers. I am raw as a skinned cow, thinking on all the holes I can't fill. All the holes I can't mend.

Captain keeps talking. 'That's where Lee will come from, if he comes back. For now, we'll be staying here.'

Sully is still missing. Jeremiah is buried in the ground. But Captain leaves Sergeant to set up pickets and teams of men to go scavenging for rations and weapons scattered on the fields. Sergeant calls out my name along with Ambrose and Will and Thomas. My throat closes again thinking on working a detail without Jeremiah keeping between me and them. But I've got to keep myself hidden, keep moving, acting like the man I am trying to be, until I find my own way, until I can see what is next for me.

All I know is there is nothing I feel useful for.

Sergeant's voice booms but I don't care a thing about what he is saying. The only thing I care about is gone and I must be still. I stare at the Company flag until it is a blue blur moving against the lighter sky. Until I don't even see the clouds or the trees off in the distance. Until there is nothing.

'Ross!' Will calls. 'You coming?'

I take a steadying breath and set my fingers loose. I blink to see clusters of men already broken off, walking to their camp-fires and tents to get what there is for breakfast before they start working. Sergeant must have excused us to our duties. Will is with Ambrose and Thomas off to my right, and I can't remember them moving away. There ain't anybody near me, they've all gone. I wonder how long I've been standing there in front of Captain's tent. I make my feet move, go to them.

I don't say anything because I don't know what sound will come out. I nod my head.

'You sure you can do this?' Will asks.

Thomas looks at me like Papa when Betsy gets to crying, like it is the saddest thing he's ever seen but he don't know what to do about it. 'Maybe it ain't time yet. Scavenging won't be pretty.'

The smallest kindness makes me want to come apart. I steel myself, my brain snapping back to this place. I've got to do it, whatever duty Sergeant has given us, whatever my condition, because there ain't a thing else for me now but working, keeping my mind from going off and staying someplace else.

'I can do it, if it needs doing,' I say, my

voice jagged.

Thomas, Ambrose, and Will sit on the ground, eating fast and silent. Will watches me. Thomas too. I make myself swallow bits of sowbelly whole, swigging water to wash it down. It makes me gag, but I keep at it until even water makes me retch.

After breakfast, our duty is to look for anything we can still use to fight those Rebels, anything we don't want them getting. The whole Company, those that ain't on picket, walks in clumps down the ridge, boys spattering the slope, seeping across the hill, no lines or rows now. I keep with these three.

We trample through the grass, trouser hems damp with the dew. Up on the ridge, at camp, things don't look so bad, the land still grows. From there, the pretty farm below looks white and clean, like it might be running. But when the ground flattens, we pass that farm and its cluster of outbuildings and I can't look. I can't think about anything. I just move my feet.

Ambrose tells us, 'That house is being used as a hospital now.'

Will says, 'Sully might be there, or maybe they need help nursing.'

We move into the woods, shaded and cool.

425

And then we are out of the trees and into the sun. The sickly sweet smell gets stronger. Things lie about. Hats. Haversacks. Buckles. Buttons. All laid out before us, sprawling across the last low hill before the plowed fields and the fields that used to be corn. Ten horses lay scattered. Pieces of a rifle carriage. Our legs slow and then our feet stop. We stand there, silent, looking.

'Union battery must've been here,' Ambrose says. 'Firing over our heads. Trying to help.'

The horses lay there, dropped out of their teams, harnesses tight around swollen bodies, looking like they just lay down for a nap in the sun. Some with thick legs twisted and torn, some with legs stiff and straight. To the far right is a broken-down caisson. One wheel splintered, three horses still harnessed to it, piled almost on each other, the ground torn up in front of them. The smell of rotting is everywhere. I retch before I get smart and hold my breath. Will has got his arm across face, covering his nose.

'Waste of good plow horses,' Thomas says.

No one has a thing different to say.

It's all a waste, I want to say, my life, this whole war, this country too, but I keep my mouth shut.

'We won't find what we want here,' Ambrose says. 'There won't be any muskets, not with the artillery.'

He starts walking again. They all do. I follow down the hill. We move closer to the woods, beyond the bare land where the cornfield was, to where Jeremiah is. Everything in my body pulls my feet to him but I only let my eyes go, looking for his tree. There it is, stretching out above the others. I take a sharp breath and hold it or else I will go to making noise. It's near enough and I've got a job. I make myself do it.

We walk through the same fields we marched on only three days ago, the same fields Will and I passed through this morning. This time, I make myself see, I don't have no choice. Jeremiah's tree off in the distance. This whole valley bound by woods and low mountains the color of Mama's lavender sachets. The ground ripples and rolls down to the town of Sharpsburg, land meant to be harvested, land I would have been proud to farm, if it could be had, before all this. Across the valley, near the trees, thin trails of camp smoke rise into the air. In the open fields, thick dark smoke rises from fires burning more than just sticks and kindling. The smell of singeing hair and roasting meat comes on the breeze. Burning carcasses.

Everywhere there are scattered clothes blown like laundry from the line, so soiled there's no reason to gather it back up. And then there are the Rebel dead, their pockets turned out, their faces turned black from the sun, like tomatoes left too long. Touch them and they burst. I can't stop myself from thinking of Jeremiah's blue eyes. The freckles across his cheeks. How pale he looked.

'You okay?' Will's voice, his head turned over his shoulder. Ambrose and Thomas spread apart, casting about.

'Fine,' I say. But I ain't. I feel so sick, like sitting down on that field and never picking myself back up, like crying and tearing at my own clothes or the ground or anything. But I can't. I make my legs, legs that don't even feel like mine anymore, keep moving.

Ambrose bumps me with his elbow.

'Want some?' he asks, holds out his flask to me. 'It's a powerful help.'

My voice ain't trustworthy so I shake my head. He lifts that flask to his mouth, taking a long pull.

'You sure? Ever since my wife — It's the only thing that makes it easier.'

And then I am not sure. I reach for that flask, its metal warm from Ambrose's hand. He watches me take a swig. It tastes awful, like being back in Doc Cuck's surgery, but there is something good about the heat down my throat.

When I take my mouth away, Ambrose says, 'Have another,' and I do.

It don't make a thing better, but I say, 'Thank you,' and get out in front of Thomas and Will so I don't have to see their faces. So none of them can see my feelings. So Will don't look at me like I've done something bad, taking Ambrose's drink.

Three muskets hang across my back, but there are more sad things than I can count. Bodies twisted out of any shape. Hands puffed so big the skin pulls tight away from the bones. Soldiers killed so young they look like schoolboys curled up to sleep. Men killed so slow they took out pictures of sweethearts and wives, of children too young to remember their fathers. All these boys, all these men, they are something to someone. There are people back home, waiting on them and the waiting ain't never going to end now. For the rest of my life I am waiting too.

I search the grass, letting my tears fall as I walk.

I blink. There at my feet is a small leather book, not much bigger than my palm, its cover an engraved spiderweb. There ain't a single body anywhere near.

It is sodden, its binding cracked and worn. I can't bring myself to touch the metal clasp that closes it. I straighten and turn, the book still in my hand.

'Will!' I call. He is twenty paces behind me and off to my left, but his head pops right up, his face drawn and tight. 'Come here!'

He jogs, his forehead creased with worry. 'What is it?'

I hold it out to him.

He says, 'Oh,' and a ghost of a smile crosses his face. 'A Bible.'

'We can't leave it here,' I say. 'Ain't right.'

'May I?' Will asks, and puts his hand out.

I set the Bible in his hand. He looks at it. Turns it over. Flips open the clasp.

'It's got a name in it,' he says, real quiet, and there on the first page, in someone's fine handwriting, is the name *Benjamin Harlin* and underneath *32nd Virginia.*

He turns the thin paper, looks to see if there is anything else written in that Bible. He flips ahead and the book falls open right in Psalms: *Blessed be the Lord my strength, which teacheth my hands to war, and my fingers to fight.* And flattened between the pages are two four-leaf clovers.

'You keep it,' I say.

'No,' Will says, and looks at me. 'It should go back to his people.'

'Not going to any and looking strange all should go back to his people.'

CHAPTER 34

The dark creeps from the mountains toward the valley and the fields where all our dead are buried. I hug my knees and sit next to the pit fire Will is tending, the cold air at my back. Loud singing and laughing drifts down the ridge, the glare of campfires lighting the tents like lanterns. Shadows swallow up the tents scattered at the edges of the battlefield until all that's left is the bright spots of flames flickering in the night.

I am working at keeping my mind swept bare when Will asks me, 'You going to write Jeremiah's folks? Send them that letter of his?'

Every feeling comes rushing over me. I just shake my head.

'You've got to send it. At least his letter,' Will says.

'Don't want to.'

Will looks at me like that is the worst thing. 'What do you mean?'

I can't explain it right. How all I've got left is two letters. How I can't send any more of him away.

'Long as I don't send that letter, he's still living to them,' I say.

That stops Will right as he's poking one of the logs with a stick. 'They'll be hearing news of the battle,' he says real quiet. 'And it won't be long before they see the casualty list. They'll be starting to think if they haven't heard word . . .'

Will is right. I know he is.

'You want me to write them?' he asks.

It is a kind offering, but it is wrong. 'No,' I say. 'I've got to do it.'

Will nods. After that we are silent. Nothing passes between us but the cracking and popping of the logs in the fire. The flames work their way through the biggest log so that it glows orange behind the black bark.

Will shifts and stands, saying, 'I'm going on over to find Thomas. He's been wanting to read the Bible.'

He looks at me so if I weren't sure before, I know now what he is doing.

'I'll be back in a bit.' He hands me the stick he's been using to work our fire and digs that tattered Bible, the one from the battlefield, out of his knapsack.

He steps away from the small circle of

light the fire casts, a dim shape moving along the ridge back to camp, to where the rest of the boys are.

I take Jeremiah's letters out, the cold air chilling my breast before I can get my jacket buttoned again. How did he ever think I could send the last of him home to his family, that I could do these things without him, that I could push everything aside, and live with only memories of him?

I drag my knapsack to me, telling myself I am going to do what is right, but that don't help one bit because I start crying.

I get hold of myself and dig inside my knapsack to find my letter paper. It is rumpled and I don't have a thing to write on but my knees. I iron a sheet against my pants, but those wrinkles stay and I want this letter to be nice. I think about waiting, finding some fresh paper. But the paper don't matter and maybe writing it I will feel something of him flutter through me again. I ain't doing right by him, keeping the truth of things from his folks.

September 20, 1862
Near Antietam Creek and Sharpsburg

Dear Mr. and Mrs. Wakefield and family,
It is only because My Heart breaks to
do it and is Broken already that I did
not Write sooner. You will have heard, I
think, how this Army met the Rebels at
Antietam Creek and how we have had
Victory. From what I saw there was
Nothing that we won with this fighting
and now we have Lost so Many. Our
Regiment saw heavy fighting in a Cornfield and I was there with Jeremiah. I
did not see how the enemy got him but
with his Wounds I think it was canister. I
Found him after it happened and he was
still Living and he knew me and was
Very Brave. There wasn't a thing to be
Done for him but I do not think he Suf-
fered long. I Tried to get him to where it
was Safe, but he was Gone too quick. I
held him when he Passed to the Other
Side and the Last words he said was,
Home. Home. So you can know that his
last thoughts were of You and of Good
Things and He died in the Company of
Someone who Loved him. There are
others here who Miss him but that is not
the same as what it is to lose a Son or

Brother or Husband.

They told me his body would not make the Journey home, so he is Buried here. He is Resting under a very Tall tree near to where we Fought. It is a Pretty place, with farms and trees all around and there is a Marker there so if you wanted to Visit you would know him. I have Gone to see him there.

I am sending the Letter he wrote for you if the Worst should happen. He wrote it before we saw our First Battle and I Know he Never wanted to Send it. He was Always Thinking on Coming Home and the Farm. Now he is Gone to his Other Home and waits for us there. It is a help for me to know that and I hope for you too.

I am Ever his,
Rosetta

I don't know if any of those words are right but there ain't a thing to make the news better, except news I ain't ready to share.

I fold that paper up and address the cover. I look at Jeremiah's letter and wonder what words he might have set down, if he said a thing about me, if he told his Ma and Pa anything of me going home to them.

Maybe come morning, I will put my farm clothes on, Jeremiah's old clothes, and desert the whole Union Army, walk away from this place, just like I walked away from home. This time I could keep heading West until Nebraska. Even now, I can cover near to twenty miles a day if I walk hard, maybe more if I find farmers willing to take me along in their wagons. Maybe I could make it there before the worst of the Winter weather and get myself settled in time for Spring planting, in time for the baby coming on. I can see it now, raising that baby up inside me and Jeremiah's dream.

That lonesome wildness whirls about me again, to think of living without Jeremiah, with no kin or family beside me, my whole life stretching out before me. I could do it if it meant living as I have a mind to, being just the way I am with no one to answer for it. But there is not just me and Jeremiah now and I can't go on living as Ross Stone. That path is gone.

All I see is blood. Lint soiled with blood. Flannel strips smeared with blood. Bed linens drenched in blood.

I gasp, my eyes flying open.

'It's only me,' Will says, from where he is sitting on his blankets next to the fire, poking at the cinders with a stick.

'You still got that Bible with you?' I ask.

'I do,' he says.

'Can you read Ruth to me?'

'Course,' he says, bringing his blankets closer to the fire, turning those onionskin pages slow and careful. And then there is his voice, saying words I ain't heard since home with Papa reading.

Tears start and I wonder what I have done, asking Will to read this, but I don't stop him. The words wash over me, his voice saying, 'And Naomi said unto her two daughters in law, Go, return each to her mother's house: the Lord deal kindly with you, as ye have dealt with the dead.'

I try to think on the words, but I can't. Home and Mama and Betsy sewing for my wedding get all mixed up with Jeremiah and his hands shaking as he took mine on our wedding day, and our wedding night and how I got the shivers.

But those words cut through my thoughts. 'And Ruth said, Entreat me not to leave thee, or to return from following after thee. For whither thou goest, I will go; and where thou lodgest, I will lodge. Thy people shall be my people, and thy God, my God. Where thou diest, will I die, and there will I be buried.'

And then I can't stop the tears from running and I try not to make any noise, but Will stops reading.

'You've got to hear the rest,' he says.

I don't know how he can say what I've got to hear. I think how Mama wanted these words read to me before my wedding. I can't tell if it is wrong of me to leave this place or wrong of me to stay.

Will reads, '. . . thou hast left thy father and thy mother, and the land of thy nativity, and art come unto a people which thou knewest not heretofore.'

And the tears keep falling.

CHAPTER 35

The sun is well up when Will drags me out of my blankets, saying, 'Sergeant asked for volunteers to guard the hospital. I put us forward.'

'I ain't good for any of it,' I moan.

'We have to find Sully,' he says, like he knows just what will get me moving.

It is late morning by the time we walk up to a farmhouse, a red H flag flying out in front. It was a good farm before all this, that much is plain. But now there ain't a thing of farm about it except the house and its wide porch and the whitewashed barn and its weathered gray plank fences with crescent moons chewed into them. Men are all around, spilling out of the house, the open barn doors. Complaining, coughing, crying, sprawling, filling any shade, lying under tents put up quick. The boys outside ain't the worst ones but they don't look good. Wounds need tending. Letters need writing. Prayers need saying. The smells of fever sweat and old meat hang over the whole farm. I cover my nose. Boys lie in crooked rows, faces streaked with dirt and gunpowder and blood, lined with pain, eyes wide with fear or closed tight against it. Men too hurt to be hungry. Men too sick to get to the outhouse in time. Black smells. Black thoughts.

I search for a face I know and catch myself looking for one I ain't ever seeing on Earth again, except maybe in the echo of some other face. I have to stop myself or there ain't hope for me being useful.

Will is up the stone steps to the house. He walks through the door left open to catch any breeze and I make myself go after him. He turns from the dark hall and its stairs, all of it stained with blood that ain't ever scrubbing out, and pokes his head into the parlor, moving closer to sounds I don't want to hear ever again. I'm scared of seeing more hurts I can't fix. This ain't the right place for me, but Will is here. I've got no one else to follow.

He steps into that parlor, says something. A voice answers. His footsteps move away into another room. Inside it ain't a proper house no more. The rooms and all the furniture are being used for the wounded.

Taking up every bit of floor are boys and men, weeping and moaning worse than the boys outside. In here, surrounded by yellow walls, it is close and hot even with the doors and windows flung open, whatever drapes there were pulled down for bedding or maybe bandages.

A shadow moves in the corner, makes me jump out of my skin. A soldier stands up from a wooden chair, moving to a man calling for water. I nod and follow Will into the next room, what was the dining room.

Boys lie on the floor in rows, one along each side of the narrow room and one down the middle, making me think of the Judiciary Square Hospital. Most of these boys are missing something. Feet. Legs. Arms. Hands. Jaws. Or else those parts are shattered so bad, they'll be missing soon. There's whimpering and moaning and rasping breaths and praying, all of it calling up things I can't bear, how there weren't a thing to be done for Jeremiah.

Down the long side of the room, Will talks to a lady kneeling to pass a hand across a boy's forehead, her skirts puddling around her. I stop in my tracks when I see who it is.

That thought don't but last a moment. This woman ain't Jennie. She might be my

Mama's age. She straightens up and moves to the next soldier with a stiffness, the way she holds herself apart telling me this house ain't hers.

I march down that row of weeping wounds and dirty bandages, right to Will and that woman, my feet pounding, making the wood floor creak. He is speaking to her. She has a wide face, round cheeks, dark-circled eyes.

'He's with the surgeon,' the woman tells Will, and that is all I need to hear.

'You've got to give me something. Something to do,' I say right over Will, hoping my stomach will hold for the work.

She looks at me straight on, an eyebrow raising. Then she stoops over the next soldier and says, 'I've been working alone. The surgeons are kept in constant work.'

'I can work alone,' I say. 'Just tell me what needs doing.'

'There are rooms full of needs here,' she says. 'And the barnyard out there.' She checks the soldier's bandage. He groans at her touch and she lays the back of her hand to his forehead. She grabs supplies from a basket behind her, her own arm wrapped in gauze below her shoulder. Her sleeve, her deep blue dress, is blood-stiffened, stained to almost black.

'We've only got our canteens,' I say.

'We want to help,' Will says. 'It's better than what else we could be doing.'

She looks at us again. Lets out a short breath through her nose, like a sheep before it charges. 'You.' She points at Will. 'You take both canteens and give water to those soldiers in the yard. They must be thirsty and there hasn't been a spare moment for me to see to them. And you, you stay here. The wounded here need bandage changes and water. There's water there.' She points to a side table, pushed against the wall by the doorway. 'I'll leave my supplies,' she adds, holding out the basket of bandages and lint.

From somewhere in the house, there is a sound worse than weeping and shrieking put together, and it keeps getting louder as the woman lifts her skirts and steps past us, grabbing a glass vial from her basket as she passes. 'Sounds like the surgeon needs my aid,' she says, whisking out the doorway.

'You need anything, you come get me,' Will says to me.

'I can do this,' I say, and give over my canteen, Jimmy's old canteen, and go to work helping the boy in front of me. Anything to drown out the feeling.

■ ■ ■ ■

When we are let to see Sully, he don't look like Sully no more. He ain't got no spark, either from sickness or hurt or his leg already being gone. He lies long and lean on his pallet, his eyes closed, the place where his leg used to be a flat space under the blanket. He won't be crisscrossing the fields anymore, or flushing birds from bushes, or making side trips on every march.

'Sully!' I say. His eyelids flutter open as I sink to my knees.

'Rosetta?' he asks, his pupils big from whenever they last gave him laudanum.

'Yes, but it's Ross.' I don't look at Will. Sully's forehead feels hot under my hand.

'I remember,' he says. 'Ross now.'

'That's right,' I say. 'We're here now. Ross and Will. We've been looking for you.'

'You took a mite too long,' he says, coming round, a flicker of a smile on his face as his hand sweeps toward his missing leg.

'Looks to be the truth,' I say.

'Got my adventure,' he says. 'Had to give the Rebs my leg for it. Still hurts.'

'I can see,' I say.

'Where's Jeremiah?' Sully asks.

'Just us,' I choke out.

Sully looks at me, his eyes bright all of a sudden.

'No,' he says.

I nod, tears spilling.

'The cornfield?' he asks.

I nod again and he turns his face away. There is a long silence.

Will finally speaks. 'You want to tell us what cost you the leg? We've been worried about you for days.'

'You both know about that cornfield,' Sully says, and we nod. 'I was coming out of that corn, like everyone was, and all those Rebs were right in front of me. Seeing them made me think about Jimmy and I wanted to bring his revenge on them.'

He stops talking, his Adam's apple still bobbing. His fingers scrabble across his sheet. He sucks in a breath and then he talks again. 'I ran out of that corn shooting, but you know how it was. I almost couldn't see what I was aiming at. But I know I got some Rebs.'

'But how'd they get your leg?' Will asks.

'Well, I saw our flag waving and that deserter — Levi? — carrying it shot right down and our colors lying there. I knew it was for me to go and raise it. It don't take long to get shot when you've got a flag waving over your head.' Sully's smile ain't a happy one.

'It hurt something awful,' he says. 'Burning and crushing and tearing all at once. It wasn't good right from the start. I would have laid where I fell, but for the fighting all over the field. I dragged myself off, got in a ditch, and prayed the whole night for it to be over and for someone to find me, praying I wouldn't die like a dog.' Sully's eyes close, tired from talking.

At least I spared Jeremiah that, at least he had me with him 'til the last.

Then Sully looks right at Will. 'I thought a lot about salvation. I ain't never asked forgiveness so many times in one night, but I got a clean soul now.'

'Well, that's one good thing,' Will says. 'There's more adventures coming for you.'

'You saying this hospital is an adventure?' Sully asks. 'Because I ain't about to argue on that.'

We laugh even though it ain't really funny. I reach for Sully's hand. He holds tight but he is so weary, he don't say a word or even move. When Will holds out the opium pills, Sully takes them, holding on to my hand until he dozes off, his soul clean and his leg festering.

When the nursing woman comes back through the parlor, making her rounds, she tells us, 'He only had a cornhusk wrap on that leg before I got here with my supplies. Looks as though that dressing ought to be changed again.'

She sets clean bandages, iodine, and a small cup half full of sugar down next to me. I kneel and peel away Sully's bandage. The flannel snags against his skin, making the stitches across his stump seep. My eyes swim to think on Sully with Jeremiah, with the O'Malleys. My cheeks burn and I don't know if I am ashamed or angry. Ashamed I can't ever bring myself to trust anyone but Jeremiah. Angry at Jeremiah for getting us into this war, for leaving me, for the baby on its way, at our plan that's smashed to bits and moldering in the ground. I want to wail, thinking on how he tried to protect me. I want to scream at all of it. And then there is a tenderness in my heart for Sully that I ain't never felt before as I mix a slurry of iodine and sugar and paint over those stitches until my hands are stained a burnt red.

I keep vigil over Sully. The nursing woman comes to kneel beside the young man on the pallet right next to us, a bandage wrapped around his head. The soldier's chest barely rises.

'He hasn't woken since being found,' she says, looking me over. 'Every time I look on him, he's worse than before.'

I can't help but think how things would be different if I'd got Jeremiah here in time. I wonder if Sully, still worn out from what that surgeon done to him, will ever be healed.

She steeples her hands and bows her head. Her lips barely move, the words coming in a whisper. So sudden, my tears spill. I bow my head to hide. I ain't even thought to say those words for Jeremiah. The tears come faster.

She finishes those last rites for the head-bandage boy. It is silent like she has moved to another patient, but she is watching me, finding something in me. I look back at her.

I ask, 'You got kin fighting here?'

'Every man fighting here is my brother,' she says.

'You ever been a teacher?'

A small smile curves her lips.

'You've got that way about you,' I say.

'I suppose we all get marked by what we've done,' she says. She gives me a measured look before moving on to another patient, leaving me thinking how I've been marked.

■ ■ ■ ■

Sully sleeps. I make rounds, change bandages, offer water to the other boys, try to forget everything.

Near dusk Sully twists and curls on his thin bed of blankets, the coming dark making the hurt greater. My sorrow ain't much different than those boys' wounds, all of us needing more distraction from our pains.

When I find the woman, I ask, 'You ain't got kin here, how'd you get the Army to let you come?'

'It irritates me to be told how things have always been done,' she says, 'so I would not accept their refusal. Or they finally had enough need, they'd take even my aid,' she smiles. 'Maybe I shamed them enough. Or they saw I could do what I said.'

'You got a name?'

'Miss Clara Barton,' she says. 'And you?'

'Private Ross Stone.'

'I see,' she says, and gives me one of those teacher looks.

I go still but my heart don't go to jumping. I ain't nervous if she sees what I am.

I say, 'I don't have to stay here now, but I ain't sure what else to do. This Army is the only thing I ever belonged to, but I've got other things to think on now. Other people.'

'Is soldiering the thing you want to do?' she asks. 'Is it your best service to offer?'

'There ain't a place else I want to go,' I say, and it is the truth, even now.

CHAPTER 36

The next morning the air has got an Autumn bite to it, but still Captain don't bring no orders. Those sick boys out in the chill, alone, need nursing and cleaning and water. They can't all have stayed living through the night.

Even so, when Will and I walk into that dooryard there are more soldiers than before, men with the flux and camp fever. As we pick our way among the boys, stopping now and then to give water or else a kind word, I get to fearing for how Sully fares, with this sickness catching, and me carrying Jeremiah's baby.

'We've got to get Sully out of doors, if he seems like himself,' I say to Will's back.

Will nods, but he don't talk until we are in the parlor where Sully lies right where we left him. He is wrapped in a blanket and I think of cocoons and wonder how he can stand it. His chest rises and falls, deep and slow.

'We oughtn't wake him,' I whisper.

Sully's eyes pop open. 'I ain't sleeping,' he says. 'Just waiting for you to tell me you heard.'

'Heard what?' I ask.

'The news about that nurse, Miss Barton,' Sully says.

'What about her?' I ask. 'We ain't seen her.'

'She worked herself 'til she dropped. The surgeon's making her leave first thing tomorrow, said we're getting supply wagons from Washington now, and he's sending her back on the next wagon.'

'How'd you find this out?' I ask, my mind working.

'I got ways,' he says, and smiles real sweet, pointing across the hall, to where a woman in charcoal-gray skirts bends over a soldier, a neighbor woman, or someone's kin, come to be of help.

'You get any other news with that smile of yours?' I ask.

'Nope. It's tough gathering information when you only got one leg.'

'Speaking of that, we've got to change your bandage,' Will says, pulling back Sully's blanket and starting to unwrap that leg. 'Then we'll see about getting you some air.'

Sully's leg don't look good. The red stump oozes with bubbling blood and thick yellow pus, and the stain of the iodine I painted Sully's stump with is gone. Sully reads what is on my face and there ain't a thing to tell him that'll make things better.

With Miss Barton leaving, there is only one way for Sully to get good nursing. And that is when a path opens before me.

'We need to get Sully on that wagon with Miss Barton,' I tell Will when we leave the hospital, the sun low and golden across the ground, dancing in patches under the trees. It could almost be pretty, except for the dead stench hanging over the whole place.

'What do you mean?' he asks.

'That's the only way he'll get well,' I say. 'He can't stay here without good nursing and what if we get orders? He's got to get back to the Capital, to a real hospital.'

Will is quiet, thinking.

'But what if he won't hold up for the journey? It's more than sixty miles — and Miss Barton isn't fit to nurse him all that way.'

'I'm going with him,' I say.

'But —'

'But nothing. I've got to get away from this place.' There is no other way about it,

I've got to tell him the whole of it. 'Jeremiah got a baby on me,' I say.

He stops where he is, the color going out of his face. 'We ought to tell Sergeant —'

'No! I'm getting on that wagon a soldier. I ain't about to get myself drummed out of the Regiment and clapped in jail for not doing according to regulation.'

Will says, 'You aren't in any condition —'

'There ain't anything wrong with me,' I say.

'I'm going with you,' Will says.

'What?' I ask.

'To ask Sergeant. I'm going with you.'

'There ain't no need,' I say.

'There is a need,' is all he says, his eyes on my belly, his mouth set in a line. 'All you have got to do is tell the truth and Sergeant'll let —'

'Until I get paid, I ain't leaving this Army any way but honorably. I aim to get the money that's owed me,' I say. 'You give me your word. Promise you ain't going to tell Sergeant. We both got secrets ain't no reason to go telling.'

Will sighs. 'I promise I won't get you pushed out of this Company, if it can be helped.'

I don't think, I just put my hand out.

The air is still around us, the sun lighting

up his hair, making it bright. He looks at my face and then at my hand before taking it. I close my fingers tight, holding him there until our eyes meet again, and I know I've got to say this right so there ain't broken feelings between us.

'It is a kindness, what you're doing, and I thank you. But Sergeant won't say no,' I tell him.

He nods and then shakes my hand hard, like he is trying to prove he is still more of a man than I'll ever be, like our hands clasping is a test and he aims to pass it.

We march through the rows of tents, popped up like mushrooms on a dung pile. Boys sit in little clumps, getting fires going, the rising and falling sounds of talking too far off to make out any words.

Sergeant sits on a stump outside his own tent, scraping his razor across days' worth of whiskers, a mirror in his left hand. When he sees us, he nods. We stand silent, watching while he finishes and goes into his tent.

'You won't say one thing?' I ask Will under my breath. He don't answer and I don't press.

When Sergeant throws the tent flap back and comes out dressed in his jacket, I talk before Will even has a chance.

'Sir, I got worries that need discussing, if you're of a mind.'

Sergeant waves his hand at the stumps around his campfire, nothing more than a few embers giving off heat. 'Let's sit,' he says.

I'd rather stand but I sit across the fire from Sergeant. Will sits next to me.

'What is it, then?' Sergeant asks once we are settled.

'Sullivan Cameron, Sir. He's in that hospital down the way, where we've been guarding.'

'How does he?' Sergeant asks.

'That's just it, Sir. He's only got the one leg now, and what's left of the other don't look too good.'

Sergeant nods so I keep talking.

'There's a good nursing lady there, but she's worked herself sick and come tomorrow she'll be on a wagon headed for the Capital.'

'You're worried for Private Cameron's life, I take it?'

I nod. 'There ain't proper nursing here. If he could get to the Capital, maybe he could get better doctoring.'

'You said there's already a wagon going that way?' Sergeant asks.

'That's right. You think there might be

some way for Sully to be on that wagon?'

Sergeant don't even have to think on it long. 'I can't see the harm in sending him back. If you think he can make the journey?'

'Sir, I can't see as how he will, if he don't have a proper nurse.'

'Well, then. What do you propose?'

'I'm asking permission to go along, Sir.'

Sergeant don't say a thing, looks from me to Will. That is when I see Will's lips are moving. Maybe he ain't as calm as he looks.

'Just to see him settled in the hospital there,' I say.

But Sergeant is shaking his head. 'We'll be moving soon,' he says. 'I can't spare another soldier. Perhaps Private Cameron would be better staying put. Captain has sent for his wife and she's due any time now. She's as fair a nurse as any.'

That almost stops me cold. But Jennie being here don't stop me from needing to leave this place.

'Sir, I don't doubt Mrs. Chalmers is a good nurse, but Sully needs good *doctoring*. I only aim to stay long enough to get him in a hospital bed. Surely there's time enough before we move?'

He don't answer, so I try something else.

'Every other boy who joined up from Flat Creek is gone.' My throat closing around the word. 'Except Sully. He's got to make it home.'

Sergeant stands up and says, 'Excuse me a moment.'

That is when Will sees fit to talk.

'Sergeant, it isn't only Sully — Private Stone has something more pressing —'

But Sergeant just disappears into his tent like he don't even hear.

I grab Will's arm. 'Don't you dare.'

But Will shakes his head, facing straight ahead until Sergeant comes back.

When he does, he is holding a slip of paper.

'I can't send you to the Capital,' Sergeant says, holding out a slip of paper. 'This is a pass for Private Cameron. If you think he needs to be on that wagon, you see to it.'

'But, Sir! I can be back in a week or two at the most,' I lie.

'Not now,' Sergeant says as he turns to go back into his tent. 'I can't spare any more soldiers.'

CHAPTER 37

I can't even move. Sergeant turns tail and disappears into his tent. I keep sitting there, waiting for him to come back and say he was wrong. Only he don't.

Will leads me away. 'Ross, you've got to go to Captain —'

I march myself off across the ridge, to where Jeremiah and I looked over the valley. To where I can watch Jeremiah's tree fade as the sun sets. I ain't got another plan.

'I'll tell him, if you don't want to,' Will says. 'I bet he won't make a big to-do about it —'

'This ain't for you to decide,' I say. 'You just leave me be —'

Only he don't.

'If you tell him, what's to stop you going home?' he asks. 'They must care for you there. I've seen you get mail.'

'I told you — I ain't going any way but honorably. I've got to at least get my back pay. I won't be no charity case.'

'Even if you tell Captain, there's still widow's benefits —'

Just hearing that word, just the thought of going home as Jeremiah's widow, makes me want to fold into myself. I don't want those benefits. I don't want anything except Jeremiah.

'I don't want to go home, not without Jeremiah,' I tell Will. 'What is there for me in that place? My Mama will make me dress in mourning, and Jeremiah's Ma will try to make me a proper farm widow the whole rest of my life. Every friend I ever had in that place is gone, save Sully.' And then there's Eli. But he must've joined up himself by now, and even if he comes back alive, his gripes don't carry importance for me no more, and maybe he can't scare me now I know I can do just as much as any man.

'It can't be all bad,' Will says, looking down at his hands and swallowing. 'But maybe I've got a place, if you don't want to go home.'

'I told you, I don't want to be nobody's burden.'

'That's not it. I'm asking — I'm offering you something,' Will says, watching the sun. 'I've been praying and I want to do right, but —'

He don't say anything more, looking at everything but me. I stare at him, watching his mouth working, waiting for more words to come tumbling out.

'I can give you a place to go,' he says, and his gaze flits away. 'So you don't have to be alone.'

He looks around, and then he speaks in a low voice, even though the tents are still far enough off. 'You can be my wife. I've got family, a place you can go to. It's not much' — his eyes meet mine — 'but it's not a hospital or battlefield neither.'

I shake my head, but he doesn't stop talking.

'It won't have to mean a thing but in name,' he says, like it is a struggle getting the words out. 'We can be the same as we are now. Like friends. And you can live your life as you see fit, and so can I — but I'll be — I'll be a father for your child, I'll give you the protection of a husband.'

That's what does it, that's what sets off the bird flapping panic wings in my chest.

I think about me and Jeremiah's honeymoon, Jeremiah curled at my back, his breath against the nape of my neck, his fingers tracing lace across my collar. It is like a fresh-scabbed wound I am testing to see how much it still hurts.

'You've got a good heart and I thank you kindly for offering, but I don't want to be wife to somebody else,' I say.

'I know who you are,' Will says, still staring at me. 'You know what I am. We can help each other — Friendship is more than plenty of men get from their wives.'

'There's better things for you than taking me and a baby on, and I don't want to keep you from what you've got coming,' I say, thinking he don't know what he is offering.

'But I'm trying to give you a safe place!' Will says it loud before starting again, more quiet, 'I'm trying to be a good friend, give you somewhere to go if you want it, to help you. If you want to live like a lily of the field, I can't stop you, but the Lord sayeth, "If brethren dwell together, and one of them die, the wife of the dead shall not marry without unto a stranger." Maybe this is my way to do what's right.'

Maybe if I were smart, I would take the life he is offering. Will is taking care of me and if it ain't love, it is still something. But something ain't enough. I stare out into the dusk and wonder what my best life is now.

Will won't let me alone.

'If you won't take my offer, you've got to go to Captain,' he says. 'Or I will.'

I only let him pull me away from the ridge, from that pretty farm, because I can't see any other way.

The nerves wash right out of me when I see Jennie Chalmers there outside Captain's tent, sitting beside Captain, clasping his hand, leaning her head against his shoulder. Seeing the two of them like that, Captain with his free arm around Jennie's shoulders, looking down at her like she is some angel from Heaven, I turn myself right back around. But it is too late.

'Ross!' Jennie calls, jumping to her feet, startling Captain and making his face go serious. It is a good thing I aim to tell Captain everything, the way she's acting.

Will pushes me forward, stands at my back.

'I've only just arrived,' Jennie says. 'Captain Chalmers hasn't had time to tell me — I'm so glad you're — but however are you?'

I can't do a thing but shake my head and her hands go to her mouth.

'Private Stone —' Captain nods, working up to telling me I have been inappropriate and disruptive, but there is never going to be a good time for what it is I have to say.

'Sir — I — there's something I've got to — something that needs telling.'

Jennie moves closer, comes to my side. All

my breath comes out of me and the words too.

'I ain't what you think,' I say. Captain's piercing eyes move across my face, but his mouth stays closed. I swallow but my mouth is so dry my tongue sticks to myself. I try to say what I ain't had to tell anyone before.

'I ain't supposed to be here. I ain't a man,' I say, looking at Jennie. Captain stays sitting there on his folding chair, his brow furrowed.

I have done something so stupid I must be touched in the head. I can't tell him the whole of it.

Behind me, Will whispers, 'Go on,' and that sends Jennie to her husband's side. She puts her hand on his shoulder. He don't say a thing, but something about her touch takes the edge out of him. When Jennie gives me a nod, I keep talking.

'My name ain't really Ross. My folks call me Rosetta. Jeremiah was my husband.'

Captain looks at me like he ain't ever really seen me before, harder than he looked at me back when I enlisted. 'Private Stone,' he says, his voice making me start, 'this is most irregular —'

'Only I ain't got Jeremiah no more and now —' A gust of wind comes, blows smoke from the fire in a swirl. I gulp a breath. 'Sir,

465

I've got a baby coming.' I say it quick, staring at Jennie's hand on Captain's shoulder. 'I ain't ever planned to do a thing but follow the term of my enlistment, and I am grateful to this Army for giving me a life with my husband, but I can't see a way to stay with the Regiment and keep Jeremiah's baby safe.'

'You admit you are an impostor, then?' Captain says, and ain't none of this going right.

'Sir, I ain't ever done a thing but my duty —'

'This is grounds for a dishonorable discharge,' Captain says.

'But Alexander!' Jennie says, pulling at his arm. 'After all the good Private Stone has done? Helping me. Nursing the wounded? Surely —'

I can see the moment the knowledge of it hits him. 'You knew this?' Captain asks Jennie.

'Why else would you send me to the Capital with a strange man?' she asks, so innocent. 'I thought you found it so obvious as to be unworthy of mention.'

'I've falsified records on Private Stone's behalf! And now you're asking for an honorable discharge?' he says, and turns back on me.

'Sir, I've got need of my back pay and the widow's benefits coming to me. I earned them just as much as any other soldier,' I say. 'Please — you ain't got to give me an honorable discharge. My family — there's death benefits —'

Captain narrows his gaze. I am a fool for speaking so plain but I ain't ever known how to do another way, I ain't ever been one to turn a thing so clever or sweeten it the way Jennie can.

'I'm asking you for the truth,' I say, swallowing. 'I'm asking you to list the person of Ross Stone as killed at Antietam.'

It is still dark when me and Will climb the stairs inside that hospital, our boots making too much noise on the creaky wood floor. I keep my mind on the steps. On this one thing. It is Will who raps lightly on the door.

A woman's voice says, 'Come in,' and it is that nursing woman sitting at Miss Barton's bedside, a lantern burning. Miss Barton lies there, her eyes half open.

'We can take over now. You must need some sleep,' Will says.

'Oh, that's kind,' the nursing woman says, standing. 'She's been restless.'

'Are Miss Barton's things packed?' I ask, when all I can think is I can't have no one else watching.

'That's her valise there,' the woman says, pointing to the foot of the bed.

'We'll see her downstairs when the wagon is ready,' Will says. 'So you can attend to others once you're rested.'

The woman nods, and then she is gone out the door. Maybe I ought to say something to Miss Barton first, but she looks so sick, I don't think it's worth bothering her over what I aim to do. I kneel at the foot of the bed and open my knapsack. What I need is inside, rolled up neat.

I unfurl Jennie's navy dress. Hold it at arm's length. It is what I have to do. There ain't nothing else for it.

'You go stand in the hall,' I tell Will. 'Make sure no one comes in.'

He nods, looking from me to the dress, before going out.

When that door closes, I set my knapsack on the floor. My fingers shake but I make them work. I take off my coat, fold it up careful, so Jeremiah's letter, still in the pocket, don't get bent. My letter home to Papa and Mama and Betsy is in there too, just like I hoped when I wrote it. Only I ain't going home to visit like I wanted. I unbutton my shirt, stuff the flannel from around my bosom down in my pack. I almost get to crying. But there ain't time for that, not now.

I slip that dress over my head, and work my pants off over my shoes. I lay them on top of my shirt, buckle the flap. Everything inside me freezes, to see the name *Stone* painted there, and that part of me, that part of my life, the last of me and Jeremiah's life together, the last of our dream, all of it packed away. Just like Jeremiah, moldering under that tree, his bones calling to me, going unanswered, and my Mama's words echoing about how we won't speak of it. I almost sink to the floor, missing a place that ain't even on this Earth.

Henry said this war was all for nothing. But that can't be the truth. Only it weren't for any of the things I thought. I ain't ever going to have that farm off in the territories, but I will always have my place beside Jeremiah.

I've got to do this. My fingers move fast over the buttons up the front of that dress. Even sucking every last bit of me in I can't get them all done, not the ones at the waist, not without a corset only I ain't ever worn such a thing. But it don't matter. Even with my hair hardly past my ears, there ain't a soul to care how I look so long as I've got that dress on.

I go to the cracked mirror over the wash-stand but when I look at myself in it, I see the life I ain't ever wanted, alone in that Little House on someone else's farm in that same town, a basket full of mending, a baby my husband ain't ever seen, my family embarrassed into silence. Like my best days are done.

But I ain't alone. If there is the least little thing of Jeremiah left to me, there ain't a thing else to do.

And so I go to the door.

In the barely light, Will helps me settle Sully onto the wagon's boards, Miss Barton already bundled beside him, moaning in her fever. From where he squats inside the wagon bed, Will reaches down to help me, and I gather up the long blue skirt in one hand and let him help me up with the other.

For a moment before he jumps down, Will holds me fast to him, the words *Heavenly Father* coming from his lips, not bothering to keep his prayers for me and Sully to himself.

I've got nothing to offer him.

'I'll send you letters,' I say. 'And you come visit when this war is done.' A gentle smile moves slow across his face, but my words ain't enough, nothing is ever enough, and then he is jumping down to the ground.

He knocks on the wagon bed for the driver, who clucks at the mules. We lurch forward, the wagon creaking, leaving Will standing there in the darkness, his hand lifted to wave as we rumble off into the mist.

I lean against the back of that wagon, the soft sounds of leaves blowing in the wind rising and falling, Sully's breath coming long and slow from the laudanum.

'Jeremiah said I might have to force you,' he mutters as he sinks into sleep, and then Jeremiah's tree rises up over the valley. I watch it one last time, all my love going to whatever is left of him until that tree disappears into the dawn before me. I close my eyes against the tears and there is Jeremiah rising early, kissing my forehead, whistling under his breath. Mama and Papa stir in the dim morning light, Mama feeding the stove and boiling water, their voices coming through the walls. There is the warbling trill of a bird, so close I could see it winging off to the trees, but there ain't no birds left here; they have all flown and my eyes ain't opening, they want to stay closed. And then it is me winging across the land, the battlefield stretched out below. I see where the cornfield stood before the war harvested it too soon, the soil soaked with blood, the farms scattered with the dead in rows, an orchard full of rotten fruit. Somehow I am in a cellar, all that dead fruit plucked and canned and forgotten on the shelves. I take up a jar, holding it up to the light, breaking it open, the berries spilling over me, covering my hands, and I will always be stained, the land will always be scarred by what we've done, its harvest will always bring the taste of blood to our mouths.

I look up then, and it is the nicest blue I ever saw spreading against the whole sky and it is Jeremiah looking down on me. I want to lift myself up to him, to feel him again. A smile spreads across my face and I think on asters opening with the sun.

'You came,' I say.

'You knew I would,' he answers.

I close my eyes.

And then I am dreaming again, dreaming of our farm, the farm we might have had. I stand at the stoop, chickens squawking away from me. Cows grazing on a gentle hill. A stand of woods off in the distance. I watch those trees, waiting for someone to come out of them, always waiting. I see all these things, standing there alone, but then I feel a small hand in mine.

Something like peace settles into my bones. There ain't no place for this baby but to be back home, with our people, in the one place where I can still find Jeremiah, where I can make him come alive for this baby I'm carrying. One place where every room has something of his love in it, where I can talk about what Jeremiah was to me, what he was to his family, where every person left alive who ever really knew him will be. One place where I can swim in the creek and feel the water rush past me like it is him swimming fast, where I can walk across the fields he worked with his own hands and he will be near to me again, living in my memories.

That does it then. I see how Jeremiah has worked it so I ain't going back the same as I left, so there won't be no shame for me over what I've done, not carrying the only gift he has left to give. There is no one now who can say I should not have gone.

Going home don't mean I've got to go back to how things have always been. Even wearing this dress, I can still do as I please, like Miss Barton or even Jennie Chalmers. Eli don't hold any sway over me, or Jeremiah's Ma neither. I have seen something bigger than that old neighborhood and I have done something of real service and I ain't keeping it secret. Anyone who tries to say different will see I'm independent as a

hog on ice.
And then my mouth is working.
'Home,' I say, and it echoes. 'Home.'

OFFICIAL LIST OF KILLED, WOUNDED, OR MISSING SINCE SEPTEMBER 17

The Late Battle at Antietam
97th New York State Volunteers
Company H

KILLED

Blalock, Levi
Price, Josiah
Stone, Ross
Wakefield, Jeremiah

WOUNDED

Cameron, Sullivan
Winship, Silas

MISSING

Bile, Andrew
Holeyhen, Ephraim
Keller, Milo

August 21, 1862

My Dear Wife, Rosetta, Always Rosetta, I can see us even now sitting on our Porch, Old and Weathered together and that is how I know we will have Our Farm. Maybe I will read this letter to our Children, to teach them something of their Mother, my Fighting Wife, my Stone Lady. Or maybe I will keep it until we are in our Last Days and show you then. Or some day when you are fussing at some fool thing I done. And you will see these words and know that even in my Dark Hours you are First in my thoughts.

It is my Hope that I can Provide for you and Protect you. That is what I aimed to do when I left Home and you there. You know I never meant for you to come here and that is why I want you to go back if anything should happen though I cannot believe I will die in this War.

I want for us to have everything we ever dreamed and spoke of. You belong on that Farm and me There with you. I am Grateful for Every Moment we stole, for Every Bit of Time Together we ever had, but if there is one thing I wish it is for more Years to Love you and be a better husband to you.

I don't regret not for one day the things we done together or having you by my side but that I put you in Harm's Way by being here. Even more than our Farm, I want for you to have a Long and Happy Life. If it is not God's Will for us to share this life more than we already done, when I am gone you should go Home and be Safe. I will wait for you in Heaven and Look on you and see the Life you make and be happy for it.

I Shall be Near to You, Always,
Your Husband,
Jeremiah Wakefield

AUTHOR'S NOTE

There was a real Rosetta who fought in the Civil War, though not in the 97th New York State Volunteers. That regiment did, however, see action at the battles of Second Manassas, South Mountain, and Antietam, all battles at which women soldiers disguised as men are known to have participated, including one woman who fought at Antietam during the second trimester of her pregnancy. And though this novel focuses on the Union side, there were women who fought for the Confederacy as well.

Studying the photograph of her in uniform, it is hard to imagine the real Rosetta, Sarah Rosetta Wakeman, as anything other than a soldier. As a private in the 153rd New York State Volunteers, she performed guard duty at Old Capitol and Carroll Prisons where she guarded two female Rebel spies and a Major in the Union Army who was discovered to be a woman. She saw combat during the Red River campaign in Spring 1864, contracted dysentery, and died on June 19, 1864. Buried as Lyons Wakeman in New Orleans, her true identity remained a secret until her family came forward with her letters, which were published in Lauren Cook Burgess's *An Uncommon Soldier: The Civil War Letters of Sarah Rosetta Wakeman alias Pvt. Lyons Wakeman, 153rd New York State Volunteers, 1862–1864.*

The fictional Rosetta is greatly informed by the feisty and strong-willed voice that shines through Wakeman's letters home. The questions her letters raised and yet never answered were the seed for this novel: How did Rosetta conceal her identity for so long? What did her family think of what she had done? What was she apologizing for in her letters home? Why did she get into a fistfight with a fellow soldier? What was it like, being a woman hidden among men? How did she feel guarding women imprisoned for what she herself was doing? Did she tell anyone her real identity? This book is my attempt to imagine the answers to those questions.

Though my primary inspiration was Rosetta Wakeman, Sarah Emma Edmonds's *Memoirs of a Soldier, Nurse and Spy: A Woman's Adventures in the Union Army,* provided a valuable firsthand look at the experiences of a woman in the ranks, as did the story of Jennie Hodgers, who after the war lived as a man for most of her life. Indeed, the fictional Rosetta's experience as a soldier is an amalgamation of the experiences of the more than two hundred women who are known to have enlisted, and whose record of service is much more thoroughly catalogued and articulated in Deanne Blanton and Lauren M. Cook's *They Fought Like Demons: Women Soldiers in the Civil War.* Just as the fictional Rosetta followed Jeremiah into the Army, many women joined up to be with fiancés, husbands, brothers, fathers. Not only did these women manage to pass the Army's physical exam (often just a handshake), some of these women even managed to conceal their identity until the very moment they delivered their babies in the ranks, a fact that seems unthinkable to us now, but perhaps is more understandable during a time when seeing a woman in pants was a rarity and gender roles were more strictly delineated.

Women served their country in various capacities, not only on the home front but also as spies, nurses, doctors, sutlers, "Daughters of the Regiment," laundresses, and prostitutes. Mrs. Rose O'Neal Greenhow (aka Rebel Rose) was in fact incarcerated for being a Confederate spy at the Old Capitol Prison until May 31, 1862, and Clara Barton did indeed serve as a battlefield nurse at Antietam until she collapsed of exhaustion, but they and other historical figures who appear in the novel are entirely fictional creations. All names, characters, places, dates, and geographical descriptions are either the product of the author's imagination or are used fictitiously.

I have attempted to render life during this time period and soldiers' experiences of battle as accurately as possible, consulting soldiers' and civilians' letters for details, especially those collected in Robert E. Bonner's *The Soldier's Pen: Firsthand Impressions of the Civil War* and Emmy E. Werner's *Reluctant Witnesses: Children's Voices from the Civil War.* Other works that were extremely useful were William P. Craighill's *The 1862 Army Officer's Handbook* and Howard S. Russell's *A Long Deep Furrow: Three Centuries of Farming in New England.* I also strived to portray the movements of the 97th New York State Volunteers faithfully, relying on John J. Hennessy's *Return to Bull Run: The Campaign and Battle of Second Manassas,* Stephen W. Sears's *Land-*

scape Turned Red: The Battle of Antietam, Vincent J. Esposito's *The West Point Atlas of War: The Civil War,* and my own experience marching the ground Rosetta would have covered as a member of that regiment at both Bull Run and Antietam. I pored over the many battlefield photographs taken by Mathew Brady, Alexander Gardner, and also the more current ones in William Fassanito's *Antietam: The Photographic Legacy of America's Bloodiest Day.* That said, in many places the activities and surroundings of the 97th New York State Volunteers have been condensed, combined, or created out of whole cloth, all in service to the story.

Which is to say, though inspired by real people and events, this book is entirely a work of fiction.

ACKNOWLEDGMENTS

Love and gratitude to my family, who supported this endeavor in every possible way. Doug, who dared this novel into being and has been wholeheartedly devoted from the very first. My parents, Neil and Sue McCabe, for reading to me, teaching me to value words, and being my first readers and editors. Matt and Kristy McCabe for their faith and enthusiasm. The Jastrows, Korpis, and Spragues for their encouragement. The Lindsays for teaching me to play poker and allowing me to step back in time at Tehama.

For their steadfast friendship and reassurance: Mariah DeNijs, Ali Kelly, and Michelle Nye. Michelle, too, for her perspective on the creative process and for telling me that sometimes what's important is just the doing; your words kept me going many times. Chris DeNijs for the line "punch and don't get punched."

I am indebted to the community of writers who have inspired, supported, and enriched my work. M. Allen and Katie Cunningham for showing it was possible. The Jaguar Fiction Collective: Steve Dershimer, Matthew Cunningham (what you told me about fighting should be a story in its own right), and Andrea Kneeland for the courage and fortification I needed, especially at the beginning — RAWR! The Fictionistas: Mikaela Cowles, Rosa Del Duca, Analisa Falcon, Kevin O'Neill, Skye Price, Isaac Smith, Toby Wendtland (who spurred me on in our race to ninety thousand words) — there are traces of your insight throughout this book. The Saint Mary's College of California creative writing faculty, notably Marilyn Abildskov and Rosemary Graham, for their unparalleled warmth, generosity, and perception; your confidence made all the difference.

I am grateful to my first editor, Sarah Rainone, who helped immensely to shape this novel. To my brilliant agent, Dan Lazar, who believed and kept believing, and always impresses with his dedication, energy, and keen judgment. To Christine Kopprasch for championing Rosetta and Jeremiah, honing their story with such care, crying at all the right spots, and shepherding it into the world with kindness and conviction.

I owe much to the historians upon whose knowledge I relied and research I consulted. Lauren Cook Burgess, for bringing the real Rosetta's letters to light, and for her work, along with DeAnn Blanton, to find the other women who fought. Ted Alexander, historian at Antietam National Battlefield, for answering my questions about the days after the battle. The re-enactors at Civil War Days in Duncan Mills, California, most especially the members of the California Historical Artillery Society, for answering my questions about artillery, caissons, and horses. While I have strived to be faithful to the history, any inaccuracies in or inadequacies of this novel are entirely my own.

ABOUT THE AUTHOR

Erin Lindsay McCabe studied literature at the University of California, Santa Cruz, and earned a teaching credential at California State University, Chico. After working as a high school English teacher for seven years, she completed her MFA at Saint Mary's College of California in 2010. She has taught composition at Saint Mary's and Butte College and resides in Northern California with her husband and son and a small menagerie that includes one dog, four cats, two horses, ten chickens, and three goats.

The employees of Thorndike Press hope you have enjoyed this Large Print book. All our Thorndike, Wheeler, and Kennebec Large Print titles are designed for easy reading, and all our books are made to last. Other Thorndike Press Large Print books are available at your library, through selected bookstores, or directly from us.

For information about titles, please call:
  (800) 223-1244

or visit our Web site at:
  http://gale.cengage.com/thorndike

To share your comments, please write:
  Publisher
  Thorndike Press
  10 Water St., Suite 310
  Waterville, ME 04901